THIRST

The Vampire Syndicate

REBECCA RIVARD

Wild Hearts Press

THIRST

Wanting her just might destroy me—and I'd still go back for more.

A gritty forbidden romance set in Rebecca Rivard's award-winning Vampire Syndicate world

THE VAMPIRE SYNDICATE

Powerful vampire mafia who will do anything to possess the women they crave. Perfect for fans of dark fantasy romance, forced proximity romance, and morally gray heroes.

Learn more: rebeccarivard.com

CAIN

Talon looked wrecked. Dark stubble shadowed his jaw, his curly hair a wild mess, his olive skin washed out.

He needed to feed, but nothing, not even the blood thirst, was prying him from his mate Eden and their newborn spawn.

Something twisted in my chest, jagged and raw.

My best friend—hell, my brother in everything but DNA—had a son now, and I was standing there like some idiot kid with his nose pressed to the glass.

I knuckled my sternum, trying to rub the ache away.

Pathetic. I should be happy for him.

I'd been wearing a track in the stone floor outside Castle Leclerc's birthing suite since midnight, wishing I could do something to help. Around three in the morning, Brien, our syndicate primus and the third man in our band of brothers, had joined me. We were seated against the wall, passing a bottle of blood-whiskey back and forth, when a loud cry sounded on the other side of the thick door.

We exchanged a look and scrambled to our feet just as Eden's parents, who'd been waiting in the castle above, hurried up.

"Talon told them to get us," Gigi told Brien. "What's going on?"

Before he could reply, Talon yanked open the door, grinning from ear to ear. "It's a boy." His Adam's apple bobbed. "I—we have a son."

With a happy cry, Gigi brushed past us to hug him.

Eden's father, a weathered lobsterman named Wes, eyed Talon over his wife's blond head. "They're okay?"

"Yeah. He's pissed off at the world and Eden...she was fucking awesome. Olivia says they're both doing great."

"Thank the Dark Goddess," Brien murmured, as Gigi and Wes released Talon to go to their daughter.

I nodded, unable to speak. All I could do was pound Talon on the back.

Then we were all in the suite. Talon returned to Eden's side, but I hung back while the others crowded around the bed, oohing and aahing over the kid. The midwife tidied up, her rubber-soled shoes soundless on the tile floor.

Eventually, things settled down and I got a closer look at Jude Talon Montgomery Esposito.

Talon grinned up at me, one hand on the tiny dhampir's head.

I gave him a thumbs-up and mouthed, "You did good."

He ran a fingertip over the kid's dark tuft of hair. The tang of disinfectant mingled with the musk of sweat and blood. Underneath was the smell of baby Jude, all soft, sweet innocence.

The jagged thing in me screwed deeper.

Talon's gaze locked on Eden, cradling their spawn to her breast. Like Talon, she looked like she'd been through a war. Her golden hair clung to her damp skin, and smudges shadowed her blue eyes. But at Talon's smile, she bit her lip, then smiled back—bright, unguarded.

He pressed a kiss to her cheek, and together, they looked down at the kid. He was red-faced and crumpled but you could tell they thought he was the most beautiful baby in the world.

Envy burned low in my chest, and I hated myself for it.

I could count my friends on one hand and still have fingers left over. And Talon? He was at the top of the list, above everyone, even Brien.

The man had my back. Always. We'd been turned to vampire the same night, had sworn the same oath of loyalty to Brien, shared the title of Maritime Syndicate lieutenants.

Talon and Brien were my brothers, but Talon had been the first, the guy who'd saved me from the hell that had been my homelife even though he'd only been a kid himself.

But now, Talon had Eden, too. A mate.

I slipped my lucky metal from beneath my sweater, thumb tracing the worn engraving. I only wore it when I needed the odds bent in my favor. Tonight, I'd worn it for Talon.

The jagged ache increased. My fingers clenched on the cold steel disc.

He's still your friend, you idiot.

Eden wasn't good enough for him, but hell, what woman would be? She was head-over-ass in love with him, and that was what mattered. And now they'd mated, losing her would gut him. That made her my people, too.

Twilight, Brien's mate, slid between me and Brien and jabbed me in the ribcage. When I scowled at her, she angled her head at Brien.

"Wake up, dude," she said in an undertone. "He's making a toast."

Resisting the urge to rub my side—the woman had bony elbows —I took a glass of the blood-champagne that someone had passed me and joined Brien and the others in congratulating the new parents.

Jude gave a tiny, very Talon-like growl. A chuckle ran around the room.

Then it was my turn. I saluted the new family with my glass.

"To my oldest friend and his beautiful mate. May Lilith bless you both." I met Eden's eyes. "I hope you'll allow me the honor of sponsoring Jude at his naming ceremony."

Talon was already nodding, but she was the kid's mom. We exchanged a long look—she knew damn well I'd urged Talon to cut her loose, but she also knew I'd had a good reason—then raised her orange juice to me. "Of course."

I swallowed. That was okay, then. I'd been forgiven—or at least, she was willing to give me another chance.

The impromptu party continued—Talon even gave Eden a ring —but I'd had my fill of sparkles and happiness. When they called for another round of champagne, I made my excuses, then raised my fist to Talon, a ritual that went back to when we were both kids.

Always our left fists, the hand that had once born the mark of our blood brother pact. The scar had disappeared after we were turned, but I still felt its phantom burn. I knew he did, too.

He solemnly bumped my knuckles with his own. "When will you be back?"

When I have Nazaire by the balls.

I shrugged. "Can't say."

Brien and I were keeping the details of this operation from Talon. He might insist on coming, and right now, he belonged here with Jude and Eden.

Talon's eyes narrowed. Then Eden yawned and shifted uncomfortably on the bed, and whatever he'd been about to say died. He rushed back to her side. "You're tired, sweetheart." He glanced around the room, voice commanding. "Okay, everyone. She needs to rest."

That was my cue. I nodded at Brien and headed for the door.

He followed, catching me in the hall. "You sure you don't need backup?"

"Too risky." I jiggled my leg, eager to get going. "I don't wanna spook my contact."

"About this contact—"

"Don't ask."

His pale green eyes frosted. "I could order you to tell me."

My hackles raised. Brien didn't usually play the primus card with me. "Or you could trust me."

"At least take someone with you—Adrian, for example."

I pretended to consider his suggestion. The young dhampir was smart, tech-savvy, hungry to prove himself. But I couldn't risk him finding out who my contact was.

"No," I said. "I go alone. It's the only way I can get what I need."

"Damn it, Cain."

I met his eyes. Brien wasn't just my alpha, he was my friend, and he was in danger, too. But I knew he didn't give a rat's ass about that, so I went for his weak spot. "You want them to come for Twilight again? Or Eden and the baby?"

"You know I don't. It's the only reason I'm allowing this." Brien dragged a hand over his wheat-colored hair. "Check in every few days, understand? Or I'm coming after you myself. I won't lose you over this."

"Chill, would you? I can handle myself. I've saved your skin a time or two, haven't I?"

Didn't he know my life didn't matter? The only people I cared about were in this room, and I'd gladly take a stake to the heart for any one of them.

Brien just shook his head and stepped back into the birthing suite. I took a last look at Talon. The guy's happiness was almost indecent, the kind of joy that didn't leave room for anything else.

He's still your best friend. Your blood brother.

Nothing could erase that. But things had changed, and we both knew it. Eden and the baby were his whole world now. They came first. They should.

And I was okay with that.

Or I would be. Eventually.

What I couldn't stomach—what had me wanting to chew nails, in fact—was a rival enforcer kidnapping a pregnant Eden to strike at the syndicate. She'd nearly died, Talon's spawn along with her. As it was, we'd almost lost them both to blood slavery.

I headed for my quarters, jaw tight. Time to end this. Nazaire had been behind Eden's kidnapping, and we all knew it. The same Nazaire who'd tried to buy Twilight at an illegal blood-slave auction.

The man was a fucking thorn in our side. Every time trouble crawled out of the shadows in the past few years, the Quebec City Syndicate enforcer was either lurking nearby or pulling strings from a distance.

But going after another syndicate's women? That was gutter-level even for him.

Still, without proof, we couldn't take him out. Not unless we wanted a blood feud with the QCS.

So I intended to get that proof.

A lead-filled balloon sloshed around in my insides.

My first major show—and it was in *Paris*.

I pressed my hands to my stomach, eyeing myself in the hotel suite's floor-to-ceiling mirror. My eyes were wide and uncertain, my mouth pulled into a worried line.

"What were you thinking?" I asked myself.

The elite of the European vampire syndicates would be in the gallery tonight. Sure, I'd sold a dozen paintings in the past couple of years, but all had been handled privately through my gallery rep.

Tonight was different. This was Paris, the beating heart of the vampire art world—and it was judgment night for the mysterious artist who'd exploded onto the scene a few years ago. The one who never appeared in public and signed her work, "The Haunt." Not even my gallery rep knew the name I was born with.

The lead-filled balloon expanded. Pressed against my lungs.

I didn't have to go to the opening. No one knew I was the artist. I could stay tucked inside this candy box of a hotel, sipping blood-champagne and eating handmade chocolates and calling it self-care. Hiding somewhere pretty enough that I could pretend it wasn't hiding.

But that would mean my father was right. The man who had no

clue I was The Haunt, yet never missed a chance to call me weak—a mistake, a blemish on his precious bloodline. A dhampir, my human half supposedly dragging me below even the lowest vampire in his syndicate.

That didn't stop him from hauling me out when convenient. Even broken tools can be useful if you don't care how they crack.

I pushed the thought from my mind and reached for the black velvet choker on my dresser. Its metal studs caught the light like secrets. Cheap, yes—but it meant more to me than all my diamonds and rubies and emeralds combined.

I rubbed the velvet between my fingers. When a vampire wrapped jewelry around your throat, it wasn't just decoration, it was a claim. A declaration that you were his. That you were wanted... special.

Luna, I hoped he'd be at the show. It had been so long since I'd felt his mouth against my skin, heard that cool voice saying my name like it tasted good.

I blew out a breath, telling myself not to get my hopes up. He didn't even know I was in France.

I clasped the choker around my neck anyway—for good luck. And because I couldn't smother a tiny, reckless hope that he'd somehow find a way to be at the gallery tonight.

I did a final twirl in my new dress, black fishnet entwined with embroidered bats—on my shoulder above my breast, the opposite arm, my upper left thigh.

It was short, edgy, bold. The party-girl Nyx I showed the world.

I lifted my chin and looked myself straight in the eye. "This is what you wanted. What you worked for. So get your butt to the gallery."

I stepped into sky-high heels, grabbed the micro-bag that held my invitation and a few necessities, and headed out of the suite.

My bodyguards met me in the hall, both in severe black suits. The younger of the two, Manny, was a dhampir like me with short dark hair, an ever-present sneer and a way of eyeing you like he was measuring how fast you'd bleed.

Jerome was much older—close to my father's age—and a

vampire with the pale irises of a shark. I'd never seen him in anything but a severe black suit, his longish brown hair slicked back from his face. He moved with a deliberate precision, no motion wasted, and spoke in clipped, one-word sentences: *Allez. Rester. Non. Non. Non.*

Either man would rat me out to my father in a heartbeat.

Outside the hotel, an SUV with tinted windows waited at the curb. Manny slid behind the wheel and Jerome settled beside me in the back. His shark eyes swept over the fishnet dress and the bare skin beneath, my only covering a bra and a thong. His upper lip curled.

I gazed back steadily. The dress was camouflage, part of my rich-girl-clubber persona. When people's eyes are glued to your legs, they tend to forget you have a mind. In my father's syndicate, that kind of distraction was sometimes the only edge I had.

And honestly? This outfit was tame compared to what half the women at the gallery would be wearing.

Manny eased the SUV onto the cobblestones, and I looked out the window. A fine drizzle blurred the glass, turning the city into a watercolor. A pair of women glided past beneath red umbrellas, tulips in motion. Streetlights cast a soft golden glow across the wet pavement, the light catching on puddles and windowpanes until everything seemed to shimmer, as if under an enchanted spell.

The gallery was a short drive away in a decommissioned Metro station. By the time we reached it, my jitters had turned into excitement.

My first major show...and it was in *Paris*. The words tasted unreal, like champagne bubbles on my tongue.

I'd dreamed of this since—forever. Had worked my butt off to get here—begging my father to hire an artist to tutor me, devouring the masters in hushed museums whenever I could slip away.

Manny opened my door and I hopped out, ignoring his outstretched hand. The air was tinged with rain and wet stone and possibilities.

I'd done it. Every sacrifice, every stolen hour had led to this.

Behind me, Manny returned to the SUV while Jerome followed

me into the subway station. A guard was posted at the top of the concrete stairs. Jerome would have to wait here with the other bodyguards.

I flashed my invitation at the guard in his dark suit. He glanced from the embossed card to me and stood aside. "Welcome, Madam Nyx."

"Merci." I descended toward the gallery, feeling lighter with every step away from Jerome.

The place was packed.

I halted on the second-to-last step, drinking it in. The subway platform teemed with vampires and dhampirs—glossy, expensively-dressed men and women who wore power like a second skin. Thralls drifted through the crowd, laughing and flirting. At one end of the platform, a blond singer crooned in smoky French, her fingers caressing the mic like it was a lover's throat.

And over it all were my oil paintings, large and lush against the gritty walls.

My fingers tightened on the steel rail. These jaded, seen-it-all vampires were here for me—Nyx. It was my art that had brought them out.

So what if no one knew I was the artist? I knew. That's what mattered.

I arranged my face into its usual blasé expression and stepped onto the concrete platform.

"Nyx!" A Paris Syndicate dhampir in a short slip-dress wiggled her fingers at me from across the gallery.

"Darling!" I gave her a finger-wiggle back and air-kissed my way through the crowd, laughing, gossiping, making promises to meet up soon. Another glittering fixture on the vampire syndicate circuit, the spoiled daughter of a Quebec City enforcer, my biggest decision which nightclub to grace next.

When I'd judged I'd spent enough time making the rounds, I merged into the cluster gathered around the nearest painting. A single white rose wilted under the moonlight spilling through a tall, Gothic window, a poison-green mamba curled possessively around the base of its vase. More serpents glided down the crumbling stone sill, vanishing into pools of deep violet shadows.

My rendering of the Quebec City Syndicate—beauty on the verge of decay, danger slithering around every corner.

But tonight, I wasn't thinking about the nest of snakes that was my father's syndicate. I was unashamedly eavesdropping on the couple next to me.

"Such unbridled power, and yet the simplicity..." murmured the woman.

"A modern take on Dark Romanticism," her companion replied.

The first speaker nodded. "She paints my dreams." (One of the few facts known about me was that I was a woman, and a supernatural.)

I moved to the second painting. The group around it was equally complimentary. In fact, the room was buzzing.

My heart swelled with pride and happiness. I had to dig my teeth into my lower lip to stop myself from grinning like a fool.

The third showed a masked couple dancing in a moody, candlelit ballroom. The gold-and-black mosaic floor beneath them had begun to crack, fissures spreading outward like the ground itself was cracking open to let in something new. Leafy vines pushed through the breaks and a cloud of blue butterflies rose into the murky light.

The vampire's platinum hair shone, his black suit molded to every line of his hard body. Heat curled low in my belly as I recalled that night...

I gulped and glanced around the gallery.

Ichika, my gallery rep, stood a few feet away—her black hair in a sharp crop, her dress a sleek, architectural gray.

I started to smile, but caught myself in time, giving her a small nod instead. She dipped her chin in return, polite but blank. Of course she didn't recognize me. The only time we'd met, I'd glamoured myself as a middle-aged, square-bodied human.

A vampire slid up to her—Baptiste, a collector and Paris Syndicate enforcer. They exchanged greetings, then he murmured, "Introduce me to The Haunt. I know she's here. Who is she?"

Everything in me came alert. I accepted a glass of blood-wine from a server in a red corset and fitted pants, pretending not to listen. I wouldn't meet with the man, of course—not even under the guise of a glamour.

"I'd love to, Enforcer," Ichika returned. "But The Haunt chose not to attend."

"Ah, oui?" he asked disbelievingly. "If she *were* here, I think she'd be eager to meet with me." He slid a hand into his pocket. "I'll make it worth your while."

"That's not necessary," said Ichika. "And it wouldn't do any good. I'm afraid The Haunt isn't present."

"Then arrange a meeting. Tell her I want to commission a painting."

"I'm sorry, sir. But she's adamant about remaining anonymous. Not even I know who she really is. And she doesn't take commissions," Ichika added, spreading her palms in a what-can-I-say gesture.

Baptiste's face darkened. "But you will pass on my request. Perhaps she will reconsider."

"Of course, Enforcer."

He inclined his head and moved away.

Ichika exhaled audibly, then slipped past me with a soft, "Pardon."

I let out a tiny breath myself. I'd half expected the enforcer to try and compel Ichika to let him meet The Haunt. But even if I'd agreed, it wouldn't have done him any good. As Ichika had said, I didn't take commissions. My process didn't work like that—I couldn't drag a painting out of myself on command. It had to rise on its own terms, unforced.

But wow. An enforcer had wanted one of my paintings badly enough to pressure Ichika. I held that fact close, a balm against my father's cutting dismissal of me and my desire to be an artist.

And on top of that, my paintings were selling. Each of the three I'd checked so far had a little red dot beside it, marking it as sold.

I hid my smile behind my wine glass.

Added to the cash I'd already stashed in an anonymous Swiss

account, I should have more than enough to fund my escape—and to stay hidden, where my father could never find me.

He kept me close—paying my bills but denying me anything resembling freedom. I was expected to charm his friends, obey his associates, carry out little "jobs" for him.

I was suffocating under his rules, his demands, his near-constant surveillance. I wanted out. I *needed* out.

But if I left without his blessing—which he'd never give—he'd cut me off without a cent. And then he'd unleash the wolves to drag me back.

His pride would never allow me to simply walk away.

I shivered and moved toward the next painting.

A man in a bright pink suit sidled up beside me, looking like a flamingo who'd flown off course and crash-landed into a murder of couture-draped ravens.

I smiled at him because hey, this crowd could use a little color.

Together, we studied the painting—an ancient gold mirror, its glass fractured like splintered bone. Each shard reflected a sliver of the dancers and ballroom from the previous piece, glittering fragments.

Pink Suit pursed his lips. "What d'you think?" he asked in French.

"Me?" I said in the same language.

"Yes."

"I—" I swallowed, unable to come up with something airy, something that might come out of party-girl Nyx's mouth. "It's good—I like it. But there's room for improvement, right? I mean—" I stopped before I pointed out all the places the work fell short, technical details that I still hadn't mastered, and said with a laugh, "I'm not a painter myself, of course."

"Mm," he said.

"And you?" I murmured. "What do you think?"

He lifted a pink-clad shoulder, let it drop. "Not really my style."

"*Ah, bon?*" I asked sweetly. "What is? Something that matches your wallpaper, perhaps?"

"You don't understand. I—these are intense. The colors, the

emotion. I wouldn't change one thing about them. But I can't see hanging one on my walls, you know?"

"Oh." He liked my work—it just unsettled him. It was the best compliment he could've given me, even if he didn't realize I was the artist.

"And for the record," he said in English under cover of the noise of the crowd, "I don't have any wallpaper to match—in case you're wondering."

I stilled, my pulse kicking up. That voice—

I flicked him a glance. Brown hair, olive skin a few shades deeper than mine—nothing like Cain, a blue-eyed blond who I'd never seen in anything but austere black and white.

On the other hand, he could've glamoured his face and coloring, and that flamingo pink would be the perfect disguise, although to get past security, he'd need an invite. Still, when had that ever stopped Cain?

Excitement flared low in my belly.

"I wasn't," I murmured, moving to the next canvas.

Pink Suit followed. When I looked over my shoulder, his gaze was on my ass.

I lifted a brow. "See something you like?"

He just smiled, lifting his eyes to mine. "I should introduce myself—Théodore Montclair." Montclair was a collector from the Paris Syndicate.

"How nice to meet you." I hid my disappointment. It was good that Montclair was here; I *wanted* him here. If he bought one of my paintings, it would be a serious boost to my reputation.

Pink Suit eased closer, eyeing the canvas along with me. When I glanced his way, a faint smile ghosted across his lips.

I caught a whiff of his scent—wild night air. A familiar scent, one I hadn't smelled in way too long.

My heart slammed against my rib cage. His head turned, and I *knew.*

That steady, unreadable look was all Cain.

"You—!" I mouthed.

His low laugh feathered over my skin. "Me."

I felt a rush of wetness between my thighs. I squeezed them together and jerked my focus back to the painting.

Beside me, he inhaled slowly. He knew about my suddenly damp panties, of course. He was a vampire with a supernatural's heightened senses.

"Missed me, have you?" Out of the corner of my eye I saw him smirk.

"No."

Yes. So much yes.

"Liar." He let his gaze drag down my body, slow enough that I felt every inch of it, then flicked his eyes back up like he'd caught me out.

Every nerve in my body lit up like a Christmas tree. I dug my fingernails into my palms and focused on the painting, when what I wanted to do was grab him by the satin lapels and fuse my mouth to his. Rub myself up against his sinewy frame. Make him burn for me like I burned for him.

"Back off," I said out of the side of my mouth. "Didn't you see Jerome? It doesn't matter if he thinks you're from the Paris Syndicate. If he hears we were flirting like this, he'll still gut you."

Jerome might not be allowed inside, but that didn't mean he wouldn't find a way to check up on me.

"You're worried about *me*?" Cain's voice was edged with amusement, like he'd enjoy taking on Jerome. He'd probably win, too. He was young for a vampire but he oozed dominance. He'd never have climbed to syndicate lieutenant otherwise.

It was me who had everything to lose if he got into a fight with one of my father's men.

"I don't want any trouble," I muttered, and to my relief, he moved back a few, socially acceptable centimeters.

I finished my wine and handed my glass to a passing server, then continued to the canvas at the end of the platform, the largest of the seven and the only item marked NFS because that painting was *mine*. A new painting, so recent it still smelled of pigment and linseed oil.

A large white tiger prowled across the canvas through a misty forest, its mouth slick with blood, its black stripes stark against its fur. Deep in the trees, a blond vampire in a wool peacoat glowered out of the canvas, his fangs also blood-tinged, a wicked silver dagger in his hand. Something about his stance suggested he was moments from erupting into motion. On a nearby cliff, a fire raged, its flames tearing at the night sky.

It was wild and emotional—and the one work I'd never intended Cain to see.

I tensed, my nerves still lit with adrenalin. But this time it wasn't from excitement—it was something colder, sharper. If I were human, I'd have broken out in an icy sweat.

I glanced sidelong at him to find he was studying me out of the corner of his eyes.

Maybe he wouldn't put it together. And if he did, there were dozens of islands off the coast of Nova Scotia. He couldn't possibly know for sure that I'd painted *that* island.

Except...yeah, right. Who was I kidding? I'd practically handed him the proof on a silver platter.

I had to distract him, and now. I edged closer, letting the back of my hand graze his.

"The washroom," I said under my breath. "Ten minutes."

Too late. He frowned at the painting, did a doubletake.

His gaze snapped to me. "What the—?"

I eased sideways. "I—"

"Stop," he bit out.

I exhaled hard but stopped moving.

He turned back to the canvas. "The Haunt," he said in an undertone. "You're—"

"Not here," I begged. "*Please.*"

He rocked back on his heels, like he hadn't really believed it. Before I could say anything else, a trio of Spanish vampires sauntered over, and we exchanged greetings.

Cain waited until we were alone again to speak—soft, menacing velvet. "If you're *her*, then you were there that night. Because that's me in the pine trees. I was wearing a peacoat just like that."

My heart kicked against my ribcage. It was him, of course—his lean, tough body, his tightly coiled energy, although I'd darkened his white-blond hair and blurred his face. Even the ghost-cat was Cain, its irises the same ice-blue.

I opened my mouth to lie. But somehow, I couldn't. "Yes. It's you."

A tense silence. Then, "Look at me."

My skin prickled. "Not here," I repeated.

"Fine. The washroom, then. Ten minutes." His tone made it clear I'd better comply.

He waited for my nod, then moved to the next painting, taking a blood-whiskey from a server and greeting a Paris soldier by name.

My heart was still pounding. Why had I been so stupid as to make that damn painting anyway?

But I'd had to. The need to process what had happened that night, to paint Cain and the fire and my shock at how fast things had gone south, had surged up in me, fierce and unignorable, like trying to choke back a scream.

Of course, I could've left the painting in Canada. I'd known Cain might find out I'd be here tonight. Hell, I'd *hoped* he would. So why ship the canvas to Paris in the first place?

But I knew the answer. It was my best work yet, and I'd wanted the world to see it—just once—before I hid it away in my studio at my father's lair.

And maybe I'd wanted Cain to see it, too.

"Wine, Madame?" A bare-chested male server offered me another blood-wine.

I stared at it for a second, then grabbed the glass and drained it. "Merci." I handed the glass back to the man.

When I looked around again, Cain had disappeared into the crowd and there was no sign of Jerome—or any QCS men, for that matter.

I started for the washroom.

"Nyx." Halfway across the gallery, a sharp-jawed dhampir with ink-black hair stepped into my path. A thrall hung off his arm like a designer accessory—curves poured into a body-con dress, pouty red lips, fake adoration.

My stomach tightened. I summoned a social smile, all mouth, no eyes. "Rodrigo."

A distant cousin on my mother's side, Rodrigo had used the connection to worm his way into my father's inner circle, despite being only half-vampire like me. He leaned in to kiss me on the lips, but I turned at the last second so his mouth brushed my cheek instead.

He pulled back, a scowl marring his handsome face. "I'm going to the new casino after the show. Meet me there."

Not asking me. Telling me.

It was an effort, but I kept my smile in place. "I'd love to, but I can't."

His fingers dug into my upper arm. "Why not?"

The thrall shifted uneasily on her pointy heels.

I eyed my cousin, chest burning, itching to rip my arm free. But I didn't. I couldn't. I was my father's property—and by extension, property of every man who served him. Rodrigo wouldn't hesitate to report my insolence, and I couldn't risk giving my father another reason to tighten the leash.

Not now, when I was so close to escaping all together.

"Dussault invited me to an after-party." I lifted a brow. "You're not going?"

Dussault was Régis Dussault, the QCS primus. And I knew Rodrigo wasn't going because there was no after-party.

His thick brows drew together. He removed his hand from my arm. "No," he said, adding with a slimy smile, "Too bad. I could use the luck."

The thrall gave a cry of excitement. "Take me, cher. I feel lucky tonight."

Rodrigo slapped her bottom. "Do you?"

She smiled and whispered something in his ear, and they moved off.

A quarter of an hour had passed; Cain would be getting restless. The man was scarily punctual. I took a covert look around, making sure no one from the QCS was watching me, and slipped out of the gallery.

The hallway was lined with those white tiles you see in subway stations all over Europe and North America. I passed the first washroom, guessing Cain would be in the second. The industrial steel door opened and his hand snaked out, hauling me into the dimly lit interior.

The bathroom was also tiled—a glossy, red-and-black mosaic. I barely had time to register it before Cain had the door locked and me backed against it. He'd dropped the glamour but kept the pink, a striking contrast to his pale hair and lake-ice eyes. His tie was shoved into a pocket, and his crisp white shirt hung open at the collar, exposing the strong column of his throat.

He stopped a few inches away. I moistened my lips, taking in his face, beautiful in that stark, angular way that made him look carved rather than born.

Four months since I'd last seen him, and that had been on that godsforsaken island, with me hidden in the shadow world. And it had been even longer since I'd touched him, felt his hands on my skin...

He was looking at me with the same concentration, his gaze lingering on my lips before dipping to my cleavage, visible beneath the fishnet.

He stilled. Something dark and hungry radiated from him, so intense I could almost feel it.

This was why I'd worn this dress—on the off chance he'd hear I was in Paris without my father and find a way into the gallery. We only ever met in public places, and I hadn't attended anything but a couple of QCS events since that botched operation in Nova Scotia.

I should be explaining, asking for forgiveness.

He should be demanding it.

Neither of us spoke. Instead, I skimmed a fingertip over the wheat-brown scruff on his jaw. It was a new look for him, sharpening the cut of his jaw, deepening the hollows of his cheeks.

He shifted closer, his lips hovering over mine.

I found myself lifting onto my toes. Wanting—no, needing—to get closer to him.

Then I blinked and jerked back, the cold steel door stopping me short. "No."

He followed, stepping into my space again. His body heat—cool to a human but just right to me—warmed me from breasts to thighs.

"No?" he asked.

I bit my lower lip. I wanted this as much as he did, probably more. I didn't kid myself that he was celibate between our meetings, even if I was.

But there was that painting between us, and the edge in his voice when he'd told—no, ordered—me to meet him in the washroom.

His fingers brushed my black choker. The choker he'd given me last spring. His hand encircled my throat around the velvet.

"No, what, Nyx *Nazaire?*"

The tips of my breasts prickled against the flimsy silk of my bra. Somehow hearing him speak my full name—acknowledging that I was the daughter of his enemy—felt like both a threat and an invitation to sexy, filthy things. His gaze dipped and I knew he could see how my nipples had hardened into points.

I gulped, and his expression softened. He traced the underside of my jaw with his thumb.

"Answer me, love. No, what?"

Love.

He didn't mean it; I knew that. But the sharp pang the word elicited made me slap my palms to his chest.

"No, I won't do this. Not when you're pissed off at me."

"Pissed off?" A corner of his mouth lifted—not in a smile, something darker. "I'm a lot more than pissed off. I'm halfway to wringing this pretty neck of yours."

His fingers tightened on my throat, just a little. At the same time, his thumb continued its slow stroke up and down my jaw, like he couldn't decide whether to fuck me or hurt me. Or maybe both.

And now my own fingers had curled around his pink satin lapel, pulling him closer.

My show was a success, and the high of that still fizzed in my veins, begging for an outlet. It made me reckless. Made me want to take, even if it meant bleeding for it tomorrow.

I needed this. Needed Cain.

It had only ever been him, from the moment we met two summers ago in Montreal.

No one else tempted me.

No one else felt right.

His gaze dropped to where I was holding his lapel. He quirked a brow. "You want me to stop touching you? Then let me go."

I filled my lungs with some much-needed oxygen. So what if he knew I'd been on the island? I could explain. Later.

"If we're doing this," I said, "we have to be fast, before someone tells Jerome I disappeared."

The fingers around my choker tightened a little more. "Oh, we're doing it."

With a hum of approval, I dragged at Cain's shirt, yanking it out of his waistband, needing skin—his skin—under my hands. My palms skated over the hard lines of his abdomen, up his narrow waist, then around to the solid strength of his back. Every inch of him a dare I couldn't help answering.

His knees bent, his hips rocking into mine. I gasped as a ripple of pleasure went through me.

His lips twitched into an arrogant smile. "I shouldn't let you get away with this," he said, almost to himself.

"Shut up."

I lifted up on my toes, angling my pelvis so he touched where I ached. His hand moved around my throat to my nape, and he sank his teeth into my lower lip, just hard enough.

My mouth opened and then we were kissing, the current between us going haywire, jumping and sizzling.

I moaned and sucked on his tongue, nipped at his lips. His hands moved over my body, finding all my most sensitive places like a heat-seeking missile.

When he drew back, I whimpered in protest. His lips moved to my neck, his stubble an erotic rasp against my skin.

When his mouth opened against my throat, I tensed, prepared

for him to switch up on me—demand answers. It would be like Cain to soften me up, then go for the jugular.

But he didn't ask about the island. Instead, he said, "Who'd you wear this choker for?"

"No one," I said, instinct making me lie. Because that was the world I'd grown up in, the kind where you protected your vulnerable parts if you wanted to survive. "It matched the dress, that's all."

He growled against my skin. "If you can't tell the truth, I guess I'll take it back." His fingers went to the catch.

My hand shot up, catching his wrist. "No—it's mine."

His head lifted, eyes searching mine. "So you wore it for me. Say it."

I swallowed. "Yes. I wore it for you."

"Fucking right you did. Because this throat is mine."

A delicious shiver went over me. I liked hearing that, liked pretending Cain had a claim on me.

"Yes," I said, voice husky.

"Good girl." He dragged his fingertips from the clasp down my upper spine, then hooked a hand around my nape for another deep kiss. When he released me, he slapped my ass. "Take off the thong."

I reached under the fishnet skirt. If anyone else had tried to order me around like this, I would've been out of the washroom like a shot.

But this was Cain. I obeyed.

He watched, eyes hooded, as I dragged the tiny black thong down my legs and over my high heels. He held out his hand and I gave it to him.

"That dress—" he muttered, shoving the scrap of lace and satin into his jacket pocket.

I smirked. "You like it?"

"Hell, yeah." He shrugged out of the jacket and hung it on a hook, his gaze never leaving me. "Every hetero male in the gallery liked it."

"I didn't wear it for them."

"I know."

"Cocky."

It was a game we played, teasing each other. Making it clear that this thing between us was about sex, nothing more.

Or at least, it was a game for him. At some point it had stopped being a game for me, something I tried not to think about.

"You like me cocky," he said and crowded me against the cool tiles. He dragged up my skirt and cupped my mound, sliding a finger through my pussy lips. "You're so wet. This is all for me, isn't it?"

Sweet Luna, it felt good. I drew an audible breath through my teeth.

"Answer me," he said sternly.

I pursed my lips, pretending to think. Playing the game one last time. "Maybe."

He fisted his free hand in my hair, pulling my head back so his eyes bored into mine. The firm hold sent heat straight to my core. "The truth, Nyx."

I licked my lips, drawing out the moment.

That wicked finger brushed over my center, right where I most wanted it, then lifted again.

I whimpered and wriggled my hips. "Yes."

His voice dropped. "Yes, what?"

"Yes. It's because of you."

Satisfaction flickered across his face. His hand moved to the back of my nape, and he leaned in, nuzzling my cheek.

"Gods, I want to fuck you," he muttered. "But first, I need answers."

A ragged exhale escaped me. "Don't stop. *Please*. I'll tell you whatever you want, but please don't stop."

"Damn you." He pushed two fingers into me, a little too hard. "I can't...tell you no."

I moaned and clenched around him, so slick, so turned on, the roughness felt good...necessary.

"Don't—" I said.

"Don't what?" He dragged the fingers out. "Touch you?" He circled the heel of his hand on my clit, sending a sharp thrill deep into my belly.

I took his face in my hands. "Don't...talk," I said against his lips. "Just—" I gave him a raw, open-mouthed kiss.

He pulled back long enough to mutter, "We *will* talk," and then he kissed me back, his hand still between my legs, working his fingers in and out of me. Then he added the knuckle of his thumb, massaging my clit as his fingers continued to stroke my inner walls.

His mouth moved to my jaw, my throat—and then I felt his fangs against my skin just above the choker. At the same time, his knuckle touched a sensitive spot.

I groaned and nearly came on the spot, but I forced myself to grab his wrist. "No! You can't leave a mark. They'll see."

He swore under his breath and pulled his fingers out of me.

"Please," I begged.

"Shh. I want to..." He sank to his knees, hands on my hips, and dragged his fangs over the vein on my inner thigh. He glanced up, his irises rimmed with the electric blue of an aroused vampire. "You're going to let me, aren't you?"

He wanted to drink from me. I twisted restlessly in his grip.

Cain didn't usually ask. He took.

But this—letting him drink my blood—was different. Intimate in a way we'd never crossed into. People like us, with access to entire stables of syndicate thralls, didn't drink from each other. We drank from humans.

He slid his tongue up my dripping center. "Nyx," he rumbled, a low, give-in-to-me sound.

Everything female in me clenched in need.

I forced myself to focus on him. The glowing eyes, the sharp white fangs. The thirst on his face.

And then I wordlessly widened my stance, opening to him.

Offering myself—my blood—as a gift.

An apology for what had happened on the island, even though I'd done what I could. Still, it hadn't been enough and I knew it.

His eyes flamed an even brighter blue. "Good girl."

His free arm banded around my waist, holding me captive as he licked the tender skin above the vein. Slow and soft. So patient in a way I both loved and hated.

I squirmed against the cold tiles. "Just do it," I pleaded.

He hummed an assent against my skin—and sank his fangs into me.

"Sweet Luna," I gasped and went stiff, thigh stinging, nerves sparking.

He kept me where I was, lapping at the tiny punctures, sending the aphrodisiac in his saliva into my bloodstream. The sting turned into something hot...essential.

He followed that with a hard pull on my thigh, drinking from me.

Pleasure slammed into me, massive waves of it. My mouth opened in a silent scream. I grabbed his head, anchoring myself to keep from flying away, as I climaxed, long and hard, chanting his name.

He threw a hand up to cover my mouth, muffling my voice. A tiny part of me, the rational part, knew enough to be grateful.

He didn't feed long, and yet, it seemed to go on forever. Taking his hand from my mouth, he withdrew his fangs and licked the small wounds clean, speeding their healing.

His mouth returned to my clit, drawing the swollen flesh into the warm cave of his mouth. Sipping and stroking and sucking until I felt another orgasm speeding at me like a runaway train. I whined and slapped my palms against the tile, hips bucking.

His fingers dug into my ass, keeping me still as he sucked hard. I lost all sense of time, knew nothing but Cain and his mouth on me.

And then I was coming for a second time, heart racing, thighs shaking.

I wasn't one of the turned. I hadn't died to become a dhampir. I'd been born this way, to a human accidentally impregnated by my vampire father. But I was pretty sure this was what dying felt like: a white-hot detonation behind your eyes, then a plunge into darkness.

I rasped Cain's name, my legs melted wax, and collapsed forward.

When I could think again, I was in his lap, his arms around me, his mouth still wet with my blood.

I lifted my gaze to his, my defenses shattered, my mind as naked as my body.

More, I wanted to plead.

Not just more sex, but more everything.

Ask me to run away with you—even if I have to tell you no.

Because my father would stake me before letting me go to a Maritime Syndicate lieutenant.

Holding my gaze, Cain licked the blood from his lips like a big, satisfied cat. "I like how you taste, firefly."

Then his eyes hooded. I could almost hear the slam of his shutters closing. My stomach dropped.

"Now," he said. "Talk."

❦   3   ❦

CAIN

Nyx's head had fallen back, her hair spilling over my arm in dark-red waves. Godsdamn her anyway for being so beautiful. An off-beat, one-of-a-kind beauty that kept dragging me back, again and again, risking my life just to be inside her.

I toyed with a silky curl, just taking her in. The wide, expressive mouth. The high cheekbones. The clear hazel eyes under arrow-straight eyebrows.

A tiny diamond glinted in her left nostril and she wore her bangs chopped high on her forehead.

I hadn't wanted to stop feeding. Her flavor lingered on my tongue, a hot temptation. I'd wanted to drink my fill, then fuck her against the wall until she was chanting my name again.

When she'd strolled into that art gallery, all long legs and attitude, heads had turned like she was a living magnet. Not because of the black dress clinging to her like sin, but for the way she wore it—like the world existed to admire her. She was hot, and she knew it.

A redheaded, golden-skinned firefly. Unique, incandescent.

But beneath the bravado, the rich-girl attitude, was something vulnerable, something no one else seemed to notice. It was that hidden need, that softness, that had me twisting myself into a pretzel, chasing the daughter of a man I despised.

She drew a breath, her tits shifting beneath that cobweb of a dress, and my dick twitched in response.

Down, boy.

The clock was ticking. Any minute now, some asshole from her father's syndicate would notice she was missing and come looking for her.

And I wanted answers.

She'd been on that damn island.

That forest painting was a signed confession, even if part of me still didn't want to believe it.

If Nyx had known about Eden's kidnapping—if she'd been on that island watching Lemaire's secret lair burn, knowing Eden was trapped inside—then why in Hades hadn't she done something? Gotten Eden out herself, or told us the moment we landed on the island.

Eden had come close to dying in that lair.

Talon had nearly incinerated himself to save her.

Anger and betrayal burrowed into me, an animal with teeth and claws, tearing at the reality of Nyx in my arms—the warm, relaxed woman who'd let me feed from her.

"*Pathetic*," my uncle Baker sneered in my head. "*Too soft. Just like your father.*"

My jaw clenched, a dull ache rising in my teeth. What if Baker was right?

Crashing the art show had taken a fuck-ton of effort. I'd had to hack into the invite list, then send the collector whose invite I'd "borrowed" to the other side of Paris on a trumped-up errand.

I gave Nyx a shake. "I said, 'Talk,' damn you. And make it good."

Gods, now I sounded like my fucking uncle—but not enough to back off.

She blinked as if surfacing from a dream, her pupils blown wide, then sat up, pushing away from me. My fingers tightened on her— even now, I didn't want to let her go—but I did.

She scrambled off my lap and sat against the wall, arms wrapped around her bent legs.

"I'm sorry about Talon's mate," she said in her faint, sexy Québecois accent. "I didn't know anything about her being kidnapped—not until I reached the island. I did what I could—made sure she had food and water."

"That motherfucker locked her—a pregnant human—in a dark, underground cell with barely enough to eat and drink. That was you doing what you could?"

She tightened her grip on her legs. "Lamaire would've let her starve. He said a hungry woman was more compliant. So yeah, I did what I could."

Footsteps sounded in the hall outside. The other washroom door opened, then shut.

I eyed her, my knee bouncing. I'd been hunting for proof in Quebec City. I hadn't expected to find it here in Paris—in a fucking painting. The one with me and the fire.

Well, I had my proof. But I wanted something more. A better apology? Nyx on her hands and knees begging forgiveness?

The door shuddered under a hard knock. "Nyx?" Jerome called in French, his voice muffled by the thick metal. "Are you in there?"

Nyx's head snapped up. "Yes," she called back. "What?"

"Are you all right?" Despite the question, he didn't sound concerned, he sounded stern, like she had to ask his permission just to go to the bathroom.

"I'm fine," she answered. "I'll be out in a couple of minutes."

"I'll wait here."

Our eyes met. Nyx moved a shoulder in a what-can-I-say shrug.

Silently damning Jerome to Hades—and not for the first time—I stood, bringing her with me.

We'd run out of time, but I wasn't finished because what I really wanted wasn't an excuse or an apology. I wanted a reason.

"Why?" I demanded, low-voiced. Vampires hear like wolves—any louder and Jerome would know someone else was in here, door or no door. "Why didn't you get word to me? Eden spent two days on that island—in a cold, wet cellar. Lamaire almost got away with her all together."

"How?" Nyx lifted her chin in that way that made me want to

shake her... or drag her closer and kiss the defiance off her mouth. "It's not like I could just text you."

We hadn't exchanged numbers. A mutual decision, one that had seemed smart at the time.

"Fuck that. You could've found a way to reach me."

"By then I was on the island. I went dark—we all did. We couldn't risk one of you intercepting our communications. I couldn't even contact Nazaire. And I didn't know Eden was on the island until I got there." She held my gaze. "I swear I didn't."

My anger wavered, which only pissed me off more. "Why should I believe you?"

She flinched like I'd hit her. "I have never lied to you. Not once."

I stared down at her, gut knotted. She smelled like guilt and adrenaline and the same impossible-to-resist pull that had wrecked my judgment from the start.

She felt it, too. Her eyes darkened, and she wet her lips, the air between us tightening.

Jerome knocked again. She jolted and tried to slip away from me. "I have to go."

I spun her to face the wall. "Not yet."

⚜ 4 ⚜

NYX

Cain pinned me to the red-and-black tiles, his breath hot against my nape, one hand clamping my wrists behind my back.

"Let me go, damn you!" I bucked against him, struggling to break free. "You got your answers. What else do you want?"

He easily controlled me. "I told you," he said, slapping his free hand to the wall beside my head. "I want a fucking reason."

"You're not my lieutenant," I hissed. "I don't answer to you."

He didn't like that. His powerful body pressed mine harder into the tiles. "Then I guess I'll have to give Brien and Talon the name of the other person on that island. Better start watching your back because I can't promise what Talon will do when he hears."

I sucked in a breath. The last thing I needed was a vampire with a grudge hunting me. "You wouldn't."

"Wouldn't I?"

Something in my throat pinched. Cain would never choose me over his friends, I knew that. But it hurt.

"You can't prove anything."

"This isn't a court of law. That painting is all the proof I need."

"Only to you. To anyone else, it's just one of The Haunt's weird, made-up creations. Bengal tigers don't live in Nova Scotia, and a fire can burn anywhere."

"It's proof enough that Nazaire's behind this. You don't do anything without Daddy's say-so."

I went rigid. Was it that obvious to everyone else that my father pulled my strings like a puppet?

"He'll laugh in your face. You'll look like an ass."

He ignored that to muse, "And I wonder what Dussault will think?"

A chill ran up my spine. My father had no idea I was The Haunt, and I was desperate to keep it that way.

If Cain and Brien took this to my father's primus, my secret would be exposed. Dussault wouldn't care that I was The Haunt—he'd probably consider it a feather in his cap—but my father would be livid. First, that I'd revealed my presence on the island, tying him to Lamaire's op. And second, that I'd been hiding something this big, something that let me earn an income he didn't control.

I swallowed sickly. I could feel Cain's gaze on my profile. I had the eerie feeling he could see straight through skin and bone to the frantic thrum underneath.

I forced a scoff. "You think Dussault gives a damn about a Maritime thrall?" Or any thrall, for that matter.

"I trusted you," he ground out. "Or was that the plan? Were you laughing at me the whole time?"

"I *helped* you," I snapped back. I'd risked my life, meeting him in secret, feeding him intel. "Brien and Twilight would never have gotten in the door of that blood-slave ring if I hadn't passed along that info to you. If Dussault ever finds out that was me, I'm toast. Literally. He'll stake me out in the sun and let me fry."

The QCS primus wasn't known for mercy.

"As for why I was on the island, my father sent me—you're right about that. He said he wanted someone he trusted to keep an eye on Lemaire." I gave a self-mocking laugh. "Ironic, huh?"

Cain turned me to face him, his fingers locked around my wrists. We were so close, I could feel his heat even through my clothes. My nipples tightened, my hormones not getting the message that this man wanted to wring my neck, not fuck me.

Something in his expression shifted. "You were the other person on the island," he said slowly, like he'd finally figured the last piece of a puzzle out. "The operative we never saw."

My heart lurched into my throat. "So?"

"The explosion." His face went cold, every line sharpening. "That was you. You're the person who booby-trapped our boat."

A punch of real fear stole my breath. This was a side of Cain I'd never seen. I had to fight not to shrink back.

"I—you're vampires. I knew you'd survive."

"Really?" His lip curled. "Kinda hard to heal yourself when your brain and body is scattered across North Atlantic. The sun would've risen before we found all the pieces. And Eden's human. We barely got her off the boat in time, and then we had to row her to Lilith Island in a fucking inflatable dinghy."

Shame heated my skin. "I knew you'd save her, that you'd find the leak in time."

"And if we hadn't?"

I licked my lips. "I—it was a calculated risk, yes. But I had to make it look good, because—" My gaze slid from his. He was right. The simple, ugly truth was that I'd been too afraid to help Eden escape. "I'm sorry," I said, low-voiced.

Gods, I was a coward.

And now I'd lost Cain's respect. Or maybe he'd never respected me.

Maybe he'd been stringing me along, trading orgasms for information.

His growl made every muscle in my body tense up. "Sorry doesn't cut it. By the time we got back, Eden was dehydrated and half-frozen. You're lucky she didn't lose the baby."

My shoulders slumped. I nodded dully. "I'm sorry," I whispered.

"Nyx!" Jerome thumped on the door again.

Cain's mouth snapped shut. Like magic, a switchblade appeared in his hand. He touched the point to my throat above the choker, a silent warning.

I stared back, shocked. He couldn't have cut deeper if he'd driven that switchblade straight into my heart.

Maybe he was right not to trust me. I was Nazaire's daughter, after all, and even though I wanted out, I was only willing to go so far to help Cain.

It's not like the Maritime Syndicate were saints. They were vampires with blood on their hands, same as my father. Same as me, if I was being honest.

It still felt like a betrayal. My whole life, the people closest to me had lied to me, used me, discarded me. Starting with my mother, who'd handed me over to Nazaire the day after I turned four—for a million euros.

Was I that easy to give away? That unlovable?

"Answer me, Nyx." Jerome again. The door handle jiggled. "What are you doing in there?"

"Answer him," Cain mouthed. He'd retracted his fangs, but he didn't look any less dangerous.

"Une minute, s'il te plaît," I called back.

Cain leaned in, voice ice-cold. "We're not done."

I worked my jaw from side to side. I just wanted to go back to the hotel and lick my wounds in peace. "Yes, we are," I said wearily.

"The Hotel de Nuit," he said like I hadn't spoken. "I'll come to you—midnight."

I heaved a breath. Since that fiasco on the island, my father had increased the eyes watching me. Slipping away got riskier each time. But Cain wasn't going to let this drop.

"Not in my suite," I told him. "I'll meet you in La Cave." The vampire speakeasy beneath the hotel.

A curt nod. "I'll be at the bar—the man with the stainless-steel pin on his lapel. And clean up." He sniffed my throat, an insulting drag of breath. "My scent is all over you."

He grabbed his jacket, tossed me my thong, and vanished into the shadows.

Jerome banged again. "Open this door. *Now*, Nyx."

I ground my back teeth together. "I said, *in a minute*."

I quickly washed up and smoothed on some of the Dioriviera

lotion on the washroom counter. Now I smelled of roses instead of Cain.

I stepped into my thong, biting my lower lip when it brushed against my sensitized skin. I'd be feeling Cain for the rest of the night, including a phantom pain where his teeth had sunk into me. I tugged my skirt down, aware he must be watching.

A frisson went over my skin. Fear and a messed-up kind of arousal.

I drew a slow inhale and eyed my reflection—wrecked hair, smudged makeup. I hadn't brought a purse, but I made use of the makeup samples in a glass bowl on the counter, touching up my eyes and mouth, finger-combing my hair. Then I unlocked the door, pulled back my shoulders, and sauntered into the hall.

Jerome was waiting, his mouth in a thin line. He pushed past me without a word.

I kept walking.

He wouldn't find anything. Cain would've slipped out of the door behind me.

Jerome might be my bodyguard, but he wasn't allowed to touch me. All he could do was report back to my father, and what would he say? That I'd spent too long in the washroom?

Back in the gallery, I inserted myself into the circle that had formed around the painting of the island.

"Why the fire?" asked a vampire from the Madrid Syndicate, a woman named Viviana. "What's its significance?"

"Fire cleanses," said the man with her.

"Fire represents rebirth," murmured a third women.

Viviana smiled. "Perhaps the vampire in the forest makes her burn."

They were close, but nobody quite got it. "Maybe," I offered, my gaze flicking toward the washrooms, "she's saying nothing's permanent. Love. Alliances." I kept my tone light, even as something bitter rose in my throat. "Even the promises we give people right before we throw them away."

"Deep," said a ponytailed dhampir from California.

I nodded, but I'd drawn the wrong kind of attention. Several people had turned their heads to eye me, brows raised.

Jerome had returned to the gallery. He sent me a last, scowling look that made my skin tighten, then headed back upstairs.

I dredged up a light laugh. "But what do I know?" I added and melted into the crowd.

CAIN

The La Cave speakeasy lay three floors beneath the Hotel de Nuit. Neutral ground where out-of-towners were tolerated, if not exactly welcome.

I stopped by my own hotel to change into loafers and a Tom Ford smoking jacket, a slim steel bar pinned to its black velvet lapel. For my glamour this time, I borrowed the face of a Kral Syndicate soldier who happened to be in Paris but was busy elsewhere.

I reached the hotel at a quarter to midnight, deliberately early so I could be in position before Nyx arrived. Downstairs, the doorman looked me over, then waved me into the speakeasy. The place oozed fifties-style glamour: red leather booths, marble-top tables, a Marshall jukebox humming in the corner.

I claimed a spot at one end of the gleaming walnut bar and ordered a blood-whiskey. "A double."

Glass in hand, I leaned against the bar and surveyed the crowd. You had to hand it to Parisiens, they knew how to dress. Even the thralls looked sharp—polished up and put on display, all shine and bored expressions.

I took a long pull of whiskey, anger simmering in my gut.

It had been Nyx the whole time. We'd known there was another operative on the island, someone who'd slipped away scot-free. Someone who'd blown up our motorboat.

The boat we'd all been on—me, Brien, Talon, Twilight, Eden—when it had exploded in the North Atlantic, hours from any help.

I'd never suspected her, even though there'd been a moment on the island when I thought I'd caught her scent. I'd figured I was wrong because Nyx was on our side, wasn't she?

Hell, six weeks before Eden's kidnapping, she'd passed along the location of a QCS lair running a blood-slave ring, intel that helped us take the whole operation down. She'd seemed genuinely concerned about the men and women ensnared by the ring.

I'd admired the hell out of her for risking her syndicate's wrath to help them.

And I'd taken that as proof she was with us.

Now I didn't know what to believe.

Doubt crawled up my nape. Had anything between us been real, or had it all been one massive mind-fuck orchestrated by her Machiavelli of a sire?

Somebody flipped a switch and a 45 dropped into place on the jukebox turntable. The opening bars of "Heartbreak Hotel" slithered through the air, all smoke and sorrow.

Right on cue, Nyx appeared. She paused, framed in the doorway, golden skin shimmering in that cobweb of a dress. And like in the art gallery, heads turned, every vampire in the speakeasy—male or female—eyeing her tight little body.

She sauntered inside, hips swaying in time with Elvis's soulful cry. Manny followed, a few feet behind.

Something primitive awoke in me. My chest tightened with an unfamiliar, unwelcome possessiveness. Mixed with the anger and doubt, it was a potent brew.

In the gallery, my first sight of Nyx had been from behind. Her thong had been visible through the fishnet, a narrow black line that bisected her ass, showcasing two plump cheeks. I'd wanted to drop to my knees and take a bite of that firm flesh. Forbidden fruit, like the apples me and Talon swiped from a neighbor's orchard when we were kids. They'd tasted even sweeter because they were stolen.

So I knew exactly what those hot-eyed vampires were thinking.

My hand fisted around the glass. I stared down at my white-knuckled fingers and forced them to ease. Slowly, deliberately.

I didn't get jealous over women. I controlled them, like I controlled everything else in my life.

Manny muttered something in Nyx's ear, then joined a couple of QCS vampires at a marble-top table. She drifted deeper into the speakeasy, pausing here and there to chat. Her gaze skimmed over me, snagging on the steel pin on my lapel. Her lashes flickered, a tell I caught only because I was looking for it, and then she turned back to the asshole she was flirting with.

Five minutes later, she was at my side. "A blood-cognac, please," she told the bartender.

I remained where I was, my back against the bar, as she slid a look in my direction. When I didn't react, she slid her hands under her mane of curly hair, lifting it off her neck. The dress rode up, gliding over her round ass, tightening across her high, firm tits.

My breath hissed in. She flashed a sly *gotcha* smile—and released her hair. It tumbled over her shoulders in thick red waves.

"Your cognac," the bartender murmured, his gaze on her tits.

Finishing my whiskey, I put the glass on the bar and relieved the man of the bowl-shaped snifter. "Allons-y," I suggested. "Before I decide you've insulted the lady."

He took a hurried step back, Adam's apple bobbing. "I beg your pardon, M'sieur. Madame."

Nyx took the cognac from me. "And you are?" she asked with a sex-kitten of a grin.

"Henry," I said, unsmiling.

"And what brings you to Paris, Henry?"

My fangs tingled, itching to drop. Hearing her call me by another man's name, especially in those fuck-me tones, amped up the murky, prowling possessiveness.

"Business." I caught her fingers and lifted them to my mouth. A casual touch, one even Manny couldn't object to, but I made sure she felt the tips of my fangs before releasing her hand.

Reminding her who was the alpha vampire here.

Her eyes darkened, and her heartbeat sped up. The primal thing liked that, liked knowing how I affected her.

That much, at least, wasn't a lie. I relaxed a bit.

I released her fingers and she rotated the snifter between her palms, warming the cognac. "What do you want?" she asked under cover of the music emanating from the jukebox.

"Two hours," I said, matching her low tone. "You and me—alone. I booked a room on the third floor."

"And if I come, will it make a difference?"

I shrugged. "I'm not making any promises."

"Then no."

I smiled like we were sharing a private joke. "Did you think I was giving you a choice?"

Her breath hitched. "I see." She set the cognac snifter down with a soft clink. "Look, I—please just drop this. If you care for me at all... let it go."

I eyed her. Something in her voice—thin, frayed—bothered me. She wasn't teasing anymore. She was anxious, maybe even afraid.

Or maybe that was what she wanted me to think. Maybe this was just another layer of the act.

A smart man would let her go. We were through, weren't we? She'd made it clear that she was Nazaire's creature.

But I had the feeling that if I backed off now, let her walk away, I'd never get her alone again.

Something hollow and icy opened up in me. Something that swallowed my common sense. I couldn't let this end here. I wouldn't.

"Figure it out," I said in a hard voice as I slid a keycard into her palm. "Or I'll go straight to Brien and Talon. Room three-oh-three."

I left without looking back.

She'd come. I'd bet a case of my favorite single malt on it—and not because I'd threatened to tell my friends.

Nyx didn't want this thing between us anymore than I did. If her bodyguards caught us, we'd be neck-deep in shit. I'd be tortured, staked. And if I knew Nazaire, Nyx would be hustled back to Quebec and kept under lock and key for the next couple of decades.

So yeah, we both had everything to lose by meeting like this.
But like me, she wouldn't be able to stay away.

✤ *6* ✤

NYX

Back in my suite, I waited while Manny swept through the rooms, checking for anything out of the ordinary. When he finally left for the night, I locked the door behind him and sank onto the velvet couch. The keycard Cain had slipped me lay in my palm, small and innocuous—yet it felt heavier than anything I'd carried all day.

I stared at it, unsure whether to laugh, curse, or hurl it across the room.

I didn't have to meet him. When it came down to it, his only evidence was a painting by an anonymous artist. It was only damning if you'd been there that night.

Which Brien and Talon had been.

I briefly closed my eyes. The last thing I needed was a pair of alpha vampires out for revenge breathing down my neck.

Even worse, Cain *knew*. Knew I was The Haunt. He could ruin everything with a few words in the right ears.

He wouldn't. Not to me.

At least, that's what I told myself. But I didn't know for sure.

Cain was a vampire to the marrow—ruthless, cold, a man who'd clawed his way to stand just one step below his primus in barely two decades. And my father had pushed him and his friends to the brink.

Why had I put that painting in the show?

I'd known Cain might crash the opening night party—hell, I'd hoped he would. But I'd felt safe; no one had yet connected it-girl Nyx Nazaire to The Haunt.

And maybe, deep down, I'd wanted him to piece it together. To see this part of me my father never had. My paintings were my soul, unbared.

I grimaced. That had gone well, hadn't it?

And I was wasting time.

I pushed back to my feet. In the bedroom, I exchanged my heels for a pair of short leather boots, then cracked open a window. The rain had ended, but a patchy fog had rolled in. On the sidewalk below, streetlights rose out of the mist like wrought-iron stems tipped with golden glass buds. Across the street, the Seine was a dark ribbon flowing through the white wisps.

I fingered the keycard. I should cut it into confetti and toss it out the window, then barricade myself in my suite for the night.

Anything to keep myself from doing something stupid.

I was so close to getting out—one wrong move and everything could blow apart.

But I couldn't.

Because tonight was it—my last time with Cain. Once I left my father and the QCS, I'd have to disappear completely.

Nyx Nazaire was going to meet her end in a dark alley, leaving behind nothing but ashes and a few pieces of charred jewelry.

No forwarding address, no trail, no loose ends.

Keycard in hand, I stepped into the shadow world, then slid through the narrow gap between the window sash and the frame. I flowed down the exterior wall, weightless as the mist, until my feet touched the sidewalk below. I ducked into a recessed doorway and exited the shadows.

Safely shrouded in the fog, I pulled a glamour over myself—the face and body of another dhampir I'd seen around the hotel. Back in the foyer, I headed for the elevators, head high, steps unhurried. I waited until I was certain I was alone, then stepped into an empty car and jabbed the button for the third floor.

When the doors reopened, my previous glamour had been replaced by a forty-something maid in a black Hotel La Nuit uniform, a tiny gray gargoyle embroidered above the left breast. I walked briskly down the hallway, my low heels tap-tapping on the marble tile, the illusion settling around me like a second skin.

It was my superpower, my secret weapon—the ability to glamour my appearance as quickly and easily as the oldest, most powerful vampires.

And no one knew about it, even Nazaire.

Cain's suite appeared empty. Without dropping the glamour, I continued through the tasteful maroon-and-cream parlor and peered into the bedroom. The massive pedestal bed hadn't been slept in, and the washroom held only toiletries stamped with the hotel's gargoyle logo.

He clearly wasn't staying here at La Nuit.

Back in the parlor, I cleared my throat. "M'sieur Cain?"

I had no idea what his last name was. Maybe he didn't have one — some vampires shed them, cutting loose anything that tied them to the past.

"Here." He spoke from behind a pair of thick black-out curtains. "On the balcony."

I released the glamour and pushed through the heavy curtains. They swished shut behind me.

Cain stood with his hands behind his back, staring down at the mist-shrouded people strolling along the Seine. He looked so alone, his face shadowed.

Sometimes I thought that was what had brought us together. Not the sex, as good as it was, but this need we both had for connection, for someone to ease the loneliness. For a few hours, anyway.

He turned to face me, hands on the wrought-iron railing behind him. His right leg started jiggling.

I waited for him to start on me again, but all he said was, "Come here."

Fine by me.

I crossed the balcony, the night air cool on my skin, and unbuttoned his midnight-blue velvet jacket. No shirt. I eased the jacket open and spread my fingers over the firm planes of his chest.

He stilled, his eyes silver in the dim light. Even the jitter in his leg cut off like someone had flipped a switch.

A shark tattoo—the mark of a made man in the Maritime Syndicate—curled over the pale skin of his neck. I didn't know what he'd done to earn it; he wasn't the kind of vampire who bragged about the lives he'd taken.

I lifted a hand, tracing the shark tat with my fingertips. His throat tightened. It was an intimate act, and a bold one, especially with a vampire so dominant to me. I should've asked his permission first.

But fuck that. I stretched up and pressed a kiss to the shark's curved body.

Beneath my lips, the blood in his carotid pulsed. Unable to resist, I flicked my tongue out, tasting salt and Cain.

His chest rumbled, the beginnings of a growl, and I stilled.

"No, don't stop." His fingers wrapped around my skull, keeping me where I was. Taking control and yet indulging me. The combination sent a curl of heat through me.

He liked it, too. The proof pressed against my stomach, long and hard.

I slid my hand down his belly, toying with his waistband. "I believe I owe you something," I said against his throat.

He drew a slow breath. "Yeah?"

"Yeah." I squeezed him through his pants.

"That's right." His hands settled on my hips, gathering up my dress. He smoothed a palm over my bare bottom, his voice a sexy rasp. "I made you come, didn't I? Twice. You owe me for that."

I met his eyes. The silver-blue had darkened, his irises encircled by a flaming cobalt. Tension thrummed between us.

I wet my lips. "I always pay my debts."

"Good, because my dick intends to collect."

"Yeah?" I cupped him through his pants. "I might like that."

He smacked my ass, hard enough to make me gasp. "Take off your dress."

He released me and watched, his gaze hot enough to scorch my flesh, as I wriggled out of the fishnet. "The bra, too," he ordered.

I complied, ass still stinging, then lowered to my knees in front of him, my hands on his thighs.

He put his hands on the iron rail on either side of his hips, jacket falling open, chest gleaming, like one of those blond, blue-eyed angels from the stories my human nanny used to tell me. Except this angel had teeth and hunger and a darkness that called to mine.

I undid his pants, eased the zipper down. He'd gone commando so his cock sprang out, brushing my cheek. I ran a finger up the smooth, veined length.

He regarded me from beneath thick, dark lashes. "Keep going."

"Yes, Lieutenant," I said, only half-teasing.

Closing both hands around him, I rubbed a thumb over the tip, wet with pre-cum, enjoying his hiss of pleasure. I licked the salty liquid, then drew his head between my lips, slow and easy.

He let me take the lead for a minute before moving his hands to my head, holding me still so he could stroke deeper into my mouth. I sucked harder and his body went rock-hard.

"That's it," he said, tone hoarse. "Take me—all of me. Show me how good you can be."

At his praise, I felt a pull between my legs. I wanted to please him. Wanted to replace his anger with me with something that pleasured us both. To apologize for rigging that damn boat to explode.

Sweet Luna, I was fucked up. We both were.

Like a sexual act could make up for that.

But Cain didn't seem to care about my fucked-upness, and I didn't care about his. In fact, it turned me on.

Maybe it was the same for him.

7

CAIN

My hands tightened on Nyx's head. From a room below came the muted sound of voices, but here on the balcony, we were hidden in the fog.

She took me deeper and I went with it, pushing even further. I was a bastard for letting her do this on her knees on the balcony's cold tiles, but something about Nyx brought out the prick in me. Maybe it was her fairy-princess vibe, the way she'd grown up rich and pampered while I'd been kicked around, told I was dirt.

I'd only been in the same room with her and Nazaire once—the night we met at that party thrown by the Montreal prima. But it was enough. I'd seen how her sire treated her, ordering her around, talking down to her like she was a thrall instead of his own daughter. And she'd taken it, standing there smiling and silent, the perfect little syndicate princess.

Part of me despised her for it. Were the fancy clothes, the jewelry, the status really worth letting him own her like that?

And she deserved a little hardship. The woman had nearly blown up me and my friends.

She gave my dick a squeeze that made me suck in oxygen, and I forgot everything except how good this felt. Gods, I'd missed it— and her.

Her mouth didn't quit: licking...sucking... Sweet and hot and wet. Her eyes were shut, her lips closed around me.

My gaze went to the choker around her throat. My gift.

It was nothing—a black velvet ribbon studded with brass, something I'd picked up in a Goth-punk store the last time I was in London because it had reminded me of her. I would've liked to give her something pricier, but Nazaire would've noticed. I'd figured she'd toss it the next night.

But she hadn't. She'd kept it—worn it in front of everyone at the art show. A cheap, ten-pound-sterling choker.

That unexpected, unwanted possessiveness snaked through my insides.

I heard myself grit out, "Stop."

She took a few beats before pulling off. She frowned up at me, her lips slick, reddened. "Something wrong?"

"Nothing. Just—" Hands still buried in her thick hair, I came to my knees beside her, driven by something I didn't understand to share the discomfort, the hard surface along with her.

Nyx crawled backward, my fingers still in her hair, the two of us coordinating the change in position with that rapport we'd had since the very first night, like we were in each other's minds, until she was on all fours facing me.

"Now." I drew her head in the direction of my lap.

Instead of taking me in her mouth, she pushed back against my palms so she could look up at me, her eyes a tawny gold in the night.

I tilted her head sideways, exposing her throat.

She gulped, the choker moving with her muscles, her lids drifting closed. "Cain..."

I drew a breath, my fangs pricking at my gums. Having her submit to me like this almost made this godsdamn night—and everything I'd learned—worth it.

I gave her hair a tug, just for being so damn fuckable, and she whimpered, her need scenting the air. My syndicate princess liked things rough.

"Suck me," I told her.

She immediately complied, resting that round ass on her leather boots, her lids half-lowered as she took me deep.

I stroked the side of her cheeks with my thumbs. "You look so beautiful—on your knees for me. You want this, don't you? Want me to use you."

Her long lashes lowered. I took that as a yes, especially when she sucked me deeper. Her fingers were around my root, her other hand massaging my balls.

She was good at this. Too good.

How many men had she knelt for?

I flashed on how her cousin Rodrigo had touched her, like he had a right to. Worse, the way he'd eyed her as she walked away from him, like he was thinking of making good on that right.

"Who else do you take like this?" I forced her to take me a little deeper, darkly satisfied when she relaxed her throat around me.

"No one," she said around me, two garbled syllables.

"Only me, then."

She nodded as much as she could with my hands in her hair and my dick in her mouth. All she could smell and taste was me.

"But," I muttered, half to myself, half to her, "I wouldn't know if you were lying, would I?"

A shake of her head.

A puff of laughter escaped me. "Why did I think you'd say you'd never lie to me? I can never predict you."

She pulled off long enough to say, "That's why you like me," then took me inside her mouth again.

She was right. Her unpredictability was why I liked her even though I didn't trust her—not completely, anyway.

And in some strange, *yeah, I'm definitely abnormal* way, I liked that I couldn't fully trust her. The challenge of Nyx—that edge of danger —excited me. I enjoyed seeing how far I could push her. What she'd accept.

She touched a spot with her tongue that made my eyes roll back in my head. My balls drew up tight, heat building in my lower spine.

"That's it," I muttered. "Make me come like a good girl. My good girl."

She moaned my name around my length. Her eyes were closed again, her face flushed. One hand slipped between her thighs, touching herself, and her obvious enjoyment increased mine.

Time stretched like warm taffy. The only things in the world were her hot, wet mouth and the hands that seemed to be everywhere, gripping my dick, massaging my stones.

I wanted to last longer, but she touched her teeth to my already sensitized flesh and a fireball exploded up my spine.

"Fuuu-ck." I groaned and emptied myself into her throat in a few hard pumps, loving how she swallowed it down, dimly aware that she was coming too, her cries muffled, sexy.

When she released me, she stayed on her knees, cheek resting against my bare thigh. Pulling up my pants, I lowered my ass to the marble tiles and drew her onto my lap, my back against the iron rails.

Her arms came around me in a loose hug. I rested my head against her hair, inhaling Nyx. Earth and sage, smoky and sweet.

Something in me sighed, settled. I'd missed her, damn it.

Hell, I'd been worried about her.

After that operation on the island, she'd gone missing. I'd wondered why, of course, but we weren't exactly in regular contact, and I'd already pushed things too far while we were scrambling to get Eden back from those SOBs.

When a month passed with no sign of Nyx, not even at QCS events, I'd started to get uneasy. I'd wanted to investigate, but if she was in trouble, me sniffing around could make it worse.

Still, while I was in Quebec trying to dig up something damning on Nazaire, I kept an eye out for her. Eventually she resurfaced at a couple of QCS parties—exclusive ones I couldn't crash without blowing my cover, even if I'd known ahead of time that she'd be in attendance.

So when Donald, our man in Quebec City, tipped me off that Nyx was going to be at an art show in Paris, I'd jumped on a jet.

I'd been half-crazed with an unnamed fear until I saw her in that gallery, laughing, flirting, *alive*. Only then did the tightness in my chest loosen.

Nyx lifted her head. "I'd better go. They...watch me now. I can't be gone the whole night."

I shook my head. "I don't know how you can live like that. Does the money mean that much?"

She gave a twisted little smile. "You think he'd let me just walk out the door?"

I frowned. It was the first crack I'd seen in Nyx's loyalty to her sire. "Maybe not," I answered, still trying to make all the pieces line up. "But you seem all in. Makes me wonder if you've been playing me the whole time."

She went rigid. Then she tore herself out of my hold, landing on her ass a couple feet away.

"Are you serious?" Her voice broke on the words. "These times with you? They're everything to me. When things get bad, I think about you, and that's how I—"

She sounded devastated, like losing my trust wasn't just a blow— it was the worst thing that could've happened to her.

And what did she mean, "when things get bad"?

"This is about Eden, isn't?" She scrubbed her hands down her face, barreling on before I could answer. "You don't get it. I knew you people had a dinghy, and I stalled the explosion so you'd have time to escape. Nazaire was so angry at me for screwing up—"

She rolled her lips into her mouth like she was swallowing the rest. Like explaining wouldn't change a damn thing.

I knew that look. That dark, hopeless acceptance. I'd worn it myself growing up under my bastard of an uncle.

Something shifted in me. That big, bright smile she showed the world? I'd figured it was a mask. I just hadn't bothered to think too hard about what it hid.

A black heat blanked my vision. "He hurt you?" My voice came out low and dangerous.

She shrugged—small, defeated. An answer all on its own.

I pushed up onto my knees and caught her by the shoulders.

"Tell me," I demanded. "What did he do?"

✣ 8 ✣

NYX

I stared dazedly at Cain, my body still buzzing, my mind scrambling to catch up. One moment I'd been curled in his lap, warm and loose and letting myself forget—and the next, I was undergoing an interrogation.

I shook my head. "It was nothing."

Don't tell. Never tell. Nobody will help you anyway.

Hot tears pricked my eyes. I blinked them away. You didn't show weakness to a vampire.

His expression hardened. "What. Did. He. Do?"

The weight of his dominance pressed against me, demanding an answer.

My pulse kicked up. My gaze slid sideways, my instincts screaming at me to comply, yield, survive.

Fuck that. This was one vampire I didn't have to obey. I'd already told him too much. I met his eyes and pressed my lips together until they hurt.

"You were helping me," he said to himself. "Giving me intel. If he suspects—" He halted, jaw tight. "Damn. That's why nobody saw you in public for weeks after."

"He doesn't suspect." My hands landed on Cain's naked chest.

I meant to push him away, but I didn't. He felt too good. My reward for making sure he and his friends survived the explosion, even knowing I'd pay for screwing up.

"How do you know?" he asked.

"I'm a female—and a dhampir. He doesn't think I have the guts to betray him. Actually, he blames Pascal. I told him Pascal broke when you tortured him."

"So then where have you been? He kept you locked away for what—a month? Two months?"

"Thirty days," I found myself saying.

Thirty endless days. And since then, he'd been keeping a close eye on me. I was lucky he'd allowed this trip to Paris.

"If he doesn't blame you, then why did you get locked up?"

I lifted my shoulders, let them drop. "There was no one else to take his anger out on."

The neon blue faded from Cain's eyes, but his expression remained dark. "And—?"

"He confined me to my apartment." My gaze slid from Cain's. "And ordered me not to paint—or anything."

"What's that mean—anything?"

"He had them throw out my pencils and drawing pads, too. A few months worth of sketches—all gone. Burned."

But first he'd called me a birdbrain and backhanded me across the face in front of a group of his men and their thralls. Then he'd made me stay and serve everyone drinks, my cheek still throbbing, before ordering Rodrigo to lock me in my apartment.

It wasn't the first time he'd humiliated me in front of the lair. It wasn't even the first time I'd been confined to my quarters. But before, I'd always had my art to disappear into. I guess he'd realized that I could survive anything as long as I could paint.

I was reduced to sketching on napkins with lipstick and eye liner. One night, I grabbed a bar of soap and drew a woman on the bathroom mirror, her mouth open in a silent scream, hands tearing at her hair.

Cain growled. "He burned your work?" He framed my face with his palms, his brows two fierce slashes. "What the fuck's the matter with him? Doesn't he know how good you are?"

Actually, no.

But I didn't tell Cain. Instead, I gave a tiny shake of my head.

I hadn't forgotten that threat Cain had made about going to Dussault with this. I didn't think he would—he seemed truly angered on my behalf. But I wasn't sure.

His thumbs brushed along my cheekbones. "Tell me how to get to him, firefly. Let me end the motherfucker."

I leaned into his palms. That nickname—firefly—made me want to melt, to agree to anything. If only this were a story, a painting, and the two of us could disappear into a fantasy world together.

But it wasn't. And this was my father, my sire.

"No." I caught his wrists, pushing them away from my face. "I'm not a blood-rat."

His expression tightened, but he released me. "I'll keep you out of it, I swear. No one will ever know you helped."

"*I'll* know."

His mouth flattened. "So you're protecting him, even now."

"I'm not a blood-rat," I said again. "Honor means something to me."

Maybe I'd given up on ever winning Nazaire's respect. But you didn't betray your sire. It was drilled into us—vampires and dhampirs alike—from the moment we could walk.

When I left the QCS, I was leaving with my head high and my conscience intact.

"I see." Cain rose, zipping his pants in one swift, final motion.

I got dressed just as fast, not caring when the fragile lace tore under my hands.

He shrugged into his jacket and leaned back against the hotel's limestone wall, head tipped toward the single star that had managed to punch through the fog.

I ached to go to him, give him a last, hard hug. But he was once again the Maritime Syndicate lieutenant.

"Goodbye," I said in a low voice.

"Lemaire was going to sell Eden," he said. "Did you know that? To Nazaire—as a blood slave."

"No. He—what?" I took a step backward. "Where did you hear that?"

He brought his gaze back to me. "Lemaire told Eden himself."

"Then he lied," I returned, on surer ground now. "Lemaire, yes. He and Fleur were running that blood slave ring, the one your syndicate broke up."

"And Nazaire's still pissed off about that."

"Not because he was a part of it. The entire upper hierarchy is seething. You think they don't know why your primus invested in that casino? He won't stop until the QCS is under Maritime control. Already, he's pressuring Dussault to allow more investment, more oversight of our private business."

"You really don't know, do you?"

Uneasiness skittered along my skin. "Know what?"

"Nazaire was up to his neck in Fleur and Lemaire's shit. In fact, before Twilight mated with Brien, your father tried to buy her, too —at a private auction. At the Black Dahlia."

My stomach dipped. I had a childish urge to clap my hands over my ears, like if I didn't hear it, it wasn't true.

The Black Dahlia wasn't just any QCS club, it was *the* club, the one reserved for the upper hierarchy. Nazaire had never taken me there. I used to wonder why, used to think it was because I wasn't important enough. These days, I knew enough to be grateful.

"She told you that?"

"She didn't have to. I saw it for myself—I was there that night. Dussault invited Brien personally, and Brien didn't want to turn him down; they were in the middle of the casino negotiations. Me and Talon went along as bodyguards. And in case you're wondering, until Brien saw Twilight, he had no plans to bid on anyone."

"Maybe my father was there because of Dussault, too. It's not like he can refuse him. When your primus invites you to something, you go."

"Nazaire didn't drop out until the bidding on Twilight hit four mil. That's a nice chunk of cash just to keep your primus happy."

"It is." I gulped, my uneasiness creeping back. "But if he was part of Fleur & Lemaire's ring, why would he try to buy Twilight and Eden?"

He moved a shoulder. "Maybe he wanted exclusive access. Or maybe he was just fucking with us. I'm not sure he knew what Twilight was to Brien, but he definitely knew Eden was carrying Talon's spawn."

It made sense. It even sounded like my father.

I still shook my head, rejecting his logic. "I'm telling you—my father doesn't keep blood slaves. I'd know."

Wouldn't I?

"That you're aware of," Cain murmured like he'd read my mind.

"I've been in all three of his lairs. My guess is Dussault wanted him to push up the price so Brien would have to pay more."

"So you're saying they tried to cheat Brien."

"He didn't have to bid."

The QCS primus pretended to be willing to work with Brien, but behind his back he called him the "princeling." He resented that Brien had been groomed to be the next Maritime primus, that he hadn't had to work his way up through the hierarchy like Dussault had. And, like my father, Dussault hated how powerful the Maritime Syndicate had become. The two of them would've happily cheated Brien if they believed they could get away with it.

"True," Cain said. "But I was there, and it sure seemed like your father wanted Twilight. You should've seen his face when Brien outbid him. That wasn't a man trying to keep his primus happy."

"Maybe he had a reason I don't know about."

Cain grunted, clearly unconvinced. I was grasping at straws, and we both knew it.

I worried my lower lip. "Well... if he had bought her, I would've helped her."

"Like you helped Eden?"

The words hit like a slap. I flinched, and he exhaled.

"I'm sorry. That was low."

I jerked my chin in acknowledgment. It hurt, but I deserved it. "I really have to go. But first, can I ask you something?"

He eyed me moodily. "What?"

"If you go to Dussault, don't bring The Haunt into it. You can tell him you found out I was on the island. Just don't out me. Please?"

His brows lifted. "They really don't know?"

I shook my head. "Only you. I know I don't have the right to ask this, but..." I spread my hands.

His chest heaved. "Only if you promise me something in return."

"What?"

"If it gets too much—if Nazaire goes too far—you get word to me, and I'll come for you. Or just get the hell out. We'll take you in, give you sanctuary. He won't lay a hand on you again. Just get yourself to Halifax and I'll send a chopper for you. There's a bar on the waterfront." He gave me the name. "Tell any of the bartenders to contact me."

My heart squeezed painfully. "You'd do that?"

Yeah, Cain had his own agenda, but that didn't make his offer any less generous. If I accepted, his syndicate would be painted as the villains. You didn't steal another man's spawn without consequences.

"Fuck, yes," he said.

I swallowed over what felt like a handful of grit. I wanted that sanctuary, wanted it so badly it scared me.

But wanting and taking are two different things.

"Think about it," Cain urged. "You could have your own studio. A big one. There's more than enough space in the castle. You could keep painting, keep showing your work. Your father doesn't have to know. And if he finds out—tough shit. I won't let him touch you."

"He'll find out. He'll come for me. You know he will."

"Let him."

I studied the hard line of his jaw. "But maybe that's what you want," I added slowly. "Maybe you're hoping he'll follow me to the island so you can take him out."

A muscle jumped in his cheek. "It's a genuine offer, damn it. Yeah, I want your father in his final grave, but that doesn't mean I don't want to help you. And yes, you have my promise. I'll keep The Haunt out of it."

I nodded, more grateful than he knew. "Thank you. And Cain? That you offered me sanctuary? It means a lot. But I'll be okay. I can take care of myself."

I'd survived a childhood in Nazaire's lair, hadn't I?

I started the fade.

"Hold on." Cain crossed the balcony, pulling me into his arms. "When will I see you again?"

Never.

I halted the fade—if I didn't, I'd take him into the shadows with me—and touched his cheek, memorizing the feel of him. Cool, a little rough. "Wait a couple of months. Let things settle down."

"Nyx..."

Hope welled up in me. "Yes?"

My defenses were down and it all poured out of me. An aching yearning, a wish that we could actually be together.

He shouldn't have been able to sense my emotions—I was a dhampir, not a human. But he went taut, then released me like a hot coal.

It was all the answer I needed. A sad smile tipped up my lips. "Goodbye, Cain."

"We're not done," he insisted. "I *will* see you again."

I just shook my head. I stepped sideways, putting more space between us, and vanished into the shadows as he watched, tight-jawed.

It took me less than a minute to crawl down to the second floor and along the wall to my suite. I flowed back into the bedroom, eased the window shut and dragged the blackout shade down. I shed my clothes and headed into the washroom.

I barely had time to scrub Cain's scent off my skin before Jerome's knock rattled my door. I opened it, dressed in a tee and yoga pants, an open bottle of blood-champagne in my hand.

"What?" I flashed him a loopy smile.

Disgust flickered over his lean face. It wasn't easy for a dhampir to get fucked up, but I'd faked it enough over the years that my bodyguards figured I had a low tolerance.

"Everything all right?" He scanned the suite behind me.

"Absss—absoluutely," I mumbled. "Everything's perrrfect. Wanna drink?" I waved the bottle at him.

His lip curled. "No," he said shortly, and left, locking the door behind him.

I took another gulp of blood-champagne and put the bottle on the wet bar, then crawled into the massive bed.

My sex felt empty. We hadn't finished. Not really.

I sighed.

My hand crept beneath the waist band of my yoga pants. But after a few rubs, I gave up because the emptiness was coming from elsewhere, somewhere deep inside me.

I'd just left Cain for the last time. If all went as planned, I'd never see him again. The moment the gallery money hit that secret Swiss account, I was gone. Out of my father's lair. Out of the syndicate world.

I'd backpack across Europe, moving only by daylight, supporting myself by selling my paintings. At night I'd lock myself away, safe behind bolted doors where no vampire could reach me.

Safe—and alone.

I should've felt a spark of excitement, a flicker of the freedom I'd dreamed about for years. Instead, I felt...flat. Like someone had drained all the color out of me.

With a low, unhappy exhale, I pulled the soft sheets over my head.

9

CAIN

Back on Lilith Island, I dropped my gear in my quarters and made straight for the war room. The place hummed with low voices and the glow of the security feeds—familiar, grounding. Brien was talking to the soldier on duty when I walked in, but he cut it off when he saw me.

"Cain." He smiled and crossed the cavern, still in tactical pants and scuffed trainers like he'd come straight from the gym, and clapped me on the back. "Good to have you back."

"Good to be back." I shook his hand, giving it a firm squeeze. Maybe firmer than necessary, like I had to prove to both of us that everything was fine. "Everything all right here?"

"Yeah—quiet, actually. What about you?"

I'd kept my promise to check in every few days, but otherwise I'd stayed silent. A good hacker—and vampire syndicates had the best in the world—could intercept even encrypted messages. No way I was risking that.

Too bad I wasn't bringing good news. "I'll tell you in your office."

"Of course." He waved me ahead of him and closed the door behind us.

I stopped a few steps in, waiting as he moved past and leaned a hip against the edge of his walnut desk. I'd had the whole flight back to Nova Scotia to decide what to tell him, and I'd settled on the bare truth.

"I got the proof we wanted. Nazaire was definitely the man behind Eden's kidnapping. But I can't use it without compromising my source."

He lifted a brow. "Go on."

"That's it." I dropped moodily into the leather armchair in front of his desk. "I promised myself I wouldn't come back until I had Nazaire by the balls. And yet here I am."

He zeroed in on the important part. "What d'you mean, you can't use your proof?"

My fingers into the chair's padded arms, frustration chewing at me. "I just can't."

Nyx had left Paris early the next evening. I'd gone back to the hotel, determined to talk to her one more time. Instead, I'd wasted a couple of hours confirming she was really gone, then contracted with a hotel-provided thrall for blood and sex. But I hadn't been able to bring myself to fuck the woman. After drinking my fill, I paid her and sent her on her way.

By then it was too late to catch a flight home. I spent the rest of the night prowling around Paris—restless, wired, and wanting Nyx in a way that made my skin feel too tight.

I had this bad feeling that might've been the last time I'd see her, alone, anyway. I'd probably spot her at some syndicate party, flanked by guards or that asshole Rodrigo. The thought made my jaw clench so hard I was surprised my molars weren't dust.

"Why not?" Brien asked.

"Because the proof—" that damn painting—"would out her to her syndicate. So I can't use it. But she was on the island at Nazaire's orders."

He straightened. "Your contact was the other person on the island that night?"

Too late, I realized I'd made a mistake. I gave a reluctant nod. "Yes."

"So she blew up the boat."

My stomach sank. "Yeah. But she rigged it so we had time to get off before it exploded."

"Or that's just what she's telling you. And you're protecting her? What are you playing at, Cain?"

"Nothing. I gave my word she'd remain anonymous. She wouldn't have helped us otherwise."

He folded his arms over his chest. "I'll allow you that. I won't even remind you that as your primus, your first loyalty is to me, because you're also a friend. A good one."

"Thanks," I started to say, but he wasn't finished.

"I think I know who she is anyway." He was too close, his gaze too knowing. I fought not to squirm on the hard leather cushion, but if I stood with Brien in this uncertain mood, he might see it as a challenge. "So the question is, what are we going to do about her?"

"Do about her?" I straightened in the chair, upset. "Look, she did what she could. She was the one who made sure Eden got food and water, and she bought us time to get off the boat."

I realized I'd accepted Nyx's explanation as the truth. That I'd begun to trust her.

"I see." His expression iced over. "So let me get this straight—this bitch was there on the island with the bastards who kidnapped Eden. The ones who were trying to take Twilight, too. My fucking mate. And you want to let her off."

"She didn't have a choice, damn it."

"Is that what she told you?"

"Yes, and I believe her. Didn't you wonder why we had enough time to get a dinghy out and away from the boat before it caught fire? She was caught between us and Nazaire. She had to make it look like she tried to stop us from escaping."

Brien's lip curled. "Sounds like you're thinking with your dick."

That brought me to my feet. If I stayed in that chair one second more, I'd go for his throat. That was unacceptable—and not just because he was my primus, but because he had a valid point.

He made a low, gotcha sound. "So you are fucking her."

"So? You got the intel you needed to take down Fleur and Lamaire's blood-slave ring, didn't you?"

His eyes narrowed. "Stand down, Lieutenant."

I met his stare, refusing to blink. The air between us tightened. A long, dangerous beat stretched—two predators sizing each other up.

Then I spun on my heel and paced away before I did something I'd regret, like pulling a blade on my fucking primus. When I turned back, I had myself in check.

"You're wrong about her," I said evenly. "She did everything she could for us. Anything more and Nazaire would've figured out she was the reason we got off that boat alive. As it was, he punished her for screwing up."

Brien unfolded his arms. "I don't trust her, Cain. And if she's who I think she is, you shouldn't either. Nazaire is a snake. It would be just like him to use his own spawn to seduce one of my lieutenants."

"Not this time. I made the first move. I'm the one who went after her, not the other way around."

Or had I? A sliver of uneasiness worked its way under my skin. Looking back, I couldn't say for sure.

Our first meeting at the Tremblay Castle had been like something out of a fucking rom-com. Across a packed ballroom—a high-class gala hosted by the new Tremblay prima and her mate—we'd locked eyes. Nyx had wet her lips. Then she turned and sauntered toward the exit, her short purple skirt swaying like bait. At the doorway, she stopped and thrown me an over-the-shoulder glance.

I'd followed, telling myself she might be a useful contact. Someone I could cultivate, pump for information.

She'd been waiting in the castle's sweet-smelling garden, the moonlight turning her red hair into dark fire. Ten minutes after that, I had her up against the wall in one of the stone turrets, that tease of a skirt flipped up, my fingers inside her...

Brien circled behind his desk and dropped into his chair. "Yeah, her intel has been solid. But she had to give you something to gain your trust. How useful has that intel really been?"

"We couldn't have taken down Fleur's lair without it."

"True—and yet, Lemaire wasn't there that night. How do we

know Nazaire didn't tip him off? Maybe he wanted Fleur out of the picture. The three of them were splitting the profit for that blood-slave ring. Take Fleur out of the equation and suddenly he and Lemaire get a bigger cut—and Nazaire's hands stay clean."

I eyed him, jaw working. "Maybe you're right. But whatever she did was because of Nazaire's orders. He's the one you want, not her."

Brien made a sound—half grunt, half warning—that said I was only seeing the part I wanted to see. "What I'm wondering is just how deep your involvement with this woman goes."

"About that..." I leaned against the door, deliberately loose, like I wasn't dropping another bombshell. "I offered her sanctuary—here, on the island."

"You did what?" His whole body went rigid. "Yeah, it sucks she was punished for letting us escape, but you only have her word for that. And—"

"She turned me down flat," I cut in. "Says she's no blood-rat."

"Yeah?" He blinked. "Well, good for her."

"But the way I see it," I continued, "she has a right to our protection. She's stuck her neck out for us twice now. And Nazaire treats her like shit—locks her up, orders her around." *Doesn't let her make her fucking art.* "She's treated more like a thrall than his—"

"Daughter?" Brien finished helpfully.

I hesitated, then nodded. "Yeah." I wasn't breaking my promise; he'd obviously figured out my contact's identity. "If she—Nyx—changes her mind, we owe it to her to take her in."

"And give Nazaire the high ground? I can just picture how he'll spin it."

"You didn't see how it was in Paris. Nazaire has always kept her on a tight leash, but now she doesn't go anywhere without a body-guard. And she seemed different—on edge. Afraid, even. She's good at hiding it, but—" I swallowed. "We know Nazaire's an abusive, controlling sonuvabitch. I just figured Nyx was an exception, that the fact that she was his own spawn means something to the man."

I should've realized it before now. Should've recognized the signs.

The way she jumped to please him but was never good enough. The fact that she was rarely seen in public without Nazaire or one of his men nearby.

She couldn't even claim her paintings as her own. She was a fucking world-class artist, and no one knew it. Why was that?

A sick feeling gathered in my gut.

I knew what it was like to be under someone's thumb. To never be good enough. To swallow your tears because crying only makes it worse.

"Something doesn't smell right," I told Brien. "What if he's starting to suspect she's helping us? If he gets any proof, I'm not sure what he'll do to her." I blew out a breath. "You may as well know—I told her if she changed her mind, the offer was open."

"Hades." He pinched the bridge of his nose. "You couldn't have run it by me first?"

I frowned, silently cursing that promise I'd made Nyx not to out her as The Haunt. Brien owned three of her paintings—hell, he'd been one of her earliest supporters—and I couldn't give him the one truth that might've tipped the scales in her favor.

"There wasn't time. I had to make a decision then and there." I shoved my hands in my pockets. "I have a bad feeling about this, Bri. Like time is running out for her. Nazaire isn't stupid. He may know more than she thinks."

"You're not some damned white knight," he said between his teeth. "The last thing I want is to hand that SOB a legitimate excuse to come after us. This way, when we finally take him down, Dussault can't claim he didn't bring it on himself. Let it go, Cain."

"I have to," I said. "Like I said, she turned me down."

But if she came to me for sanctuary, all bets were off. I'd be damned before I'd let her twist in the wind.

She wasn't the only one with honor.

Or that's what I told myself. The truth was more complicated: that primitive thing in me couldn't let this go. Couldn't let *her* go.

Like I'd told her—we weren't done.

"What about here on the island?" I retook my seat. "Everything okay?"

"Yeah—quiet, actually. Talon's been glued to his suite. Dude's afraid to let Eden and Jude out of his sight for more than a few minutes." Brien grimaced. "Can't say I blame him after everything that went down."

I jiggled my knee, hating that he even had to worry about that kind of crap. "How the fuck did this happen? Lilith Island's ours. We rule here, for gods' sake."

We'd ramped up security—doubled patrols, increased the number of hidden cameras, sent up drones—but the island was too big. Forty-five square kilometers of tangled forest, jagged cliffs, scattered orchards, and open fields. Too many places to hide. Too many angles to defend.

Brien exhaled. "It all goes back to my mother, doesn't it? They got to her right here on the island."

"Yeah, but that was the slayers, wasn't it? They've got no reason to go after us these days."

"That was my father's theory, yeah. But he never found out for sure, and Lilith knows he tried. If he'd gotten even an ounce of proof, he would've personally hunted down the slayer responsible and damn the consequences."

I nodded grimly. Jules Leclerc had never really come back from losing his mate. Something in him had broken. He'd haunted the castle walls, eyes locked on the blood-soaked ground where the prima had been staked. Like if he stared long enough, hard enough, she'd claw her way out of her final grave to him.

"And meanwhile," Brien said, voice tight, "they keep coming at us. I don't blame Talon for keeping Eden and Jude close. I'd do the same with Twilight if she'd let me." He blew out a breath. "But as she likes to remind me, she's as good a fighter as anyone I'd assign to guard her."

❧

M y next stop was Talon's quarters. He opened the door with Jude tucked against his shoulder, swaddled in a tiny purple sweatsuit, soft brown curls just like his dad's springing up all over his head.

Talon lifted a finger to his lips. "Eden's asleep," he said in a hushed voice. "But Jude keeps vampire hours." His mouth twitched with amused resignation.

"Should I come back?" I asked in equally quiet tones.

Jude lifted his head, straining to turn in my direction. His gaze found me—or tried to. His head wobbled, then dropped back onto Talon's shoulder, a small, trusting collapse that did something to my chest.

"No, come in. Just keep it down, okay?"

"You got it." I stepped inside, easing the door shut behind me, watching as Talon stroked a hand over his son's curls. "How's he doing?"

"Growing like a weed." Talon gave Jude a proud look. "Olivia was here earlier for his two-week checkup. Said he's already up six ounces."

"Six ounces, eh?" I eyed the small, sweatsuit-clad lump. "Kid's a bruiser."

Talon chuckled. Jude gummed his dad's neck.

"Hang on there." My friend made a face at me. "Little mofo's already got a taste for blood."

My brows lifted. I shot a look at the kid's round, toothless mouth. "Doesn't he need fangs?"

"Not to suck. I opened a vein for him." Talon held up his wrist, showed me the faint, silvery line where the skin had healed.

"They drink blood this early?"

"Depends on the kid, I guess. He was trying so hard to get to my vein that we gave it a try, and he took right to it."

Jude moved his head around again in uncoordinated, jerky starts and stops, somehow managing to land on top of one fat wrist, which he promptly started gnawing on.

"See what I mean?" Talon rubbed the little guy's purple-fleece-clad back. "Kid's always hungry. Eats every couple of hours or so. Olivia says my blood is just as important as milk while he's growing this fast."

I stared at Talon, half-incredulous, half-bewildered. He was juggling the kid like he'd been doing it for years and bragging about a six-ounce weight gain. Who was this man, and what had he done with my best friend?

"Right," I muttered.

Talon dragged his gaze from Jude—who was trying to shove both fists into his mouth now—to meet my eyes. "I've been waiting for you to get back. Eden and I wanted to ask you something."

"Anything."

"We want you to be Jude's syndicate sponsor."

"Me?" My pulse hitched. "I'm honored, Tal. But I can't. I don't know a thing about kids."

He scoffed. "Like I do? You'll learn, same as me. Brien is Jude's primus, so he's out. And I would've picked you anyway. You're the closest thing I've got to a brother. No, screw that. You *are* my brother."

Damn, damn, damn.

My gaze flicked from Talon's face—open, earnest, terrifyingly certain—to the tiny, helpless bundle on his shoulder. Jude shifted, letting out a soft whimper, and suddenly, the air got thinner. Like the room had shrunk around me and left no space to breathe.

I stepped back, palms up. "I'm the wrong guy. I'm honored— gods, I am. But if something happens to you, I'd be responsible for him. Right?"

Talon's thick brows pulled together. "Where the syndicate is concerned, yeah."

"So I'd be like his godfather. The way Wayne Baker was my godfather."

My uncle Wayne Baker, to be precise, although he'd never let me call him "uncle." I called him *sir* when I was a kid, and now, I didn't speak to the bastard at all.

"That's what a sponsor is. But don't forget Eden—"

"If we disagreed, as his syndicate sponsor, I could overrule her. You know that."

"Hey." Talon crossed the room toward me. That's when I realized I'd backed up until my shoulders hit his door. "First, I'm not going anywhere. So this is a ceremonial position. And I want you, no one else."

"Don't say that." I pressed against the thick wood, knee bouncing double-time. "I can't do it. What if something did happen to you? I won't risk it. *You* shouldn't risk it, and if Eden knew how messed up I am, she'd say hell no."

Talon was wrong to even ask. No way should I be the one standing behind his son in any official capacity. Not as a sponsor. Not as anything that implied I was whole.

I was too broken inside.

"Listen to me." Talon crooked his free arm around the back of my head, bringing my face to his, Jude between us. "Are you listening?" He waited for my muttered agreement before continuing, "You are nothing like that motherfucker. I was there, remember? I know what he's like and I know what you're like. You might not know what you're doing, but you'll figure it out. The one thing you would never do is terrorize an innocent kid. I trust you, bro. Understand? I. Trust. You."

His powerful arm around my head grounded me. That, and the small weight snuggled between us. The fear and anxiousness—and *anger*—subsided to a level where I could think more clearly.

"No, *you* don't understand. I don't have any good memories about being a kid, and I know nothing about raising one. I never even knew my mom, and I don't remember my dad."

Yeah, maybe I had a couple of memories that might be my dad —tickling me until I was laughing hysterically, kicking a ball around with two-year-old me. But I wasn't sure if those were real or imagined, something I'd made up to comfort myself when my aunt and uncle had punished me yet again for breaking some rule I hadn't even known existed.

Talon had pretty much adopted ten-year-old me, even though he'd been only a few months older, and I'd been an angry, insolent little shit who only went to school for the free lunch.

The man had literally saved my life, giving me a place to hide from my dick of an uncle. By thirteen, I'd been planning Wayne Baker's murder. In detail.

It had been Talon who talked me down, pointing out I'd go to juvie for years. "When we're older," he'd promised, "we'll stick it to the sonuvabitch."

"Yeah," I'd said around the lip my uncle had bloodied. "We will." Then I'd punched a hole in Talon's bedroom wall, and he'd taken the blame for it. Together we'd patched the wall and repainted his whole damn bedroom so his mom wouldn't forbid me from coming over.

My eyes had closed. My face had blanked. I could feel myself retreating into numbness. My safe place, the place where no one could hurt me. I kept my knee going, though, the rhythm both soothing and a reminder that I could run like the wind now. Nobody touched me now if I didn't want them to.

Nobody.

"Hey." Talon gave me a shake. "You still with me?"

I forced my eyes open again. "I'm sorry, but—you were there, Tal. You saw what he was like. What if I'm like him? What if I...lose control?"

"You won't," he said, voice steady, firm. "You're always in control. You used to scare me a little when we were kids. You'd get that look on your face—that laser focus—and even the bigger kids would back off."

I pulled back, shaking my head.

He released me but stayed close. "Please, Cain. There's no one else I'd rather have looking out for Jude. Brien will be his primus. I know he'll do his best, but he has the syndicate as a whole to consider. You'll be Jude's person—the guy he can count on to always be on his side. If you're worried, let Brien and Eden make the major decisions. You just be his advocate."

"Fuck." I scrubbed a hand over my face, eyeing the tiny dhampir.

He was so small. So breakable.

So damn easy to hurt.

"Look, forget I asked." Talon turned away, rubbing slow circles on Jude's back. His voice was quiet, but I heard the disappointment in it. "We'll just have to find someone else."

A hot, acid shame spilled into me. Talon had fed me, given me a place to sleep, made sure I got to school—when he'd still been a kid himself. His own life had been almost as screwed up as mine, with an alcoholic mom and a dad who spent half his time off-island.

Man up, dude. This is Talon's son.

He was right. No one would fight for Jude like I would.

"No." I straightened. "I'll do it."

Talon broke into a grin. "You'll be fine, you'll see. Practice for when you have your own someday."

I grunted. I *did* want to have my own spawn someday, but not for a long, long time—like a couple of centuries or so. And I'd hire experts to raise the kid so I didn't mess him up.

"Here." Before I could stop him, Talon had shifted his son to my arms. "He likes to be upright so he can look around."

"Whoa." I froze, clutching Jude like he was a live grenade and one wrong move would set him off. "Give a man some warning. I told you—I don't know how to do this."

"Then you'll learn. First lesson: support his head." Talon moved the hand I had on Jude's shoulders to the back of his skull. "He's getting stronger, but it's still too heavy for his neck muscles to hold up."

I wrapped my fingers around the baby's fragile cranium, heart thudding like I'd just stepped off a cliff.

"Sweet Lilith, he's small. The size of a rugby ball."

"Right?" Talon gave a wondering shake of his head.

Jude squirmed, whimpering.

My stomach dropped. I shoved him at his father. "Here. He's not happy."

"Loosen your hold." Talon gently pushed him back to me. "You won't drop him."

"Says you," I grumbled, but followed his advice.

Jude scrunched up his small face and dragged in air. What I knew about kids would fit in a thimble, but I was pretty sure he was gearing up to scream bloody murder.

I tried again to pass him to his father. "Take him, damn it."

He backed away. "Try jiggling him. He likes that."

"Yeah?" That, I could do. I gave Jude a tentative bounce.

He unleashed a loud cry. I gulped, shooting Talon a helpless look.

My friend crossed his arms. "More."

I started bouncing in earnest, and to my shock, after letting out a couple more cries, Jude burrowed his head into the space between my shoulder and neck, snuffled for a few seconds, then fell silent.

When I chanced a look at him, he was sucking on his fist and staring into space. "Huh," I said without ceasing my up-and-down movement. "It worked."

"You're a natural," Talon returned.

I snorted and gathered Jude closer, sniffing his nape. "He smells good," I said when Talon chuckled. "Like powder and baby."

Talon grunted, and I glanced up to find him watching us with a sappy smile. "Look at you, Uncle Cain."

I went rigid and Jude murmured unhappily against my neck.

"No 'uncle,'" I gritted, bouncing like a demented rubber ball until the kid calmed again. "Just Cain."

"Got it. Should've realized." Talon's tone was apologetic. "I'll make sure Eden knows, too."

I gave a tight nod, jaw locked.

"So we're good?" he asked.

"Yeah, yeah." I adjusted Jude, who'd gone boneless against me, eyes shut, mouth slack with sleep.

I'd put him out. Me. And damn if that didn't spark a flicker of pride in me.

I met Talon's eyes. "I'll be a good sponsor, I swear. The best. Anything he needs, he's got it."

He just smiled. "Why d'you think I asked you?"

10

NYX

The journey back to Quebec seemed endless. I had a first-class seat to myself, Jerome and Manny in the seats behind me. I stared into the darkness beyond the window, fighting the slow creep of doubt. Had I made a mistake? Should I have taken Cain up on his offer, escaped Quebec City while I still could?

But it was too late now.

We crossed into Canadian airspace, and I forced myself to lean back. To breathe despite the tight band wrapped around my chest.

You made the right choice. The only choice.

The lights of Quebec City appeared, shimmering against the blackness. And then we were gliding over the St. Laurence River and descending toward Jean Lesage Airport.

Just one more month. I only had to hold out until the gallery money came through. I'd survived this long; I could make it another four or five weeks.

A discreet black limo met us at the airport, a QCS soldier at the wheel. He conveyed us to the outskirts of the city and my father's sprawling lair beneath a decaying cemetery. Nazaire owned a gorgeous Old Town mansion and a ski lodge in the Laurentians, but this was his favorite lair—and the one I'd grown up in.

We left the limo in an underground garage, the air thick with exhaust and old stone. Jerome led the way into a tunnel that burrowed underneath the street to the cemetery. I fell in behind him, Manny and the driver bringing up the rear with the suitcases. The damp walls swallowed us, our footsteps the only sound in the dark.

We surfaced in a crypt, the Marchand family vault. The Marchands had died out long ago, and the dead didn't care that their bones guarded the entrance to a vampire lair. I breathed in the crypt's familiar dusty scent as Jerome touched his palm to the biorec pad, hidden in the base of a shrine to the family's patron saint.

When Nazaire first brought me here, he'd tucked me into a nursery as far from his apartment as possible. I'd never left, just traded the child-sized bed for a bigger mattress, the toys for paint brushes.

But somewhere along the way, this place had stopped feeling like a home and started feeling like a prison.

A hidden door slid open, revealing a flight of worn metal steps. We descended into the hushed, stale quiet below. At the bottom, Jerome peeled off toward the main part of the lair, leaving the others to deliver my suitcases to my apartment. We wound through a series of smaller tunnels lit by kerosene torches, their flames throwing restless shadows across the stone walls. The air grew cooler, the silence heavier, each step pulling me farther into an underbelly I no longer wanted to belong to.

As we neared my apartment, brisk footsteps sounded ahead, and Perla emerged from the gloom—rich brown hair coiled into a neat bun, her curvy showgirl frame wrapped in a gray silk blouse and tailored black pants. A former thrall in her mid-forties, she was the closest thing I had to a friend.

"Welcome back, Madame," she said, dipping her head with practiced grace.

I gave a slight nod, aware of Manny just behind me, observing.

Perla and I both knew the rules—show too much warmth to a servant, and they disappeared. So I kept my face blank, my happiness at seeing her buried.

She unlocked my apartment door and ushered me inside. As I crossed the threshold, my lungs expanded on the first deep breath I'd taken in hours. These two rooms, along with the art studio next door, were the only places I could be fully myself.

The velvety green walls of the living room enveloped me like a forest at twilight. Pumpkin-colored throw pillows warmed the space, and the massive fern beside the couch unfurled its fronds in welcome. Along the far wall was a collage of paintings and second-hand treasures—ornate frames, tarnished mirrors, and other oddities. It was part boho, part goth, and all mine.

Perla directed Manny to put the suitcases in my walk-in closet. He complied, and then with a jerk of his chin in our direction, left.

The door clicked shut behind him, and Perla opened her arms, pulling me into a warm hug and kissing both my cheeks.

"How was Paris? You enjoyed yourself?"

I hugged her back, letting myself lean into her for a moment. Her scent, lavender and fresh soap, wrapped around me.

"Yes, of course," I said, the words I wanted to say crowding my throat.

That the gallery had been packed. That the crowd of world-weary vampires had lined up to buy my paintings like they were newly unearthed Rembrandts.

Perla had encouraged my painting from the time she'd taken over management of the lair. I'd been a lonely thirteen-year-old aching for someone to talk to about art, and she'd listened to me ramble on for hours about everything from oils to natural-hair paintbrushes. Then she'd helped me set up a studio, working it so my father believed it was his own idea, something that would improve my worth in the vampire world. Not because I'd become an artist, but because I could talk like one.

In a syndicate full of ancient, cultured predators, being able to toss around talk of technique, provenance, and artistic lineage—superficially, of course—made me useful. Someone who could smile and nod and glide through the circles my father wanted access to.

Art wasn't just art; it was social currency, a way to play the charming, well-bred accessory his associates expected.

So yeah, I wanted to tell Perla what a triumph my art show had been. But I couldn't do that to her, couldn't put her in the position of having to choose between keeping my secret or lying to my father.

I gave her a last, hard squeeze and let the words die on my tongue.

She released me and stepped back. "Did you go out with your friends?"

"Friends?" I flashed on Cain, on his knees in the washroom.

The pleasure he'd given me. And then later on the hotel balcony when I'd returned the favor. The pure need on his face...

Stop it. It's over. Done.

"What?" A knowing smile lifted my friend's lips. She was a former thrall, after all, and one who'd enjoyed her work.

I mustered a shrug and changed the subject. "Bien sûr, I enjoyed myself. I mean, Paris... The shopping was fabulous and the art show was wonderful. I even bought a painting."

The oil painting of Cain and the tiger was being shipped back to me under the ruse that I'd purchased it.

"But no men?"

Twice now, Perla had covered for me when I'd slipped out to meet Cain. Not that I'd told her outright, but I could tell she'd guessed—and that she approved, was silently cheering me on.

At my grimace, her perfectly plucked brows climbed. "So there was a man."

My shoulders slumped. "*Was.* It's over."

"Then he is an ass."

"No, I'm the ass for thinking he wanted me for myself." I rolled my lips into my mouth, trying to swallow the pain.

"I'm sorry. But he can—" She made a graphic gesture that drew a reluctant laugh from me. "That's better." She patted my back. "I'll unpack, yes?"

I trailed her into the bedroom, the familiar palette wrapping around me like Perla's hug. Purple and black, walls soaked in shadow, the kind that felt protective rather than oppressive. The ebony headboard was my own design, etched with a crescent moon and a sprinkling of shooting stars.

"It's okay," I told her. "I can do it later."

"It's no trouble." She was already in the walk-in closet. She swung a suitcase onto a wide shelf and opened it. "What about the famous Haunt? You met her?"

I sent my friend a sharp look, opening myself to her emotions just to be sure, but all I sensed was natural curiosity. The Haunt had become something of an obsession in the vampire world, especially after Brien Leclerc—Cain's primus—had bought three of my early works.

I shook my head. "No. She didn't show."

"Too bad."

She sorted my clothes into small plastic laundry baskets—whites in one, colors in the other. When she reached the fishnet dress, she held it up, letting it dangle like a question. "This is new."

I touched it. "I bought it in Paris."

Her gaze flicked to mine. "Ah, oui? Very sexy."

"I wore it to the opening."

I flashed to Cain, the way his eyes had seemed to eat me up. Like I was the only thing in the gallery worth looking at. That look had made me feel seen. Wanted.

Now it just hurt.

"For this man?" Perla asked, her voice gentle.

I just shook my head.

She eyed me for a few seconds, then nodded. Allowing me my secrets because we both knew they were dangerous.

I swung the second suitcase onto the shelf and unzipped it.

She clucked over the tear I'd made in the fabric. "But it's ripped. I'll mend it."

"Just throw it away, okay?"

I scooped up my dirty underwear and shoved it into the laundry basket. Like if I did it forcefully enough, I could bury the memory of Cain and what I'd done in that dress.

"Very well." She stacked one basket on top of the other. "Nazaire is in the lair," she said with a sidelong glance at me. "He'll be calling for you in an hour, maybe less. But you didn't hear that from me."

"Merde." My pulse kicked up. "I'd better clean up."

My father liked to surprise me. Not because he didn't trust me—like I'd told Cain, he believed I was exactly what he'd made me: obedient, broken in, too weak to rebel. But he liked to keep me off balance. It amused him.

"Yes." She faced me, her teeth worrying her lower lip. "I wish… things could be different for you."

My gaze snapped to hers. A beat passed. I almost said it—almost told her that that I was leaving. That by next month, I'd be gone.

But I didn't.

"It's not so bad," I said instead, turning away so she wouldn't see the lie on my face.

There was a short pause, then she said, "You go clean up. I'll finish up here. Oh, and I ordered steak frites. It should be here by the time you're ready."

My favorite meal.

Gratitude squeezed my chest. I met her eyes. "Thank you," I said, hoping she'd hear everything I wasn't saying.

Her face softened, and I knew she understood—that I wasn't just thanking her for steak frites, but for standing by me when it gained her nothing and could cost her everything.

"Of course. Now go." She shooed me away with a flick of her pearly nails.

I headed for the shower, already feeling the weight of Nazaire's presence pressing in from the walls. The performance would start soon, and I needed to be flawless.

After, I dressed in a silky pink camisole and cropped black pants. In the living room, Perla had left a covered dinner plate on the coffee table. I sprawled on the couch, the plate balanced on my lap, feet propped on the distressed oak table. I was midway through my steak frites when I received a text from my father's PA, summoning me to his apartment.

Abandoning my meal, I pulled on a fitted leather jacket, the buttery black hide molding to my torso like armor, then stepped into low boots and hurried through the lair's twisting corridors.

Nazaire was alone in his parlor except for Yvette, the thrall who doubled as his PA. Both were dressed for the evening, my father in a tailored suit, his black hair gleaming like a raven's wing. Yvette wore a short crimson dress and heels, her dark brown hair loose around her shoulders, her softness—round breasts and full lips—a foil for his hard, polished lines.

"Bonsoir, my dear." Nazaire watched me cross the parlor, the barest smile on his lips—all I ever got from him.

"Good evening, Father." I kissed each of his cool cheeks in turn.

"You'll have some wine." He snapped his fingers and Yvette hurried to the inlaid ebony sideboard.

She handed the wine to me with her eyes lowered. I frowned, a small, inward pinch. I didn't know her well—she lived with my father along with the other thralls, shuttled between his lairs like luggage—but for the first time it struck me that she wasn't just cautious around him. She was afraid. Not uneasy or wary. Afraid.

I thought of what Cain had said about my father, about how deep his involvement in the blood-slave ring ran, as deep as Fleur or Lemaire.

An acrid taste filled my mouth.

Nazaire jerked his chin, and Yvette retreated to the other end of the parlor.

He touched his wineglass to mine. "Santé."

"Santé," I murmured.

He regarded me through heavy-lidded eyes as I sipped my wine. "How was your trip?"

"The usual—shopping, clubbing, a few art galleries."

His nod oozed condescension. "You and your little hobby."

"Mm." My hand tightened on the glass. I wanted so badly to tell him that my "little hobby" had packed the gallery with collectors eager to buy my work.

The last time I'd shown my father a painting, I'd just turned eighteen. I'd still been chasing his approval, hoping he might see something in me worth loving.

He'd barely glanced at the canvas before patting my arm. "You're improving," he'd said, the way someone might praise a child for coloring inside the lines. "Maybe, when you get better, I'll hang one of your paintings in my parlor."

The message beneath it—that my art was a waste of time, that I was a waste of time—hit with surgical precision.

I didn't paint for weeks.

And I never showed him anything again.

Nine years later, I was grateful he had so little interest in my work. I'd never have been able to hide my secret life as The Haunt otherwise.

He raked a look over my black leather jacket and cropped pants. "Did you buy anything?"

"A couple of dresses."

He made an impatient sound. "I meant at the galleries."

"A painting, that's all."

"I hear this artist—The Haunt—is getting well-known. I'm surprised you could afford her work. Rodrigo said the paintings went for fifty, sixty thousand euros each."

So this was about money. He'd heard I'd bought a painting and wondered how I'd been able to afford it.

"Oui?" I served up an innocent smile. "I really wanted that one, and you're so generous with me." With Nazaire, it never hurt to stroke his ego. "I had money left over from last year's allowance, and I added some of this year's to it."

"I see." He still hadn't taken his gaze from my face. "How frugal of you."

A warning tiptoed up my spine like a line of ants. I put my half-finished wine on the sideboard and busied myself rearranging the five red tulips in a glass vase.

"Not so frugal," I said, my tone carefully light. "You should've seen what I spent at the shops."

"Hm." His shoulders eased a fraction. "Bien, I didn't call you here to talk about money. I've a job for you, mon lapin."

My rabbit. A pet name dressed up as affection, but really just another reminder of who held the leash.

I came close to snapping a tulip stem.

I am not your damn 'rabbit.'

As a child, I'd have done anything to win Nazaire's approval. I'd begged to learn martial arts and knifework like the other syndicate spawn. I wasn't as fast as a vampire, but I'd trained hard, putting in extra hours, determined to prove I was as good as any spawn in Quebec.

My father might not love me, but at least he'd respect me.

But I was done trying. I no longer wanted his respect. I just wanted out.

I still trained a few hours a day, but not to make my father proud. Now it was about survival. He kept me around for one reason—I was useful. The moment that changed, I'd be handed off like a party favor to one of his men or traded to an ally in another syndicate. Already, at least two men had expressed interest. Being the daughter of a high-ranking enforcer came with its own twisted currency.

Releasing the poor, blameless flower, I turned back to Nazaire. "Of course. Whatever you need."

He acknowledged that with a dip of his chin. My consent had never been in question; we both knew that.

"You know that asshole princeling."

"You mean the Maritime primus?" I asked warily.

"Who else? Anyway, I'm in contact with a human who lives on that accursed island."

"Lilith Island." Goosebumps popped up on my arms.

Impatience flickered across his face. "Yes. You'll meet this man and assess his offer, then report back to me. Yvette." He snapped his fingers, and the PA hurried back to his side.

"I'm texting her the name and address right now, Enforcer."

My phone buzzed. I glanced at the screen. I didn't recognize the name, but the meeting was in Nova Scotia. Maritime Syndicate territory.

"Are you certain about—?" I caught myself. Nazaire hated having his decisions questioned.

But he hadn't been on that nameless island when Brien, Cain

and the other Maritime Syndicate members had arrived. They'd been out for blood. I'd only survived by concealing myself in the shadows, my energy draining away the longer I spent there until by the time they left, I was weak and shivering.

And then they'd come back—a half-dozen of them. To hunt me.

I had no juice left to return the shadows. So I'd dragged myself into an abandoned fox den, clawing at the earth with bloodied fingers as I sealed the entrance behind me with dirt and raw panic. I'd nearly suffocated before they gave up and left.

At first light, I fought my way out of the burrow, stripped to my underwear and started swimming. An hours-long journey through the icy North Atlantic, to an uninhabited island nearby where I'd stashed a few supplies—a handful of freeze-dried pouch meals, a change of clothes, a sleeping bag, a radio. I'd hunkered down in a cave, on edge and listening for footsteps, the whisper of a blade in the dark. Only after two nights had passed did I dare risk radioing for a boat to take me back to the mainland.

My father's expression shifted—not much, just a slight tightening at the corners of his eyes—but it was enough to make my skin ice. "You have something to say?"

I swallowed and returned my phone to my pocket. "No, sir."

"That's what I thought," was the silky response.

I ground my back teeth together. He was so sure I wouldn't dare question him. That, paired with the queasy feeling in my gut over what had happened the last time I was in the Maritimes, made me lurch into speech.

"Actually, I do. Lilith Island is their territory."

His face darkened. "And?"

My throat cinched, my instinct to back down, soothe, apologize.

But I was done being a rabbit in a predator's world. I wanted to be something with fangs and claws and a killer instinct.

"You weren't there that night. They *played* with Pascal like he was a—a—toy. I didn't see what happened to Lemaire, but I know he didn't last long."

"And where were you, mon lapin?"

Heat crawled up my cheeks. There it was—the insinuation that

I'd cowered in some hidey-hole rather than help Pascal and Lemaire.

"Following orders," I told him evenly. "I stayed hidden so I could rig their boat to explode."

He crossed the Turkish carpet to me, slow and deliberate. "But those Maritime bastards all survived, didn't they? And meanwhile, Pascal and Lemaire are in their final graves, while you—a dhampir—lived. Interesting, no?"

The unfairness of his accusation stole my breath, especially after I'd turned down Cain's offer of sanctuary—because I wasn't a blood-rat. Because loyalty still meant something to me and I refused to sell him out to those "Maritime bastards."

"If you're saying I double-crossed you," I said, chest burning, "then you're wrong. You're my sire. I take my orders from you and Primus Dussault. No one else."

His hand lifted. I tensed, bracing myself for the slap. It never came. Instead, his eyelids dipped—slow, savoring—before his finger-tips traced down my cheek with a softness that felt more insulting than a strike.

"So passionate," he said. "And you want to please me, don't you?"

My throat worked. There was only one right answer. "Yes, of course."

"Then you'll meet this man for me—assess his offer. If it goes well, perhaps I'll reward you. A little bonus. Enough for another weekend in Paris, yes?"

"Thank you," I said, the words tasting like ash.

"Good. The meeting is set for Thursday night. Tomorrow, there's a party, an above-ground one, with humans. Wear one of your new dresses. Régis asked that you attend, and you'll want to look your best. He's looking for a new companion."

I forced a nod. "As you wish."

A companion?

Fear knotted in my chest. I wouldn't even be a thrall with a contract. I'd be the primus's property. A blood slave, in other words, dressed up in silk and jewels.

I hesitated, then risked a last question. "This man I'm meeting... May I ask what he's offering you?"

My father's mouth curved. "One of Brien's lieutenants."

❧ 11 ❧

CAIN

In life, you get two choices: break—or break others.

Wayne Baker's favorite saying played through my mind as I stood on a hill swallowed by darkness, staring down at his white clapboard farmhouse. When I was a kid, it had seemed like a mansion—four bedrooms, two full baths, a whole dining room I wasn't allowed to set foot in. It had dwarfed Talon's two-bedroom cottage.

Now it was just a tired old house, paint peeling off the siding, porch sagging under its own weight. Like Baker himself.

Still, I couldn't look away.

When my father had gone over that cliff in his car, I was too young to understand we'd been on Lilith Island that night. To this day, I didn't know if Baker had a hand in it. My dad was his wife's brother, not his, and I remembered a huge argument right before it happened.

The Bakers had moved immediately to take custody of me, even though my mom's sister had wanted me, too. The moment the ink dried on the legal documents, Wayne took control of my dad's assets. That money was meant to be mine at twenty-one, but by then, he'd drained every cent to pay for my "care."

In reality, he and Aunt June had used it to build a farmhouse and fill it with expensive antiques, then invested the remainder. All of it in their names, of course.

Some men would've killed Baker the moment they realized he'd stolen their inheritance. I'd even considered arranging an "accident" like my dad's. The symmetry had its appeal.

But I didn't want to kill Baker. I wanted to break him.

And as a syndicate vampire, I had the power to do it.

First his farm failed. I didn't harm the small herd of Holsteins. Before Talon, those cows were my only friends. Yeah, I attended the island school—most days—but I didn't make friends there. I was the freak, the kid with holes in his shoes and too-short pants and the thousand-yard stare.

So instead of killing the cows outright, I'd made sure Baker's luck turned. A few missed repairs here, a couple of years of failed crops. Enough to push him into taking out a second mortgage on his house—from a bank the Maritime Syndicate effectively owned. When he fell behind on the house payments, I made sure he wasn't offered any extensions or leniency.

One by one, he sold off the herd. Then his investments tanked, and to stay afloat, he was forced to sell all that pricy furniture.

Baker made it all too easy. The man couldn't hold a steady job to save his life. He was too much of an asshole to work for someone else.

Somewhere in there, Aunt June died of cancer. When the news reached me, I celebrated with a bottle of blood-whiskey and three thralls, my only regret that she didn't live long enough to see her beautiful house, the one she'd been so proud of, collapse around her husband's ears.

These days, Baker survived on odd jobs and growing what he could on the half-acre that was all that remained of his farm. On Tuesday nights, he had a few friends over for beer and poker. But other than that he was alone, brooding about what the world, the syndicate, and most of all, me, owed him. In his warped mind, anyway.

But he'd finally crossed the line. Me, I didn't care about—it was entertainment, watching his feeble attempts at payback. Like a kitten batting at a toy mouse.

But when he'd involved another syndicate? He'd signed his own death warrant.

In the kitchen below, the light went out. A short time later, a lamp came on upstairs and my uncle's silhouette appeared behind tattered lace curtains.

When I was a kid, Wayne Baker had been like God to me. He who must-be-obeyed, with a powerful build and hard fists. You didn't question him. You didn't even breathe wrong in his presence.

Now he seemed to be slowly caving in—hollow-chested, shoulders sloped.

The island bank had moved to repossess his house. Baker had apparently realized by now that I was behind his bad luck. He'd contacted the QCS—using his own phone. He'd used an app with end-to-end encryption, but I was the syndicate's resident tech guy along with the dhampir Adrian, and together, we'd unlocked the code.

My lips curved.

Time to play, Wayne.

I trotted down the hill to the house.

⚜

I didn't bother with the front door. Instead, I swarmed up the siding to the bedroom. The windows were locked. I punched a hole in the nearest one and shoved my bare fist through the shards to undo the catch.

Baker burst out of the bathroom in boxers and a dirty gray tank, a toothbrush in his hand. His jaw dropped. Then his face reddened.

"You!" he snarled, sending toothpaste flying. "Get the hell out of my house."

I pushed the window up and swung into his bedroom, feet first. "No." I straightened to my full height. "I'm not that kind of vampire, Baker. I don't need an invite to come inside."

Without taking my gaze from his, I brought my bleeding hand

to my mouth and licked the blood. His whole body went motionless, and his eyes jumped from side to side, unable to hold mine.

I sensed fear—and gods, it was sweet. I lapped up his apprehension like I lapped up my blood. Slowly, and with an unholy satisfaction.

Baker swallowed noisily, the toothbrush clenched in one fist.

Oh, yeah. Let him feel that heart-stopping dread, the terror that freezes you in your tracks like a hunted animal. Let him learn that some monsters smile when they come for you.

When my hand was clean, I prowled forward, enjoying how he stiffened. It freaked humans out when they realized I could move without them hearing me.

I stepped into his space, close enough that he had to tilt back his head to look into my face. His jaw hardened.

It was the first time he'd seen me since I was turned. Gods, how it must burn him that I'd grown into someone taller and more powerful than him.

"Go ahead and finish brushing your teeth," I said.

He didn't move. His throat bobbed. His gaze dropped to my chin. For the first time he looked a little unsure.

I let my lips curve. "Unless you're too chickenshit to turn your back on me."

His grizzled face darkened, a slow, ugly flush. Without a word, he turned, putting the toothbrush in its holder before filling a cup with water. He rinsed his mouth, spat deliberately into the sink, then faced me again.

"We'll talk downstairs." He walked forward.

I stayed where I was, forcing him to halt in the bathroom doorway. "See, that's a problem. You think you're in charge here." Ignoring his angry flush, I stepped aside and gestured at the bedroom. "We'll talk up here."

His fury spiked. "You're a screw-up, boy. Always have been, always will be."

I leveled a stare at him. I wasn't the scared, broken kid who'd had to bite his tongue—or else.

His mouth tightened. But he obeyed. No one ever said the man wasn't smart. Mean as a junkyard dog, yeah—but smart.

He took a wide-legged stance on the worn blue rug, arms crossed over his caved-in chest, trying again to hold my stare—and failing. "What d'you want?"

I pursed my lips, pretending to think it over. "To make you sweat. To hurt you. Actually, I've been doing that for years." I let the words settle, then added, almost lightly, "But I guess you finally figured out I'm the reason you lost the farm, and now the house, too."

His face twitched, just enough to satisfy me.

"But then, you bought them with stolen money," I went on. "My money. Money you took when I was too young to stop you." I tsked and shook my head. "Karma's a bitch, ain't it, Wayne?"

"Why, you—" He lunged at me, hammer fists swinging.

For a moment, I was a kid again, facing that same raging bull. My breath jammed in my lungs, my heart pounding double time.

His fist shot toward my jaw. Feet planted, I instinctively tilted my head—too fast for a human to track—and his hand cut past my face with a *whish*. The other fist came for my temple. I evaded that, as well.

A frustrated growl tore out of him.

I snapped back to myself. I wasn't that small, defenseless boy anymore. I was a fully grown vampire—stronger, faster, and more than able to stand my ground.

I pivoted on my heel, slicing a roundhouse kick through the air. It connected with his chin with a solid crunch. He dropped like a stone, hitting his head against the bedframe on the way down.

He lay there for a good ten seconds, breathing hard and staring up at me with murder in his eyes, while I waited to see if he was concussed. Not that I cared, but I didn't have the patience to babysit him until he was well enough to talk.

"What the hell are you looking at?" he snapped.

"A dead man." I flashed an it's-payback-time smile. "You fucked up, asshole."

He blinked a couple of times. Then he rolled laboriously onto his side and sat up, the bed at his back. "I don't know what you—"

I cut him off. "I'm doing the talking."

He had the nerve to wave for me to continue like he had the power here.

My jaw clenched. I grabbed his hand mid-wave and broke his fucking index finger.

He let out a girly shriek. A downpayment on the pain he'd dealt me in the years between the time I was three and when I moved out at age sixteen.

He looked from his hand to me, outraged. "You're fucked now, bloodsucker. There are rules. Laws. When the other islanders find out about this, you and your fancy-pants primus are toast."

That startled a laugh from me. "Like you're squeaky clean. But if you want to go there, sure." I was happy to explain exactly why he was going to die. "Those rules only apply to humans who don't fuck with us. And Wayne, we caught you trying to sell intel to another syndicate. That nullifies the agreement between the islanders and my syndicate, which means"—I brought my face close to his—"I. Can. Do. Anything. I. Fucking. Want."

The color drained from his face except for two dull red spots on his cheekbones. He scrambled sideways along the bed on his ass, pushing himself with his feet and uninjured hand.

"Who told you that?" His eyes darted from side to side. "Because it's a goddamned lie."

I stalked the short distance between us and squatted next to him. "We hacked your cellphone, *Uncle*. You offered to help the QCS get to Brien. He's our primus. Our alpha. And we *like* the man. Even if we hadn't sworn an oath to follow and protect him, we'd be out for your blood."

A pungent, fear-soaked sweat oozed from his pores. "I—you—"

I spoke over him. "But you had a problem. The QCS didn't believe you could deliver Brien, so you offered them someone else instead—me. For a million dollars, cash. Told them you're my uncle so they'd know you were legit. I don't know why you'd think I'd go even five yards with you, let alone off-island. But maybe you weren't going to ask me. Maybe you had some stupid-assed idea of trying to kidnap me."

"It's not what you think." He licked his lips. "I was stringing them along, okay? Waiting for them to set up a time and place, and then I was gonna come to you people."

I closed my hand around his throat, not enough to injure, just enough to make the untruth catch in his windpipe. "Uh-uh, Wayne. We hate liars. Don't we?" That was the one lesson he'd beat into me that I hadn't thrown away.

"It's the truth." Face turning purple, he clawed at my wrist, panic edging his voice. "I swear."

"You know we can sense a lie, don't you?" I rose to my feet, bringing him with me, so that he was forced to stand on tiptoes. Allowing him just enough air so my fun didn't end too soon.

He gave up trying to defend himself. "You—" he gasped. "You won't—get away with this. I have—friends."

I snorted. "Nobody cares about you except your poker buddies, and my guess is they'll miss you for two weeks, tops. If they do come to the castle asking about you, we'll stonewall them. Maybe I'll even burn down this damn house. In a few years, no one will even remember you ever lived here."

His eyes bulged. He slammed his knee up toward my balls. I blocked it with my thigh, then lifted him above me and walked across the floor with him. When he realized where I was heading, he went wild, kicking and twisting in my grip. He was still fighting when I tossed him, headfirst, out the window.

He flew toward the graveled driveway below, arms and legs flailing in a useless scramble. At the last second, he twisted, landing on his side instead of his head. His left arm gave with a satisfying crack.

I landed in a crouch beside his crumpled form. He sucked in a sobbing breath, his heart thrashing against his ribs like it wanted out.

"You're still alive." I smiled down at him. "Good. I'm not done playing."

12

NYX

The human that Nazaire wanted me to meet was Cain's uncle.

The Maritime Syndicate lieutenant he'd mentioned? It had to be Cain. The man wanted to sell his own nephew to us.

My stomach churned.

I lowered my head to my hands.

I can't do this.

I pressed my fingertips into my closed eyes, like I could somehow gouge out what I'd just pieced together.

I'd spent most of today trying to figure a way out of this mess. But there wasn't one. If I backed out now, my father would demand to know why. What was I supposed to say—that Cain was my lover?

I could picture how *that* conversation would go.

Besides, did I even want Nazaire to send someone else? This was Cain.

They wouldn't just capture him, they'd torture him and laugh at his pain. And when they were done, they'd stake him.

Nazaire might even make me watch.

I couldn't let that happen. Not to Cain.

I hadn't been able to dig up much on Baker—he barely existed online—but I did find a foreclosure notice. He was about to lose his house, and Cain, a syndicate lieutenant with money to spare, could've saved it with a single wire transfer. If Baker was drowning, it was because Cain had let him sink.

Then again, Baker was trying to make his nephew disappear, so I guess the "love" went both ways.

Nazaire, of course, hadn't been able to resist. He'd do anything to hurt Brien. I was starting to think this vendetta against Brien was personal. I just wish I knew why.

But why me? This was the kind of assignment my father gave to his inner circle, not to me.

My head jerked up, a horrible suspicion sinking its talons into my brain.

Maybe it wasn't a coincidence. Maybe Nazaire had found out about me and Cain.

We'd been discreet, meeting only a handful of times, and always when we were both in the same place for other reasons.

Except Paris.

Cain had made that trip for one reason: me.

Had Jerome or Manny seen something? Heard something?

A knock on my door brought me to my feet, heart racing.

It was only Perla, breezing in to help transform me into something glittering and presentable. The last thing I wanted was to play dress-up at a party. But if Dussault had asked for me by name, staying home wasn't an option. So I let her choose a dress—a sparkly pewter slip—and pull my curls back with a diamond clip, leaving a few tendrils to soften my face.

"There." She handed me a pair of diamond-and-platinum hoops. "You'll outshine every vampire in the place. If I looked half that good in sparkles, I'd bathe in them."

"Thanks." I dredged up a smile.

She caught my gaze in the mirror. "Nyx?"

I reached for the second earring. "Mm?"

"If you ever leave...take me, all right? I don't want to be left behind."

I stilled. "I don't know what you're talking about."

Hurt flashed across her face, and I cringed inwardly. But why was she asking tonight of all times? I'd been so careful.

"Of course," she said. "Forget I asked." Her teeth caught her lower lip. "You won't tell anyone, will you?"

We both knew who she meant.

I inserted the second earring, the platinum cool against my skin. "Tell them what?"

She gave a half-hearted smile and held up a sheer silk shrug. "How about something for those bare shoulders?"

"Perfect." I took it from her, the fabric delicate between my fingers. A breath passed. Then I made the decision to trust her. "The next time I go to Paris, I'll take you, oui? Or maybe Madrid—it's been a few years since I was in Spain."

She understood. Her smile spread to her eyes. "I'd love that," she said.

✵ 13 ✵

CAIN

I showed up to the meeting with Nazaire's representative wearing my dead uncle's clothes—his battered leather bomber, his best blue shirt. The fabric still stank of him, a sour bite that dragged up old memories I'd rather leave rotting. But it lent weight to my glamour, so I put up with it.

And Baker? He was feeding the sharks. Literally.

I hadn't drained him—my stomach turned at the thought—but the great whites weren't so picky. They showed up seconds after I dropped his unconscious body off a cliff and took over where I'd left off, nature's perfect executioners: indifferent, efficient.

Before that, I'd taken his phone so I could set up the meet at a dive bar on the mainland, chosen at random. Anonymous and forgettable.

The flight to a helipad just outside of Halifax took less than fifteen minutes. I left the pilot with the chopper and switched to a rented truck that smelled of fish. Overhead, the sky pressed low, clouds heavy and swollen, the air thick with the hush that comes before a storm.

As the last coastal town faded from my rearview mirror, I flicked on the radio and pressed harder on the gas. A cover of "Heartbreak Hotel" came on, John Cale's version, all grit and shadows.

Nyx flashed into my mind, gliding through the speakeasy to Elvis's accompaniment, all long legs and attitude. And later, on her knees on the balcony, giving me the best head of my life.

My dick pressed against the front of my fly. I shifted in my seat, jaw tight, that prowling frustration riding me. If only I could rewind, say something different. The right words. The ones that would've made her come back to Lilith Island. Made her choose me.

But I'd disappointed her somehow. Even then I knew it. She wanted something from me—needed something—and I didn't know how to give it. Or maybe I knew and just couldn't.

So she went back to Quebec and her bastard of a sire.

A hum started in my chest, a restless thrum. It climbed into my throat, vibrated through my bones.

Keep driving. Cancel the meet. Go to her.

Quebec City wasn't far. I could be there by daybreak, find somewhere to hide. Be with her by tomorrow evening.

The bitch of it was, on paper Nyx Nazaire was my ideal woman.

Talon and I had made a pact after we were turned—vampires only. Then he went and mated Eden, a human. It made me dig in harder. I'd be the one who held the line. The man who didn't bend.

The road narrowed as I entered a pine forest, the trees crowding close under the dark clouds.

If things were different, I'd make an all-out play for Nyx. Yeah, she was a dhampir, not a vampire. But her father was a powerful enforcer, and his sire was the Paris primus. With a lineage like that, she was practically vampire royalty.

Too bad Nazaire would rather rip out his own throat than let one of Brien's men claim his daughter.

Not that it mattered—because when push came to shove, she hadn't chosen me. She chose him.

My mouth filled with something harsh, regret tangled up with want.

Nyx was so much more than her bloodlines. She was smart, talented, magnetic. A beautiful, just-wicked-enough firefly, all glitter-dusted wings and starshine.

And I wanted her. I couldn't shake it, couldn't let it go.

Even though wanting her might be the thing that finally broke me.

The GPS informed me my destination was coming up on my right. Exiting the forest, I passed a row of clapboard houses, a grocery-slash-gas station, two weatherbeaten churches, and a school. Finally, there was the bar, a slow-slung building on the opposite end of a parking lot from a brightly lit Tim Horton's.

Glamours eat energy. I'd made the drive as myself, knit cap tugged low to hide the blond. I parked the truck in a dark corner of the lot, killed the engine, and peeled off the hat.

Wayne Baker.

I summoned his image like a curse, let it settle in my bones. Then I drew deeply on my vampire magic. It surged up, cold and greedy.

Glamours didn't just change your face—they somehow picked up the details and transformed you into a near perfect facsimile. In under a minute, I was Baker. Gray hair, sagging jowls, caved-in body.

His voice, low and gravel-thick, I could do in my sleep.

I put a switchblade in my pants pocket and slid a pair of silver cuffs, tucked into a leather pouch, into the bomber's pocket. Not that I was expecting trouble. Why mess with Baker when they were fishing for something bigger—me?

Still. Preparedness was survival.

I climbed out, pointedly avoiding the rearview mirror so I wouldn't see that SOB staring back at me, and lumbered toward the entrance, Wayne-Baker-style. Head down and forward like a bull readying itself to charge, fists swinging at my side. Dragging his ghost behind me like second shadow.

The interior was done in smalltown bar—grimy wood paneling, black vinyl stools and a wall full of neon beer signs. A trio of TVs behind the bar were tuned to a hockey game out west, and an electric fire danced beneath a pair of crossed hockey sticks.

I ordered a Moosehead from the bartender and nodded at the two guys in flannel hunched over a platter of nachos and a half-drained pitcher of beer. When my Moosehead arrived, I took it and claimed an empty booth with a good view of the front door. I kept my gaze on the game, making a show of sipping my beer. As a vampire, I could ingest a small amount of alcohol, but I preferred mine with a splash of blood. Without it the beer tasted like stale bread.

The door swung open and a couple stepped inside along with a blast of wintery air. They greeted the bartender like old friends and took seats at the bar.

Then a skinny dude in jeans and a navy windbreaker arrived. Trying to blend in, but a little too polished, a little too French for small-town Nova Scotia.

My nape prickled.

His gaze flicked to my Moosehead, the agreed-upon signal. It was Nazaire's man, all right.

I gave the smallest nod in return.

He stopped at the bar for his own bottle before taking the bench across from me. "Colder than a witch's tit tonight," he muttered in Québecois-accented English.

I gave the correct response, mentally rolling my eyes. My uncle had watched too many B-grade spy movies. "Then come on in," I rumbled in my best Baker-tones, "before you freeze your ass off."

The man's angular shoulders eased. He unbuttoned his windbreaker, leaving it open over a sleek gray T-shirt. "I believe you have a package for us."

"For the right money, yeah."

"And that would be—?"

"A million. Like I told you."

He pursed his lips. "You understand you must deliver the... package to the mainland. We can't come to you. The island security is too good."

"Understood."

"Then perhaps we can make a deal." He lifted the bottle to his lips.

I eyed his lean throat as he swallowed. Something about the

movement made me flash to Nyx, how her skin had felt beneath my lips, soft and warm. And its flavor—*her* flavor...

My cock stirred. I tore my gaze from the guy's throat and sat back. *What the hell?*

For one thing, this was a dude—and I was solidly Team Vagina, except for the occasional three- or foursome. But on top of that, it wasn't like me to get distracted like that, especially with so much at stake.

His eyes met mine, and I just knew he was rocking a glamour, too. It made sense. Why take a chance Baker might be able to identify him?

Come to think of it, the guy smelled familiar. I inhaled, trying to place him, but couldn't quite put a name to the scent. The other man's eyes narrowed, and I took a sip of beer, trying not to make a face at the yeasty, blood-less liquid.

"So, Baker." He placed his bottle on the battered slab of oak between us. "What makes you think you can get Ca—the package—to leave the island with you? From what I hear, he doesn't like you much."

How the fuck did he know that? I didn't talk about Baker—ever —to anyone but Talon or Brien. I eyed the other man, both irritated and impressed. Someone had done their research.

But I knew how Baker would've responded. I pulled my eyebrows into a scowl that could curdle milk. "You let me worry about that."

"That's not good enough. I need details. This won't be easy to pull off even with your help." The guy started to stand. "So if that's the best you can do..."

I growled. "Slow your horses. I can deliver, okay?"

He leaned back against the vinyl. "How?"

"Not here." I dropped my voice. "Too many ears. Around back— five minutes."

A brief nod. "Alright."

The bar erupted into cheers. The Canucks had scored a goal.

By the time the frenzy had died down, Nazaire's rep had slipped out the door.

I rose to follow, muscles coiled, mind already shifting to the next move—when my phone buzzed.

Brien, asking me to call ASAP.

I locked myself in the men's washroom and hit the call button. "It's me—what's up?"

"Donald contacted us with some new intel. About my mother."

Donald was the vampire "overseeing" our stake in the Quebec City casino—a polite way of saying he played poker, drank blood cocktails and doublechecked the take at the end of the evening. He leaked just enough to the QCS hierarchy to convince them he had a grudge against Brien, while reporting everything he learned back to us.

"Your mother?" I furrowed my brow. "But isn't Donald in Quebec City?"

"He is, which is what makes this interesting. He overheard a couple of QCS men talking. Turns out they believe Nazaire was behind her assassination. Actually, they think he staked her himself."

"Nazaire?" My jaw dropped. "But what about the slayers?"

"He could've made it look like they were responsible. It's been done before."

"But why your mother? Did these guys give a reason?"

"No. But Donald said they're convinced it was all Nazaire—Dussault's name never even came up."

A dark excitement slithered through my blood. Finally, a legitimate excuse to bury the sonuvabitch. "You think that's true?"

"Donald seemed convinced. I told him to keep digging, but if he keeps asking questions, it will get back to Nazaire. What about you? Did Nazaire's rep show up?"

"He did, and we were just about to discuss terms. You want me to abort?"

"No, that's why I called. Bring the guy back to Lilith Island. Let Nazaire wonder what the hell happened. I'm tired of dancing with the motherfucker. I want him rattled. Even if he didn't stake my mother, he's out there arranging to have you kidnapped—or thinks he is, anyway. Not to mention that whole shitshow with Eden."

"Will do."

"And Cain? We'll get what we can out of this dude—and then we're going hunting."

A smile curled my mouth. "About damn time."

It wasn't until my phone was back in my pocket that I realized what this meant to Nyx. If we went after her father, she could get caught in the crossfire. And I couldn't let that happen.

So I'd get her out first. Even if I had to fucking drag her out of there. I'd act first, explain later.

Because protecting her wasn't optional. It was instinct, something I'd have to think long and hard about when I got back tonight.

Outside, fat white flakes had started to fall, turning the parking lot into a snow globe.

Booted footprints in the fresh white stuff circled around the side of the building. I removed the cuffs from their leather bag, careful to handle them by the plastic-coated outside so the silver wouldn't sear my flesh, and returned them to my pocket. Then I followed the prints to the alley behind the bar.

The QCS man leaned against the concrete wall, the single bulb over the backdoor illuminating half his face. His skin and eyes gleamed in the dim light, confirming he was a supernatural. A dhampir, if I had to guess.

"Talk." He straightened from the wall. "Explain how you think this would go down."

"Show me the money first," I returned because that's what Baker would've said.

"You get nothing until I'm sure you can deliver."

"A downpayment, then." I moved closer. "You syndicate bastards are rich. You can afford it."

"We'll pay when—" He never finished the sentence because I was on him, spinning him to face the wall and snapping the cuffs on his wrists from behind before he could react. The tiny spikes on the cuffs slid out, digging into his skin. An invention of mine to increase the pain and deliver the poisonous silver directly into the bloodstream.

He hissed and arched his back—and slammed the heel of his heavy boot at my instep. I jerked my foot away just in time.

A whisper of sound made me throw myself to the side. A silver dagger grazed my shoulder and hit the wall between me and my captive.

I spun around to find Jerome coming at me with a dagger that was a twin of the first. I snatched up the first dagger as it hit the snowy asphalt and dove left, hitting the pavement in a roll and springing back to my feet.

The other vampire's eyes widened. Clearly, he'd expected a human.

Surprise, mofo.

Dropping my glamour, I bared my fangs and lunged at him with his own dagger. He parried my thrust, and we went at it, hard and dirty. Out of the corner of my eye, I caught the skinny dude edging along the wall, hunched forward, cuffed hands stuck out awkwardly behind him. He was going to escape.

I snarled. This had to end now. But Jerome was good. Every strike I threw, he met with equal force, his own blows fast, practiced, controlled. He wasn't just fighting; he was moving with the kind of precision that came from knowing exactly how close death was and refusing to blink.

Then his boot hit ice.

He cursed, arms flailing as he fought to keep his balance.

I lunged, slamming him into the concrete wall, and drove the dagger into his chest. The silver bit into his heart. A raw groan tore out of him, but even then he wasn't finished. His arm jerked in a last, desperate strike meant to punch through my ribs and find my own heart.

I felt the impact, but the point snagged in the leather jacket.

I wrenched the dagger from his hand, then tore the other from his chest. Blood sprayed and I jumped back as a dark, magical fire ignited, licking through his veins. Smoke poured from his eyes, and blood dribbled from his mouth.

He slid down the wall, crumpling into the snow. A beat passed. Then black-edged flames burst out of the open wound in his chest.

Behind me, boots crunched in the snow. I whipped around in time to catch the guy I'd cuffed lurch around a corner, doubled over. I sprinted after him.

He skidded left and veered into the nearest backyard, but I was faster. I caught his upper arm, jerking him to a halt. He let out a low, despairing sound and tried again to jam his heel into my instep.

"Enough." I swung him around and frog-marched him back into the alley. Behind the bar, I shoved him into a corner and patted him down, turning up a silver switchblade, a phone and a rental car remote. I kept the blade and tossed the remote into the snow. The phone I stowed in a pocket before grabbing his upper arm again and pulling him around the bar toward the parking lot.

He wrenched his arm from my grip and tried to take off.

I grabbed him by the back of his collar and hauled him back, my switchblade to his throat. "Listen, you bastard. Stay put or I'll slit you open like a trout." I'd lost the gruff Wayne-Baker voice.

The man's nostrils flared. "Cain?" he breathed.

He twisted his head, straining to see me. His glamour wavered, and I was staring into Nyx Nazaire's wide hazel eyes, a diamond winking in her left nostril.

Son of a motherless goat.

That's why he—no, *she*—smelled familiar.

The glamour dropped, leaving her in the outfit from the bar, her soft red curls tumbling down her back. I lifted the switchblade from her throat and yanked her around to face me.

We stared at each other as the snow fell around us.

"You?" I gritted. "You're part of this?"

She'd come here to negotiate with Baker. To have me kidnapped. Delivered to her father like a gift.

She hadn't even tried to warn me.

A dull ache opened in my chest. So much for wanting her. So much for much for my thrice-damned protective instincts.

Gods, I was an ass. Baker had been right after all. I was a weak excuse for a man, too blind to see she'd been playing me all along.

"Cain." She licked her lips. "I—I can explain..."

I bet you can.

My body unlocked from its stunned posture, cold fury pouring into the dull ache like fuel on a slow burn. I snapped the switchblade shut and shoved it into my pocket.

"Call me *Lieutenant*," I said through my teeth, and started for the truck again, dragging her with me.

❧ 14 ❧

NYX

A trap. They'd found out about Baker, and they'd sent Cain instead.

The realization stabbed into my brain. My breath hitched. My pulse stumbled.

But Cain hadn't expected *me*. His expression had contorted—first with shock, then with anger. For a beat there, I was sure he'd send me to my final grave alongside Jerome.

"Move," he bit out, adding a shake for good measure.

My stomach dropped to my lug-soled boots. I tried to plant my feet, but the parking lot was a slick mess, and Cain didn't slow, just propelled me in the direction he wanted me to go. I skidded, wrists burning as the spiked silver cuffs dug in.

"You don't understand," I said. "Please—just listen. You owe me that much."

"Talk, then." He halted, staying behind me like he couldn't bring himself to look at my face. "Explain why you were meeting with Baker—who wanted to sell me to your sire."

I winced. Goddess, it looked bad. "He contacted us, not the other way around."

"Yeah—so?"

"So my father was interested, of course. He's obsessed with Brien—you know that."

"Go on." His breath was warm against my cheek and smelled faintly of beer.

"He asked me to meet with Baker. I didn't have a choice—I couldn't turn him down. And I didn't want to once I knew it was about you. I didn't expect you to come instead." I drew a slow inhale. "Was your uncle even a part of this or was it all a trick?"

"Oh, he was a part of this. We intercepted the texts."

"Was?"

"He fell off a cliff. Sharks got him."

"Oh." I absorbed that.

Fitting, really. The man had tried to hand his own nephew over to a rival syndicate; even a human had to know what that would've meant for Cain.

"Well," I said, "my plan was to talk to him, see what he had to say. Then I'd go back to Nazaire and tell him to forget it, that Baker couldn't be trusted. That it could be a trap."

"You don't say?"

Cool fingers curled around my throat. Not tight. Just enough pressure to remind me of other times he'd controlled me like this, how the world would narrow to the heat between us, his body against mine.

For a few seconds, I forgot the bite of the cuffs and the danger I was in. Forgot everything but how that grip had meant something else entirely, something that made my knees weaken and my thoughts scatter.

"I can't tell if you think I'm a fool," he said, "or just too blinded by you to notice what's right in front of me. You didn't have to meet Baker. You could've contacted me—sent word through that bar in Halifax. I would've shut him down from my end. But you came yourself—with a vampire for backup. And I'm supposed to believe you're not here to negotiate."

I swallowed sickly. "I didn't have time to contact you—I just found out two nights ago myself. And I didn't want to bring Jerome, but I didn't have a choice. My father insisted. I think he's getting suspicious. In Paris, when you and I, you know—"

"Fucked," he finished for me in a flat voice.

I dipped my chin, wondering why I hadn't been able to say it aloud. I suppose I wanted it to be more than fucking.

"Anyway," I pushed on, "I was afraid my father had found out about us, that we've been meeting. He said Jerome was for my protection, but then why send me at all? This isn't the kind of op he usually sends me on. What if it was a test? So I had to do exactly what he said—no deviations."

Something shifted deep in his eyes—small, but real enough to make me think I'd reached him.

Behind us, the bar door creaked open. Two humans exited and picked their way through the slush and ice to their vehicle.

"Get moving." Cain used the hand at my throat to turn me in the direction of a big black truck, guiding forward with his fingers clamped on my nape. "You can tell me the rest on the way."

The cuffs burrowed deeper. I stifled a moan. The pain didn't matter. What mattered was making things right with Cain.

"Please. It's the truth. You have to believe me."

"Right now, you could tell me your blood is red and I'd doublecheck it."

I went limp, but he lifted me by the waist and kept moving, my feet dangling above the snowy pavement. The spiky teeth bit harder. This time, I couldn't hold back a yelp of pain.

"Put me down," I begged. "I can walk myself."

"No." He didn't set me down until we reached the truck.

"Where are you taking me?" I asked.

"Lilith Island."

"What? *No.*" I jerked at the cuffs without thinking. White-hot pain shot up my arms, and my knees buckled.

I knew all about Lilith Island. How far out in the Atlantic it sat, a dark speck of rock and forest and syndicate law. Once you crossed its borders, you weren't just isolated; you were under Maritime Syndicate rule. They ran that place like their own private Sicily.

If Cain took me there, I might never leave. He could lock me away and no one would stop him. And if I did manage to escape, I'd be branded a blood-rat for the rest of my life.

"Please." Forcing my legs to straighten, I threw a pleading look over my shoulder. "You have to believe me. I wasn't here to hurt you. You can't take me to Lilith Island. You'll ruin—"

"Can't I?" he interrupted as he turned me to face him, making sure I saw his fuck-you smirk.

Even being moved was agony. I inhaled, a small, hurt sound.

Cain muttered a curse. Reaching behind me, he pressed something on the cuffs and the spikes retracted. I released a breath. My wrists still burned, but it no longer felt like a silver-toothed dog was gnawing them.

The humans got into a small red car and pulled out of the parking lot.

"You don't have to do this." The words spilled out, scraped raw by panic. "You can pretend I didn't show. I'll tell my father that Baker never showed, that something must've happened."

His lips quirked in a nasty little smile. "Now why would I lie to my own primus for you?"

I swallowed hard.

Why indeed?

Something inside me caved in, piece by crumbling piece, leaving a gaping crater where my heart had been.

Clearly he felt nothing for me. He'd been stringing me along to get what he could. Yeah, he'd liked the sex, but the end game had never been me. It had been my father.

I searched his coldly handsome face, looking for a crack... a flicker. Something that said I'd mattered. That I'd been more than a convenient route to intel about the QCS.

But his expression was unreadable.

And I was drowning in his silence.

"You don't believe me," I stated dully. "You think I'm lying."

"Yes."

A wild hurt bloomed in my belly. I'd been trying to *help* the man. The man I'd begun to believe was my mate, even though I hadn't dared say it aloud. I'd barely let myself *think* it.

And Cain? He'd leapt straight to the worst possible conclusion.

The weight of it crushed the air from my lungs, tearing up the last of my hope along with it. Anger surged up through the ripped pieces, hot and blinding.

I let my forehead drop to his chest, my voice going bedroom-husky. "Cain..." I breathed, savoring the way his whole body stiffened.

Then I drove my knee toward his groin.

I didn't expect to escape. He was more powerful even when I wasn't handcuffed and fighting silver poisoning. But I wanted to see him doubled over in agony, wanted him to feel a fraction of my pain.

The man moved like a ninja—half-demon, half-nightmare—twisting out of reach almost before I was in motion. My knee glanced off the outside of his hip.

At least I'd made him jump back.

I feinted left, darted right. I made it three steps before he grabbed me by the arm. "Try that again and I'll take it out on that ass of yours."

What?

Red hazed my vision. I went rigid, breathing hard.

"That's better. Now, *move*." His hand landed on my bottom—harder than necessary—propelling me toward the truck's passenger side. He had to reach around me to open the door.

His mistake.

As his fingers touched the handle, I reared back, smashing my head into his nose. There was a satisfying crunch, and the air filled with the scent of his blood.

Point to me.

Cain didn't give me time to enjoy my victory. In the time between one breath and the next, he spun me around and shoved me up against the truck. His fingers clamped on my chin in a punishing grip, his body pressing closer, a reminder that I was fighting a man who could literally rip my head off my body.

"That was a mistake," he said, blood trickling down his face.

My nape tightened at his set mouth and the heightened blue of his eyes. I'd aroused his vampire—and not in a good way. But I was too hurt and angry to back down.

My glare should have turned him into a pile of smoking ash. "*That* wasn't a mistake. My mistake was trusting you."

"You've got that backward. My mistake was trusting *you*. Now get in the fucking truck."

Caught in the moment, we both forgot that I couldn't move with him holding my chin, his body blocking my path.

I held his gaze, even though every instinct I had urged me to drop my eyes for a dominant vampire. "No."

His answering growl tugged at my core. "I'm not giving you a choice."

To my humiliation, a tingle raced up my spine. My nipples prickled against my tee. No bra because I was pretending to be a man.

"Fuck you," I spat back.

The tension between us shifted, took on a sexual edge. His nostrils flared, and his gaze dropped to my lips.

"Beg me," he said in a rasp like the velvety sandpaper of a cat's tongue. It licked over my skin, made my sex hollow with wanting.

I squeezed my thighs together, hating how easily he could get me revved up, even with my wrists aching and silver seeping into my bloodstream.

His hips rocked against mine. Something about his expression told me his reaction was as involuntary as mine. That like me, he both wanted this, and yet despised himself for it.

I eyed the blood on his face. The rich, salty aroma amped everything up another notch.

My mouth watered, thirsting for a taste. For *his* taste.

For him, inside me.

His lungs gusted. "You're going to get me killed, you know?"

And then he had me up against the truck, my arms trapped between my back and the metal door. The handcuffs pressed into my skin, burning into the already blistered flesh.

I hissed and bucked against his body. "*My wrists.*"

Cain jerked back and pivoted me sideways so he could examine them. His expression darkened. He muttered something vicious and worked the catch. The cruel silver circles opened and a moan of relief escaped me. He slid the cuffs off and yanked the passenger door open.

"In the truck," he ordered, but instead of giving me a chance to obey, he swept me up himself and deposited me on the seat. "Arms out."

I wordlessly extended them. He eased up my sleeves so he could examine my wrists. The spikes had tattooed a ring of raw, weeping blisters into my skin.

"Damn it, Nyx," he said like I'd somehow wounded myself. "These look bad."

I curled my lip. "Go to Hades."

He muttered something that sounded like, "I'm already there," and snapped the handcuffs on my wrists again.

Then, to my shock, he eased the soft cotton of my long-sleeved tee between my wrists and the silver bands, protecting my injured skin from further exposure.

"As soon as we get out of town," he told me, "I'll stop somewhere for salt and water to wash out those wounds."

I shrugged. It would help, but the poison was already spreading through my bloodstream, a prickling, painful burn that would only grow worse. At least my hands were in front of me now.

"And Nyx?" He speared a hand into my hair, tugging it so my chin was elevated, my throat exposed to him. Making it crystal clear that, here and now, he was my alpha.

This time, I couldn't resist dropping my eyes—a quick, instinctive response. "What?"

"Try anything and I will hunt you down and make you sorry you were ever born. Is that clear?"

I pressed my lips together, hating how easily he read me.

"Nyx?" he prompted.

"Got it," I mumbled.

He released me. "That's better."

He shut the door, scooped a handful of snow, and scrubbed the blood from his face before rounding the truck. A few minutes later, we were heading east out of town, farmland and scattered houses sliding past.

The truck hit a rut, throwing me against the door. I smothered a whimper. Silver wounds heal slowly, and I was especially susceptible. Even without the spikes biting into my skin, the welts throbbed painfully. And these handcuffs weren't just restraints. They'd been engineered to force the poison deeper, to flood my system as quickly as possible.

Cain swung the truck into a gas station with a convenience store attached.

"I'll be right back," he said with a frowning glance at me and hit the remote, engaging the locks, before loping off.

I watched him enter the store. My last chance to run.

I even unlocked my door and grabbed the handle.

But I was weakening by the minute, exhaustion weighting my limbs, my body aching like a human who'd caught the flu. I wouldn't get a hundred yards like this.

And how would I remove the cuffs? I might even do something that would cause the silver spikes to dig into my skin again.

My breath leaked out in despair. I rested my forehead against the window, the glass cool against my heated skin.

I was still there when Cain returned. I heard his approach, but I couldn't seem to make myself react. When the door swung open, I spilled forward toward the pavement.

He cursed and caught me, bobbling the two bottles of water he'd bought. He dropped them on the truck floor and eased me back against the seat. Through slit lids I watched him tear open several salt packets and empty them into one of the bottles. He capped it and shook it, mixing the salt in, then pushed up my sleeves and eased me forward so my arms dangled out of the truck.

"This is going to hurt," he warned—and poured the salt water over my left wrist.

He hadn't lied. Pain exploded through me. I gasped and jerked against his hold.

"Don't move." Cain tightened his grip on my upper arm and grimly cleaned my other wrist.

I stifled a shriek. Mercifully, my mind went blank. I came back to myself to hear myself whining like a hurt animal. Dragging in a breath, I dug my teeth into my lower lip so hard I drew blood.

"Almost done," he muttered.

I focused on his strained face. A muscle in his cheek flexed like he was hurting right along with me.

That emptiness inside me swelled, pressing against my ribs. He had no right to feel my pain, not when he'd caused it.

I looked past his shoulder. *You're nothing to me.*

Not a lover. Certainly not my savior.

An enemy. A lying, two-faced enemy.

He rinsed the salt away with the second bottle. "That should be better," he said, helping me to sit back against the seat.

I let out a long exhale. The throbbing hurt eased, although I wouldn't have admitted that to Cain even if he'd held a knife to my throat.

He touched my bleeding lower lip without saying anything. I just looked at him until, with a distorted little smile, he released me and closed the door.

We continued east through the falling snow, the only sound the swish-swish of the wipers. Shortly after, we entered a thick forest.

We could've been driving into one of my paintings.

Headlights carve a path through the snow-choked night, their glow swallowed by the dark. A single set of tire tracks disappears into the trees. Ahead, a wall of thorns—razor-sharp, tangled, draped in roses so red they seem to burn against the cold.

Somewhere beyond the thicket, she stands, eyes wide. Watching and waiting. This is no Sleeping Beauty. She won't be claimed by just any man who cuts his way through the thorns. He'll have to prove himself—earn the right to her. And even then, she might refuse him.

Yeah, my paintings were repositories for all my bottled-up longing.

Cain glanced at me. "We'll be at the coast in another thirty minutes or so."

I nodded without speaking. To talk felt like too much of an effort. I felt feverish and lightheaded, as if my head had morphed into a balloon and was floating somewhere above my body, while the rest of me sagged in the seat, heavy with pain.

I stared dazedly out the dark window at the thick white flakes. Picturing the prince who'd come to my rescue. Funny thing was, he looked like Cain.

I snorted, and Cain exhaled. "Something amusing about this?"

That made me laugh out loud, a cracked, unhinged sound I barely recognized. "You h—have no idea."

I felt rather than saw the look he shot me. "Just go to sleep already."

"Noway," I muttered, the words slurring together. "To sssleep, I'd have to feel ssssafe."

But the next thing I knew, my eyes were closed, my head lolling against the seat. I jerked upright, heart pounding. My fever had worsened, my body burning, my head still floating around some-where in the stratosphere.

We'd left the forest and entered another town, this one larger. We must be nearing the coast.

I forced myself to focus. "What happens when we get to Lilith Island?" I asked because if I didn't say something, I might pass out again, and the vulnerability in that terrified me.

"You're going to tell Brien everything you know."

My smile was a bitter sliver. "Like Hades I am."

I'd helped this man, and Brien, too.

And it still wasn't enough. I was never enough.

"Then we'll lock you up," he said.

"I guess you'll have to because I'm done helping you."

"Up to you," he said and turned on the radio.

I focused on the dark scenery again, the silver burning its way through me like a slow-moving fire. The snow stopped.

When my eyes drifted shut, I forced them open and asked another question, trying to keep myself from slipping into uncon-sciousness. "Why did your uncle hate you so much anyway?"

"Because I exist."

"He raised you?"

"Yeah." A beat passed, his profile carved in stone, giving nothing away. Then he muttered, "My mom died when I was a baby—I never knew her. And my dad... a car crash when I was three. I barely remember him."

My heart clenched. I ignored it. I was *not* going to feel compassion for the man who'd abducted me.

But I found myself sharing something about myself. "My mother left me with Nazaire when I was four. She couldn't handle a dhampir kid. Said I was too needy—always wanting blood." Mama had called me a "needy little bitch," with a smile, of course. To her, everything is a joke. "But I think she just wanted to party without tripping over a kid."

"I know."

Of course, he did. His syndicate probably had a book-length file on me.

Maybe he'd even targeted me from the beginning.

Although it had felt mutual to me. Two strangers stunned, even a little afraid, at how much they wanted each other.

"Do you ever see her?"

"Not really. She'd rather pretend I don't exist." Head pounding, I closed my eyes. "The dhampir thing, you know."

"So she wasn't at the show."

I gave a tiny shake of my head. "She doesn't even know I paint."

"So it really is a big secret. Not even Nazaire knows."

"He knows I paint."

"But he hasn't figured out you're The Haunt? Wait, does he even know how good you are?"

"I don't show him my work. Not that he ever asks to see it."

"That's fucked up. You know that, don't you?"

His voice came from a long way away. I had the odd feeling he wasn't even there—just a figment of my imagination.

"As fucked up," I replied, the words slurred again, "as your uncle trying to sssell you to usss."

This time, when my eyes closed, I couldn't force them to open. The next thing I knew, the truck had stopped. Cain scooped me up and carried me to a waiting helicopter.

Keeping me on his lap, he slipped headphones over his ears,

then mine. The pilot lifted us into the sky. The chopper lurched, the wind off the ocean tearing at the frame, then steadied. We swung out over the black water.

I was too hot. Skin too tight, head too late, my whole body aching. My eyes shut again.

Lips brushed my forehead. I thought I was dreaming until Cain grumbled, "You're burning up."

"Silver," I rasped. "I'm...allergic."

His curse vibrated against my temple. Then I felt him removing the cuffs. "I've never seen it wipe someone out like this."

"Lucky me." Keeping my wrists out so they didn't touch anything, I curled into myself, refusing to read anything into how he held me—like that he might actually like care.

"Nyx."

"Lemme sleep... Tired."

"No. Here." He pressed his wrist to my mouth, the skin smooth and cool against my dry lips. "Drink."

I made a half-hearted attempt to feed, but I was too out of it to puncture his skin. The effort drained me. I sagged against the solid wall of his chest. "Just...leave me alone."

"I fucking wish I could," he said under his breath.

He shifted me around, fumbling for something out of sight. Then his wrist pressed against my mouth again. This time, blood seeped through my lips, warm, salty. Life-giving.

I lapped at it greedily.

"Suck," he urged, and I obeyed.

I managed to swallow a few mouthfuls before darkness took me under again. Five minutes later—or that's how it seemed, anyway— the chopper touched down.

I raised my head, still weak and achy, but Cain's blood had sent a shot of energy into me, thinning the fog in my brain enough to let me take in my surroundings. We'd landed in a courtyard, hemmed in by what had to be Castle Leclerc. Four black towers rose around us, their silhouettes carved against the moonlit sky like a threat carved in stone.

Cain stood, still cradling me, and dropped to the worn cobblestones.

I pushed at his chest. "I can walk," I said above the *thump-thump* of the blades.

"Why don't you just shut up," he suggested and strode up the castle's granite steps like I weighed nothing.

The wooden doors groaned open and a broad-shouldered man in a blue Maritime Syndicate uniform filled the threshold. He glanced at me, but his expression didn't change, as if Cain carrying a woman into the castle was nothing remarkable.

"Good to have you back, sir." He ushered us into the domed foyer.

I caught only flashes of the foyer as we stepped inside—a sweep of night sky painted overhead with swirling stars and a golden moon; faded tapestries sagging on the walls; sea-serpent sconces with glowing pearls of light clamped between their teeth; and a mosaic of a great white shark, jaws parted wide, beneath Cain's feet.

"Impressive," I muttered, and for a second, Cain's gaze locked with mine, like he understood exactly how I felt.

Then he wrenched his gaze away and shifted me in his arms so that as little of our bodies touched as possible. Like I was a sack of hazardous waste, in fact.

"William," he said, "could you let Brien and Talon know we're back?"

"I already have. And the lady?" The big man's gaze flicked to me. "Will she require a room?"

"No," was the clipped reply. "We'll be in my quarters. Have Brien and Talon meet us there, would you."

"Of course, lieutenant."

15

CAIN

I carried Nyx down the flagstone steps. As I entered the lair's winding tunnels, she glanced up at me. I braced for more of her excuses, maybe a demand to be put down. Something to justify the anger banding my chest. But she said nothing—her gaze just drifted past my face, dull and unfocused.

I turned toward my quarters. I should've taken her straight to the dungeon, but she was still feverish, the silver chewing its way through her system. She could barely stand on her own. And we needed her healthy, didn't we?

I slapped a palm to the biorec pad beside my front door. Inside, I lowered Nyx onto the Eames couch, leaving the door ajar for Brien and Talon. She slumped against the chrome arm, legs on the gray leather. I reached for her boots, but she moved her feet so they hung off the couch.

"Let me keep them on," she rasped. "Please?"

I shrugged and rose back up.

She stared up at me, smudges bruising the skin beneath her eyes, chest hitching in shallow, pained breaths.

My gut knotted. I wanted to fuck up whoever had done this to her, wanted to make them bleed for hurting her.

Too bad that someone was me.

"You need food," I said gruffly. "And liquids. I'll have the kitchen make you soup." With red meat—she needed the iron.

I already had my phone out. That handled, I crossed to the wet bar, poured her a glass of blood-wine and carried it back to her.

"Drink," I said.

Instead of obeying, she looked from the blood-infused liquid to my face. Her forehead wrinkled, like she couldn't figure out why the man who'd injured her was now trying to heal her.

That makes two of us, firefly.

But I couldn't help myself. Even with the sting of her betrayal still flaying my skin, I couldn't stand seeing her hurting.

She sighed and stared up at the ceiling.

"That wasn't a request." I slid my hand behind her head and lifted it, pushing the wineglass into her palm. "Drink."

Her soft lips turned down, but her fingers closed around the stem.

"All of it," I told her.

She exhaled audibly. But she drained the glass.

I took it from her. "More?"

"No, thank you," she said. Polite, stilted words that made me want to crush the thin crystal bowl in my hand.

I put the wineglass on the bar. When I turned back, she'd inched herself higher on the couch arm and was gazing around curiously. I'd noticed that about her—how she *looked* at things.

It was an artist's way of taking things in, I realized now. Observing, cataloguing, filing away for future reference.

She blinked. "This is... you." Her eyes met mine. "You chose everything yourself, right—the palette, the furniture? No decorator."

"Yeah."

A small smile tugged at her mouth. "I knew it."

Knew what?

I glanced around the living room. To me, it was practical. Expensive, yeah, because I could afford the best. But practical, with clean lines and no clutter—white walls, mid-century leather-and-chrome furniture, a walnut bar with flat, almost-invisible panels. No rugs, just black terra cotta tiles that could be heated with the flip of a switch.

Nyx eyed the trio of photos behind the Eames—my sole effort at personalizing the place. Big, moody things, shot in silvertone because I liked how the intense black-and-white let you see the bones behind the colors. The first one caught a midnight storm rolling in over the ocean, the clouds heavy, restless. The second showed a pale pre-dawn fog slinking up to the base of the castle's coal-dark walls. The third was the simplest: a lone pine against a glowing full moon.

When I caught myself waiting for her reaction, I tore my gaze from her face and sank into the Barcelona chair beside the couch. This wasn't a social visit. The woman was a prisoner, not a guest.

"You took these, didn't you?" she asked. "On the island."

I jerked my chin in assent. "Yeah."

"You're good," she said. Short and sincere.

I couldn't stop the ripple of pride that went through me— ridiculous, but real. An artist like The Haunt liking my photos. I actually started to smile.

Then suspicion kicked back in. Of course she'd flatter me. That was the game. Make me think she was on my side, so I'd forget who really owned her loyalty—Nazaire.

She was his. His creature. His weapon.

The enemy.

My smile faded.

An awkward silence fell. Nyx's eyelids drooped. She massaged her forehead, let out a pained exhale.

The sight of her, clearly hurting, caused something hot and restless to flare in my chest. I eyed her, my knee bouncing. Her gaze flicked to my leg, a faint line forming between her brows.

I forced the leg to still and glanced at the door. Where the hell were Brien and Talon?

I'd pulled my phone out to check on them when I heard them in the hall.

With an obvious effort, Nyx pushed herself upright on the couch, feet on the floor, her injured wrists hanging loose in front of her. The navy jacket drowned her frame, made her look like something she wasn't—small, breakable, like she needed saving.

My jaw tightened. "Tell them the truth and you don't have anything to worry about."

"Yeah?" Her thick lashes lifted, her golden-brown eyes burning into mine. "I told you the truth and look where it got me."

The door opened and Brien entered, wearing power like his custom-made suit. He stopped on the far side of the coffee table and stared down at Nyx—his eyes cold slits, his jaw set.

Meanwhile, Talon closed the door with a soft click and leaned back against it, arms crossed, his lieutenant mask firmly in place.

They were trying to intimidate her, and it worked. Her shoulders hunched and her breath quickened.

My heart lurched, demanding I put myself between her and danger. One second I was standing by the chair, the next I'd stepped past Nyx to put myself between her and Brien. My primus.

Brien scowled, sharp, disbelieving.

Talon straightened from the door. "Cain," he warned in his deep voice.

I froze. *What in Hades are you doing?*

I was acting like she was mine. Mine to protect, to shield.

"Sorry," I muttered to Brien and edged back to my side of the coffee table.

He gave me a long, unreadable look before shifting his attention to Nyx, who was eyeing me, her forehead wrinkled again.

"So," he said to her. "Just so I understand this—your sire sent you into my territory to negotiate a deal to kidnap one of my men. Do I have that right?"

She visibly summoned energy, pulling back her shoulders, lifting her chin. "Yes."

"And you knew it was Cain?"

"I was told it was one of your lieutenants." She clasped her hands together, her face open, her eyes pleading. "I swear, I was only there to find out what I could. I figured I'd listen to what Baker had to say, then go back to my father and tell him to drop it, that Baker couldn't be trusted."

A muscle worked in my jaw. If only our truth-sense worked on vampires and dhampirs, not just humans. She could be spinning us a tall tale and we'd never know.

Brien's lip curled. "But you would say that, wouldn't you? To save your own skin. And if that's true, why bring Jerome? He would've listened in on the negotiations, known you were lying about Baker."

Nyx's gaze jumped to mine, a cry for backup...for trust.

I looked back, stone-faced. But my knee started bouncing again.

She rolled her lips between her teeth, then blanked her face.

"I didn't have a choice about Jerome," she told Brien. "I didn't even know he was coming too until right before I left." She dragged in a breath. "Everything happened so fast—which I *told* Cain. I had no way to get him word."

"And Nazaire?" Brien asked. "You don't think he would've followed up with Baker? He would've taken your word on it?"

She spread her hands. "I think so, yes. But either way, I'd have bought some time. Time for me to contact Cain or someone in your syndicate. By the time my father followed up, Baker would've been neutralized, right? My father might've wondered what happened to him, but he wouldn't have been sure."

"Mm." Brien fell silent, letting the pressure build.

Nyx kept her eyes carefully down.

"Say I believe you," he said at last. "Say I even invite you to remain here on Lilith Island. I understand Cain offered you sanctuary with us."

Her spine went rigid. Her gaze lifted to Brien's face. "And I said no."

"Does that decision still stand? Jerome is—?" He glanced at me.

"In his final grave," I confirmed.

"Won't you take heat for that from Nazaire?" Brien asked Nyx.

Her fingers dug into her thighs, a quick, almost imperceptible movement. "He knows I'm loyal to him."

Which wasn't an answer. Not really.

"You can't go back," Brien told her. "You know that, don't you? Cain tells me you were on that island with Lemaire and Pascal. You were the only one to return from that, too."

Her eyes slid sideways. Probably remembering how the SOB had punished her for that mess on the island. As if a single dhampir could've stopped four vampires. She was lucky she'd survived.

"And now Jerome," Brien continued, voice soft but relentless. "Three vampires Nazaire trusted. And instead of returning to Quebec, you vanish."

"Because of Cain," she protested.

"We know that. But will your sire?"

Her throat worked, a small, betraying swallow.

Time to turn up the heat. I placed my palms on the coffee table, forcing her attention to me.

"Brien's right—you can't go back to Quebec. Cut your losses, Nyx."

Her chin notched up, defiance in every striking, impossible-to-ignore angle of her face. "Maybe I can't go back to Quebec, but if you let me go now, I can leave the country. Nobody ever has to know I was here."

I snorted. "You think crossing a border changes anything? Your sire will hunt you no matter where you run. With us, at least you stand a chance."

"So then I'm a prisoner here," she said flatly.

An unwelcome sliver of guilt slid under my ribs. I set my jaw and ignored it. She deserved everything we threw at her.

I rose back up. My friends' eyes jumped between the two of us like they were watching a tennis match.

"That's up to you," I told her. "You can be our prisoner—or our guest."

I stepped back, and Brien took over, calmly listing what we knew about Nazaire. That he'd been pocketing a third of the profits in Fleur and Lemarie's blood-slave ring. That he'd intended to buy Eden and her unborn baby, and enslave them as well.

Most of it, I'd already told Nyx. But Brien ended with the newest—that we had credible intel Nazaire had orchestrated Prima Lenore's slaying.

Nyx looked a little sick. "Your mother?"

"That's right."

Her brows pinched. "But why?"

"Fuck if I know." Brien dragged a hand over his nape, his cool exterior slipping so that he looked almost human, a grief-stricken son missing his mom. "But this is my mother we're talking about. If you know anything, can help us in any way..."

Nyx folded in on herself, arms around her middle like she was trying to hold herself together. "He doesn't tell me anything. But—"

"Go on," Brien encouraged her.

She let out a breath. "He's ambitious. He'd challenge Dussault if he thought he'd win. So maybe—and this is just a guess—but maybe he wants this." Her gaze drifted around my quarters. "The castle. The island. Everything."

Brien shook his head in disbelief. Talon swore. I rocked back on my heels.

Talon spoke first. "He wants the Maritime Syndicate?" he asked, incredulous.

"Maybe?" Nyx cut Talon a short, unhappy look. "He's targeted Brien, you, and now Cain. And before that, Brien's father. Either directly or through the women close to you. You've been playing defense for years, right?"

The three of us traded a look. It tracked. But damn, the guy had balls.

"I don't think he expected Brien to consolidate power so quickly, though," she added.

"His mistake," I muttered.

Nyx turned back to Brien. "You're young. To my father, that makes you vulnerable. Unworthy of being primus."

Brien just shrugged. He was used to that kind of crap from older vampires, which just showed how they let their power and centuries blind them to the truth. The man was fucking dangerous.

"Stay here on the island," he told her. "I haven't forgotten the intel you passed us. I owe you for that."

She blinked several times. For a heartbeat, I thought she might soften. Then her lips pulled into a knowing smile.

"Let me guess," she said. "Your offer comes with strings. You want my help to get to my father. Quid pro quo, isn't that how this works?"

My fists clenched at my sides. She was going to refuse. Of course, she was.

But I couldn't help respecting her for the way she held her ground, refusing to betray that sonuvabitch who'd sired her.

Infuriating. And the Dark Gods help me, impressive.

"Yes," Brien admitted without hesitation. He lifted a hand as she started to shake her head. "Hear me out. We can't let him keep striking at us without retaliating. With or without you, we're going to move on him. You can make it easier on yourself by helping us. You'd take a blood oath, swearing your allegiance to me and the syndicate. You wouldn't be a full-fledged member, but you'd be under our protection. We could use someone with your skills."

Nyx drew a long, deliberate breath, then said, "No."

It was clear her mind was made up, and Brien saw it, too. "That's your final answer?"

"Yes. Like I told Cain, I'm not a blood-rat. And I'm done being *used*." She spat the last word like it tasted foul.

His face hardened. "Put her in a cell," he told me. "We can't have Nazaire's spawn running around loose."

I gave a clipped nod. "Understood."

Talon waited until Brien left to move closer. "Need any help with—?" he jerked his chin at Nyx.

At Brien's order, Nyx had shuddered. Now she sighed and seemed to wilt, her shoulders curved forward, her mouth turned down. Apparently, she'd been holding herself together with spit and string.

I worked my jaw, furious that she'd tossed Brien's offer back in his face. "No. I've got it."

I poured another glass of blood-wine and thrust it into her hand, standing over her until she drained it.

Talon frowned. "What's up with her?"

"Silver poisoning. I used the new cuffs."

I took her left hand and showed him the still-weeping wounds encircling her wrist. She didn't resist. Didn't even look at me, just sat there, staring at the coffee table like I wasn't even in the room.

Talon whistled. "You rinsed them with salt?"

"Yeah—before we left the mainland. She says she's allergic."

"So what are you going to do?"

"What Brien ordered me to do." I hooked my hands under Nyx's armpits and hauled her to her feet. "Lock her in the fucking dungeon."

❧ 16 ❧

NYX

Cain steered me into the torch-lit passage outside his apartment. Talon muttered something about checking on Eden and disappeared into a nearby door.

"You can still change your mind," Cain said.

I forced my spine straight. The boost I'd gotten from his blood had worn off, and all I wanted to do was curl into a ball and whimper. The only thing keeping me upright was pride. "I won't."

His winter-sky eyes flamed a dangerous blue. "Up to you," he said and urged me into motion.

We walked without speaking. The few people we passed nodded to Cain. As for me, I got the side-eye. They knew.

I notched my chin a fraction higher.

Cain halted at the top of a flight of rough-hewn stairs, the air below damp, heavy. "Can you manage the steps?"

The distance to the bottom looked impossibly long. "Of course." I set my jaw and started down. But I was tired and my foot slipped on the narrow steps. I stumbled into the wall.

He made a sound that was close to a snarl. "Stubborn," he bit out and scooped me up, taking the narrow steps at an easy jog.

Our destination was a short hall with five cells, their thick, silver-reinforced wood doors ajar. Apparently, I was their only prisoner.

Cain set me down in the first cell, bare but for a sink and a seatless metal toilet. The air inside was damp, heavy.

The gleam of silver made me turn my head—a manacle, attached by a chain to the stone wall. My swallow sounded loud in the silence.

He followed my gaze, then looked back at me.

Don't cuff me to the wall. Please, don't...

The thought of being chained like an animal made my knees turn to rubber. And I was pretty sure I couldn't survive another bout of silver poisoning.

A small muscle tightened along his jaw. "Sure you don't want to change your mind?"

I shook my head.

"Suit yourself." He exited, the heavy door thudding shut behind him.

Not the manacle, then.

My breath whooshed out. I lowered myself, body shaking, to the dusty stone floor. I heard the muffled sound of a bolt sliding into place. Then...nothing.

The darkness was complete. Not even a sliver of light that would allow me to see.

You're okay. You're okay.

The pep talk didn't take. My heart hammered a fist against my ribcage, like it was demanding to escape. I curled up on the hard floor like a pill bug, all my vulnerable parts tucked inside, trying not to whimper.

I gulped in oxygen. *You got this, girl.*

I'd survived my mother dropping me off at a vampire lair. Survived Nazaire's tests, his punishments, his fucking mind games. I could survive this.

But it hurt so damn bad.

And not just because of the silver poisoning. That was a different kind of pain. Sure, my muscles ached, my head pounded, and I was pretty sure my fever had spiked again. Not fun, but I'd live.

This hurt went soul deep.

This was I'm-in-love-with-a-man-who-was-only-using-me hurt. It coiled around my ribs like wire. Even breathing was painful.

How could I have been so stupid?

I forced myself to inhale, then exhale. Took another breath, and then another. Slow and easy.

A shiver shook my whole body.

I was so cold... and hot.

A couple of tears dripped down my cheeks. I wiped them away, not because it helped, but because I refused to lie here and cry.

The door swung open. I pried my eyelids apart and pushed upright, back braced against the wall, teeth rattling like they were trying to escape my skull.

Cain strode into the cell in a crisp white shirt and black pants, his hair still wet from a shower.

"In here," he said over his shoulder and turned back to me, composed, controlled—and clean.

The contrast to my own self—filthy and shivering—couldn't have been greater. Right then, I'd have given every penny in my secret Swiss account to call down a thunderbolt and knock him flat on his perfect, freshly washed butt. I ground my chattering teeth together and wrapped my arms around my bent legs, trying to still the shaking.

Two men followed Cain into the cell with a mattress and a folded-up metal frame which they assembled into a cot while shooting furtive looks at me. They made up the bed, then turned to him.

"That all, sir?" asked the taller man, a redhead with an open, freckled face.

"Get her some soup," he said. "The kitchen should have it ready. And a metal cup."

"I'm on it," he said and the two jogged off.

I remained on the floor, hugging my knees.

Cain pulled back the covers. "Get in."

I mustered a sneer. "That an invitation? Because thanks, but no thanks."

His mouth thinned, dangerously so. In two strides he was on me, hands closing around my upper arms as he lifted me into the air and set me down on the cot. My boots were removed, and he pressed me down, tucking the covers around me with clipped, efficient movements.

"You're welcome," he said.

"Oh, excuse me," I returned from my prone position, voice wavering despite me. "Thank you, Lieutenant, *sir*. Except why am I this sick in the first place? Oh yeah. You."

Something flickered across his face—regret? Guilt? Whatever it was, he quickly buried it.

"I went easy on you. Anyone else would be in way worse shape right now. And I'd be interrogating them instead of tucking them in."

My mouth opened, but he pressed a finger to my lips.

"Uh-huh. No more talking."

"You—!" I pushed his hand away, sputtering weakly.

His growl raised every hair on my body. "You need to rest, damn you. Then you can fight me, okay?"

I shut my mouth.

"That's better," he murmured as he straightened.

I shot him another glare, but he was right. I had no fight left. Just keeping my eyes open took all my energy.

I rolled onto my side, snuggling into the covers, and gave a last shiver before going still. I sensed him watching me, but I kept my eyes shut until the freckled redhead returned with the soup.

Cain thanked him by name—Jasper—and took the small basket of food from him, adding, "Let Adrian know we'll need a guard during the day, okay?"

"Will do." Jasper glanced at where I lay huddled under the quilt. "PM me if you need anything."

When we were alone again, Cain sat on the cot next to me, the basket on his lap. "Can you sit up by yourself?"

For answer, I struggled upright.

His handsome face went rigid. "You can ask me for help, you know."

I snorted. "I'd rather chew silver shavings."

A muscle ticked in his cheek. He focused on the basket, removing the lid on a bowl of Mediterranean meatball soup. The rich, meaty aroma made my stomach rumble. Suddenly, I was ravenous.

Handing me a cloth napkin, Cain took out a spoon and placed the basket on the floor next to the cot. I spread the napkin on my lap, hating that Cain would see my shaking fingers, and reached for the bowl and spoon.

He moved them out of my reach. "I'll feed you."

I shrugged, my gaze on the steaming bowl.

Another tremor shook my body. Cain gave a frustrated snarl and scooted closer until his thigh touched mine through the quilt.

"Here," he said, voice rough, and lifted the spoon to my lips.

The soup was delicious and blissfully hot. Within a few mouthfuls, my shivers eased.

I held out my hands for the bowl and spoon. "I can do it now."

He handed them to me, remaining on the cot until I'd finished. I silently handed them back and he stowed them in the basket.

"Thirsty?" He dug a stainless-steel cup from the basket.

I swallowed thickly. "Yeah."

"The water in the sink is drinkable." He filled the cup and handed it to me.

I drank every drop, the liquid cool and tasty, then swung my feet to the floor.

Cain's fingers clamped on my shoulder. "Where d'you think you're going?"

I stiffened. "To the WC."

He grunted, but helped me up and walked me to the toilet, his hand firm around my arm. Steadying me whether I wanted it or not.

"I've got it from here," I said, trying to pull free.

"I can help." His grip didn't budge. "It's not like I haven't seen it before."

I just looked at him.

He exhaled, a rough, resigned sound. "Fine. I'll be right outside."

He left the cell door cracked open, leaving me enough light to see what I was doing. The instant I flushed the toilet, he stepped back inside. I washed my hands and face, then made my way back to the cot. He was there, holding the covers for me, tucking me back in.

I looked up at him. "I'm not going to change my mind. You're wasting your time being nice to me."

His jaw went rigid, but he didn't reply. He just turned and walked out. I assumed he'd leave then, but he stayed in the hall, the door open. I could see him pacing back and forth, phone pressed to his ear when he wasn't firing off texts.

I turned my back on him.

He was still there a few hours later when my fever spiked. He rolled up his sleeves and sponged me off, then changed me into yoga pants and a fresh T-shirt. My head felt like it was bobbing somewhere above my shivering body again. I watched him care for me as if I were observing a video of the two of us.

He looked...different. It took my fogged brain a second to understand why. Then it struck me: his white shirt was untucked, the pristine cotton splattered with water, and his short hair stood on end like he'd been dragging his hands through it.

For a moment, I just stared. Cain didn't come undone. Ever. But right now he looked like someone had yanked a thread loose and the whole man was starting to unravel.

No—don't read into it. It doesn't mean anything.

Toward dawn I drifted into an exhausted sleep. When I woke, the door was shut, but a battery-powered lantern glowed in the corner of the cell, and a cashmere sweater lay folded at the foot of the cot.

I pulled it on. The fit was perfect, the cashmere warm against my chilled skin.

I released an agitated breath.

I know what you're doing, Mr. Maritime Lieutenant. And it won't work.

But I smoothed a hand down the soft blue fabric.

17

CAIN

When I let myself into the cell that night, Nyx's cell phone in my hand, she was curled up in the blankets, asleep, her mane of wine-colored hair spilling over the pillowcase.

It was long past sunset. I'd expected her to be awake—she had been earlier when I'd checked with the guard on duty—but she must've lain down again. At least she'd eaten—steak tartare, blood-wine.

She stirred, blinking up at me, dazed and unguarded, a crease marking one downy cheek.

Damn her, anyway. I hated how she could get to me even now, hated the guilt I felt at using the spiked handcuffs on her. I kept picturing them clamped around her wrists, biting into the tender skin...

I was a vampire, for Lilith's sake. I wasn't supposed to feel like this. I wasn't supposed to *regret*.

I thrust the phone at her. "Nazaire's been texting you," I said gruffly.

She shot upright. "My father?"

I just held the phone out until she took it. Her fingers brushed mine, warm from her body. I ignored the spark it sent up my arm.

She opened her messages. I already knew what she'd find. He'd written in French, naturally, but I understood enough to read them, enough to know he was furious that she'd slipped the leash.

> FATHER: Where are you.

> FATHER: Why isn't J answering his phone.

> FATHER: Why are you headed to the coast.

As I'd suspected, Nazaire had tracked her phone.

> FATHER: You are on Lilith Island. Answer me at once. Where's J?

And finally:

> FATHER: You're with that lieutenant. Respond immediately.

Nyx's brow pinched beneath her cropped bangs. Her thumbs moved, typing a reply.

I plucked the phone from her fingers. "Uh-uh."

"I don't understand." She lifted her eyes to mine, pushing her curls back with a shaking hand. "He thinks I'm helping you?"

She looked so confused and unhappy that I felt a fresh twinge of guilt. But this was war, and her sire was the one in the wrong here, not us. Play this right, and we could finally take the motherfucker out.

"Maybe," I said. "My guess is that he's not sure, but he has to be wondering how a human could've taken out both you and Jerome. And Jerome's phone burned along with his body, so Nazaire can't track it. Your phone, though..."

"You—!" She swore in French and lunged for her phone. "Give me that."

I lifted it above my head. "No."

She launched herself off the cot, hands clawed, going for my eyes. I tossed the phone on the cot and grabbed her by the arms.

She reared back and slammed her head forward, aiming for my nose. Again.

I dodged right and she hit my shoulder instead. She reared back a second time, but I'd had enough. I spun her around, twisting her arm behind her back, and shoved her face-first against the nearest wall, cheek pressed to the hard stone.

I put my lips to her ear. "I wouldn't piss me off if I were you."

She bucked against me, trying to throw me off, grinding her ass into my lap. We both went motionless. My dick pulsed against her crack. Those thin, stretchy pants didn't hide much.

My lower body moved before I realized it, rubbing myself against her round globes. Her glutes clenched. I groaned, low and ragged, and did it again, a slow rotation of my hips that dragged the aching head of my cock over her firm bottom.

It was dirty and all kinds of wrong, but I was angry and aroused and my body was thinking this was Nyx, who liked it a little rough. It wouldn't be the first time we'd wrestled for control.

She emitted a harsh exhale. "Get off me."

"No." I kicked her feet apart and thrust my thigh in between hers, testing. She was warm, the soft fabric damp.

I cupped her mound with my free hand, and her body arched, pressing back into me. I chuckled darkly, and she tensed.

"Knock it off," she gritted.

I touched my lips to the delicate knobs of her spine above the blue cashmere sweater. "Doesn't feel to me like you want me to stop," I said against her soft skin. "It feels like you want more."

Her throat worked, her body sagging against the wall. "Are you trying to break me? Is that what this is?"

I stilled because her tone didn't match mine at all. She sounded...bleak.

Like I was the asshole who'd imprisoned her and figured he could get his rocks off without her consent. With a sick, injured woman.

Something hot and tight balled in my chest.

Bringing her bent arm down, I released her and stabbed my finger at the cot. "Sit."

She didn't obey, of course. Instead, she slid behind it, keeping the thin mattress between us. But I noticed she leaned on the wall for support.

I dug my fingertips into the bridge of my nose. "For the love of Lilith, sit down. I won't touch you, alright?"

Her lip curled. "And when I'm better? What then?"

"Not then, either. That's not why I brought you here." I blew out a breath. "Look, I was out of line. It won't happen again—you have my word."

Her gaze moved over my face, assessing my truthfulness. Then she gave a jerky nod.

I gestured at the cot. "Now, would you please sit?"

"I'm fine." Her mouth thinned. "I know what you're up to, Mister I'll-Give-You-Sanctuary. You want my father to know I'm on Lilith Island. You don't care if he thinks I double-crossed him. You're trying to goad him into coming for me."

I gave a single, unrepentant nod. "All true."

Her mouth slackened like she'd expected me to deny it. Then her eyes squeezed shut, her face a mask of fury.

I braced myself for the explosion. The Nyx I knew was fiery, emotional.

When her eyes opened again, vampire-blue rimmed her irises. She didn't explode though. She accused.

"I wondered why you wanted me. You're a lieutenant—you could have anyone you want. But you never wanted me at all, did you? Not me, Nyx. You wanted Nazaire's spawn." She practically spat the last two words at me.

I scowled, stung. "It wasn't like that. I would've wanted you no matter whose spawn you were."

Her lips pulled into a scornful smile. "Yeah, right."

Now she was pissing me off. The woman was in my fucking head, night after night, and she thought I didn't want her?

"Did I seem like I didn't want you a few minutes ago? Because my cock was damn hard for a guy who was faking it."

"You're a vampire. You're always ready."

I growled. "Don't twist this. I wanted you. Every fucking time. And you weren't pretending either, love." My voice dropped, cold with the hurt I refused to show. "You were more than happy to take it anyway I wanted to give it to you."

Nyx's eyes narrowed to dangerous slits. Then she visibly gathered herself, pushing off the wall and slipping around the cot. She sauntered forward, hips swaying in the tight black pants, and stopped an inch from me. So close, when she drew a slow inhale, the tips of her nipples brushed my chest like a dare.

"Do you want to give it to me now, Lieutenant?" She toyed with my collar, sending me a look from beneath thick lashes. "Maybe you want to punish me. Would you like that? I've been a bad girl, haven't I?"

I knew she was messing with me, that she was angry, that she was out to wound me any way she could. My dick didn't know it, though. It pressed against my zipper.

Yes, please.

The gods knew, I ached to take her up on her offer. To pin her to the stone wall and grind into the heat of her pussy until she begged me to let her come.

And then I'd peel her clothes off and show her what I did to bad girls.

"Nothing to say?" She undid the top two buttons of my white shirt.

When she pressed a kiss to my throat, I drew in some much-needed oxygen and reminded myself that she wasn't the one in charge here.

"Enough." I thrust my fingers into her thick curls and tugged back her head.

She met my eyes, not a trace of fear on her face. I felt an unwilling flicker of admiration. Not too many dhampirs could hold my gaze.

Her fingertip traced from the hollow of my throat to the top of my sternum. "You don't want me to stop. You want to fuck me—don't you?"

Hell, yeah.

I dipped my head, unable to resist nuzzling that tender spot beneath her ear that always made her moan. She did it now, a sexy whimper that made my balls tighten to the point of pain.

I moved lower, nipping her throat, dragging my tongue up the side of her neck. She must've washed up in the sink, because she smelled of the plain bar of soap, a clean note on top of her own, familiar earth-and-sage.

I inhaled deeply. Without my wishing it, my other hand closed around one firm ass cheek, urging her up against me. My knees bent so I could press my aching dick into the notch of her thighs.

But even as I licked and kissed my way to her mouth, I was looking at the cell out of the corner of my eye. I'd made it a little more comfortable, but it was still a prison cell.

In the castle's dungeon.

And me? I was the man who'd put her there.

Even if she did want this as much as she seemed to—and I was ninety-nine-percent sure she did want it now, even if this had started as an attempt to either punish me or coax me into letting her out of the cell—I'd still be crossing a line if I took this any further.

A bright, flashing red line.

Godsdamn it anyway.

Especially since I could feel her damp heat seeping through the thin layers of fabric separating us. Not to mention that I was as hard as a slayer's stake.

But there was that promise I'd just made her. Even if she released me from it now, I'd given my word, and if I broke it so soon, she'd never trust me again.

And that bothered me. She'd probably hate me before we were done, but the thought of losing her trust bothered me.

I wasn't even sure why. After all, I didn't trust her, did I?

I needed to put a stop to this game—now.

First, though, I allowed myself a taste, sliding my tongue into her mouth, eating at her lips the way I'd like to eat out her pretty pussy.

She moaned and rocked her mound against me, more proof she'd forgotten that damned promise.

But I hadn't.

With a rough exhale, I unwound my fingers from her hair. Moved both hands to her hips. Pushed her away from me.

Her whimper of protest went straight to my cock. I deserved a blue ribbon for this. No, a fucking gold medal. Somewhere up there a couple of angels were high-fiving each other and laughing their asses off at me.

"Cain." She strained to get closer to me. "Please."

"I can't." I rested my forehead against hers. "I gave you my word. And you're sick—still recovering."

I waited for her to say something. If she released me from the promise—told me she felt better now—maybe we could continue this. Find a loophole. She could touch me, for example.

But she didn't say a word. We stayed like that, eyes closed, breathing the same air, my hands resting on her hips, the firm, warm shape of them both grounding me and tempting me in equal measure. The seconds ticked by, heavy and slow, stretching out around us like they didn't want to let go.

Then her hand pressed lightly against my chest.

I swallowed the frustration, the want, the whole mess of it, and let her go.

She took a long step backward. "You're right. I—" She bit her lip and turned away.

I buttoned up my shirt and tucked it in, then shook out my hands, that twitchy need to move, *to run*, pressing at me.

Nyx eased up the right sleeve of her sweater so she could rub her wrist.

I focused on her, my agitation less important than her pain. "That should've healed by now."

"The other one is better. This one was worse."

The one I'd grabbed. I winced inwardly.

"Lemme see." I held out my hand. When she hesitated, I added, "Please?"

She put her hand in mine. The blisters had closed over, but the wrist looked painful, red and swollen.

I sucked a breath between my teeth. "Damn it, Nyx. You should've said something."

"You had my arm locked behind my back. Was I supposed to ask you to play nice?"

I worked my jaw, conceding the point with a low exhale. I let go of her hand and reached for the phone on the cot.

"I'll get you another salt-water rinse."

"Don't bother." She sank onto the thin mattress. "It wouldn't help—the silver feels like it's spread everywhere. I just have to ride it out. I'm better though. Just tired." She steepled her fingers, shoved them between her thighs. "Look, what are you going to do about the texts?"

"Answer them."

"Answer them how?"

"I'll say you're on Lilith Island. That you came willingly, and that you'll be living here from now on."

Her mouth hooked sideways, a joke's-on-you smile that didn't reach her eyes. "You might as well stake me now. Because if he ever gets me back, I'm—" She shook her head.

"What d'you mean? You're his only spawn, aren't you?"

"But I'm a dhampir," she responded, that odd smile still on her lips. "An embarrassment, proof he slipped and sired a child on a human. He's obsessed with finding his 'true' mate." Her fingers carved air-quotes between us. "A vampire, someone he can make a perfect little pureblood with—like Brien—and when that happens, I'll be nothing to him. I told you, I think he was getting suspicious, that he might've heard something about us, and this will just confirm it. He might just leave me here to rot."

The guilt was more than a twinge now. "He'll come," I muttered. "If he doesn't, we'll leak that we have his daughter. He won't risk looking weak."

Nyx went still, like the words had brushed a bruise she'd been pretending didn't exist. "Yeah. That would work."

"You don't have to go with him," I pointed out.

"Right." She gave a short laugh. "You've thought of everything, haven't you? Almost makes me think this was your plan all along."

"Wrong," I ground out. "Yeah, it crossed my mind, but I never acted on it—and I could have. You've been alone with me more than once. Paris. London. Montreal. If I wanted to kidnap you, I could've done it in then."

She only shrugged, unconvinced.

The guilt was a thrumming in my blood now, hot and insistent. When I stripped everything else away, was I any better than Nazaire?

I'd gone to Paris to try and weaponize Nyx, turn her against her sire. To twist whatever spark that existed between us into something that served me. I'd wanted proof, and she was my best shot at getting it.

And if she'd resisted? I'd even toyed with the idea of snatching her, retribution for Nazaire hunting our women.

I opened my mouth. I didn't even know what I meant to say, but Jude's small face flashed through my mind, the trusting way he'd burrowed into that space between my neck and shoulder. If Nazaire had gotten his way, that kid would've been born a blood slave.

My teeth clamped together. I pulled up Nazaire's messages and drafted a reply in French.

> NYX: I'm with the lieutenant. He offered me sanctuary & I said yes.

I showed her the message.

A shadow passed over her face. "Please don't send that. If you care for me at all—"

I punched *Send*.

Because I didn't care for her—I couldn't. My brothers were the important ones here. Them and their mates—and Jude. Most of all, Jude.

Her swallow was noisy in the small cell. "Why are you doing this to me?"

My chest tightened. "I'm not doing it to you. I'm doing it to him."

"Got it." Another bitter laugh. "I'm just collateral damage."

I exhaled, reminding myself of the stakes if we didn't neutralize Nazaire. But I had the stomach-churning sensation of something slipping through my fingers, something good. Something I hadn't appreciated until now, when I was about to lose it.

"You remember telling me Nazaire didn't give you a choice? Well, he hasn't given me one either. It's him—or us."

Her gaze dropped to her hands. "Understood. This isn't personal."

I ground my teeth together and turned toward the door. But I couldn't leave it like that.

I swung back to Nyx. "Look at me," I demanded.

Her eyes lifted. "What?"

"You're wrong about me and you. I fucked you because I couldn't stay away. I'm a Maritime lieutenant—I have a duty to my syndicate, to my brothers. Yeah, I was looking for an edge, a way to get to your sire, and you know why. But you and me?" My voice dropped, low and rough. "That was real. You were never a job. Believe that if you believe nothing else."

❧ 18 ❧

NYX

The door clicked shut behind Cain. For a long moment, I just sat there, feeling like he'd kicked a hole in my chest.

Somehow, even after everything that had happened last night, I'd been holding out hope that he wouldn't send that text. That he'd leave me out of this, find another way to get to my father.

I dropped my face into my hands, digging my fingers into my temples.

Too late.

Because Cain was right. My father would come for me. Not out of concern, but because the idea of his spawn under the protection of another syndicate—especially the Maritime Syndicate—would be a stain on his pride, a shame he couldn't stomach.

Luna knew what he'd do to me after he "rescued" me—and he would get to me. Cain and Brien might think this island was locked down, but my father had gotten to Brien's mother, hadn't he?

I brought my hands down, blinking rapidly.

You're so screwed.

Even my stupid little seduction had blown up in my face. The plan had been to distract Cain long enough to snatch my phone from him and smash it. To take myself out of this game.

But Cain hadn't been distracted, I had. He'd stayed in control, and I'd melted like chocolate on a hot stove.

I squeezed my inner thighs together, still wet for him. Still wanting him.

Even when reality slammed back into me—who he was, why I was here—I hadn't made an attempt for the phone. I'd forgotten everything his mouth on mine, his body hard against mine.

The last thing he'd said reverberated in my brain. Words he'd gritted between clenched teeth, like they were torn from him against his will.

"You're wrong about me and you. I fucked you because I couldn't stay away.... That was real. Believe that if you believe nothing else."

"Damn you," I rasped

Because I wanted to believe him. Even locked in the dungeon of his syndicate's castle, I wanted to believe it had been real. That *we* were real.

But we weren't. Because that would mean we were mates, and a vampire mate wouldn't be able to lock his woman in a cell. He couldn't. The bond would tear him apart if he treated me like that.

I wrapped my arms around myself, uncaring of my wrists, fighting a soul-deep, aching hurt.

Focus, Nyx.

Escaping was all that mattered, getting out of this cell and finding a way off Lilith Island. Not to Quebec City. Brien was right —I could never go home.

But maybe I could still have that life I'd dreamed about?

Then it hit me. Those texts—my father had sent me to meet Cain's uncle, not Cain himself. So why, when I'd disappeared, had he immediately assumed I was with Cain?

Fresh pain fisted my stomach. This whole thing had been a set-up—there was no other explanation. My father had found out about Cain, had sent me to the meeting to watch me squirm.

If I'd come back saying it was a no-go, he would've accused me of double-crossing him.

And if I'd gone through with the deal? He would've had the

satisfaction of forcing me to arrange the kidnapping of my own lover.

Either way, he won.

But instead of an aging human, Cain had come instead. And now Jerome was in his final grave, and I was trapped on Lilith Island with a syndicate that didn't trust me...and a man who didn't love me.

That last part cut deeper than anything my father had planned.

The lantern flickered and died, plunging me into darkness. It was the final straw. I threw up my hands, cursing my father—and myself for getting dragged into one last game instead of leaving when I had the chance.

My cursing ended in a moan. Everything inside me just... gave out.

I let myself collapse back onto the mattress, staring up at the dark ceiling. The fever, the cell, my burning wrists—it was all bad enough. But the betrayal? That was the part that hollowed me out. Every person I'd ever trusted had either used me, lied to me, or handed me off like I was nothing.

And now here I was, sick in a dungeon, proving them right. Proving I wasn't worth choosing.

The weight of that settled on my chest, like the whole castle was sitting on my ribs.

I didn't care what Cain said; it was hard to believe he hadn't planned something like this from the start. He was that ruthless. I'd heard the stories.

Naïve, thinking he wouldn't turn on me. I felt like that firefly he liked to call me, drawn too close to a torch and somehow surprised when my wings caught fire.

Maybe he'd even been the one who leaked that we were secretly meeting. Nazaire paid well for any scrap of intel on the Maritime Syndicate, and that would've been monumental.

How well did I know Cain, after all? I flashed to those photos behind his couch, the ones he'd taken—the dark, understated romanticism they had, like French New Wave. Who would've guessed the controlled Maritime lieutenant had a romantic streak? There was so much more to him than he'd let me see.

But then, I hadn't told Cain much either. He hadn't even known that I was a painter, let alone The Haunt.

I huffed a laugh.

Gods, we were pathetic. Sharing bodies but no real trust.

One thing was clear. He wasn't on my side. He could've let me go last night when he'd realized it was me, not one of Nazaire's men. But he hadn't. No, he'd taken me prisoner.

Maybe my father had been right all along. Maybe I wasn't the predator I tried to be.

I was the rabbit.

Soft... vulnerable. Toothless in a world built for wolves.

Sleep pulled me under like a suffocating wave, dragging me into a feverish dream. I saw Lilith Island from the sea—the coal-black castle crouched on its cliff, unnatural vines snaking down its walls, its four towers soaked in a blood-moon light.

Then I was running through the castle halls—arched ceilings, torchlit corridors, the echo of my own footsteps—but every door I opened landed me back in this same small, airless cell.

Someone was coming. Nazaire... Cain... I didn't know, but whoever it was meant to hurt me.

Goosebumps prickled my skin. I was running out of time. I had to escape. Panicked, I pounded on the thick, silver-reinforced door until my fists were raw. It didn't budge.

I crumpled to the stone floor, breath ragged—and jolted awake to find myself huddled against the wall next to the cot.

The door banged open. Cain stood framed in the doorway, legs apart, hands fisted. "Nyx?" he asked hoarsely, his gaze sweeping the cell.

"Cain?" I squinted up at him. Was it really him—or was I still dreaming?

"What the—?" He scooped me up. Cool lips touched my forehead. He swore under his breath, saying, "Your fever's up again."

I shivered. "Cold," I whispered through chattering teeth in case he was real. Too miserable to care if it made me appear weak.

"Get a fresh lantern," he barked at someone in the hall, then tucked me into bed with a rough care.

After that, I drifted in and out of consciousness. His voice pierced the fog, ordering me to drink, and I swam to the surface to feel a metal cup against my lips. I turned my head, too listless to swallow whatever it held.

With a muttered curse, he put the cup down and got into the bed, pulling my shaking body against his. I pushed fretfully at his chest, trying to get away, but he murmured, "Hush. Relax."

His warmth seeped through my clothes, his arms felt strong, safe. With a sigh, I subsided into him.

He sank his fangs into his wrist and pressed the holes to my mouth. "Drink."

But I didn't; the effort was too much. I closed my eyes and floated away again, until the blood touched my tongue. My whole body contracted with thirst, and I latched my lips around the vein he'd opened, sucking hungrily.

"Is it really you?" I asked against his skin.

His mouth touched my temple. "Shut up and drink."

I exhaled, a ghost of a smile on my lips. "Yeah, you're real."

Between his blood and the heat of his body, my shivers stopped. I drank until I was sated, then dropped into a deep sleep, mouth still on his skin.

When I woke again, the inner clock all supernaturals are born with told me it was an hour before sunrise. I opened my eyes to find myself tucked into the covers, and Cain pacing in front of the open door, head lowered, hands clasped behind his back.

He halted mid-stride and rotated his head. "You're awake."

At my mumbled assent, he entered the cell, crouching next to the cot. "How d'you feel?"

"Better."

His eyes closed, a flicker of genuine relief softening his face.

My heart clenched, but I warned myself not to read into it. He might want me alive, but only because he needed me.

He lifted the covers. "Let me see your wrists."

I lifted them without a word. The burns had healed, leaving only two pale pink bands.

He touched a fingertip to one of the scars. "It doesn't hurt?"

"No."

He nodded. "Your fever broke, too, about an hour ago. You thirsty?"

"Yeah." My throat was parched, my head ached, and my mouth tasted like I'd swallowed rust. I felt fragile, not quite well, like my body was trying to find its balance again.

Cain filled the metal cup and helped me sit up. When I gulped the first cup down, he brought me another, and I drained that one, too.

As he took the cup from me, I caught his arm. "Tell me something once and for all, no bullshit, because I'm screwed no matter what. Why are you doing this? Is it only about my father?"

His dark brows pulled together. "Why am I doing what?"

"This." I gestured at the cot, the cashmere sweater. "Would you still be taking care of me if you didn't need me to get to Nazaire?"

Something flickered across his face—something that looked almost like hurt. Then his expression shuttered, his walls slamming back into place. "We can get to him without you."

"Then why am I here?"

Instead of answering, he rose to his feet. "Try and get some sleep. I'll have them bring you something to eat in a few hours."

And then I was alone in the cell.

I stared at the closed door, bereft and confused. I forced my shoulders back.

I would not break. I would not care.

When I woke next, it was mid-morning. I washed up and sat on the cot, bored and hungry.

Wishing I had a paintbrush.

And some paint.

And a canvas.

My fingers kept flexing like they were trying to sketch the air.

The door swung open and I scrambled to my feet. A tall, broad-shouldered woman in a Maritime Syndicate uniform, black hair scraped into a ponytail, poked her head through the door and scanned the cell like I might have a small army crouched beside the cot.

"Breakfast," she told me and jerked her chin at someone in the hall.

A scrawny teenager with a shock of pink, blue and purple hair sauntered into the cell. Human. Despite the cocky grin he threw me, underneath he was wary... watchful.

"Morning." He indicated the covered basket in his hands. "I brought food."

The guard remained in the doorway, arms folded beneath her breasts. When I glanced at her, she moved a hand, making sure I saw the switchblade concealed in it. *Don't try anything funny.*

I dipped my head. *Message received.*

She didn't have to threaten me. I already knew I wasn't leaving. I was in a dungeon, buried in a castle, marooned on an island owned by the Maritime Syndicate. Even if I escaped the cell, what then? They'd haul me back before I reached the castle gates.

This was their fortress—guards prowling, cameras watching, and doors bound in silver. I couldn't fight my way out. I was a dhampir, not Wonder Woman.

No sense battering myself against a wall. The only thing I'd bruise was me.

But it wouldn't hurt to make a friend or two.

I smiled back at the teenager, trying to project harmlessness. "Thank you."

"I'm Rio," he said. "And you're Mademoiselle Nazaire." He hit every syllable like an American and mangling half the vowels in the process.

"Please, call me Nyx."

"*Neex,*" he echoed. "Dope name."

That tugged a smile from me. A real one. "Thanks. It means *night*. In Greece, Nyx is a goddess—kind of an elemental force."

"*Very* dope." He set the basket beside the cot and flipped the lid open with a little flourish. "Hope you're hungry."

Inside waited a full-on feast—crisp bacon, fluffy scrambled eggs, a croissant shining with butter, and a muffin studded with blueberries the size of marbles.

My stomach rumbled. "Starving," I admitted with a rueful grin.

"Yeah? Well, enjoy." He turned to go.

"Wait—stay. I'd like some company...if that's allowed?"

I shot the guard a pleading smile.

Her expression didn't so much twitch.

"It's okay by me," Rio told her. "The lieutenant wants her to have anything within reason."

He did?

The guard grunted and pulled out her phone. A few seconds later, she looked up. "He can stay. Fifteen minutes," she added, all steel.

"Understood," said Rio. He waited until she'd stepped out of the cell, then settled onto the floor next to the cot. "Eat." He handed me the plate. "It's gonna get cold."

I sat cross-legged on the mattress, the plate on my lap, and bit into the still-warm croissant. "Ohh..." My eyes slit with pleasure.

"Good, huh?" Rio stretched out long legs clad in ripped jeans, his back against the cot. He appeared relaxed, but underneath he was alert, sizing me up. "We buy them from a bakery in Bluebeard's Cove."

"It's as good as you get in Paris," I said around a mouthful of flaky goodness.

"I'll let the baker know. I brought you coffee, too." He passed me a spoon wrapped in a cloth napkin and a cup with a sip-lid. "I figured you being from Quebec City and all—you know, French. Café au lait."

Actually I took my coffee black, but I took a sip, trying not make a face at the milky taste. "Half-French," I said. "My mother was born in Spain. But they love their coffee, too."

"Yeah? I have some Spanish in me—or that's what my abuela

says. My parents came from Mexico, but I grew up in Ohio. I've never even seen Mexico."

"So you didn't grow up here on the island?"

"Nah. I came here last fall with Eden—Talon's mate. This is the first time I've been out of the U.S."

"So you knew her in New York?"

His open expression faded. "Yeah, but how did you know that? She said you've never met."

I took a sip of coffee. "When a lieutenant mates with a thrall, it's news."

The shockwaves had rippled through the QCS. My father had gloated, said it proved how weak Brien was, how unfit to be primus. A lieutenant of his claiming a human? A thrall? That was practically unheard of.

Rio still looked suspicious, so I changed the subject, even though I couldn't help being curious about Eden—how she was doing, how old the baby was now.

"I like your hair, by the way."

"Yeah? Thanks." He ran a hand over his colorful locks. "I met Eden in New York—she saved my life. No lie. I was living in a park."

"I'm sorry."

He moved a bony shoulder. "It's all good. Here on the island, I'm her companion—and Talon's PA." He added that last part like it was nothing, but pride radiated off him.

I let my brows lift, just enough admiration to make him glow. "A lieutenant's PA? They must trust you."

His chest puffed. "Guess so."

I finished the croissant and started on the eggs, keeping my tone light. "Tell me about Bluebeard's Cove. It's here on the island?"

"Yeah." He crossed one booted foot over the other. "Other than the castle, it's the only place to hang. But it's not bad."

By the time I finished eating, he'd painted a vivid picture of his new home and its inhabitants. I hadn't realized how many people lived on the island—both human and vampire—and how self-sufficient they were.

The Maritime Syndicate owned the land, letting the local humans live on it rent free. The homes and businesses were theirs to buy and sell as they pleased. In return, the syndicate enjoyed a steady supply of thralls—locals who were paid well and bound to service for only three years.

"Impressive," I murmured. It explained how the syndicate had grown so powerful, despite their start on an island in the middle of nowhere.

"The whole freaking island is descended from pirates," Rio added. "That's how Bluebeard's Cove got its name." He gathered the remains of my meal and packed them in the basket. "Look, I gotta bounce."

I came to my feet along with him. "Any chance you could get me a toothbrush and some paste? And a hairbrush—if it's not too much trouble."

"I'll see what I can do, okay?" he said, and started for the door.

"Wait," I blurted. "Could you get me pencils and a pad of paper?"

He turned back. "To write on?"

"No. To draw on."

He brightened. "You're an artist?"

I shrugged. "I just like to draw, is all."

I wasn't sure why I hadn't told him I was an artist—I could've agreed without admitting I was The Haunt. But I'd been hiding behind my party-girl persona for so long that denying it was instinctive.

The guard frowned at Rio from the doorway. "Time's up."

"Coming," he replied and gave me a thumbs-up. "I'll see what I can do."

He was back within two hours with the requested items, including another lantern.

I desperately needed to brush my teeth—and my hair, for that matter—but I set the toiletries aside on the cot and reached for the pad of textured charcoal paper instead. "How'd you get it so fast?"

"I have my ways," he said with a smirk, handing over a box of charcoal pencils—soft, medium and hard—and the special eraser that went with them. "You like?"

"I do." I hugged the art supplies to my chest. "These are perfect."

"Thank Eden. She told me what to buy."

"Oh." I blinked, thrown. "Well, please give her my thanks."

"Will do." He set the new lantern next to the one already in the cell. "The batteries are rechargeable. I brought you another one so if one dies, you can just turn on the other one. I'll be bringing you your meals—just let me know when you need a charge, and I'll take care of it."

I nodded and opened the box. Eden had even included a pencil sharpener. She'd thought of everything.

Guilt tightened my chest, reminding me how close I'd come to having her blood on my hands, the choices I'd made that I could never take back.

"How is Eden, anyway?" I asked.

"Good." A pause. "Why d'you want to know?"

I moved a shoulder. "Cain told me she just had a baby."

A grunt.

I wanted to ask how the baby was, wanted proof they were both okay. But Rio had iced over, so I flipped open the pad instead. "Mind if I sketch you?"

His posture loosened. "Me?"

"Yeah. You've got a good face—interesting. One part nice, one part 'don't mess with me.'"

Like someone who'd seen too much for his age, been battered by life. But I kept that to myself.

"Huh." He tilted his head, considering that, then flashed a crooked grin. "Later, yeah? I've gotta run. Peace out, 'Kay?"

And he was gone.

I stared at the closed door. The lantern burned with a steady, unblinking light, but the room felt different without him—bigger, emptier. The shadows didn't move, but they still seemed to twitch at the edges of my vision, like they were waiting for me to notice how alone I was again.

The silence pressed in, thick and heavy.
I straightened my spine and opened the box of charcoal pencils.

154

19

CAIN

I rose from my day sleep with the blood-thirst chewing at my gut like a feral rat. I needed fresh blood to replace what I'd given Nyx.

The lair was stirring around me—doors opening, low voices sifting through the stone, the soft movements of bodies waking. Background noise, the familiar routine.

I sent a text, arranging to meet one of my regulars in the thralls' quarters. Unlike most of the castle vampires, I didn't bring thralls back to my apartment—that was my private space, open only to a few close friends.

My next message was to Nyx's guard, who assured me that she was better, that she'd eaten a couple of good meals and was moving around.

The thrall greeted me with a smile and a body-hugging red dress, the practiced welcome of a woman who knew the routine. With a muttered hello, I backed her to a wall, pushed her long black hair to one side and sank my fangs into her soft skin. She shivered in pleasure and let her head fall to the side.

Each suck flooded me with heat. My dick hardened, the predator in me craving the other half of the blood-sex equation. I pushed my hips against her, driven by an ancient, primal instinct.

Her breath hitched. She widened her thighs, asking for more. My hand moved over her body, cupping a firm breast, pinching her nipple into hardness.

"More," she rasped.

My hand went to her hem. But as I started to draw up her skirt, I flashed on Nyx, hollow-eyed and shivering in that musty, airless cell.

And I couldn't do it.

I moved my hand back to her waist and finished feeding.

"Cain?" she whimpered as I licked her neck clean, healing the small wounds.

"Sorry, love." I patted her ass. "Not tonight. I'll drop a bonus in your account, though—all right?"

I stalked back to my apartment in a piss-poor mood. First Paris, now tonight. Nyx was in my head, fucking with my instincts—my very self.

The last thing I wanted was to find Rio slouched against my door, contemplating the purple laces on his scuffed boots. The eighteen-year-old was Talon's project—I think he saw something of himself in this New York City street kid. Me, I figured Rio had seen an opportunity and jumped on it. And hey, all respect to him; I admired his hustle. Didn't mean I wanted to babysit him, though.

"What?" I demanded gruffly.

"Lieutenant." He uncoiled his skinny body from the door. "Got a sec?"

I grunted, hoping he'd get the hint and take his problem elsewhere. I touched my hand to the biorec pad and pulled the door open.

"It's about Nyx," he added.

My head snapped toward him. Nyx had scared the crap out of me last night—raving about doors and wolves, out of her head with silver poisoning, then losing consciousness—but by the time I'd left this morning, she'd been sleeping all right, her fever broken. And the guard was under orders to let me know immediately if she relapsed again.

"What about her? She okay?"

"She's fine," he said. "That's not why I'm here."

I lifted my brows. "Go on."

"Well, I was the one who delivered the meals you ordered for her."

"And?"

"I want to keep visiting her, that's—"

"No," I interrupted. "You can take her meals, and that's it."

"But Eden said..." He gulped at the look I turned on him.

"Go on," I prompted softly. "What did Eden say?"

"You know." Shoving his hands in his jeans pockets, he rocked back and forth on his toes. "That you...like her."

"I like a lot of people."

Rio's eyelids fluttered at that obvious untruth. He hitched a shoulder without speaking.

"And no, I don't want you visiting my prisoner."

"Okay, but..."

I pulled an irritated breath through my teeth. "What?"

"Nyx asked for a couple of other things, too—and we already gave them to her. Eden said you wouldn't mind."

"Did she now?" Eden had been a castle thrall. She knew better than to stick her nose into syndicate business.

"A toothbrush," Rio said. "And a hairbrush. Things like that."

"I guess that's okay, but that's the end of it. Understand?"

"Yes, Lieutenant."

I was pretty sure he'd have rolled his eyes if he'd dared. But he didn't.

Smart kid.

I stepped inside my apartment.

"But you should know," Rio added in a rush, "that Eden sent her a sketchpad and stuff to draw with, too."

I halted, hand on the door. "Eden isn't in charge of Nyx—I am. From now on, any requests go through me first, understand?"

"Yeah." He glanced down. "But Nyx *asked* for them," he said under his breath.

Of course she'd asked for them. An acrid shame filled my

mouth. Nazaire had punished her by not allowing her to make her art, hadn't he?

"You did say she could have anything within reason," the kid added. "You should've seen how she lit up when I gave them to her."

"Fine," I said tightly. "Let her keep them. But that's it—nothing else."

I started to shut my door.

"Nice talk," Rio muttered. "But you're going about this all wrong."

I swung the door open, pinning him with a look. "What did you say?"

"I said—" he squared his shoulders—"that you're going about this all wrong."

I jerked my chin at my living room. "Inside."

"I'm Talon and Eden's PA," he grumbled. "Not yours."

I just looked him. He sidled past me like the former street-rat he was.

"Sit." I pointed at the couch.

He obeyed, his mouth a narrow line.

I considered him. He was testing me, seeing what he could get away with. Normally, I wouldn't tolerate it, but if our roles were reversed, I'd probably be doing the same. Fuck, at his age, I would've flipped myself off and dared me to do something about it.

If I kept on like this, Rio was going to clam up and I'd learn nothing.

I sighed inwardly and offered him a drink. His mouth dropped open, but he recovered smoothly. "Sure."

I poured us each a shot of a premium, blood-free whiskey and handed one to him. "Okay," I said, settling into the Barcelona chair, "what am I doing wrong?"

"You want something from Nyx, right?" He took a gulp of whiskey. "And no, I don't know what," he added when my brows dipped. "But people talk. I know her dad's a QCS enforcer and that he's the one you're really after."

I could guess who "people" was—Eden. Talon needed to impress upon his mate the importance of guarding syndicate business.

"Go on," I told Rio.

"Well, if you wanted something from me and you locked me in a cell, I wouldn't give you fuck-all."

I sipped my whiskey. "So what would you do?"

He blinked. "You asking my advice?"

"Isn't that why you're here?"

Why I was talking this over with a teenage human, I had no clue—except Nyx was proving tougher than I'd expected and I didn't have the stomach for what it'd take to break her.

Last night when I'd found her curled up on the stone floor, I'd been nearly paralyzed with fear. I would have done anything to make her better—anything.

Letting her drink my blood was the least of it. I would've drained myself dry for her.

Lilith help me if Nyx ever realized the power she had over me.

"Huh." A faint, pleased smile curled Rio's mouth. He propped a booted foot on the opposite thigh and took another swallow of whiskey. "First thing is to let her out of the cell. I mean, it's not like she's going to escape Lilith Island."

I shook my head. "The cell's leverage. Let her out, and I have nothing to pressure her with."

"Fair." Rio eyed his shot glass, thinking. "Okay, how about this? Find out what she wants most. Use that to bargain with her."

"Tried that. She turned me down flat."

I'd offered the woman sanctuary, her own studio. She'd said no to both. I had nothing else to bargain with unless it was her father's continuing existence—and that was a nonstarter.

"Yeah? Damn." His face fell, but he quickly rallied. "You sure that's what she really wanted? I mean, did she tell you straight out?"

"Yes," I said, then grimaced because I had no idea what Nyx wanted most. I'd assumed. "No," I admitted.

Rio pursed his lips. "Tell you what. I'll work on her for you. I think she likes me."

Something panged in my chest.

I forced a slow breath through my nose. Was I actually bothered that Rio and Nyx had apparently hit it off? More likely, she was playing him. Still, it grated.

I kept seeing her face from yesterday evening. Blank, flat-voiced, saying she understood it wasn't personal. Like she'd already buried whatever we'd had, marked the grave, and moved on.

I shook my head. "You won't change her mind."

"Maybe not. But either way, I'd let her out of that cell. Locking her up like that—you're making an enemy, you know?"

I grunted, staring into my whiskey. Itching to hurl the shot glass at my clean white walls, to watch the expensive crystal shatter, the liquid exploding across the painted surface like a bloodstain. But that was teenage Cain, the feral, out-of-control kid I'd been before being turned and learning self-discipline.

The kid who'd been caged a few times himself—in the island jail —and nearly gone berserk trying to get free.

"I'll think about it." I knocked back the whiskey and rose to my feet. "Now, if we're finished, I've got work to do."

⚜

For the next couple of nights, I stayed out of the dungeon except for a quick visit each evening to see Nyx with my own eyes.

Each time she was upright, the silver burned out of her system, but she wasn't herself. Low energy. Dimmed. The sparkle gone.

No suggestive voice, no games. Just cool politeness, eyes lowered like I was a stranger. Like she'd never begged me, moaned for me, taken me deep inside her body.

And Gods, that pissed me off.

She wasn't supposed to look through me like that. She wasn't supposed to feel distant. My instincts snarled every time she dropped her gaze, every time she acted like I meant nothing.

By the third night, it was clear that she'd rather rot in that cell than sell out her father. Any other prisoner, I would've admired the loyalty. Or crushed it out of them.

But with her, respect twisted into something darker.

Possessive.

Unreasonable.

I wanted to drag her out of that cell, pin her to the wall, force her to meet my eyes.

Make her admit she was *mine*.

But wanting that—wanting *her*—felt like a weakness I refused to show. So I punished myself instead.

I got Brien and Talon to meet in the gym and drove my body past the edge. Weights until my muscles screamed, then hand-to-hand combat until my knuckles split and iron filled my mouth.

Sweat, muscle, pain. Like I could beat the weakness back one strike at a time.

After, I took an icy shower and fed from another of my regulars before heading for the war room. I opened my laptop and stared at the screen, still wound tight, the kind of tension that made the walls feel too close.

Unable to work. Unable to stop thinking about Nyx.

It was a relief when William, the castle butler, poked his square, buzz-cut head through my office door. "Chief Valente wants to see you—about your uncle."

"What about him?"

"He's dead," said William.

I sat back. So the sonuvabitch had washed up somewhere. "What does Valente want?"

William shrugged a beefy shoulder. "You're Baker's only family on the island."

"Tell him I'm busy. Brien left me in charge." He was with Twilight—the two took a nightly swim in the Atlantic (which was insanely cold in early March, even for a vampire)—and Talon was still on parental leave.

"I'm afraid Valente is being persistent, sir. Your uncle's death was suspicious. Broken bones and such. There wasn't much of him after the sharks got to him, of course."

I smiled. "I'm sorry to hear that."

"Me, too, sir." The butler smiled back.

"And Valente's here, you say?"

"Yes, sir. He insists on speaking to you in person."

I closed my laptop and rose to my feet. It's not like I was getting much done anyway. "Where is he?"

"In the upper lair. The drawing room."

"Tell him I'll be right there. And make him comfortable—give him something to drink, pastries, whatever."

"Very good," he said and left.

The upper floors were all old-world decadence. Brien's father, the first Maritime primus, had carved the place out of stone and ego. French opulence welded to Nova Scotian grit—crimson wallpaper, bone-white panels, polished marble floors, furniture that could've been stolen from Versailles. There was even a godsdamn ballroom.

Sometimes I still couldn't believe I ended up here. The luxury felt like a costume, and me a stray dressed up in borrowed clothes. Yet here I was, a fucking syndicate lieutenant.

Two decades ago, even I wouldn't have bet on me ending up as one of Brien's righthand men. I flashed on myself, wild and half-starved, trailing Brien's mother, Prima Lenore, into the castle's foyer. I'd been wide-eyed at the sheer wealth, and the power behind it.

Tall and blond like her son, the prima had appeared in the island jail where me and Talon were doing thirty days to offer us both a deal: agree to be Brien's bodyguards and she'd turn us.

The two of us had exchanged a slack-jawed look, then said "Yes, ma'am," at the same time. We were nobody then, just a pair of idiots trying to prove what badasses we were.

As the willowy blond vampire had led us through the halls to the cavern beneath the lair where she would turn us, I made myself a promise. I'd survive transition, no matter what. No twenty-year-old kid wants to die, but I didn't care that much about living.

What I wanted was payback, to shove my new status in my aunt and uncle's faces.

And I'd done it. Over and over and over.

Talon had wondered why I didn't simply off Baker, put the bastard out of his misery.

But I'd enjoyed humbling him. Had fucking loved hitting him again and again—in his pocketbook, where it hurt him the most.

It still hadn't been enough. Nothing I did could make up for my aunt and uncle's abuse. I hadn't even wanted an apology. They could've crawled to me on their knees begging forgiveness, and I would've laughed and buried my boot in their soft bellies.

In the drawing room, Valente was on his feet, cradling a coffee cup in one long-fingered hand, studying the ornate gold clock on the mantel like he was trying to figure out how it was put together. A fifth-generation islander, he was tall and lean, and steady in that way locals trusted. I didn't know him well, but he had a rep as a fair man.

"Lieutenant." He set his cup on a saucer on the antique coffee table and calmly met my gaze. "Thank you for seeing me."

"Of course." We shook hands, then I waved at a pair of green brocade couches. "Sit, please."

"I'll stand, thanks anyway." A grin creased his leathery cheek. "I spend too much time on my ass as it is.

I clasped my hands behind my back. "I hear you found Baker."

"Yes." He explained that his skull and few spare parts—a shin, a hand—had washed up on a beach a few kilometers south.

"You need me to identify him?" I asked.

"That won't be necessary. The dental records confirmed it."

Behind my back, I tapped one finger against the opposite wrist. "So why are you here?"

"Your uncle didn't leave a will. That means the house will come to you."

No fucking way.

"He has a sister," I pointed out.

"Not anymore. The sister passed a couple of years ago. And her children aren't keen on hanging onto some run-down place on a syndicate-run island. No offense, Lieutenant."

I lifted a shoulder. "None taken."

"So, that leaves you. The land will revert to the syndicate, of course, but the house will have to go through probate, which could take years. In the meantime, I'm sure you'll want to maintain it."

"Let the bank have it," I said. "I hear he was about to lose it anyway."

Valente's gray eyes turned cold as the ocean in January. "I think we both know your syndicate owns the bank. So to my way of thinking, you already own it."

My own eyes narrowed. "Then let it rot."

His jaw worked—but he didn't let up, like a terrier with a bone.

"I think we both want to avoid making waves, eh? I'll write up Baker's death as an unfortunate accident—guy went in the water and didn't survive. All I'm asking is that you patch up his old place. It's either you or the town footing the bill, and seeing as you're set to inherit the building, it seems fair you step up. We've got young families here, decent folks who'd be happy to rent a big house like that from you."

His meaning was clear. Sure, I could pull rank on him—on Lilith Island, the syndicate was the law—but keeping the locals happy was good business. If Valente put it around that a Maritime lieutenant had pitched one of their own off the cliffs, it'd cause trouble, even if the guy was an ass like Baker.

"In that case," I replied, "I'd be happy to take responsibility for the house."

He gave me an easy smile like he'd never doubted I'd see it his way. "I'll let the mayor know."

I walked Valente out. He gave me another firm handshake and drove off in his syndicate-issued SUV. I followed him through the portcullis and stood on the edge of the cliff.

The wind tore at my shirt, cold teeth chewing at the cotton, while the sea below battered itself against the rock—relentless, beautiful. I stayed until salt coated my tongue.

Wondering why I didn't feel more.

My aunt and uncle were gone. On their way to being erased from even the islanders' memories.

I should've been satisfied. Triumphant, even.

Instead, everything felt muted. Off.

And where triumph should've been, there was only...emptiness.

Back in the castle, I headed for the dungeon like a damn homing pigeon, stopping only long enough to grab the bag of clothes I'd ordered for Nyx—underwear, a camisole, another sweater, designer jeans.

I found her seated yoga-style on the cot, sketchpad balanced on her knees, hand moving in quick, graceful strokes. Too absorbed in what she was creating to notice me enter.

Curious, I edged closer.

A mysterious blond man in a peacoat—like the painting in the show—stood among the trees. Me, I guess. Only this time, Leclerc Castle loomed behind me, its battlements sprouting wings, huge bats tearing their way into a dark, furious sky.

My shadow fell across the drawing.

Nyx jolted and slammed the pad shut. "Yes?" she said without looking at me.

She'd washed up—she had that clean-soap smell—but her hair hung limply around her shoulders. Maybe I should take her upstairs for a shower? But it wasn't just her hair. She seemed smaller, her cheeks pale under her natural tan.

I raised the bag like an offering. "I brought you more clothes."

"Thank you." Still no eye contact. Not even a glance at the bag.

I dropped the bag on the cot and crossed my arms over my chest, fighting the twitch in my knee, the urge to pace, to shake off the feeling that she was slipping further and further out of my reach.

"Don't—" I ground out.

"What?" She raised her eyes, but her gaze landed somewhere around my shoulder.

"Don't thank me. You were right the other night. I don't—just don't do it, alright?"

She placed the pencil and a blobby gray eraser in a metal box— just so—and closed the lid. "Whatever you say, Lieutenant."

My lungs gusted with frustration. I had the urge to smash my fist into the stone wall behind me. "Why are you so stubborn?"

Her fingers clamped around the pad, knuckles whitening. "Why are you asking me to betray my sire?"

"Weren't you going to betray me?"

"No." Her brows formed a dark V above her nose, but she finally lifted her gaze to my face. "I told you, I was just there to hear your uncle out. Then I would've gotten word to you."

"I wish I could believe you."

The truth pulsed beneath my ribs. *I want to believe you.*

A bitter smile tugged at her mouth. "You never trusted me, did you? That whole time, I'll bet you were checking up on me, making sure I wasn't playing you. But I never did, did I? I could've tipped my father off about our meetings. You were careful, but you were also vulnerable. I could've stabbed you in the heart myself."

She was on her feet now, the pad tossed aside. Her chest jerked in short, uneven breaths, and two spots of color burned on her cheeks, her hurt and anger slamming into me like a physical blow.

I let my arms fall to my sides. Nobody could fake that kind of pain. Or at least, Nyx couldn't. Not with me.

With me, she'd been unguarded, allowing me to see the woman beneath the gloss and bravado.

My stomach caved in. What if I'd screwed up? What if she'd been telling the truth all along? And I hadn't believed her, even after she'd shown me, again and again, that she was on my side. I'd been too blind, too suspicious, too ready to see treachery in every corner.

And because of it—just like Rio had warned—I'd turned her against me. Made an enemy of the only woman who could make me feel something.

"You're a screw-up, boy. Always have been, always will be."

Now I didn't want to punch the wall. I wanted to drive my skull through it.

Nyx wasn't done. "I could've taken advantage, turned you over to my father long before the other night. But I didn't. Because I wanted you. I *liked* you. I wouldn't have hurt you for the world. But I will not betray my sire." Her finger stabbed into my sternum, one sharp poke for each word, and I kept my hands at my sides, accepting I deserved that and more. "I. Am. Not. A. Blood-rat."

She stopped and drew a serrated breath. "Think about it. If I help you get to him, how can you ever trust me to be loyal to you and your syndicate?"

I worked my jaw back and forth, unable to come up with a good answer.

She turned away, shoulders rigid. "Just go, okay?"

I stared at the back of her head, at the way she held herself too stiff, like she was bracing for more pain. She was right. Why would we trust her if she switched sides like that?

But I knew why I'd pushed her.

I'd wanted her to choose me over Nazaire.

I'd wanted her, body and soul. Complete surrender.

The admission poked a tender spot inside me. I fisted my hands. Pathetic. That was the abandoned three-year-old talking, the toddler who'd lost his father and didn't even remember his mother. Family was just a word for me until I met Talon, and later, Brien.

It was different for Nyx. She had a father, even if he was a twisted mofo. I couldn't fault her for being loyal to him. Blood chains ran deep in our world; most of us could trace our lineage back a thousand-plus years.

Didn't mean I didn't resent the grip the man had on her. I did.

Irrational, sure, but I wasn't rational about Nyx. She got under my skin, past every defense I thought I had.

But that was on me, not her.

The real enemy here wasn't Nyx. It was Nazaire.

I caught her by the shoulders. "Hey."

She tried to wrench free, but I turned her to face me so I could look her in the eyes. "You're right," I said.

She drew herself up to her full height, proud as a queen. Then she frowned. "I am?"

"Yes. You're right, and I'm wrong. You're loyal. I respect that, actually."

A scoff. "If I'm right, then why am I in a cell?"

"You're not." I released her and grabbed the bag of clothes from the cot. "Let's go."

She slow-blinked and didn't move—until I reached for the

sketchpad and box of pencils. Then she snatched them up, clutching them to her chest.

"Where are you taking me?"

"The garden suite. You'll still be confined to one area, but there's an enclosed garden, a shower, a comfortable bed."

"What about Brien? He's okay with this?"

"Let me worry about Brien." I pulled the door wide. "Now, are you coming or not?"

"I'm coming." She jammed her feet into the short black lug-soles without tying them and stumbled after me, art supplies hugged to her chest, boots clomping against the stone.

"You're gonna break your neck." Shaking my head, I handed the bag of clothes to the guard and crouched to tie them myself.

When I rose, her straight, dark brows were pinched together. "I can't figure you out."

A humorless breath escaped me. I took the clothes from the guard and guided her out of the cell.

"That makes two of us. Because I can't figure me out either."

Cain took me through a series of torch-lit tunnels—left, left again, then two rights and another left.

"Let me guess," I muttered. "You're trying to get me lost."

His reply was deadpan. "We like to fuck with intruders."

I cut him a look, and the corner of his mouth twitched upward. Somehow, that was reassuring. If he'd relaxed enough to tease me, even a little, then that was something, right?

A tall, dark-haired man stepped out of a short passage, his stride breaking when he spotted Cain. He backed up immediately, giving us space. His gaze flicked to me—curious, assessing—before he dipped his chin in a respectful nod to Cain.

The next person we ran into stepped aside as well. Then a third.

It struck me how powerful Cain had become. When we'd first met, he'd been one of Brien's personal bodyguards, a watchful shadow in the background. Even then, he left an impression. But now he was nobody's shadow—he was a Maritime lieutenant, a breath beneath the primus in the hierarchy, radiating authority.

And Luna help me, it was hot.

When he put a hand on my lower back to steer me into a short hallway, a thrill rippled up my spine. My pussy clenched around empty air.

Cain's head snapped around, and our eyes collided. His were arresting—blue ice surrounded by fiery cobalt.

I swallowed hard.

His hand slid up to my nape, gentle but firm. "Keep looking at me like that, and I'll forget the promise I made."

I was still recovering from being the sickest I'd ever been. I didn't trust him. And he was holding me captive.

I shouldn't have shivered in pleasure, but I did.

"Yeah?" I dredged up a sneer. "Well, don't fool yourself that I want it. You'd be forcing yourself on a prisoner."

"Would I?" he asked with a knowing smirk and turned me toward the only door in the hallway, reaching around me to open it. "After you, firefly."

I'd expected something like Cain's apartment: white walls and swanky leather-and-chrome furniture, that cool, immaculate order he lived in. Instead, I was enveloped in soft yellows and greens, with beachscapes stretching across seafoam walls. Through an open doorway, a massive teak bed was topped with gauzy white scarves like drifts of mist.

He dropped the bag of clothes on the pale lemon couch. "You're confined to these two rooms."

My gaze slid to the French door at the opposite side of the living room, its glass darkened to protect sensitive skin and eyes.

"No," he said firmly. "And just so you know, we have eyes on the garden and both doors."

I shrugged a shoulder, disappointed. Still, anything was better than that windowless cell and its four gray walls.

"Your meals will continue to be delivered. As for blood, you'll have to make do with blood-wine for now."

"That's fine." I didn't drink fresh blood more than once or twice a week anyway.

Cain had been meandering around the living room while he talked, fingering the books in the shelves, running a finger along the kitchenette counter. I'd noticed before how he was always moving, never still, but this wasn't his typical excess energy. No, he seemed nervous.

He poked his head into the bedroom. I put the pad and pencil box on the coffee table and trailed after him. We stopped at the same moment, caught by the sight of the towering four-poster.

Memory smacked me in the chest: London, a foggy autumn night, a viscount's Mayfair townhouse. Vampires and dhampirs and humans entwined in the halls, laughter and the pulse of beat-driven electronica intertwined with a half-dozen languages.

I hadn't brought my own security—it would've been an insult. Cain and I ditched the party before midnight and ended in a private apartment with a gauze-draped poster bed. We couldn't get enough of each other, one kiss leading to another, one position flowing into the next. In between, we shared a bottle of Dom Pérignon, debating silly things like which accent sounds sexiest when you're drunk and why sex makes blood taste better.

Near dawn, I'd ended up with my head on his shoulder, telling him how I hated being caught between worlds, always half something, never enough. He'd tightened his arm around me and admitted he'd almost broken the night he'd been turned. That when Prima Lenore had bared his neck and extended her fangs, he'd been so scared he almost pissed his pants. He'd bitten through his own lip just to keep from begging her to let him leave.

And then we'd fallen silent, but it wasn't the kind you felt you had to fill. It had been full of us.

Cain's throat worked. I knew he could hear my own gulp.

"The bathroom's over there." He tilted his head in its direction and frowned at the empty walk-in closet. "You need more clothes. I'll have them here by tomorrow."

"Thank you," I told his chin.

His face hardened. "Stop thanking me, already. I never should've thrown you in that damn cell in the first place, but when I found out it was you meeting my uncle..."

He'd moved closer. Or maybe I had?

"I could've tried harder to let you know something was up," I admitted. "But Nazaire... He was acting suspicious. I had to play along."

"Fuck." He briefly closed his eyes. "I'm sorry—you knew the situation, I didn't. I might've even done the same in your place."

My hands were on his chest now, toying with the placket of his crisp white shirt. And when his lungs lifted in a breath, mine did, too—like my body had forgotten it wasn't his.

That's when I noticed his cheeks were faintly flushed, his lips darker, redder.

Something twisted inside me. Something jagged, possessive.

He'd fed, which meant he'd had sex, too.

I could *smell* her on him, female, with a hint of apples and mint.

And me? I stank of the cell, my hair hanging limp and greasy around my shoulders. Hard to stay clean when all you had was a bar of soap and a sink.

I drew back, hurt and angry. I didn't have a right to either, but that didn't matter. Not when it was Cain.

He caught my hands. "What?"

I shook my head. "Nothing."

"Don't, damn it. It's not nothing. You're upset."

"Fine." My gaze locked on his. "You fed."

"So?" A beat. Then his lips parted, forming a silent O. "I fed. That's all."

"Right," I said flatly, tugging my hands free. He was a supernatural; drinking blood made us horny whether we wanted it to or not. "It's not my business. But you don't have to lie about it."

"It's not a lie," he growled. He seized my hand, pressing it to his erection. "Feel this, damn it. I haven't fucked anyone since Paris. Since *you*."

My breath hitched. My fingers had developed a will of their own because they stayed where he'd put them, exploring the hard ridge. When he drew a ragged inhale, I stilled, my gaze snapping to his. He was telling the truth—he hadn't had anyone since that night at the gallery.

"Why not?" I asked, then jerked my hand from his crotch. "Never mind. I don't know why I asked."

"I know why." Strong palms cupped my face. "You want to hear that it's because of you. That I can't get you out of my head. That every time we fuck it's the best ever—and then it gets even better." His thumbs caressed my cheekbones in slow strokes. "I'm right, aren't I?

"No." I was gripping his shoulders now, needing to hold onto something because the ground beneath me had tilted. "Yes. I don't know." The words tumbled out like loose stones.

"Well, it's true." His blue eyes burned into mine, like the admission scoured him raw. "I don't want anyone but you."

The air between us hummed. My pulse kicked, and the anger and hurt in me twisted into something reckless, something that felt too much like yearning.

Did he feel it too?

That pull buzzing beneath my skin a live wire, the one I'd been trying to pretend wasn't there? A knowing. A recognition.

But no, that couldn't be right. This man couldn't be my mate, not when he still saw me as the enemy.

I pulled back. "What about my father?" I asked, inserting him between us like a shield. "Have you heard from him?"

His gaze turned frosty. He released me and stepped back. "Not since that first night."

"He knows it wasn't me, then—texting him."

He lifted a shoulder, let it fall. "Probably."

"So what are you going to do?"

He just looked at me.

"I see." I turned and headed for the living room, needing to get away from both him and that four-poster bed.

Cain followed. "The floors are heated," he said, tapping an electronic panel next to the door, impersonal as a hotel manager. "Thermostat's next to the intercom. If you need anything, push *two* for Kerry—the housekeeper. Hit *three* for the kitchen." He glanced around, his gaze catching on the sketchpad. "I'll have them get you more drawing things—supplies. Make a list and give it to Rio."

"I will." I paused, then added, "Thank you." Again.

But I *was* grateful. To be allowed to draw meant a lot.

He shrugged. "You have a gift. You should use it."

I bit down on my lower lip, tempted to leave it there. He was my jailer. My captor. I owed him nothing.

But Cain valued truth...and information.

And even though he was keeping me here against my will, he'd apologized for locking me up and moved me to this apartment.

He'd bent. Maybe I could bend too.

He reached for the door handle.

"Wait," I said. "There's something I have to tell you. Nazaire knows. Those texts—he assumed I was with you. Why would he say that unless he found out we've been meeting?"

Cain nodded, unsurprised. "That's what I figured. And—?"

A chill licked over my skin. I rubbed my upper arms.

"You understand that's why he sent me to meet your uncle? He knew exactly what he was doing—he wanted to put me in an impossible position."

Cain opened his mouth, then closed it.

"What?" I asked.

"No." The corner of his mouth tilted in a crooked little smile. "I want you to figure it out for yourself."

And he left, leaving me staring, brow furrowed, at the closed door.

It wasn't until I stepped under the hot spray of the shower that it hit me. The meeting with "Baker" *had* been a test, and from my father's point of view, I'd failed it.

I'd chosen a side. Cain's.

I'd never had any intention of hurting him. In fact, I would've done anything to keep my father's hands off him, including lying to my own flesh and blood.

Somewhere along the way, something in me had shifted. Something I couldn't turn off even if I wanted to.

And the Dark Gods help me, I didn't want to.

21

CAIN

The door of the garden suite clicked shut behind me, and the calm I'd been clinging to shattered. I cursed and drove my fist into the tunnel wall. Pain flared, but I barely registered it.

If Nyx hadn't been playing me, then I'd fucked up.

I glared at the spidery cracks like the stone could somehow rewrite the past three nights.

I told myself she'd known what Baker had wanted and had come anyway, that we'd had no choice but to put her in a cell. But now that reasoning felt paper-thin.

I would've still brought her back to the island for her protection and mine. But we didn't have to throw her in a cell. I could've fought Brien on that. I could've stood up for her.

Because Nyx—she'd chosen me. She'd done the best she could to save me from Nazaire's machinations.

And me? I'd repaid her by imprisoning her.

I was still staring at the cracks when my phone buzzed. I shook out my throbbing hand and fished the device from my pocket. It was Brien, telling me to get to the war room ASAP.

No explanation, but I could guess—someone had reported that I'd moved Nyx from the cell. I grimaced and headed off.

Talon caught me at the next intersection. "What's this about you and Nazaire's spawn?"

My jaw locked. "I moved her to the garden suite, okay?"

He lifted his hands. "Hey, it was a question, not a judgment."

"Sorry," I muttered, heat crawling up my neck. "But I can't take a crap in this place without someone running to Brien. And her name's Nyx," I added because she was more than just 'Nazaire's spawn.'

"Got it," he said. "So... is Nyx still sick?"

"No, she's better. That's not why I moved her."

"Then what's up? You need me to back you, I will, but you gotta give me something to work with."

"It's something Rio said. If we want Nyx on our side, we can't keep treating her like the enemy. Keeping her locked in a cell is only going to make her hate us."

Talon gave me a sidelong look. "And maybe you were looking for a reason to let her out."

"So what if I was? She shared intel with us, Tal. That was risky, and she didn't ask for anything in return."

"Agreed. But she also blew up our boat. And she showed for that meeting with Baker."

"Yeah, about that. You really think she had a choice? The man's a vampire, an enforcer. Can you imagine her just saying no to him?"

Talon blew out a breath. "Yeah, guess not."

We'd reached the war room. I stopped, a hand on the doorjamb.

"She did what she had to do to survive," I said. "From what she said, he only keeps her around because she's useful. I'm pretty sure he'd already figured out she fed us intel, even before I sent those texts." My voice roughened. "I just made it worse."

I slapped my palm on the biorec pad and pushed the door open. "She's still a prisoner. But locking her in a cell isn't punishing Nazaire—it punishes her. And Nyx may be more of a victim of Nazaire than any of us realize."

"Fuck." Talon blew out a breath and followed me into the cavern.

Brien and Twilight were already in his office. Talon entered first. I paused to smooth down my white shirt, feeling like I was ten again, summoned to the principal's office for breaking some stupid-ass rule. I pasted on a neutral expression and followed him, closing the door behind me.

Brien was leaning against the desk, arms crossed. Twilight perched on the edge beside him, her fishnet-clad legs crossed at the ankles, deceptively dainty in gold sneakers and a blood-red dress.

I gave my primus and prima a respectful nod—playing the game —while Talon took the leather armchair in front of the desk, knowing I'd rather stand, be free to pace.

I got straight to the point. "If this is about me moving Nyx from the dungeon, then maybe I overstepped. But she's not the kind of woman you cage. Keep her in that cell much longer and she'll shut down completely, and we'll never get anything out of her. I promise, she's contained—I'm keeping her in those two rooms. I'm not even allowing her into the garden."

Brien glanced at Twilight, the two communicating in that word-less way of a mated pair. I braced myself. I had to win this argument because I was damned if I'd let them send Nyx back to the dungeon.

But when Brien turned back to me, it was to say, "Okay. We trust your judgment."

The tightness in me eased a little. "Thank you."

"Actually," said Twilight, "it's smart to keep her somewhere with access to the outside. If and when Nazaire's people come hunting for her, it may lure them into making a move. We have a camera on both doors, right?"

I nodded. "We do, and the alarms are set. No one's getting within ten yards of her without us knowing."

"Perfect." Her smile was all sharp teeth. "Hopefully, Nazaire will take the bait. Save us the trouble of goading him to retrieve his daughter."

"Might as well allow her the run of the garden," said Brien. "Make it easier for someone to get to her."

I stiffened. *No fucking way.* "Too risky."

Brien cocked his head like he'd heard something I hadn't said. "Because—?"

Because if they somehow got to her, it'd gut me.

But I wasn't ready to say that out loud.

"Our security has been breached twice in the last few years. Twice that we know of, that is. The island's too big, and we can't be sure Nazaire doesn't have someone on the island already, someone on his payroll. And I'm not letting that SOB get ahold of her. He knows about me—you read the texts."

I'd forwarded the texts to the three of them.

Brien and Talon nodded. Twilight's brow wrinkled. "You think he'll take this out on her."

"I'd put money on it. It was a test—and Nyx botched it, thanks to me. If he gets ahold of her, there's no telling what he'll do."

"Fine," said Brien. "No garden access unless you're with her. Now we've already laid the groundwork—hints about the castle's supposed vulnerabilities. How else do we turn up the heat on the bastard?"

"Hit him in the assets," Talon murmured from the armchair. "Bank accounts, investments. And maybe it's time to leak that we have Nyx here on Lilith Island—that she's one of us now?"

"The assets first," I said, recalling how Nyx had begged me not send those texts, how important it was to her not to be known as a blood-rat. "If that doesn't work, we can think about leaking the info about Nyx."

The meeting turned to the best way to inflict financial pain on Nazaire. After, I dealt with the items needing my immediate attention, then grabbed a leather jacket and headed out of the castle. Needing to get out, go someplace Nyx wasn't so I could *think*.

Outside, the moon had been up for hours. It hovered above the east turret like the eye of some enormous beast, watching me cross the cobblestones to the carriage house that housed our vehicles.

I eased my Ferrari into the courtyard, convertible top down, its gleaming black frame catching the moonlight. As I aimed toward the portcullis, Talon stepped out of the darkness, silent as one of the wolfdogs that patrolled the castle grounds.

He laid a hand on the passenger door. "Want some company?"

"You have to ask? Get in, mofo."

He slung a leg over the door, sliding into the seat with an easy grace. "So, where're we going?"

"Baker's house. Valente's on my case about it standing empty."

I hit the remote clipped to my visor. The portcullis groaned and slid upward, the metal grille parting like the top half of a jaw. I pressed the gas, and we shot out of the courtyard, tires biting into the cobblestone.

"Why were you at that meeting, anyway?" I asked, steering us along the cliffside road. "Aren't you supposed to be on parental leave?"

"You needed backup."

I grimaced because he wasn't wrong. "I appreciate it, but Eden and the little guy need you more. Which reminds me—why the hell are you out here with me?"

"They're fine. Eden's got half the castle waiting on her like she's a damn queen, including Twilight's halmoni—and you know that woman is scary."

My lips twitched. "True."

Twilight's grandmother was a former slayer herself. She'd moved in and taken over, running the castle's domestic operations along with Kerry, the official housekeeper.

"If you're sure—"

"Wouldn't be here if I wasn't."

I whipped the sportscar around a curve, hugging the cliff edge. The wind off the Atlantic slapped our faces, ice-cold and laced with salt.

Beside me, Talon drew a slow inhale, looking out over the ocean. "It's good to be out."

"Yeah," I said.

We drove in silence for a few minutes, then Talon said, "So Valente knows about Baker?"

He knew I'd offed the SOB, of course. I'd told both him and Brien that night.

"Yeah. They found him—enough to ID him, anyway."

"Valente gonna be trouble?"

"Nah. Man just wants me to do something with Baker's house. He didn't make a will, and apparently Valente's elected me the heir." I swung left. "And here's the turn."

We bumped down a teeth-rattling driveway that would probably land the Ferrari in the shop for the next month and halted in front of the empty farmhouse. I cut the engine, the old, familiar unworthiness creeping up my nape, tightening my skin.

Talon got out first, looking up at the broken window, the one I'd tossed Baker out of.

"You should've brought me with you that night," he said when I joined him on the gravel.

"I handled it."

"But you didn't have to. Not by yourself."

"I know, but—" I lifted a shoulder, let it drop.

How could I explain that final confrontation *needed* to be just me and Baker? Maybe I'd wanted to prove to myself that he didn't scare me anymore. That he was just a bitter, broken bully who no longer had any power over me.

Our eyes met, and Talon gave a slow nod. He'd been there for most of it, after all.

He vaulted onto the sagging porch and tried the front door, but it was locked. I stepped up beside him, the boards groaning beneath us.

He eyed the curtained windows. "What's it like inside, anyway?"

"Falling apart—but the same. I don't think he changed a damn thing after my aunt died. Like one of those nightmares that never changes, just waits for you to come back." I grimaced. "Valente wants me to fix it up, maybe rent it out."

A lighter appeared in Talon's hand. He thumbed it open, and the flame flared to life, small but hungry. "Or," he said, watching it dance, "you could just torch the place. Build something new."

Hell, yeah. Deep inside, the wild, unwanted kid in me leapt up, grinning and whooping: *Do it. Burn it down.*

Lilith knew, I wanted to. Wanted the fire to swallow the memories, the echo of angry voices, the rooms where I'd learned to flinch.

Talon held the lighter up. "No?"

I jiggled my leg, staring at that bright, too-tempting flame.

A beat passed. The kind where you stop running from your demons and turn to face them. Where you accept your scars are a part of you and that you're stronger because of them.

"No," I said at last. "It will make someone a good home."

He snapped the lighter shut. "You want my advice? Let the bank have it. Why should you deal with this crap?"

"That was the plan. But I promised Valente—and I think I need to do this, you know? Need to see it through."

"Then throw some money at it. Hire a contractor and let them make the decisions."

I shot him a look. "You think your mom would want to help—handle the details like trim, paint, all that?"

"Hell, yeah. Actually, she could use something to do. She's still sober." Talon's expression was half-proud, half-relieved. "And this time, I think it'll stick. She knows we won't let her near Jude if she's drinking."

"That's good, Tal." I smiled back. "Great, in fact. So she'll do it?"

"Of course. This kind of project is right up her alley. And she'd do it for you anyway. You always were her favorite." He huffed a laugh. "Thought sun shone out of your ass, in fact."

"The only person on the whole damn island who did."

"Except me."

"You were my blood brother. You had to love me."

"Blood brothers." He rumbled, amused. "We were what—eleven?"

"Twelve years and two months, and dead serious—at least I was. Figured if you were my brother, I had a chance at a family. Like your mom might see me as hers, too."

The admission scraped out of me.

Talon and I exchanged a look. Then he punched my shoulder.

"Hey, I needed a brother, too. And my mom *is* yours—she'd say so herself. She let you move in, didn't she? Even when she was drinking, she trusted you, saw something in you that nobody else did." He slanted me a lopsided smile, the one that used to mean trouble and now meant *look at how far we came*. "I saw it, too. Always knew you'd grow up to be somebody."

"Back atcha, dude." I gave him a short nod and switched gears. "I'll be in touch with your mom, then. And of course, I'll pay her, whatever she asks. She's doing me a favor. If you talk to her first, make sure she knows that."

"Copy that." Talon tipped his chin toward the house. "Now why don't we see what it looks like inside?"

He raised a booted foot and kicked the door open.

⚜

In the end, the farmhouse held no ghosts, just dust and silence. The bones were solid, although the roof sagged and the house needed painting, inside and out, and the porch replaced.

I pulled out my phone, taking photos for Talon's mom and the contractors. I'd warmed to the idea of taking the house on, of gutting the place, erasing every trace of my aunt and uncle and handing it off to a young family.

"We'll have to rip out the kitchen and bathrooms," I told Talon. "Start new. And that porch has to be replaced."

"Up to you," he returned.

I stilled, struck by the idea. "Yeah, it is."

I could do whatever the fuck I wanted. The irony was satisfying.

After everything the Bakers had done—the arbitrary rules, the constant punishments—I was the one left holding the keys. Their precious house and what was left of their fancy antiques? I got to choose what stayed and what burned.

As the Ferrari rattled and bounced its way up the driveway, Talon said, "You know, I think you're right to do this. You need some—what d'you call it?—closure."

"Revenge," I corrected, turning onto the cliff road.

"Nah. You already got your revenge. This is something else. Tying up loose ends...letting go."

"Maybe. But it's also revenge."

We shared a wolfish smile.

I liked to think that somewhere out there, Baker saw my smile —and flinched.

22

NYX

I toweled off, my thoughts ricocheting between two impossible choices: Nazaire or Cain. Honor or love.

The fact that it even *felt* like a choice made my chest constrict. I wasn't supposed to hesitate when it came to Nazaire. Hesitation went against everything I'd been taught to believe.

But it was time to face facts. The story I'd always told myself about my father—about what I was to him—was a lie. I was never going to earn his approval. He was never going to love me. I'd been a tool, at best.

What I'd called discipline had always been domination. What I'd told myself was training had always been control. And the way he watched me, corrected me, punished me—it hadn't been about making me stronger. It had been about molding me into something he could use.

I'd spent years pretending his cruelty had purpose, that there was some logic behind it. But there wasn't. He hurt me because he wanted to. Because he could. Because it pleased him to see me bend.

It was time to accept I'd never be enough for him, not as an heir and not as a daughter.

With the decision came a kind of peace, the weary clarity that settles in your bones when you stop resisting what you know is true.

Nazaire couldn't "rescue" me if I refused to leave. This wasn't his territory. Anyone he sent would be counting on my cooperation.

Well, fuck that.

I wasn't completely powerless. I could disappear into the shadows, glamour myself. Even if my father came himself, he'd have to knock me out before I'd leave because I wasn't going quietly.

Which left Cain. Some of the bravado drained out of me.

You could stay. He wants you to.

The Dark Gods knew I was tempted.

But not like this. Cain might want me, but his offer came with conditions.

I'd never come first with him. He'd said himself that his duty was to his syndicate. If I stayed on Lilith Island, I'd be tying myself to a man who hadn't chosen me freely.

A man who'd never choose me, Nyx, over his syndicate brothers.

The thought left a hollow ache blooming under my ribs.

I hung up the towel and straightened—not much, just enough to feel my spine. I was done accepting second best. I deserved better.

If Cain couldn't give me everything, then I was better off walking away.

The Maritime Syndicate couldn't keep me on Lilith Island forever. Either they'd finally get to my father, or they'd get tired of keeping me prisoner. Either way, they'd release me.

And then I could finally enact my plan—take my cash and vanish into the anonymity of a big city, one without a powerful syndicate. Stay in at night, fly under the radar.

I twisted my damp hair into a messy bun and drifted through the suite, examining the art without really seeing it, picking up books and putting them down again. My fingertips skimmed over the couch, the chairs, the cool granite counter—touching everything because I couldn't touch the one thing I wanted.

In the kitchenette, I poured myself a glass of blood-wine and carried it to the bedroom doorway. The gauze-draped bed blurred at the edges as I stared at it. A trace of Cain's spicy midnight scent still clung to the suite, faint but unmistakable. I pressed my knuckles to my mouth, throat clogging as the memories rose.

How that night in London, his frost-blue eyes had locked on me like I was the only thing that mattered.

How, when he touched me, all that restless, kinetic energy in him went still. He'd gone quiet, intent, like wanting me cost him something he didn't know how to give.

I dragged in a breath.

This is what you wanted. Freedom—from Nazaire, the syndicates, the games...

I padded back into the living room, sipping wine and gazing out at the moon-drenched garden, picturing how I'd paint it. Because that's what I did when my heart hurt.

The garden must be gorgeous in the summer; even now it had a haunting, stripped-down beauty. Fairy lights followed a path through skeletal trees and ornamental grasses, tiny stars in the darkness. Grape vines clung like dark veins to the weathered stone walls, and fruit trees raised their branches among pots of dried-up herbs.

A white cat with a single black ear appeared out of the shrubbery and picked her way through the snow-covered path to butt her head against the glass. I tried the door, but it was locked, as Cain had said.

The cat sat on its haunches, regarding me through citrine eyes.

"Sorry," I told her. Somehow, I knew the cat was a *her*.

Annoyed, she flicked the black ear at me and vanished back into the bushes. A few seconds later I saw her sleek body trotting along the top of the wall, and then she was gone.

A reel flickered to life behind my eyes, vivid as a movie. The moon casting silver shadows over a forgotten garden; vines creeping like fingers; and the snow-pale cat—no longer just a cat, but a shapeshifter, a guardian, a queen cloaked in fur and mystery.

Then one day, a vampire comes searching for the queen...

My fingers twitched, hungry to capture the scenes on canvas. To escape into a world where I controlled the ending.

I curled up on the couch, pad in hand, and began to sketch.

23

CAIN

I took my time on the drive back, keeping the Ferrari to a smooth, steady glide. Talon sat beside me, the two of us talking about nothing much, just like old times. For a few miles I let myself pretend things were simple again. We rounded a curve, and the castle came into view, rising out of the cliffs, its four black towers stark against the moonlit sky.

I glanced at Talon. "Remember that night we came back with Prima Lenore?"

He chuckled, shaking his head. "I was scared shitless."

"You, too? My pulse was banging in my ears so loud I couldn't think."

"I almost threw up all over the shark mosaic. And then she marched us down to that cave beneath the lair. Tide was high enough that it was half underwater. I figured if we didn't make the cut, she'd toss us in and let the great whites clean up the mess."

My lips twitched. "She would've, too. She was efficient like that."

A short laugh. "Yeah."

We fell silent, and somehow I knew he was back in that cavern with me, our throats bared for the prima's bite. I'd been shaking in my cheap boots, but I'd held my ground, feet planted, refusing even to blink.

I would've sold my damned soul for some of Lenore's strength, her power, her pitiless will. But she hadn't wanted my soul. She wanted my humanity.

And I gave it freely, shedding it like a snake's brittle, used-up skin. What remained was cold, ruthless, heartless—like the old ones who'd walked this path before me.

But I guess I wasn't as untouchable as I believed. Every vampire's got a crack in the armor—their mate.

And mine was named Nyx.

And I'd fucked it up.

Something real had been growing between me and Nyx, and I'd torn it out with my bare hands.

Because I'd listened to Baker's voice—the one that called me weak for wanting her, that said needing her made me soft.

And in trying to drown him out, I'd hurt her.

I swallowed over the boulder in my throat and glanced at Talon. "Can I ask you something?"

"Shoot."

I flexed my fingers on the steering wheel, made a tiny correction to the rearview mirror. "What's it like—being mated?"

"She... completes me." A corner of his mouth tipped up. "It's like finding the piece you didn't know was missing. And she's always in here." He brought a fist to his sternum. "Even when she's not beside me, I feel her. Like a heartbeat that isn't mine."

Last year—hell, even last month—I would've laughed off something as sappy as a missing piece of yourself. Soulmates, destiny, all that poetic bullshit.

But I wasn't laughing tonight. The truth of it smacked me in the chest, leaving me exposed and off-balanced.

Nyx felt like my missing piece, too, the one thing my money couldn't buy. Her unhappiness was now my unhappiness.

When I didn't say anything, Talon sent me a look from beneath his brows. "You still think I should've held out for a vampire?"

I shook my head. "Maybe at first, but not now. You two have something special—even I can see that. You find your mate, you claim her."

He nodded, slow. "Yeah. You just know. And when you do..." He exhaled, shoulders rising and falling like the weight of it lived in his lungs. "It's everything. Nothing else on Earth even comes close. It doesn't matter that she's not a vampire. She's just Eden."

He eyed me, waiting.

I glued my gaze to the road. Saying it aloud would make it real, break open something I'd never be able to close again.

He snorted. "You gonna make me drag it out of you?"

"I'm thinking," I growled. "This is—" I shook my head.

"Alright, then tell me this. What would you do to keep her?"

"Anything." My voice was low, guttural, the words ripped from my heart. "Burn down the world. Bleed it dry. Whatever it took."

"Does she know?"

"I offered her sanctuary, didn't I?"

"So? She's an in, a way to get to Nazaire. You would've done that for anyone close to him—right?"

"Probably," I admitted. "But I wasn't thinking of him when I made the offer. I was thinking of her, that she needed a safe place. Somewhere away from that controlling sonofabitch."

"So you want to protect her," Talon said, "and you'd do anything to keep her." He shook his head. "You, my friend, are well and truly fucked. Because right now, she thinks that all she is to you is bait. Those texts—"

My back teeth clamped together. That was the curse of brothers. They were world-class bullshit detectors.

"I did it for the syndicate. For *you*—all of you."

"So she *is* bait."

"Fuck you." I swung into the next curve, tires screaming.

Talon gave a little half-smile and braced himself so he didn't get flung out of the convertible.

"Okay," I conceded after the car righted itself. "I saw an opportunity and took it. But she's not bait—he's not getting anywhere near her. I'll take him apart with my bare hands if I have to."

"Then you better make sure she knows that," he said. "Because if she thinks she's just a pawn, it won't matter what that bastard does. You'll lose her anyway."

"Not going to happen." I eased off the gas, every muscle locked tight at the thought of Nyx walking away for good.

Mine.

My Nyx. My forever.

It wasn't love. That word felt too pale, too soft for what burned in me. Love was for humans. What I felt was older, hungrier—something forged out of blood and bone and magic.

She was the only woman for me. The one who could break me just by turning her back.

And I'd smashed her trust.

"I'll make this right," I told Talon. "Whatever it takes."

❧ 24 ☙

NYX

I worked in a feverish white heat, absorbed in my story and the pictures that grew from it. Minutes melted into hours as I sketched, erased, shaded, redrew—the images coming faster than my hands could keep up.

Wild roses twined around a silver-haired prince, their thorns biting into his skin. A princess shaped from heartbeat and shadows, her face tight with the kind of love that could bring down a kingdom. A striking blond vampire sprawled on the cobblestones, a dagger jutting from her ribs, and a long black-scaled snake gliding past her head, its body thin and elegant as a tailored coat.

My nape prickled. With an effort, I dragged my gaze from my sketch. Cain stood on the other side of the coffee table, watching me.

I snapped the pad shut, sliding my mask into place—practiced smile, head tilted in fake interest. "Hi."

Something passed over his face, like he was physically hurting. Like fake-me upset him. "Just checking on you."

I placed the pad on the coffee table, the stick of charcoal and eraser beside it, and came to my feet. "Well, I'm fine."

He remained where he was on the other side of the table, studying me through hooded eyes.

"What?" Uneasiness tightened my shoulders. "Is it about my father? Something happened?"

"No," said Cain. "He's gone dark."

My mouth twisted. "Sounds like him. He likes pressure, likes making people crack." He was probably waiting and watching, hoping the Maritime vampires would make a mistake.

Cain made a noncommittal grunt and crouched, rearranging my art supplies until the bottom edges formed a perfect line. Something about that made my chest clench. It was so him.

That night in London, he'd had flowers delivered to the hotel suite: calla lilies the deep red of garnets, wrapped in a black velvet ribbon. When I'd emerged from the shower early that morning, I found him in the suite's kitchen, slicing the end of one stem so it would match the others. He'd glanced at me, lips tugging into a crooked half-smile, laughing at himself a little. Then he'd said, "I want them to be perfect for you," and my heart had gone all stupid and syrupy.

I dug my nails into my palms. "You don't have to do that," I told him. "I'll only mess them up again."

He straightened and gave me almost the same crooked smile. "Habit."

When I didn't say anything, his smile dissolved. "What were you drawing, anyway?"

"Pictures."

He waited a moment and when I didn't add anything, gave a tiny sigh. "D'you need anything? Food? Blood-wine?" His gaze landed on the untouched tray on the kitchenette counter and he crossed the room, lifting the lid on a blue earthenware soup bowl. "You didn't eat?"

"I forgot," I said just as my stomach growled.

He shook his head. "Go wash your hands. I'll heat it up."

My hands? I shot a glance at my smudged fingers and winced. There was probably a streak across my cheek, too. Correction: two streaks, according to the washroom mirror.

I scrubbed up and brushed out my now-dry hair, this time

leaving it loose around my shoulders. When I returned, a steaming bowl of lobster bisque waited on the counter alongside a crusty baguette and a glass of ruby-colored blood-wine.

My mouth watered. "Thanks," I muttered, sliding onto the stool and curling my fingers around the spoon.

Cain took the stool beside me, close enough that I could feel his warmth along my arm and thigh. When I chanced a look at him, he was watching me eat with an indulgent smile, though something darker edged it.

The answering pull in my body was immediate. I shifted on the seat, my skin tight, needy.

"You forget to eat much?" he asked.

I tore off a piece of the baguette. "No. Perla doesn't let me."

"Perla?"

"The lair housekeeper."

"Yeah? You two close?"

I nodded. "She's like the big sister I never had."

"Human?"

"Yes, but she's a former thrall. She's smart, knows how things work. She looks out for me."

"And you need that? Protection?"

My fingers dug into the baguette. "I didn't say that."

"No," he said. "You didn't."

"Anyway, that's all I'm saying about Perla—or the lair." I popped a piece of bread into my mouth.

He blew out a breath. "I just want to know more about you. I'm not fishing."

"How do I know that?"

A muscle in his jaw worked. "Fair enough. But I am interested. You never said anything about this Perla before."

"You didn't ask."

He made an exasperated sound deep in his throat. A warning.

A danger-tinged thrill shivered through me, and my pulse beat in my ears, wild and hard. Goddess help me, I was enjoying this, wanted to see how far I could push him.

Which was why I had to stop.

"Hey, I understand." I gave him my widest fake-Nyx smile. "It's not like we had that kind of relationship. It was just sex, right?"

His hand caught mine, halting the soup spoon midair. "The hell it was."

He rubbed his thumb over the sensitive skin between my thumb and index finger, slow and deliberate. Heat pooled low in my belly. My thighs tightened, and the spoon slid from my nerveless fingers into the bisque.

My heart thudded once, then again—like it was trying to speak for me. Send a message.

I stared at his slowly moving thumb.

This was bad for me—letting him touch me, and worse, enjoying it. I knew that. But I couldn't bring myself to pull away.

I licked my lips. "You..." I trailed off, then tried again, louder this time. "You know that's all it was."

He kissed my hand and fished my spoon from the soup, wiping the handle before handing it back to me. "Eat—you're still healing."

I grimaced. There was my answer—a nonanswer. At least he hadn't lied. I took another bite, the richness too heavy now, but I managed to eat a little more.

Cain waited until I put the spoon down, then took my shoulders and turned me toward him. "It wasn't just sex for me. You remember me telling you it was real for me? That you were never a job?"

My heart constricted. Of course I remembered. "Please, don't."

His jaw flexed, but his gaze didn't waver. "The time we had together was never enough. I couldn't get you out of my head—kept thinking up ways to see you again. Please—"

He exhaled roughly. Then his expression cracked wide open, leaving him unguarded, raw. "Give me another chance, firefly. You never have to tell me a single thing about your father again. I want you, not your intel."

All the air seemed to have been sucked from the room. I closed my eyes, the burn in my chest begging me to give in, to *believe*.

But my trust had been all used up.

"I can't," I rasped, my voice breaking on the last syllable.

He stroked my upper arms, his thighs bracketing mine. "Look at me and say that."

I forced my lids open, met his gaze squarely. "I can't," I said again, steadier this time. "I *won't*."

His Adam's apple worked. He looked like he was in as much pain as I was, which couldn't be true.

"I'm not your enemy," he said lowly.

That word—*enemy*—struck like a lash. I flinched, and he instantly released me, his eyes bright with hurt.

I slid off the stool and backed away from him. "I want you to go now."

His shoulders slumped, just a little. Then he got off the stool. "If that's what you want."

"It is. Yes."

He nodded once, then just stood there, like he was waiting for me to take it back. When I didn't, his chest heaved in an audible breath.

"I'll see you tomorrow, then. And Nyx? Whatever you need, ask for it—alright? I'll make sure you get it."

"Okay," I managed, lips numb. I turned away, arms wrapped around my ribs as if pressure alone could keep me from coming apart.

Footsteps sounded, then the door opened. Closed.

Emptiness swallowed the room.

I stood there, hollowed-out and aching, reminding myself he had reasons—good ones—for lying to me. That I had to stand firm. That he absolutely was my enemy.

But he'd seemed different. Like he'd meant every word this time.

And he'd respected my request, left me alone the moment I'd asked, without pushing or trying to change my mind.

Or maybe that was just what I wanted to see. The same way I'd once mistaken my father's crumbs of approval for anything but manipulation.

I gave my head a hard shake. I'd never felt more confused, more alone.

Eventually, I moved back to the counter, picked up the spoon and took a mouthful of bisque. It had gone cold.

So had I.

25

CAIN

A stillness settled over the castle, like the thick, oppressive calm before a nor'easter.

Four nights since I'd brought Nyx back to Lilith Island, and Nazaire still hadn't come for her. We'd laid the bait: the texts I'd sent him, posing as Nyx; the breadcrumbs we'd scattered, carefully planted lies about the castle's supposed vulnerabilities. Security was on high alert, the ferry watched on every run to and from the mainland, and the few inlets where you could beach a boat without shattering it against the rocks were under covert surveillance.

As for me, I didn't go anywhere without a couple of blades.

What in the name of the Dark Gods was the bastard waiting for? He wouldn't go away quietly. Not Nazaire.

No, he was plotting something. I could feel it like a spider crawling under my skin, making me twitchy, tight.

Gods, I hated these waiting games. But the next move was Nazaire's. I just hoped we'd done enough to provoke him.

To add to my tension, Nyx had blocked me. Those flashes of emotions I'd been getting from her? They'd stopped, like she'd thrown up a wall between us and locked the gate.

And I missed it. Missed *her*.

She seemed further away now than when she'd lived in Quebec.

Monday bled into Tuesday. When I awoke that evening, I took Nyx a box of chocolates and her favorite blood-wine. Like the night before, she was hunched over her sketchpad, laying down a drawing with fast, urgent strokes, like she couldn't get it on the page fast enough. This time she didn't even register me, and when I returned later that night, the wine and chocolate sat untouched on the kitchenette counter and she was still hunched over the pad.

I was pretty sure she hadn't moved since I'd left her.

I studied the drawing over her shoulder. Castle Leclerc crouched in the fog like the photo I'd taken, only transformed. Vines rose from the mist to snake their way up the black walls, winged creatures flapped against a midnight sky, and a sliver of a moon lurked behind a tower like it was keeping a secret.

It was so her, classic *The Haunt*—dark and moody as an old-style fairytale.

She finally noticed me standing there. She jumped and slammed the pad shut before pasting on one of those bright smiles that didn't touch her eyes.

It made me want to punch a wall—again.

"Hey," I said. "Everything okay?"

"Yes, thank you," she said, so polite my teeth clamped together.

I loosened my jaw and scanned the living room for something else to say. At the French door, Demon was on her hind legs, batting at the glass in a frenzy of feline indignation.

I glanced at Nyx. "Wanna go outside?"

"Outside?" she echoed, her gaze going to the specially darkened glass. "The garden, you mean?"

"Yeah."

She bit her lip—hard enough to leave a dent—and I caught myself holding my breath. When she said, "Yes," it felt like I'd won something I hadn't known I was playing for.

"C'mon then." I thumbed open the security app and unlocked the door.

Outside the castle walls, the March wind shrieked off the ocean, but inside the enclosed garden, the air was cool, almost gentle. Nyx walked beside me, taking everything in—the early buds, the tiny lights threaded through the bushes, the narrow stream ending in a frozen waterfall above a small, ice-covered pool—but her shoulders stayed tight, her expression guarded.

It wasn't until Demon slinked up beside her, brushing against her leg, that I saw her ease.

"Salut, belle," she murmured in French, crouching to rub the small white devil behind the ears.

Demon—who usually treated me like furniture—melted against Nyx's leg, purring like they'd been soulmates in another life.

Nyx glanced up at me. "What's her name?"

"Demon."

"Ah, a perfect name for une belle chat."

"She's Brien's. She ignores everyone else except Twilight."

"You're particular, aren't you, pretty cat?" Nyx combed her fingers through Demon's soft fur.

The cat leaned into her, eyes slitted.

"She likes you," I said.

"Mm."

"Cat's got good instincts."

Nyx flicked me a look. "Better than some people."

I winced. "Sometimes you don't listen to your gut because your head's telling you something else."

She just shrugged, eyes fixed on the garden. The moon cast shifting shadows over her beautiful, off-beat face—her long cheekbones, her full mouth, the diamond in her nostril—like it couldn't decide what version of her to show me.

"Look," I told her, "I'm sorry it came to this. But I'm not sorry for getting you away from that bastard. Maybe I wanted to use you—fine. But only to protect my friends. What's his excuse?"

Her fingers stilled in Demon's fur.

"You can't even put your name on your own art," I said. "You're hiding the best part of yourself from your own father. That's fucked."

A beat passed and I thought she wasn't going to say anything.

Then she met my eyes. "I wanted him to love me. I kept thinking if I was only good enough, worked a little harder..." One corner of her mouth lifted in a self-mocking smile.

Something hot and ugly twisted in my gut. I'd been there, been in her situation, but I'd gotten out by joining the Maritime Syndicate. She hadn't had that option. She'd been stuck in that SOB's sticky web.

My voice came out a low growl. "And you'll never be good enough, will you?"

She briefly closed her eyes. "No."

"That's what I thought," I said. "And I would've taken you away from him for that alone. Even without the history between him and us. If that makes me the bad guy, fine. Hate me. Because I'd do it again."

Her gaze lifted to mine. "I don't hate you," she said, so quiet I had to strain to hear her.

I stared down at her, fighting the urge to haul her against me and claim what my instincts already knew was mine. But it was too soon. Push now, and I might lose what little ground I'd managed to take.

"So where do we go from here?" I said.

"I don't know." She rose, chin lifting that fraction that always sparked something primitive in me. Not fear. Defiance. A reminder she was her own woman, with her own agenda.

"I'm still your prisoner, even if the cage is more comfortable. You're still using me as bait. Maybe you don't need me to get to my father, but you haven't let me go. So you tell me."

"I have to see this through. We both know that."

"Yeah." Her nod was small, resigned. The look on her face—the hopelessness, the understanding that nothing had changed—hurt. The fake smile was gone, a small mercy. But I'd do almost anything to see the real one again. "You made your choice. And I've made mine."

"Nyx..."

Her shoulders hunched. "Leave it, Cain." She headed for the

door, Demon trotting alongside her.

Yeah, I really wanted to punch something.

Back inside, my gaze fell on the sketchpad, thick with the pictures she'd made in the past couple of nights.

That was it. That was what she needed.

She wasn't just sketching to pass the time. She was an artist, starving for the tools she didn't have.

I couldn't give her freedom. Things with Nazaire had gone too far; letting her leave now would paint a target on her back.

But this? I could give her.

As soon as I left her, I contacted an art shop on the mainland and paid extra to have art supplies expressed to the island on the Tuesday ferry: canvases, paints, brushes, a palette and a palette knife, the whole arsenal. That night, I brought them to her myself.

When I let myself in, she was stretched out on the couch, dark red curls spilling around shoulders, glowing against the deep blue cashmere sweater I'd bought her. She glanced up—eyes dull, flat—until she saw the canvases under my arm.

"What's that?" She sat up, gaze flicking from the three canvases to the bag in my other hand.

"A gift." I put the canvases on the floor beside the couch and handed her the bag.

When she peeked inside, her breath hitched. "You brought me paints?"

She brushed her fingertips over the tubes, slow and reverent, like they were something precious. And for the first time in days, her hazel eyes had some light in them. Just a flicker, but something in my chest warmed in response.

I crouched beside the couch, looking into the bag along with her. "I don't know if they're the right kind, but—"

"No, these are perfect." She lifted one of the brushes. "This is even the brand I use. And bristle brushes, not synthetic. How did you know?"

"I asked the owner of the store. She's a painter herself—seemed to know what she was doing."

She nodded. "Well, thanks.

"You can thank me by painting something."

My reward was a brief, real smile. "I will, yeah."

Our gazes snagged, and my own lips lifted in response. The warmth in my chest flared brighter. My heart smacked against my ribcage, a near-painful beat.

For an instant, I caught a flash of emotion from her—hope and something else, like recognition. Like she was seeing something she hadn't let herself believe.

An answering hope ignited in me.

A curl had fallen forward over her shoulder. I reached out, taking my time, giving her a chance to pull away. When she didn't, I rubbed the silky strands between my thumb and forefinger.

Her chest expanded in a slow breath. Then she rolled her lips in and leaned away. The curl slid from my fingers.

I sank back onto my haunches, reminding myself to be patient. We were on opposite sides of a war, and no amount of touches or gifts could change that. I had to see this thing with Nazaire through and hope that someday she'd forgive me.

She turned back to the paints, lifting each tube from the bag and lining them up on the coffee table with the brushes and the rest of the supplies. Focused. Careful. Already slipping away from me again.

I pushed to my feet. "I should go. Let you paint."

Another jolt of emotion, disappointment this time. "Oh," she said.

"Unless you want me to stay—"

She looked up. "Only if you let me sketch you."

I blinked. "Sketch me?"

"Mm-hm. I prefer a live model." She was already reaching for her pad.

I dropped into the armchair across from her. "This feels like a setup. Tell me you're not going to give me horns and a tail."

She glanced up, eyes gleaming now, and I wanted to high-five myself for putting that playful spark there. "Depends."

"On what?"

"On how nice you are." Her voice had a huskiness that slid over my skin like a slow, hot lick.

I slung an arm over the chairback, pretending I wasn't reacting, that she hadn't just flipped the power between us with a single line. "How nice do you want me to be?"

She cocked her head, a subtle challenge that made everything masculine in me go tight. "Nice enough to sit still. Nice enough not to ask to see what I'm drawing."

"Done," I said immediately.

Her lips tilted up, like she hadn't expected me to fold that fast. But she flipped open the pad and took out what looked like a black piece of chalk, although it was rectangular, not round.

"Don't move," she muttered and started sketching.

I watched her watching me, long glances from beneath thick lashes. From anyone else, it would've made me edgy. But when it was Nyx, I wanted to preen like a peacock, give her something worth looking at.

The primitive creature in me growled.

Go ahead and stare, firefly.

This attraction—this electric pull—between us wasn't one-sided. I could work with that.

"When I make a picture," she said, "I tell myself stories about what I'm painting."

"Yeah?"

She nodded. "It's part of my process. You're definitely a prince, maybe a faerie royal with those blue eyes and platinum hair. You're on your throne, your court around you. But you're bored."

I raised an eyebrow. "Bored?"

"That's right." A corner of her mouth lifted. She was teasing— and yet she wasn't. "Restless. You can have anything you want, but it's never enough."

Her strokes grew sharper, more deliberate. The gray chalk left smudges on her long, elegant fingers, but she didn't seem to notice.

"You're powerful," she continued, voice dreamy. "But something's missing. You're waiting for something."

I held still, willing her to go on. She wasn't talking about the sketch anymore, and I wanted—no, needed—to see what she'd say next.

"Maybe someone," she added, eyes flicking up to meet mine.

Something in my chest kicked hard.

"Maybe I've already met her," I said. "Maybe I'm waiting for her to catch up."

26

NYX

I'd been wrong. Cain didn't look bored. He looked hungry under that relaxed façade.

My throat bobbed. My fingers tightened on the charcoal stick, laying a dark slash across the fae prince's shoulder where he lounged on his throne, jewel-studded crown tilted, shark tattoo curling up the side of his throat, hands resting on the worked-silver arms.

I rubbed the slash with my fingertip, softening the edges, then deepened the crescents beneath his eyes, making them darker. Less glamour, more danger. The kind that would never fade, that lived in the bone.

"Maybe I've already met her. Maybe I'm waiting for her to catch up."

The way Cain had said that, low and raw. Like he meant it clear to his soul.

I swallowed hard and switched to a pencil, adding embroidered leaves to the prince's velvet sleeve.

"Maybe she doesn't want to be caught," I said when the silence had gone on too long.

Cain leaned in, elbows braced on his thighs, gaze locked on my face. "Maybe I can change her mind."

I stilled, the pencil loose in my fingers. For a moment, neither of us moved, the air between us charged, expectant.

He drew an audible inhale. "Nyx?"

I shook my head. "You can't. I'm done, Cain."

The spell broke. His eyes shuttered and he sat back, resuming the first pose.

I started the embroidery on the prince's other sleeve.

Cain watched me draw, jiggling his knee. He wasn't upset, though. It was a measured, thinking-it-over bounce.

Several minutes passed. "Whatever names you're calling me, I'm calling myself those and more."

That got under my guard. My lips twitched despite myself. "I don't think so."

"That bad?" he asked, so deadpan I couldn't help grinning.

"Don't ask."

His gaze moved over my face, settling on my mouth like he was drinking in my smile. "You know I have to ask now."

I added a pair of horns to the prince's platinum-blond head. "I can insult you in two languages. Gives me an edge."

His eyes crinkled, and my breath caught in my throat. Unfair, how he could still do that—slip beneath my defenses and jab me right in my soft, unprotected parts.

He studied me while I pretended I didn't notice. "You're not what I expected," he said finally. "I figured you were vampire royalty —a princess. You don't walk into a party, you *arrive*—like it's your stage and the rest of us are only there to admire you. But I was wrong. You play a good game, but that's all it is to you, isn't it? A game. And if you didn't have to play, it wouldn't bother you at all."

"Because I don't give a damn about the game."

"So it was all for your father."

I went still. "We're not talking about him."

"You're right." His voice softened. "I'm sorry."

I picked up the charcoal stick again and added a shadowy tiger curled at the prince's feet. "You're not what I expected, either," I admitted.

"What did you expect?"

"An entitled lieutenant."

"Meet a lot of those, do you?"

"Oh, yeah." I gave a humorless chuckle. "But if anyone's vampire royalty, it's you, Mr. Maritime Syndicate Lieutenant. You and Talon are next in line to be primus."

"So? Brien's not going anywhere. The man will probably be primus for the next few hundred centuries at least."

I glanced up. "Does that bother you?"

He shook his head. "I like my place in the hierarchy just fine—me and Talon both. Brien respects our opinion, treats us like brothers."

"Vampire royalty."

"Nah. I'm so far from being a prince it's funny." His laugh rasped out of him, like it was scraped from somewhere old. "I was the island fuckup."

I stopped drawing. "Seriously?"

Cain, a fuckup? I couldn't make the pieces line up. All I saw was the man in front of me, all coiled control and lethal competence.

"Baker sure thought I was." Something flickered across Cain's face, quick and raw. "Kept telling me I'd end up in prison. He wouldn't have lifted a finger to help me, either."

"He sounds like an ass."

I didn't say *cruel*. I didn't say *the kind of man who leaves marks you can't see*. But Cain's jaw tightened like he heard it anyway.

"He was, but he wasn't wrong. Me and Talon were one bad decision from doing something that would've gotten us permanently banished from the island when we got lucky. Prima Lenore offered us a shot—bodyguard detail for Brien."

"Lucky?" I frowned. Didn't he see it? The distance between that kid and the man he was now? The power he'd accrued, the respect —and not because of his bloodline, but because he'd earned it. "Luck's only half it. You took that shot and made something of it. You couldn't have done that if you were such a fuckup."

He shook his head. Then a slow smile spread over his face.

"Brien was only sixteen himself, then. But I think that's why we hit it off—we were both just twenty ourselves. We were supposed to be protecting him, but we were nearly as wild as him."

I resumed drawing. "Maybe his mother knew he needed that.

Because he's still here, isn't he? He survived until he got old enough to take care of himself."

"He was born with a lot of power, but yeah. We were damned if he was gonna get hurt on our watch. And now we're like brothers."

Something lodged in my throat. I swallowed over it. "You're... that's good. Having people like that."

His gaze met mine, and his face softened. Somehow I knew he was thinking of my family—or lack of one. Of how I had no one like Brien and Talon in my life. No one who'd bleed for me, no questions asked.

"I am," he said quietly.

$$\text{❦}\quad 2\,7 \quad\text{❦}$$

CAIN

"So," Talon asked, "make any headway with Nyx?"

It was early the next evening, and we were sipping whiskey on his battered leather couch. Talon had handed Jude off to me so he could kick back on the couch, and the little guy had fallen asleep on my shoulder, gumming my collarbone. My white button-up shirt had a damp spot from his drool, but whatever. It would wash out.

I wasn't wired for families, for fatherly love. That had been burned out of me at a young age. But when Jude snuffled and resumed gnawing like I was his favorite chew toy, something a lot like love smacked me in the heart. The last, jagged edges I'd carried since his birth—loss, jealousy, the dull ache of being on the outside—smoothed out.

I cupped Jude's small round head and met Talon's eyes.

"She's good. We're talking."

My mouth tugged up before I could stop it. Last night we'd talked for hours, broken up by her drawing a version of me in velvet and a crown, then sending the poor bastard into battle against murderous pixies.

"Talking?" Talon smirked. "S'that what the kids call it these days?"

My eyes narrowed a fraction. "Yeah, talking."

"And?"

I glared at him over Jude. "Since when do we gossip about women?"

"Since my best friend forgot all his charm and kidnapped his mate."

"I didn't say she was my mate."

Talon snorted. "You're mooning around like a teenager with his first crush."

"The hell I am."

He just lifted his brows.

"Seems like I remember you doing the same thing," I muttered.

"That's why I know the signs."

I feathered my fingers over Jude's soft curls. "Well, I made some headway with her. We're not there yet, but..."

Talon lifted his whiskey to me. "My money's on you, bro."

"Thanks." I put my glass on the coffee table and shifted Jude to my other shoulder.

He mumbled in protest, eyelids fluttering.

Talon came to his feet. "Let me put him down. I want Eden to get some sleep before he wakes up for his next feed."

I handed the baby over. "Anytime you need help with him, just say the word. I like holding the little guy. I don't even mind him chewing on my shoulder, even if he has the jaws of a baby shark."

Talon's cheek creased. "Now I'm really worried. Who are you and what've you done with my best friend?"

When my mouth flattened, his smile only widened. "I like the new you," he said and headed into the bedroom with Jude.

When he returned, he refilled our glasses and sprawled onto the chair next to the couch, legs outstretched on the copper-and-gray rug.

I rolled my glass between my fingers. "You know I'd do anything for you, man? You and the little dude and Eden, too."

His thick brows climbed. "Of course I know, you ass."

"Just making sure."

I took a long pull of whiskey, then almost choked as the phone in my pocket buzzed. Nyx's phone.

I put down the glass and shot to my feet. "Nazaire must've got back to us."

One look at the screen and my heart dropped to the soles of my shoes. "That motherfucker."

Talon was up instantly. I angled the phone so he could see the photo—a woman in a cell.

His jaw hardened. "Do you know who that is?"

I met his eyes. "No. But I bet Nyx does."

"Hades," he muttered.

I pocketed the phone. "Brien and Twilight need to see this. And then I'll have to show Nyx."

He shoved his feet into low boots. "We'll both go."

Funny, how I hadn't really known Cain until he'd kidnapped me. Not the man behind the reputation, the man who'd grown up wild and unwanted.

I'd only known the Cain who could make me burn with a single, hooded glance.

But last night had changed something.

I sat at the kitchenette counter, doodling on a blank page. My gaze drifted to the canvases he'd brought me, the ones I hadn't touched yet because starting a painting felt somehow permanent. Oils took time—to paint, to dry.

I was still his prisoner. I should've been plotting my next move.

Instead, I kept circling back to his face when he'd opened up. I'd seen no calculation, just painful vulnerability.

He'd shared a part of himself with me. A truth.

And I felt honored.

That was the part that unsettled me the most. Not the confinement, not the maneuvering to get to my father. But the way he'd handed me a piece of his story, exposed himself without asking anything in return.

Now I was doubting everything. Did I want to keep fighting him? Did I really want to leave?

That bright new life I'd pictured for myself—freedom, safety—had lost its shine. Instead, it looked like one of my charcoal sketches, a world without color or heat. Without Cain.

That's when I realized I'd forgiven him. That I respected him for his loyalty to his friends and syndicate.

Of course, he hadn't chosen me over Brien and Talon. They were his family. I hadn't truly understood how deep that bond ran until now.

I sketched a wall of moonflowers opening as the sun went down behind a black turret. A threshold scene—something shifting, something beginning.

Because I'd felt something, last night. Something that had sparked my hope again, small but stubborn.

Maybe—just maybe—there was a place for me in Cain's family.

A place for me with him.

A knock on the door made my heart leap. "Nyx?" called Cain.

"Come in," I called back, closing the pad.

I swung around, smiling, as he entered, until three more people crowded in after him—Brien, Talon, and a slim woman in cropped black pants and a metallic pink shirt—the new prima, Twilight.

The entire upper hierarchy of the Maritime Syndicate.

My pulse picked up, and not in a good way. I slid off the stool, searching Cain's face. "What happened?"

"We got a text from Nazaire—a photo."

I didn't like how the corners of his mouth had pulled downward, like he was sorry in advance. A chill snaked down my spine. "And?"

He held out my phone. "Do you know this woman?"

I snatched the device from him. My throat closed.

"It's Perla," I managed.

The housekeeper sat huddled against a stone wall, face bruised, eyes empty. Barefoot, her hair tangled around her face, her navy dress torn. More bruises were visible on the arms she'd wrapped around her legs, like she was trying to fold herself into a smaller target.

"Sweet Luna." I pressed my free hand to my mouth.

Everything I'd been wrestling with—my freedom, forgiveness,

my stupid, fragile hope—collapsed in on itself, suddenly unimportant.

"Nyx—" Cain started.

I drew a ragged breath. That tiny, reckless optimism I'd let myself feel—that maybe, somehow, we'd get our happy-ever-after—dried up like a salt-soaked plant.

Because while I'd been sitting here sketching moonflowers and imagining a place in his world, Perla had been suffering.

Because of *us*.

"You should've never brought me here," I told him, voice shaking. "You should've let me go back to Quebec."

He reached out, slow, unthreatening, and eased the phone from my grip. "I'm sorry, firefly. I—"

"Don't!" I reared back. "Don't call me that."

His fingers twitched on the phone. "Okay—Nyx." He exhaled heavily. "Look, we need information. Why would he go after Perla? I thought she's his housekeeper?"

"Because she's the one person I care about in that fucking lair." The words tore out of me. I dug the heels of my palms into my eyes. "I should've guessed he'd go after her. But I didn't think he knew."

I shook my head slowly side to side. "I shouldn't have made friends with her. I knew better. But we were careful. And now she's —" My voice splintered.

"Nyx." Twilight appeared between me and Cain. She gripped my shoulders. "Listen to me."

I jerked against her hold, one heartbeat away from a scream. "Let. Me. Go. This is your fault—all of you."

She hung on, mouth grim. "You're upset. I get it. But you need to calm down. Not for us—for Perla."

A red-hot buzzing filled my head. "What do you care?"

"Oh, I care." Her laugh was humorless. "Cain said he told you the story—that Nazaire almost bought me at a blood-slave auction. At the Black Dahlia."

That brought me up short. I focused on her concerned face. "Yeah. He told me."

"So I saw what the QCS is like firsthand. Trust me, I know we have to get your friend out of there." She paused. "Are you listening?"

She waited until I nodded.

"I get that you're angry, but this isn't on Cain and it sure as hell isn't on you. It's on Nazaire."

The angry buzz returned, even louder. I twisted against her grip. This time, she released me.

"It is so on Cain," I bit out. "I wasn't part of any auctions, my father was." I rounded on Cain. "You had to tell him I'd taken sanctuary with you. If you didn't need me to get to him, then why bring me into it? But you had to use me. The weakest link," I added bitterly.

Cain didn't even try to deny it. "You're right."

The admission hit like a slap. I flinched.

"Except," he went on, "I never thought you were weak. From the start, I thought there was more to you than anyone saw, and once I got to know you, I was sure of it." His gaze locked on mine, steady, almost pleading. "You're fucking incredible, Nyx. If anyone's strong, it's you. You'd never have survived the QCS otherwise."

I stared at him, chest tight. His praise slid under my skin, painful as a silver blade.

Not because I didn't believe him. I did. But it was too little, too late.

It couldn't undo those texts to my father. It couldn't undo Perla, sitting broken in a cell.

"You would say that, wouldn't you?" I said over the grit filling my throat, deliberately echoing Brien's statement from that first night.

Let him feel what it was like to be misjudged. Doubted.

He met my glare head on, his stark with sorrow. "Because I mean it."

"We miscalculated," Brien said. "Based on everything we know about your sire, we expected him to strike at us here on the island. He got to my mother, and he was obviously aware Lamaire kidnapped Eden right outside her parents' home." He squeezed his nape. "None of our intel suggested you had anyone in your life he could use against us. That's on us, and I apologize."

His apology sliced through the buzzing in my brain. That he, a primus, was accepting the blame? That meant something.

Twilight spoke again. "We'll help you. You want to rescue your friend, we'll go in with you. You want us to ransom her, we'll do that too."

My gaze swung to her.

"Let us help you," she said. "For Perla's sake—and for all the other Perlas that he could still hurt."

I nodded slowly. Seeing again my friend's bruises, the empty look in her eyes.

"He's your sire." Twilight's face held a compassion I didn't expect from a vampire. "We understand that, respect that you owe him your loyalty. But he has to be stopped."

My throat worked once. She was right.

The hot, buzzing anger contracted, settling cold and hard in my belly.

This time, Nazaire had gone too far, and I was going to take him down. But I couldn't do it without their help.

I drew a shaky breath. "Ransoming her won't work. He doesn't want money. He wants you. All of you, but especially Brien." I met his eyes. "This won't end until one of you is in the ground. Permanently."

"And I'm such a charming guy," he said, deadpan.

Twilight flicked him an unamused look, which he met with a crooked grin. "Hey." He ran his thumb and first finger down her shiny brown braid. "They're not going to get to me. They haven't yet, have they?"

They exchanged a look that felt like an entire conversation. Envy flashed through me. I couldn't help glancing at Cain, wishing... Well, it didn't matter what I wished.

Twilight turned back to me. "Why don't we sit down, talk this over?"

She gestured at the nearest chair and waited until I was seated before lowering herself with a dancer's grace onto the couch. Brien sat beside her, and Talon dropped into the other chair.

Cain didn't sit.

He shoved my phone into a pocket and planted himself behind me, his hands on the chairback like he was aligning himself with me. When I sent him a frowning look, he met it coolly.

Like *of course I'm on your side*.

I dragged my focus back to Brien and Twilight, forcing Cain and whatever there was between us into the background where it belonged.

"What about your primus?" Twilight leaned forward, her braid sliding over her shoulder. "Does Dussault know about your sire's vendetta against Brien?"

"Maybe," I said. "They don't talk business around me. But I do know Dussault is angry about how the Marine Syndicate's been throwing its weight around. I wonder if—"

The pieces slid together, clean and inevitable, halting me mid-sentence.

Brien rested a sinewy arm on the couch behind his mate. "Go on."

"What if Dussault is using my father, letting him take the blame? If he takes you four out, then Dussault can move on the Maritime Syndicate. Even if he only manages to send one or two of you to your final graves, it still weakens you. The hierarchy would be scrambling, fighting to see who becomes the next lieutenant...or even the next primus. And if my father gets caught, Dussault can swear he had nothing to do with it."

Brien nodded. "It tracks. Dussault's the type to hang back, watch how the chips fall, then make his move. An opportunist."

"Back to Perla," said Twilight. "Can you tell where she is from the photo?"

"Yes—his lair in Quebec City. He has a cell beneath it."

Talon had been watching from the other chair, his long legs stretched out and crossed at the ankles, his deep-set eyes taking in everything. "You sure?"

"Yes." The memory of others locked in that same cell flickered through me—people my father had taken me down to see as a lesson, people I hadn't been able to help. I dug my fingernails into my thighs, and added, "Very sure."

"So how do we get to her?"

"You can't," I said. "Not on your own. You need me."

"Or a map," Cain said from behind me. "Along with the appropriate codes and instructions."

"No." I craned my neck to look at him. "It won't work without me. You can get through the first door with a code, but you need my palm print for the next two."

"We have ways to get around that."

"It'll be faster with me."

His brow lowered. "I'm not letting you—"

"Can you do it?" Brien cut in.

I swung back to him. "Yes. There's a tunnel. No cameras—my father likes to have a private route in and out of the lair. Only a few people even know it exists. I can get in, open doors for whoever goes with me."

"And we'd be in the shadows, of course." Twilight pursed her lips, thinking. "Could work."

"If it's not a trap," Talon interjected. "Nazaire will be expecting something like this, especially if he believes Nyx has flipped to our side."

"Good." Brien's handsome face hardened. "I want the motherfucker watching his back. I want him worried." He glanced at me. "You can map it for us? Draw diagrams?"

"Do I have your word that you'll take me with you?"

The four exchanged glances.

"You won't have much time," I pointed out. "The cell is in the center of the lair. The only way you'll make it that far is the shadows, and there are multiple doors between the tunnel and the cell. You can't open them in the shadows. You need someone with you, someone the cams recognize."

"We'll probably have to fight our way out." Twilight looked me up and down, sizing me up. "You won't slow us down?"

I straightened. "I've been training with vampires my whole life."

"And you were the other person on the island," she said, almost to herself. "The boat—our boat—you rigged it to blow."

I stiffened, but she didn't sound angry. She sounded impressed.

"I won't go in as myself," I added. "I'm good with a glamour."

I swept my gaze up and down her and let the change roll over me. Within thirty seconds, I was Twilight's twin, from her coffee-colored braid to her raspberry pink sneakers.

Her dark brows rose. She glanced at Brien. "She's resourceful. I say we take her."

"Agreed," he said.

Relief washed through me. I dropped the glamour just as Cain's hand closed on my arm, hauling me from the chair.

"We need to talk," he said between his teeth and marched me into the bedroom, kicking the door shut behind us.

He backed me against the wall, forearms braced on either side of my head. His warmth surrounded me, his breath brushing my cheek.

"No," he ground out. "It's too risky."

I met his glare with one of my own. "You don't get a say, *Lieutenant*."

A muscle in his cheek ticked a warning. "Like Hades I don't."

I lifted my chin. "We're nothing to each other. And Perla's my friend—I have to go."

"No, you don't. You can give us all the info we need, and we can get through the damn doors on our own. If this goes sideways, Nazaire will come straight for you."

"Let him," I shot back, even though the thought made me a little nauseous. "But nothing will go wrong."

Cain's nostrils flared. He slid his fingers into my damp hair and dragged my head back, rough and possessive.

My pulse stuttered.

He gave my hair a little tug. "Even the best-planned ops can go to shit. You're not going, are we clear?"

I licked my lips, and his gaze dropped to my mouth. An electric heat sizzled between us. My tongue felt suddenly thick.

"I'm going," I managed to say.

His lips came to my throat, sending a shiver sliding over my skin. "No," he repeated, softer now, almost tender.

"Brien said—"

"Fuck Brien." He bit my neck. Not hard. Just enough to let me know he wasn't pleased with me. "He knows better than to come between a man and his woman."

Pain shredded my heart. I turned my head away, my cheek against the wall.

"But I'm not your woman," I said evenly. "And Perla needs me."

His chest rumbled in displeasure. He straightened from me, taking his warmth with him. "Nyx—"

I rushed into speech. I didn't want to hear his excuses—or worse, an apology.

"Please, Cain." I touched his arm, dropping my defenses. This was more important than me or my pride. "I know that lair—I grew up in it. And Talon's right—it's probably a trap. You go in without me, who knows what will happen? You want your friends to end up dead?"

A short, charged silence fell. Then he swore and stepped back. "Come, then, damn you. But you'll do exactly what I say, understand? No going off-book."

"Understood," I told him.

And I did understand. That didn't mean I wouldn't improvise if it was the only way to save Perla.

Back in the living room, Cain's friends looked up, faces questioning.

"She's coming," he said, mouth tight.

Brien nodded.

Twilight straightened, her dark eyes met mine. "We'll get your friend out of there. I promise."

"Thank you," I said, voice low.

Cain fished my phone from his pocket. "Should we respond to Nazaire? Or let him stew?"

"Answer him," I said. "He hates to be ignored. I'm afraid of what he'll do to Perla if we don't." A cold prickle crept over my skin, and I rubbed my upper arms.

"Here." Cain handed me the phone. "You do it—you know him better than we do."

"Call him directly," suggested Brien.

"Yes." It was the right move, even if the thought of hearing his voice made my stomach twist. But this wasn't about me.

I set my jaw and pressed Nazaire's number.

He answered on the second ring.

"Allô," I said. "C'est moi—Nyx."

A short silence. Then he said in French, "You got my message, then."

"Yes," I said in the same language, then blurted, "Please let Perla go. She has nothing to do with this."

The others stiffened. I knew all three men spoke French, and Twilight's narrowed eyes told me she understood as well. But if there was even the smallest chance my father would release Perla, I had to try.

He chuckled. "She means so much to you, then?"

Too late, I realized I'd only confirmed that Perla was important to me. I tightened my grip on the phone. "What do you want?"

His voice turned cold. "I think you know, little rabbit."

My mouth tightened. "Why would I know?"

"Because that bastard of a lieutenant is probably standing right next to you."

"And if he is?"

"Tell him I'm waiting." He paused. "Meanwhile, Perla is, too. I've missed her taste. It would be a shame to drain her completely..."

Drain her?

"No! Please—"

But he'd ended the call.

Around me, the others had stilled.

"He's not bluffing," Twilight said.

"No." I stared down at the phone, the screen blurring for a moment. "But he'll keep her alive for now. Just keep...torturing her. And sending me photos—"

My voice cracked, and Cain's arms came around me in a hard hug.

I wanted to stiffen against him, but I couldn't. I needed that hug too badly. So I sank into it, let myself take some comfort.

He touched his lips to my temple. "Tomorrow night," he promised. "We won't let him drag this out."

His friends muttered their agreement.

"Good," I said fiercely and pulled away from Cain.

Twilight grabbed my drawing pad and the pencil box. "I know you'll be with us," she said, "but map out Nazaire's lair anyway. The more we know going in, the better."

I nodded and led them into the kitchenette, settling on a stool. The others crowded in—Cain and Twilight on either side of me, Talon and Brien across the counter. I flipped to an empty page and pulled out a fine charcoal pencil.

"Can I ask you something?" I said to Brien as I began to sketch. "Give Perla a place here on the island. She's not safe in Quebec."

He nodded without hesitation. "Of course."

"Thank you." I sent him a grateful smile. "You won't be sorry. She's a good person, and she works hard."

Twilight glanced from me to Cain. "And you?"

Cain drew breath to answer, but I got there first. "I'll manage. But I would like a ride somewhere. Europe, maybe."

Some country without a major syndicate.

Cain's hand settled on my lower back. "She'll be staying here," he said firmly. "On Lilith Island."

I made a noncommittal sound and bent over the pad. This wasn't a fight I was having in front of his friends.

But I would be leaving.

Because staying would break me.

Nyx drew a detailed map of Nazaire's lair for us. She couldn't resist a few artsy touches—a bat lurking in a corner, a Gothic chandelier marking the great room, a snake disappearing down the stairs to the lair. The others noticed, especially Brien, who'd been one of the first vampires to buy her paintings. But I figured that was just because he had a thing for good art. No way he'd ever connect Nazaire's socialite daughter to The Haunt.

She walked us through the map and together, we fleshed out the plan to rescue Perla. By the time the others finally headed out, it was well past midnight.

The door clicked shut behind them. I turned to Nyx.

She'd gotten off the stool but was holding the pad tightly to her chest, jaw set, like she was holding herself together by sheer will.

My gut twisted. "I'm sorry," I said. "About Perla."

She hitched a shoulder. "Collateral damage," she reminded me flatly. "But hey, you got what you wanted, didn't you? I'm helping you break into his lair."

"Fuck what I wanted. She's your friend, and I'm sorry she got dragged into this." I took a step closer. "I want you to be happy, Nyx."

"Really." Her hazel eyes lifted.

There was so much pain in them, my lungs closed up. That emptiness that had hit me after finally putting Baker out of his misery? This was worse. Ten times worse.

"I did what I thought I had to do," I said, giving her the truth because it was all I had left. "To protect my friends. But I'm sorry—so fucking sorry—that Perla got hurt because of it."

She kneaded her brows with her knuckles. "I want to hate you," she whispered. "I *should* hate you." Stronger this time, like she was trying to convince herself. "I thought we had something." A short laugh. "Something special. That maybe we were even mates."

I flinched.

Her eyes lifted to mine. "Scared you, didn't I? Don't worry. I know a syndicate lieutenant would never claim a dhampir as a mate."

"Like hell I wouldn't. Maybe I used to think that way, but not anymore. I'd be fucking honored."

One side of her mouth curled in a yeah-right smile.

Something deep inside me clenched. That she thought herself anyway inferior to me was just wrong.

"It's the truth, damn it. If anything, you're too good for me. You're practically a princess, and I'm the fuckup Brien's mother sprang from jail to babysit her son."

Her lips parted. "You were in jail?"

"Yeah." I scrubbed a hand down my face, the shame still a part of me even all these years later. "That shot I told you she offered me and Talon? That's where she found us—the island jail. Me and Talon both. She told me later she figured Brien needed friends who could think outside the box. And she wanted men who had no previous ties to the syndicate so our only loyalty was to him."

She nodded slowly, like that explained a lot.

"But about you and me," I continued, "when we met, I had a plan, and you weren't a part of it."

Her gaze flicked away. "Now that, I believe."

"Hey, I admit I had my head up my ass. If I could do it over again, I would."

I took a deep breath. Time to lay it all on the line.

"That night on the way to the bar? I was starting to think you could be my mate, if that was why I couldn't seem to let you go. And while I was still wrapping my mind around that, I find out you'd come to the meeting yourself—to negotiate with my uncle to kidnap me." I grimaced. "All I could think was you'd been lying to me the whole time. That when it came down to it, you'd choose Nazaire over me. Every fucking time."

"Like you chose your syndicate over me?" It wasn't an accusation. It was a soft, wounded acknowledgment that somehow cut deeper.

I spread my hands. "They're all I have. My family."

"Yeah." A sad smile ghosted across her lips. "You'd do anything for them, wouldn't you? They're lucky. And you should—I don't even blame you for it."

And then suddenly, I was feeling her emotions again, like a river flowing from her to me.

Hurt, yes, and some leftover anger. But underneath was something raw, something that hadn't given up on us yet.

Maybe I could still save this?

I dropped to my knees on the terra cotta tiles before her. She pulled back, eyes wide, mouth ajar.

Guilt tore through me at her obvious surprise. She'd clearly never expected this from me.

I reached for her hands. She let me take them, her gaze glued to my face.

"Before you, I was hunting for a pureblood mate. To strengthen the syndicate. And," I admitted, "to boost me. I guess I was still trying to prove I'm not the island loser." I swallowed something prickly. "That I didn't make lieutenant just because I'm Brien's friend."

Another rush of emotion, empathy and something steadier—velvet over steel. "Oh, Cain." Her voice softened. "You don't have to prove yourself to anyone. It's obvious that people respect you." A corner of her mouth ticked up. "They're even a little afraid of you."

"I know. I even believe it—most of me. But there's a part of me that never feels good enough." I dropped my gaze to our hands.

First time I'd ever said it out loud—even Talon had never heard it—and it felt like stripping to the skin in the middle of a syndicate ball. Exposed. Naked. Vulnerable.

"Hey," she said. "You started as a soldier, right?" At my nod, she continued, "And you rose through the ranks until now you're a lieutenant, a powerful one. I bet you worked twice as hard as anyone else to get where you are."

"Everyone but Talon," I said automatically. "He worked his ass off, too."

"There you go. Sure, Brien's your friend, but he wouldn't have promoted you unless he thought you could hold off challengers. So of course you're good enough. In fact, you're fucking impressive."

I huffed a laugh. "Fine. I'm impressive."

She didn't smile back. "You are. I knew it the moment I met you. You think you're proving yourself, but don't you see? You already have. That's why Brien chose you. That's why Talon respects you. The only one left to convince is you."

My chest pulled tight, lungs dragging in air like I'd been underwater too long. And then it spilled out—the truth I'd been choking back. "I didn't know what to do with you. You *asked* things from me, just by being you. I couldn't let myself trust you. Couldn't let myself trust *us*."

Her voice was a thread of sound. "And now?"

My gaze roamed over her beautiful face. A face I'd never get tired of seeing. A mouth I'd never get tired of kissing.

She'd turned down my offer of sanctuary. I'd known even then she wanted more from me, something I hadn't known how to give her. So I'd hidden behind duty to Brien and the syndicate. But that was a coward's excuse, an obligation Brien had never laid on me.

Enough hiding. Time to stand bare and admit I wanted the same thing.

"Now," I said, low and certain, "I want it all. Everything."

She shook her head—but it didn't feel like a no. More like I'd knocked her off balance and she had to find her footing again.

I soldiered on. "Nyx Nazaire, will you accept my mate bond? I'll fight for you. Stand with you. Believe in you. Just—be yours. If you'll have me."

Her throat worked. Her eyes held mine, peeling back every layer until all that was left was the man beneath the vampire—the needy, unlovable kid I thought I'd buried six feet deep.

My jaw flexed. Instinct screamed at me to bolt, to pretend I didn't need anyone or anything. But I stayed, holding her hands and holding her gaze. Letting her see me.

"Trust me," I said, the plea raw in my throat. "Trust *us*."

Then I felt it. A touch—a warmth, deep in my chest, as if Nyx's heart had reached out to mine.

My own heart stuttered, the primal thing inside me coming alert, stretching like a beast coming awake after a long sleep. I started to smile.

But then her eyes slid sideways. The warmth retreated, a tide dragged back into black water. "I can't," she told our clasped hands.

My brow knotted. My fingers clenched on hers, like I could chain her to me through sheer will. "You...can't?"

I dropped back on my heels, searching her features.

"No." She gave a single shake of her head, still not looking at me.

"But—why?" My stomach turned sour. "Because of your father? You're still choosing him over me?"

"No!" She reared back, tearing her hands from mine. "That has nothing to do with it."

I rose to my feet. "Then what's the problem? You feel it, too. I can tell—I've been getting flashes of emotion from you since Paris. Don't tell me that isn't the mate bond."

"Stop pushing!" Her eyes blazed. "This is too sudden. *Too much*."

That hurt. "Too much?"

She raised her hands, palms out. "I can't think when you're this close. I need space. Please."

A beat passed. Long enough for me to notice the splinter working its way into my heart.

Long enough for dreams I'd barely known I had to crash down around my ears.

"Right." I backed up, a jittery feeling running up my spine. My knee started to jiggle, like if I moved it fast enough, I could outrun the pain.

Nyx retreated to the opposite side of the couch, body shaking, breath jerking in and out, like she might shatter at a single touch.

Which made no fucking sense.

I peered at her. "What's wrong, firefly?" The nickname slipped out—a plea. "Talk to me. I can't fix this if you won't tell me what's wrong."

"This." She waved a hand between us. "It's too fast. One night I'm a prisoner and the next night you're asking me to be your mate? I just...can't."

The splinter in my heart hit the softest part of me. I dug the heel of my hand into my sternum, like I could grind the ache out. "I see."

Something flickered across her face—guilt, fear, maybe both—before she looked away. "I just need time."

"Time," I repeated flatly.

She licked her lips. Then her chin lifted in that tough, *I know you're a big bad vampire but you're not going to push me around* way that made something hot and reckless surge through me. Made me want to show her exactly how bad I could be, and then drop to my knees again and beg her to take my bond.

"That's right," she said.

I exhaled. Brought my hand back to my side. "Okay. You need time, you've got it."

Right then, she could've asked me for anything, and I would've bled myself dry to get it for her.

Anything, that is, except let her go.

I could handle the waiting, could stand here, hollowed out, and give her all the time she needed to catch up—to believe in me, in us.

But give her up?

No fucking way.

30

NYX

Cain's energy battered at the barrier I'd thrown up between us. Edgy, controlled and a little dark, like the man himself. It sang to me like a siren, a whirlpool of instinct and temptation dragging at my chest.

I tensed, fingernails biting into the couch's cotton back, resisting with everything I had.

And then, just like that, the edgy, magnetic pressure cut off.

Cain scraped a hand through his hair, leaving it sticking up like a baby chick's, the vulnerability in his face squeezing my heart. "I should go."

"Yes," I whispered, unable to say anything else without breaking, giving in.

And I couldn't—for his sake.

A muscle twitched in his jaw. "Right, well..."

Neither of us moved. We just stood there staring at each other, like the gods had pressed pause on the world.

The ironic thing was, I trusted him now, believed this thing was real for both of us. That brief connection had shown me how much I meant to him. I knew him now in a way I hadn't before. His hungers, his truths, even the lies he carried like scars.

And Sweet Luna, the bond had been beautiful, a shimmer of color and need stretching between us.

Every part of me ached to accept him as my mate, to be claimed, and claim him in turn. It felt like I'd stomped on not just his heart, but my own.

But he couldn't know that. Not until Perla was safe.

Because if our plan to rescue her failed, I had a backup. I'd lie—tell Nazaire I'd already mated with Cain—and then offer myself in trade for Perla. He'd jump at it because if he had Cain's mate, he had Cain, too. The lie would buy the Maritime vampires time to get her out.

So no—I couldn't accept Cain's mate bond tonight. If something went wrong and I ended in my final grave, I'd take him down with me.

If he hadn't shut down so fast, he might've figured out what I planned. But he'd curled into himself like a wounded animal.

Because of me.

I licked my lips.

I'd hurt Cain. My lethal, iron-willed vampire—he had a heart, and it could be wounded.

But I'd known that, hadn't I? I wouldn't have fallen for him otherwise. I'd seen how he was with his friends, how he'd do anything for them and their mates.

The heaviness of what I'd done—with what I might have to do—pressed against my chest, my throat. I could hardly breathe.

But I couldn't live with myself if I stood by and let Nazaire torture Perla.

Cain moved first. "Tomorrow night, then," he said and headed for the door.

My fingers unclenched from the soft cotton. "Stay," I said hoarsely.

He turned back. "What?"

I cleared my throat, knowing I should let him leave. But I couldn't, not like this. "Stay. Please."

His brow furrowed. "What about needing time?"

"Remember that story I told you last night?" I slipped around the couch. "About the fae prince?"

"Yeah. But—"

"Shh." I stopped in front of him.

His shoulders pulled into a stiff line, but he didn't move or speak, just watched me with hot blue eyes.

Tonight, instead of his usual black and white, he wore all black— pants, dress shirt, both cut to show off his hard-muscled frame. I undid his top button. "You know that prince was really you."

His Adam's apple bobbed. "Was he?"

"Oh, yeah." I slipped open the second button. "So here's what we're going to do. Pretend we're in the story, and the page just turned." I spread his shirt apart and touched my lips to his collarbone, breathing him in. "It's a blank page. No past, no future. Just you and me writing whatever we want." I stroked my fingertips over his chest, lightly furred with dark blond hair.

His hands came to my hips. His jaw clenched like he was in pain. "What d'you want from me?"

"This." I licked at his mouth, nipped his full lower lip. "Stranger."

"Fuck." His voice was tight, but his fingers dug into my hips, keeping me where I was.

"A blank page," I murmured and moved against him, slow and sensuous, dragging my breasts over his chest. "Like we just met tonight."

A beat passed. Then he made a low, at-the-end-of-his-rope sound and hauled me up against him. One hand cupped my chin, taking control, and his mouth descended on mine in a take-no-prisoners kiss.

I sucked his tongue deeper, drinking in his taste—heat and whiskey and Cain. I couldn't get close enough. The thin barrier of our clothing was an irritation.

I brought a leg up, twining it around his thigh, wanting him thick and hot against my center. Needing the hard muscles of his pecs to soothe my aching breasts. Even the belt buckle against my stomach felt necessary.

It had *hurt* these past few nights, to keep him at arm's length. To tell myself I hated him, knowing it was a lie, told to make myself feel better.

When he lifted his head, his irises were a thin silver rim around dark, enlarged pupils. "If this is some kind of trick, I swear I'll spank you."

"No trick, I promise."

His gaze moved between my eyes, assessing my truthfulness.

I pressed closer, running my fingers down one angular cheek, lightly scratching the stubble. "Don't make me beg," I said against his ear. "Or maybe you should—make me beg, that is. Maybe you should punish me. I did try to meet with your uncle, after all. That was very bad of me." I bit down on his earlobe.

"Fuck." He sounded tortured. "Damn you, Nyx. I can't—I can't tell you no."

Longer fingers wrapped around my nape. His other hand stroked down my back in a firm caress. He palmed my ass, urging me up against his erection.

Triumph surged up in me, along with an awed sort of humbleness. That this powerful, controlled male had a weakness—me.

He saw my lips twitch in an *I-win* smile, and slapped my bottom. "Just remember who's in charge."

My sex constricted. "You are," I said immediately.

That elicited a rueful laugh. He smacked me again, harder.

"I haven't been in control," he said, "since the night we met. I think about this—about *you*—all the time. It's eating me alive, how much I need you."

"Oh." I swallowed broken bits of glass, all pretense that we were strangers, writing on a blank page, falling away.

He'd opened himself to me, let himself be vulnerable, and I couldn't respond. I couldn't tell him I loved him, that I'd be honored to accept his bond.

But I could touch him, show him how special he was, how perfect.

I finished unbuttoning his shirt and tugged the fabric from the waistband of his pants. He took over, stripping it off in one fluid motion and tossing it on the couch.

My breath snagged. He was so damn beautiful, every line of him honed and lean, from his sculpted shoulders to his narrow hips. A man who could fuck you into a stupor—or hunt you down.

The inky shark twisted around the side of his neck, its teeth bared, menace in a single, fluid shape. I traced its outline with a fingertip, then spread my hands across his shoulders, loving the solid strength beneath my palms.

When I brushed my thumbs over his nipples, the sound he gave— half groan, half growl—made my entire body clench in response. I needed to get closer, to touch him skin-to-skin. I stepped back and tugged off my sweater and T-shirt, leaving me in the red satin bra that had arrived yesterday in a chic black box along with matching panties.

"Sweet Lilith." His gaze dropped to my breasts and the silky red material cupping them. "I knew that bra would look fucking perfect on you."

I reached for him, but he caught my hands, pressing a kiss to each palm—a tantalizing promise—before lowering to his knees for the second time that night.

This time, though, he wasn't asking for anything. He was there to take.

A muscular arm looped around my waist, pulling me toward him and a little off-balance so that I had to grip his shoulders to stay on my feet. "I have to taste you," he muttered.

He pressed a kiss to my sternum, then closed his teeth on the thin satin, biting first one nipple, then the other, just hard enough.

White-hot bolts of lightning shot down my spine. I whimpered and twisted against him.

He tightened his grip, keeping me still. He took his time, nuzzling, biting, licking, sucking—slow and deliberate, until I was close to breaking.

"Cain," I said. "I need—"

He lifted his head. "Close your eyes."

I obeyed, head tipped back, body tense with anticipation. He swept an arm beneath my knees, the other cradling my shoulders. I let out a startled chuckle as he carried me into the bedroom.

He set me down next to the four-poster and lowered his brow, mock stern. "What, you don't think I can be romantic?"

A voice command and lights glowed on around the bed's teak canopy, filtering through the draped gauze like stars just before dawn. A second command, and music spilled into the room, low and lush, the kind made for slow dancing and promises.

I touched his cheek. "Very romantic."

He framed my face in his hands and kissed me with a laser-like focus, tilting my head just so, moving his mouth deliberately, drawing me deeper until I was clutching his shoulders, every nerve alive, my knees turned to water.

He removed my bra, tossing it at a nearby chair, then said, "You deserve romance." His palm glided up my ribcage to close over my breast. A calloused thumb brushed over the nipple, the roughness good...necessary. "I should've given you more. I'll work on that."

I shook my head. "You don't have to. I—the things we've done— I would think about them for weeks after. Wake up, touching myself."

His cheek creased. "Good," he said. "I'm glad you suffered as much as me."

He'd suffered?

The thrill that gave me merged into pleasure as he kissed his way from my lips to my throat, sucking on the sensitive spot where my shoulder met my neck, his mouth hot and wet.

I caught his head, holding him to me. Almost afraid I was still in the cell, dreaming this—the bed and the lights and the music; Cain; the careful way he was touching me...*romancing* me.

"More?" he asked against my skin.

I drew in a lungful of his earthy scent. This wasn't a dream. It was too real, too detailed—and I thanked the Goddess for that.

"Please," I said, the word dissolving into a moan.

His answer was a scrape of his teeth over my already sensitized skin, his fingers busy at the waistband of my jeans. When he had it undone, he lifted his head and stripped away the rest of my clothes, leaving me in high-cut red panties.

His gaze moved over me in a look that was pure hunger. The kind of look you don't just see, you feel, like a heated lick over your skin.

He thrust his fingers beneath the satin waistband, cupping my mound in a firm, *this is mine* hold. "Tell me you haven't had another man since Paris."

I shook my head, my attention on where his hand was.

A finger probed my wet folds. "What does that mean—that shake of your head?"

"It means no, I haven't."

"Since when?" He glided a fingertip around my swollen clit.

I gasped and arched my hips, blood pulsing in my ears.

"Tell me," he demanded. "Give me that much, at least."

A jagged exhale escaped me. "Since you," I confessed. "There's been no one since you. Since that first time in Montreal."

"Good," he said against my ear. "Because I'd stake any man who'd had you. And then I'd make you pay for it—like this."

He removed his fingers. I whimpered my displeasure.

"Hush." He crouched at my feet and helped me out of my panties.

The rest of his clothes vanished in a blur of vampire speed. He drew the comforter back and lifted me onto the cool linen sheets. I stretched, arms above my head on the pillow, one leg bent and falling to the side in a deliberately provocative sprawl.

He got a condom from his pants and set it on the night table, then paused, one knee on the mattress, taking me in. "Beautiful," he said in husky tones.

I shifted restlessly, reaching for him. "Come here."

He complied, crawling over me with an unhurried grace. The canopy lights turned his platinum hair into molten silver and his eyes—impossibly blue against those dark eyelashes—locked on me with a focus that felt almost feral, like the white Bengal tiger from my painting had stalked off the canvas to claim what was his.

He zeroed in my breasts again, drawing the tips into the warm cave of his mouth, sucking them into needy points. My hands came to his head, holding him close until he finished and pressed a line of kisses up my neck to my mouth.

"Beautiful," he said again, lips moving against mine. "Incredible face. Tight, fuckable body. Even your fingers are pretty." He turned and kissed my palm.

I blinked, drugged by pleasure. "You're the beautiful one."

He snorted.

"I mean it." I toyed with the short hairs on his nape. "I love looking at you. I always have."

He was on the move again, slithering down my body to my lower belly. I bent my knees, opening to him.

"Look at this, then," he said, and waited until I met his eyes. Then he licked my clit.

Pleasure jolted through me, bring my hips off the bed. "Yes," I rasped.

He teased the seam of my sex with his fingers and tongue. "Say *please*. We agreed you'd beg, didn't we? You said it was fun."

"Did I say that?"

"Yes." He nuzzled my mound, his stubbled chin brushing over the tender skin of my inner thighs.

When I just moaned, he growled against my clit, the vibration almost too much. "Say it."

"Please." I paused and added, "*Lieutenant*."

He lifted his head and smacked me right—there. "Don't call me that."

I yelped and yet I loved it, wanted more of that pleasure/pain.

I pouted and raised my arms above my head, conscious of how it lifted my breasts, and wriggled on the sheets. "You don't answer to 'Lieutenant'?"

He bared his teeth, the tips of his fangs glinting sexily. "Not when it's you. You can call me *sir*."

"Yes, sir." I traced a slow, teasing line down my throat. "Forgive me, sir."

He rewarded me by parting my folds and swiping his tongue up to my throat. He sucked the swollen flesh into his mouth, drawing circles with his tongue until I was panting and arching into his mouth. "Please, sir. Please..."

But instead of letting me come, he lifted his head. "Not yet."

"Why not?" I asked, half-pouting, half-serious.

"Because I said so."

"Maybe I don't want to wait."

I slid my hand down my abdomen, my gaze daring him to stop me. He watched as my hand crept closer to my mound. His nostrils flared once, like he was taking my scent deep into himself.

But just as I touched my clit, he intervened, removing my hand. He flipped me over, dragging me onto my hands and knees. His hand landed on my ass. "I said, *Not yet*."

I quivered, tempted to keep fighting him, but also needing to take this. To be punished a little. That new page couldn't be written until we'd cleared the air.

"Right now, I'm in charge," he reminded me. "And I think you have a lot to make up for. After this, you're going to stay on your hands and knees and take my dick, anywhere I want to put it. Is that right?"

He spanked me again, harder this time. And then again, and again. My head dropped forward, my butt tingling, my brain scrambled with lust.

"Answer me," he ordered.

What was the question? But I knew the correct answer. "Yes," I told the mattress.

Another hard slap that made my whole body clench. "Yes, what?"

"Yes, sir."

"That's better." He smoothed a hand over my burning cheeks. I tensed, waiting for another smack. Instead, he turned onto his back and slid between my open legs. When I glanced down, his fangs were fully unsheathed. He dragged them over my inner thigh, a slow scrape.

I moaned, so wet and ready, a single touch might set me off.

"Is this what you want? Or maybe this?" He drew my clit between his fangs.

I tensed, nerves sparking. The sharp points were on either side of it. Still, knowing they were so close to my most vulnerable flesh was scary but in an erotic way, like being tied to those four teak posts, open to anything he wanted to do.

"No?" he said, voice garbled because his mouth was full of me.

I shivered and grabbed his head, keeping him there. "*More.*"

A dark chuckle. He lifted his head. "Try again, pretty girl. You used to be better at begging."

I knew exactly what he was remembering—that first night in Montreal, when he'd made me say it. Had kept me trembling on the edge, until I was babbling his name and "please," over and over.

I loosened my grip on him. "I'm begging, okay?" I said, low and raw.

He just looked at me, waiting, until I said, "Please, Cain. I mean, *sir*. Please let me come, sir."

"That's better." And then, without warning, instead of sucking my clit back into his mouth, he sank his fangs into my thigh just centimeters from my sex, injecting the aphrodisiac into my bloodstream.

Lights exploded behind my eyes. I dropped to my forearms on the bed.

"So good," I moaned. Or maybe I screamed it. "*So good, so good, so good.*"

He didn't let up, drinking and sucking until I was whimpering and yes, begging. Then he licked the small wounds closed. I knew he hadn't drunk nearly enough. He was still taking care of me even though he must be aching to feed.

My heart turned over. I wanted so badly to tell him that I loved him. That of course, I'd accept his mate bond. Instead, I pressed my lips together.

The aphrodisiac was a fever in my blood now. Cain brought his mouth back to my pussy. A few slow circles of his tongue and I shattered, chanting his name, my inner walls clenching in hard, rhythmic pulses.

I was still scattered in tiny pieces around the room when he rolled me onto my back and entered me with a low, hungry sound.

"Yes," I whispered, tightening my arms and legs around him, taking him as deep as I could. If tomorrow night went south, this might be all I ever had of him. Our forever in a single night.

He buried his face in my throat, stubble scraping against my skin, grounding me in the ache of now. In this bedroom with draped gauze and soft shadows and the man I loved.

The bond stirred again, tried to claw its way out of my heart. I slammed a lid on it, keeping it caged, silent. The effort made me gasp, and Cain lifted his head.

He stilled. A beat stretched. I held my breath, waiting for him to demand what the hell was going on.

His eyes narrowed to suspicious slits. "Not now," he said. "But when this is over, we're going to have a long talk, you and me."

Relief flooded me. I forced a smile, praying he wouldn't pick up on it, wouldn't catch the truth bleeding through. "As long as we can do it with your dick inside of me."

He cursed. "You are such a bad girl."

"You like me bad."

"Fuck, yeah, I do." His fingers slid into my hair, tugging my head back, baring my throat to him. His mouth closed over my skin, hot and claiming. Reminding me that he was in control. That if he wasn't pushing me for more, it was his choice, not mine.

He propped himself on his forearms and started moving again—a measured rhythm that was somehow both perfect, and not enough. Beneath my fingers, his back flexed with each thrust and retreat. Stroking deep until I felt myself rising again.

A low sound escaped me.

His mouth brushed mine. "Good?"

"So good," I breathed, tightening my inner muscles around him.

"Firefly," he returned hoarsely.

That name—mine alone—made my heart constrict.

"Cain," I whispered back.

He broke first, driving into me with short, uneven bursts, his restraint thrown aside.

"Take it," he gritted. "Take me."

A fierce, possessive instinct flared. I tightened my grip on him.

I'd done that, made him lose his control. The realization cracked me wide open. Waves of pleasure slammed into me. My sex clamped greedily around him.

"That's it," he said hoarsely. "Come for me. Now, love."

He came down fully on top of me, hips still working, face buried in my neck, and groaned out his release just as I soared, star-lit and ecstatic, over the edge.

After, he rolled onto his back, drawing me into the curve of his body, my cheek pressed to his chest. I curled up, my bent leg over his thigh, breathing in his spicy scent. His heart slowed to a vampire's pace, a handful of beats per minute.

He let out a rough exhale. "I missed this," he murmured against my hair. "Missed you."

"Yeah?" I snuggled closer.

"That night in Paris? I should've never let you leave. I went back the next night, but it was too late. You were already gone."

A corner of my mouth tipped up in a small, regretful smile. "You couldn't have stopped me," I said into the warm hollow of his throat.

"No?" He caught one of my curls, winding it around his knuckle. "There's something I've been wondering. That night on the island—you wanted me to know you were there, didn't you?

"Yes and no. A part of me was hoping you'd find me, force me to come back to Lilith Island with you. Then I'd tell you what I'd done for Eden—that I'd made sure she had food and water—and you'd say I had no choice. That I belonged to you now. That you were keeping me even if it set off a blood feud." My laugh sounded thin in my ears. "And in a way, that's exactly what happened. Just not how I pictured it."

His lips brushed my temple. "I wish you'd come to me that night. Because you're right—I wouldn't have let you walk away. I would've brought you back here."

His voice sank lower, slowed, like he was making me a promise. "And that fire on the island? It was nothing compared to what I'd do if someone tried to take you. Then—or now."

31

CAIN

I took Nyx a second time, this time roughly from behind, pressing deep, imprinting myself on her. The primal thing had come fully awake. It pushed me to claim her in a way she wouldn't be able to forget tomorrow, even in her sire's lair. Not out of anger or hurt. Out of the bone-deep fear that I could lose her before she really understood what she was to me.

Afterward, I gathered her against me. She yawned and fell asleep in my arms, soft and warm and trusting.

But I couldn't settle. My nerves were stretched, my thoughts racing. Too much could go wrong tomorrow night, and I fucking hated how I'd lost control of the situation.

Careful not to wake her, I eased out of the four-poster bed and made my way to the war room. The soldier on duty informed me Talon and Brien were at the castle's underground speakeasy—the Bite Club, as the thralls called it.

I headed back into the tunnels and the familiar red door. Inside the speakeasy, the bass throbbed like a second heartbeat and colored spotlights swept over the club in purple, gold and red. On the dance floor, thralls ground their hips to the rhythm, eyes heavy-lidded, bodies slick with exertion. A handful of enforcers and soldiers moved among them, their faces edged with hunger. Any other night, it would've hit me like a drug, but I wasn't here for blood or sex.

I glanced around at the curtained alcoves. Talon had just finished feeding in one nearby, the silk curtain pulled back. He wiped his mouth and eased the thrall onto the couch, signaling a server who hurried over with a fruity drink.

Talon handed it to the thrall with a murmured thanks, and she relaxed against the couch arm, sipping it. An easy night for her—Talon didn't fuck anyone but Eden these days. Same for Brien and Twilight.

I guess I'd just joined that club.

Talon rose and headed around the dancers to me. "You here to feed?"

"Nah." I shook my head, unable to drink from anyone else so soon after being with Nyx. "I'll just have a blood-whiskey."

"Brien's over there." He tipped his head toward a black velvet couch, where our friend sprawled, mouth on another thrall's neck. "Twilight's with her halmoni."

We ordered a trio of whiskeys—blood for me, straight for Talon and Brien—and dropped into the armchairs flanking our primus as he licked the thrall's throat clean. She stood, and with a friendly nod to us, sashayed off, hips swaying in her short red skirt.

I handed Brien the third whiskey. We sat watching the dancers, Brien and Talon talking about nothing much.

I turned my shot glass in my hand, replaying the past couple of hours in my mind. Something was off with Nyx. She should've accepted my bond—we were mates, and she knew it as well as I did.

Fuck needing space. Now that I'd had time to think, that excuse didn't ring true. Or at least, it wasn't the whole truth.

So if that wasn't the reason, what the hell was?

An unwelcome thought slid in: *What scared her enough to lie?*

Brien set his whiskey on the cocktail table and angled toward to me. "You okay, dude?"

I took my time answering, long enough for Brien's brows to pull together and Talon to glance from the dancers to me.

"Something's up with Nyx," I said.

Talon frowned at me from the other side of the low black table. "Like what?"

"If this is about tomorrow night—" Brien started.

"She hasn't changed her mind, if that's what you mean." I took a gulp of whiskey. "Hell, you two might as well know. I asked her to accept my mate bond."

Talon grinned. "You fucker."

Brien rubbed his chin, doubtful. "I— you sure?"

The hair on my nape lifted like he'd just threatened Nyx. My muscles locked before I forced them to loosen.

Brien was my friend. He knew Nyx was with us now.

"Very sure," I said in a hard voice. "But don't worry, she turned me down."

They both recoiled a fraction, surprise flashing across their faces.

"What happened?" Brien asked.

"I don't know." I dragged a hand down my face, like I could scrape away the ache. "I told her I believe in her, would be hers if she'd just have me. I fucking begged—on my knees—asking her to trust me."

"You begged?" Talon rolled his lips into his mouth, eyes gleaming. "On your knees? Now that, I'd pay money to see."

"Fuck you." I shot him a glare. "Yeah, I begged. More or less. She understood."

"Not the best timing," Brien pointed out. "With her friend and all."

"And you did lock her in a cell," Talon added, smirking. "And poisoned her with those new silver handcuffs."

"Not helping," I ground out.

Now they both had their lips rolled in, trying not to laugh. That was brothers for you, merciless when they smelled blood in the water.

I scowled at them. "Maybe my timing was off, but she wants this. I could *feel* it. In fact, I've been sensing stuff from her for a while, things I shouldn't feel from another supernatural."

"Emotions," Brien said, serious now.

"Yeah."

Talon scratched a stubbled cheek. "Sounds like the mate bond to me. Eden's human, so I could always feel things from her. But now that we're mated, she's wide open. Everything pours through."

"That's how it is with mates," Brien confirmed.

"Yeah?" I rubbed at my chest, right over the spot where I'd sensed Nyx reach out to me. It was tender. I had the feeling that if I lifted my shirt, I'd see a bruise. "What's messed up is that I could've sworn I *felt* her for a few seconds, like she started to bond with me, then changed her mind."

Talon pursed his lips. "Maybe she's just being cautious. It had to hurt, the way you turned on her."

"I had my reasons," I muttered. "But yeah. There was something else, though. Like she was afraid to bond with me. I sensed fear."

Brien's brow creased. "Fear of you?"

"Maybe. She's got every reason to hate vampires. You know the QCS—I wouldn't blame her for running far and fast from a syndicate vampire, especially a lieutenant."

"But she hasn't run from you," he pointed out. "Until now."

"No, and that's what bothers me. This plan of hers—we all know it's risky. Too many variables, too many ways it could go wrong. What if she's not afraid *of* me? What if she's afraid *for* me?"

His nod was thoughtful. "Makes sense, especially if she's your mate."

"Yeah." My knee started bouncing, restless and jittery. "She blames herself for what they're doing to Perla. But I'm the guy who forced Nyx to come to Lilith Island. And I'm the guy who put her in Nazaire's sights, dangling her like a piece of raw meat in front of a wolf."

"Cain—" Brien started.

"No," I said over top of him. "This is on me. Nyx's only mistake," I added, low and tight, "was trusting me."

"Fuck that," said Talon. "You made that call for the syndicate— especially for Eden and Jude. Doesn't Nyx see that?"

I gave him a stark look. "Yeah, but like I said, she blames herself —not me. For sleeping with me in the first place, for handing over intel. So if we can't save Perla—if Nazaire has some trick up his sleeve..." I paused and swallowed. "What if she's thinking of trading herself for Perla?"

Brien let out a low whistle. "They'll crucify her. And if they don't, she'll wish they did."

"Yeah." My voice came out like gravel. The crawling tension ratcheted up. "Screw it. We're not taking her. I won't risk her, damn it."

"She seems dead set on coming," Brien pointed out in neutral tones.

"Too bad. I'll toss her ass back in that cell if I have to. I don't care if she hates me for it. At least she'll be alive."

Brien leaned forward, hands braced on his knees. "Whatever you decide, the syndicate will back you. One hundred percent."

Talon nodded, silent and solid.

"But—?" I said because I knew there was more.

"But this woman—Perla—is Nyx's friend. And without Nyx, getting her out of there is dicey. If we don't take Nyx and something goes wrong, she'll never forgive you. Realistically, we might not even reach Perla without Nyx's help. It's Nazaire's lair, his turf. We're not talking a clean extraction, we're talking a dirty fight, blood and teeth, no holds barred. And from what Nyx says, we'll be outnumbered three-to-one."

"Nazaire might even kill Perla out of spite," Talon added.

My fangs pricked at my gums. "Then we bring more people," I shot back. "Fight harder."

"How do we get them in without Nyx's help?"

"I don't fucking care. We'll blow up the damn lair if we have to."

"We can do that," Brien agreed. "But if Nazaire survives, Nyx will never be safe. He'll know if he gets to her, he'll have you—her mate."

My mouth pulled sideways. "But we're not mates, remember? Because—"

"She said no." Brien sat back, one brow raised.

"Hell." Mind reeling, I gazed at the dancers without seeing them as I finally connected the dots. "That's why she rejected the bond.

She knew that if she accepted, Nazaire would try to use it against us." I dropped my head into my hands. "I have to let her come, don't I? I don't have a fucking choice."

"Yeah," said Brien. "It might be the only shot we've got at prying Nyx out of his grip for good."

"Fuck." A red haze filled my vision. I dug my fingers into my temples, fighting the panic clawing at my lungs.

Brien's laugh held zero humor. "Mating's a bitch, isn't it?"

I stared at him, fear a yawning cavity inside me. "I can't lose her. I...won't come back from it."

Talon's expression hardened. "Not happening," he said. "We know what we have to do—get to Perla first. We don't give Nazaire a chance to use Nyx as leverage. Then we end that sonuvabitch, once and for all. Brothers forever, yeah?"

He extended his left hand, palm raised, and I felt the phantom sting of the old wound, the vow sealed in blood.

We came to our feet at the same time. I slapped my palm against his and held it there, our fingers interlocked. "Brothers forever."

Brien stood, too, and for the first time ever, wrapped his hand around ours. And damn if a gold spotlight didn't swing over our heads like some kind of blessing.

"Brothers forever," he said.

My throat burned. I couldn't speak or move. I just stood there, letting it sink in—these two really were my brothers. Men who'd follow me straight into the grave if I asked.

Brien's grip loosened first. "But just in case, we need a Plan B."

"Yeah. But first—" I hauled them both in, an arm around each of their necks. "Thanks, you mofos."

I got a couple of grunts in return. But they understood.

By the time I let them go, I had our backup plan. It came to me whole, like my subconscious had been working on it for a long time.

I turned to Brien. "Can you have Twilight meet us in your quarters? I have an idea."

✵ 32 ✵

NYX

The Quebec City cemetery lay silent beneath a shroud of snow. Cain and I halted under an ancient maple, its bare branches rattling in the icy wind. Brien, Twilight, Talon, and the two enforcers—James and Adrian—had already slipped ahead in the shadows to wait near the Marchand crypt. All of us were clad in black: long-sleeved nylon tees and tactical pants that held an arsenal of silver—daggers, switchblades, stakes.

Even I'd been allowed to arm myself. I'd tucked a switchblade up my left sleeve and a dagger rested in the holster on my right thigh. My hair was in a tight French braid, a twin of Twilight's dark plait.

Cain moved closer, his lean-boned face glimmering in the darkness, his eyes molten silver, his fangs slightly elongated. He'd never looked more like a vampire.

He took me by the shoulders, his gaze skimming over me, not checking my gear—checking *me*. "You good?"

I exhaled. "As good as I'm going to be."

He nodded. "Your only job is to open doors and provide cover. If something goes wrong, you hide in the shadows—I don't care what it is. Understood?"

Perla's bruised, frightened face flashed into my mind. I swallowed and didn't answer.

247

His fingers tightened. "I can still pull the plug on this."

My stomach knotted. I hated this as much as he did, was terrified of what my father would do if he caught me. But it was a chance I had to take.

I touched the metal disc at his throat—his lucky charm, the only thing he owned of his father's. Maybe some of the luck would brush off on me.

"Trust me, cher. All right?"

A darkness prowled deep in his eyes. "I can still pull the plug on this."

"Please, don't. We both know you need me."

"You think I don't know that? It's the only reason you're here."

"Then let me do what I came for."

His eyes closed. When they reopened, the darkness remained—edgy, dominant—but this time, he let me see the raw fear driving it.

"Whatever happens," he said, "I want you to know we've got your back."

My heart squeezed. I rose on my toes to rub my lips over his. "Thank you," I said against his mouth.

"Keep your thanks." He touched his forehead to mine. "I don't need gratitude; I need you to fucking survive. To come home with me."

My throat clogged. This wasn't Cain's battle, it was mine, and I was going to do everything I could to keep him out of this.

But that he'd said it aloud, made it clear how important I was to him? That was everything.

The part of me who'd constantly had to prove her worth, who'd never been *enough*, drank it in like rain on a starved field, soaking deep, filling cracks I hadn't even known were still open.

Because I was enough for Cane, just as I was. Me—Nyx.

Then he added, "And just so you know, I'm not leaving without you. That's my promise to you. We're in this together—mate."

A cold finger tripped up my spine. "Cain, no. Don't—"

"Too bad." He drew back enough for me to see his face, his mouth firm with resolve, moonlight carving a hard line across his cheek. "You made your decision, I made mine."

"I don't want this," I said, desperate now.

He gave me a very Cain half-smile, dangerous, maddeningly sure of himself. "Have some faith. You've got four badass vampires backing you up. Get us in there and let us do the rest."

He didn't wait for my protest. He kissed me, quick and hard, and turned me toward the Marchand crypt.

"You—" I shot him a narrow-eyed look over my shoulder.

He flashed his fangs, an alpha vampire who'd made up his mind. "Some arguments you're not going to win, love. Now go. Everyone else is in place by now."

A gust of wind kicked up, scattering powdery snow across our boots. I took a steadying breath, centering myself, then pictured Jérémie, a QCS soldier and a member of the lair, and began to walk. Within seconds, my body tingled, the glamour settling into place.

Cain followed in the shadows. I crouched to open the trap door camouflaged in the grass, the one leading to a tunnel that bypassed the crypt. The secret entrance that I hoped Nazaire would've forgotten I knew about.

That's when I felt it, a fierce, all-consuming protectiveness that could only be coming from him. Every muscle in my body went tight. I flicked a glance at where I *sensed* he stood.

This wasn't good—it was bad. Very, very bad.

CAIN

Nyx hadn't lied about how fast she could pull a glamour. From one stride to the next, she morphed from a sexy, long-legged redhead into a lean-hipped man, taking on the look and gait of Jérémie like she'd been born in his skin.

From the shadows, I watched as she pulled up a square of grass under a pine, revealing a heavy iron trap door concealed in the soil. Her fingers flew over the keypad, ten digits in rapid succession, and the door opened on well-oiled hinges.

The rest of us left the shadows one by one as planned—Brien first, then the others, with me bringing up the rear. Nyx waited until we all made it through the trap door, her body angled so that the only person visible on camera was her, then followed.

By the time I dropped into the tunnel, the other five had melted into the gloom. I did the same. Nyx believed Perla was being kept on a level below the main lair, a level accessible by only one staircase near the lair's great room. Nyx set off into a narrow passage, the rest of us following in the shadows, heading for the great room.

Twice, she was forced to enter the shadows herself when other vampires crossed our path. I watched her closely. Glamouring yourself while dipping in and out of shadows was a brutal drain. If her energy faltered, she was screwed—we all were. But she had to keep it up. If any of the QCS vampires had recently seen Jérémie else-where in the lair, the whole plan could collapse.

Several twists and turns later, we reached the great room, a huge, vaulted chamber that could've been ripped straight from a German castle. Nazaire was a wealthy sonuvabitch, and his lair had been built to both impress and intimidate. Thick oak arches ribbed the ceiling like exposed bone. A hulking iron beast of a chandelier hung in the center, its squat red candles throwing blood-tinged shadows across the floor, and faded tapestries covered the stone walls.

A long black table stood at one end of the chamber, and at the other, a fire smoldered in a hearth big enough to roast a pig in. In between were a handful of couches and armchairs in rich velvets and silks. Fortunately, only a few members of the lair were present, and they barely glanced up as Nyx headed to the kitchen, still in the form of Jérémie.

In the kitchen, Nyx slapped together a sandwich and tucked it into a cloth bag along with a water bottle. The next stop was a wooden door etched with a bat, wings spread wide. Nyx rapped on the smooth wood and it creaked open. A woman in a QCS uniform stood framed in the doorway, one hand on the dagger at her belt.

Nyx opened the bag, showing her the sandwich and bottle. "Food for the prisoner," she said in French.

The guard nodded and waved her inside, and I slipped in after them. Brien and Twilight were with me, also in the shadows. Per the plan, Talon would stay at the top of the stairs and James and Adrian would wait by the door at the opposite side of the great room.

We stood on a landing, a staircase descending into darkness below. Leaving the door open, the guard unhooked a kerosene torch from the wall, its flame casting jagged shadows on the limestone walls. She motioned Nyx to follow her. I trailed after.

At the bottom, three tunnels branched out like veins. The guard veered left, stopping at a door built to hold a vampire—two-inch-thick wood reinforced with wide silver bands, crossed in an X. She slid the torch into a bracket and drew an ornate brass key from her pocket. The door unlocked with a rusty groan and she pushed it wide.

Perla sat slumped against a stone wall, arms wrapped around her legs, still in the same torn navy dress. She looked like she hadn't moved since the photo had been taken. She was barefoot, her right foot swollen, the wounds on her throat crusted with blood.

Her eyes lifted to the guard. She moaned and recoiled, pressing herself against the rough stone like she hoped it would swallow her.

"S'il te plait," she said in a cracked voice. "No more."

Something in me clenched. Whatever softness I'd been born with had been beaten out of me before I turned ten. But to brutalize a woman just for befriending Nyx? A woman who'd served Nazaire loyally for years?

This wasn't discipline. It wasn't even punishment. It was the kind of cruelty a sadist used to remind everyone who held the leash.

"A meal," the guard informed Perla in clipped French. "You get ten minutes. So eat fast."

Perla's gaze went to the bag in Nyx's hand. She moistened her lips, then snatched it, her movements jerky and uncoordinated. She unscrewed the water bottle with trembling fingers and gulped some down before tearing into the sandwich.

The guard turned toward the door. That was my cue.

I stepped from the shadows, silver dagger ready, and locked an arm around her neck. She bucked, trying to throw me off, her chest moving in panicked bursts. Her hand went to the weapon at her belt.

She never got it free.

I drove my blade deep into her sternum. Blood sprayed, slicking my arm.

She gasped, fingers plucking at the carved ebony handle. She must've realized it was hopeless because she strained to look at me over her shoulder.

When she caught my eye, she bared her fangs. "May the Black Goddess...chain your soul and cast it...straight to Hades."

That pulled a smile from me. "I never figured I'd go to heaven," I returned—and gave a last twist of the blade.

Her low scream tore through the cell. The magical fire sparked to life, dark and hungry. I wrenched the dagger free, wiped it on her sleeve, and shoved her away.

She staggered to the wall and collapsed next to the door, ending up seated on the stone floor, legs splayed, head flopping to the side, smoke pouring from her mouth like a doll out of a low-budget horror movie. The air thickened with the acrid stench of burning flesh.

In the hall, Brien and Twilight had already stepped into the physical world. Twilight leaned into the cell, taking in the scene with a professional eye.

"Nice work," she told me, giving the guard's twitching body a quick once-over.

I grunted acknowledgment and turned back to Perla. She struggled to her feet, the half-eaten sandwich in her hand, careful not to put weight on her injured foot.

Her gaze darted from me to Nyx-as-Jérémie. "What do you want?" she rasped.

Nyx dropped her glamour and crossed to her, hands outstretched. "C'est moi, ma chum."

I shot forward and caught her arm. "What are you doing?" I growled in her ear. "He could have a camera in the cell."

"Let him see me," she returned, gaze on her friend.

"Nyx?" the other woman mouthed. Then her face crumpled. "You came." She leaned into Nyx, dragging in a shaking breath. "He said you would, but I wasn't sure. Oh, ma belle, you shouldn't have."

"Fuck him," Nyx said.

Perla startled at that—eyes wide, mouth parting like she couldn't believe Nyx had said it out loud.

Nyx slid an arm around her waist, taking most of her weight. "Can you walk?"

For answer, Perla tried to put her injured foot on the stone floor and winced. "I'm sorry. My foot—he threw me into a wall and... I think it's broken."

She looked helplessly from her foot to the sandwich in her hand, as if she'd forgotten she was holding it. She tucked it into her pocket with a shaky breath. The water bottle she tipped back and drained, then let it fall to the floor.

I eyed Nyx, torn between wanting to smack her pretty ass for exposing herself this way, and getting out of here ASAP.

"Get back in the shadows. We can take it from here."

"Can't." Her slim shoulder lifted in a rueful shrug. "I'm almost out of juice."

My right hand clenched around the dagger's handle. Yeah, I definitely wanted to spank her ass.

"Lean on me," Nyx told Perla, and half-carried, half-walked her to the door.

I exhaled and went ahead to check that it was safe. Twilight and Brien had remained in the tunnel outside, watching for trouble.

As the two women exited the cell, Perla froze, her gaze pinging around the tunnel. "We have to be careful," she said in an undertone. "He's not going to let us leave."

"We've got this," Nyx assured her. "But we do have to hurry."

"My foot..." Perla bit her lip, obviously in pain. "I don't know if I can."

"I'll carry you." I stepped forward.

Perla cringed, shoulders hunching, like she was expecting a blow.

"Easy," Nyx murmured. "This is Cain. You can trust him. He's from the Maritime Syndicate—they all are."

The human blinked. "Cain? He is the one who—?"

"Oui," said Nyx.

"Ah." Perla's bruised mouth curved. "A Maritime lieutenant," she said like that explained something. She straightened back up. "Yes, please," she told me.

I shoved my dagger into a hidden pocket in my tactical pants, gathered her into my arms and headed for the stairs, Nyx on my heels.

Above, Talon whisper-shouted, "Someone's coming." The door thudded shut.

My pulse kicked. I bolted up the stairs, Nyx right behind. Brien snatched up the torch, and he and Twilight followed. We hit the landing as someone banged on the other side of the door.

Talon held up three fingers. "Three men," he told us. "That I saw, anyway."

"James and Adrian?" asked Brien.

"Still in the great room. I saw these dudes dropping out of the shadows and threw the door shut. It locked automatically."

Perla lifted her head from my shoulder. "I told you," she said, her voice flat, stripped of hope. "He won't let us go. He means to stake you all."

"He'll have to catch us first," I told her.

Brien turned to Nyx. "Is there another way out?"

She shook her head. "No."

"This is it," Perla confirmed.

Twilight bounced once in her black Adidas, fangs shining in the murky light. "Then we make our stand."

Brien's eyes flared blue. "Damn right."

On the other side of the door came the scrape of a key being inserted in the lock.

Talon planted his feet and grabbed the doorknob with both hands.

I turned to Nyx, but she was already reaching for Perla. "I'll take her—you fight."

I nodded and eased the injured woman into her arms.

The brass knob turned. Talon braced himself and hung on, as someone tried to open the door from the great room. "Ready?"

"Swear you'll leave me if it means saving yourself," Perla told Nyx, her expression fierce beneath the bruises. "I'll cover for you."

I eyed the injured human. She'd already won me over by befriending Nyx, but now she'd earned my respect.

"No." Nyx's jaw tightened. "You're coming with us. I promised you that when I left, you were going with me."

I pulled my daggers free. Brien and Twilight already had their blades out.

Brien nodded at Talon. "Open it."

Talon released the knob, whipped out a stake, and kicked the door open. We poured through the doorway as three vampires dropped into fighter's crouches, fangs bared and blades out, eyes shining in the chandelier's blood-red light.

We fanned out, trying to box them in. Then the closest vampire shifted—a barely perceptible twitch of his muscles—and lunged at Talon, silver dagger out. Talon jerked his stake up, and the blades clanged off each other.

The second man came for me. I met him with both my blades, and we fought, hot and furious, no time to breathe or even think. All I could do was react, parry, thrust. A few feet away, Brien and Twilight double-teamed the third.

Nyx scurried past, shielding Perla with her body. On the far side of the room, James and Adrian dropped out of the shadows, protecting the pair of women as instructed.

I sped up my blows. The clock was ticking. Nazaire would be here any second.

But our time had run out.

He'd already emerged from the shadows on the other side of the room along with two other men who'd engaged Adrian and James, leaving Nyx and Perla undefended.

Nazaire closed the door behind him, blocking the only other exit. Nyx halted, then slid sideways, putting Perla on a couch without taking her gaze from her sire.

I cursed—and let myself get distracted. My opponent was no longer in front of me.

I went low and whipped around, ducking the dagger that would've pierced my chest from behind. As he stumbled past me, carried by his own momentum, I popped up to slam my blade against the back of his skull. It landed with a satisfying crunch.

He faltered and turned toward me. I drove him back with a vicious kick to the chest. He smashed into the wall. Stone cracked, and his blade fell from his hand. I knocked it away with my foot.

He hissed, fangs flashing, and leapt at me, raking his claws across my shoulder. I went at him with both blades. One sliced halfway through his wrist; the second I buried in his heart.

His jaw dropped, like he was surprised I'd gotten past his guard. Gods knew what the QCS had told themselves about Brien and his people, but they clearly hadn't expected us to outfight them.

I showed him my own fangs. "Surprise, motherfucker."

He clamped his hands around the dagger's carved ebony handle, dragging it partway free. Then his strength gave out. His fingers opened, releasing the handle, and he crumpled to the marble tiles.

I swung around to see if my friends needed help. The two vampires they'd been fighting lay bloodied and silent, smoke rising from their bodies, dark fire eating through their flesh.

But Nazaire had gotten to Nyx. He had an arm crooked around her neck, a blade angled against her carotid. Red shadows from the chandelier bled across their faces—Nyx's tight and controlled, Nazaire's lit with an unholy glee.

My heart punched against my sternum, a single hard blow. Then it just...stopped.

At Nazaire's signal, the vampires James and Adrian had been fighting shoved them away and closed ranks around Nyx and her sire.

James and Adrian looked at me. "Sir?" asked Adrian.

"Stand down," I barked as the rushing in my ears drowned everything, even the ragged breaths of my friends coming to stand beside me. The world narrowed to a single point: Nyx's life balanced on a sharp silver edge.

My mind spiraled with an impossible decision.

Stay frozen—or strike.

Nearby, Talon said under his breath, "Stay calm, bro. We've got this."

I barely heard him.

Perla came to her feet, pale under her bruises. She limped her way to them, hand outstretched. "Please, my lord. Nyx is your daughter. She's—"

Nazaire backhanded her across the face.

My heart slammed into high gear. I don't even remember crossing the great room. I was just there, in front of them, my remaining dagger in my hand. Someone—me—was growling, low, feral.

Perla stumbled backward and hit the wall. She whimpered, a small, hurt sound.

My friends had moved an instant after me. Talon was in time to catch Perla. He handed her off to James and Adrian, who helped her to a couch out of harm's way, while Brien and Twilight fended off Nazaire's two men with raised daggers.

At a word from Nazaire, they backed off, returning to his side.

James and Adrian rejoined our group, and the six of us formed a semicircle around Nyx, Nazaire and his two men.

A smile curled the Quebec City enforcer's thin mouth. "Thank you, little rabbit," he told his daughter, planting a kiss on her cheek. "You brought them straight to me."

She heaved a breath. Then she lifted her chin. "You can still end this. Keep me, but let them go. If you swear to drop this vendetta against them, then they'll leave. Right, Primus Leclerc?"

Out of the corner of my eye, I saw Brien's jaw work. "If you swear a blood oath," he told Nazaire. "Then yes."

A sharp rush of gratitude hit me. Brien hated Nazaire as much as I did—wanted him gone. But he was willing to let the SOB walk for me. To save my mate.

I didn't know what I'd done to deserve friends like this.

The lean, dark-haired enforcer wasn't as savvy as I figured because he shook his head, sneering, "So magnanimous, but I believe I'll decline. I'd rather see you on your knees. Begging."

Brien simply looked at him.

The hair on my nape stirred. The air stilled, thickened, like a storm about to break, and not just because Brien was about to blow.

I glanced around, hand on my hilt.

Shadows moved—left, right, behind—then a half-dozen men appeared all around the great room. Like us, they'd come dressed for a fight, in combat-ready clothing, blades gleaming in their hands.

"Surprise," Twilight said under her breath.

The six of us moved toward each other, forming a facing-out hexagon so we covered each other's backs.

The newcomers prowled toward us. Silent, well-trained predators. But then, so were we.

I still faced Nyx, a man closing in on me from either side. I calculated the odds of reaching Nazaire before they stopped me and judged it wasn't good. I braced myself to try anyway.

Nyx's mouth moved in a soundless apology. *I'm sorry.*

My brows drew together. I gave a tiny shake of my head because she had nothing to be sorry about.

Nyx stared back, body stiff with tension. Then she flinched, and I realized her bastard of a sire had moved the dagger down, the silver point biting into her thin nylon shirt.

"Drop your weapons," he said, teeth bared, "or I'll bury this in my bitch of a daughter. And not in her heart—in her liver. That would be a shame, no? Such une jolie fille."

My blood iced. The liver was the body's filter, the organ that removed toxins like silver. Best case? Nyx would be screaming in agony for weeks. Worst case—her allergy would finish what the silver started and she'd never crawl back.

She pulled in a shallow breath, face expressionless.

"Now," Nazaire rapped out. "Weapons on the floor."

She mouthed *no* at me, eyes pleading.

I snarled lowly. Did she really think I'd stand by and let that motherfucker drive a blade into her?

"He means it," I told my friends and crouched to obey.

$$\text{❄ } 34 \text{ ❄}$$

NYX

Cain placed his dagger on the black marble floor. A soft, almost polite click that struck me like a gong.

He'd disarmed himself.

To protect me.

He'd stripped himself of his weapon, defying his hardwired, gut-level need—to dominate, to battle to the death—to keep me safe.

Something deep inside me broke open, a barrier forged of years of never being enough. Of always falling short.

Then fear detonated in my chest. My heart grew fists and pounded them against my ribcage, wild with terror.

This wasn't what I'd planned. He wasn't supposed to do that, wasn't supposed to trade himself for me.

"Cain, no!" I twisted Nazaire's grip. "Don't trust him."

My father—no, my *sire*; I refused to think of him as my father any longer—locked his arm tighter my neck. "Quiet," he spat against my ear.

Cain ignored me and started to rise.

"All of them," said Nazaire.

Cain gave him a hooded look but produced a switchblade and added it to the pile, before straightening up again.

I couldn't breathe. Not just from the arm strangling me but

from the weight of what Cain had done. It felt like all the air had been sucked out of the great room.

The other five Maritime members had gone statue-still. Nazaire looked at Brien and said, "Your weapons, too."

"No!" I slammed an elbow into my sire's rib cage, desperately trying to get free. If I could get away—even for thirty seconds—I could fade into the shadows, taking myself out of the equation. If I could dredge up the energy, that is. "Don't—that's what he wants!"

"That's enough." Nazaire's grip on my throat constricted until it felt like he was one millimeter away from crushing my windpipe. "Another word and I'll send your pretty lieutenant to the Dark Gods right now"—a jab of his dagger for emphasis—"in front of your eyes."

I stilled, chest jerking in and out. It was the only way to buy Cain and his friends time. I only prayed he knew what he was doing.

"The weapons," Nazaire reminded Brien.

"No," he returned.

Nazaire dug the blade a little deeper. This time, I managed not to react.

Cain took over, moving forward. A trio of my father's men closed in on him like wolves coming in for a kill.

He lifted his hands, loose and easy. "I'm unarmed," he told Nazaire, ignoring the other three vampires. "Now let her go. It's not her you want. You want a hostage, take me. My friends won't stop you."

This was Cain's plan? I swallowed a moan.

He flicked a glance at me. Somehow I knew he was asking me to trust him, and I managed to form my lips into a confident answering smile. Well, semi-confident anyway.

"Not you," Nazaire told him. "Your primus."

He took the dagger from my side long enough to point it at the tall, pony-tailed vampire.

"No," said Cain. "You want him, you go through me first. But let's make this interesting." His smile was cold enough to frost stone. "Enforcer Nazaire, I challenge you for your daughter. If I win, she becomes mine. Any tie to the Quebec City Syndicate will be cut. Her loyalty will belong to the Maritime Syndicate—and me."

"A challenge," my sire echoed. I didn't need to see his face to know his expression had turned calculating. "And if I win?"

"You take my place in the Maritime Syndicate hierarchy."

The QCS vampires exchanged glances. An offer like that was almost unheard of. But if Brien agreed, the challenge could go forward.

It was a brilliant countermove on Cain's part. Refusing the challenge would make Nazaire appear weak, afraid—and he'd rather bleed out on his own dagger than admit to either.

"A Maritime lieutenant," Nazaire said. "Does he have your permission, Primus?" His tone put quotes around the word "Primus," like Brien had somehow tricked his way into ruling one of North America's most powerful syndicates.

"My lord?" Cain said without taking his gaze from me. "Do I have your permission?"

Brien stepped next to his lieutenant. He didn't seem surprised, and neither did Talon. I should've guessed they'd have a Plan B.

Maxime, a slim French vampire with swept-back dark hair who was my sire's closest friend, moved to block Brien. The Maritime primus leveled a look at him. Maxime halted and retreated without a word.

Something in the room had shifted, a subtle rebalancing of power. Cain had just tilted the board, and Nazaire was too arrogant, too focused on his own maneuvers to realize he was playing under someone else's rules.

But other QCS men noticed, except possibly Rodrigo. Several of them eased backward, giving Cain and his friends a little more space.

Beneath the fear, beneath the dagger biting into my side, hope stirred. Not the fragile, flowery kind. The kind that came with teeth and claws.

"Yes," Brien told his lieutenant. "You have my permission. And you'd better fucking win," he muttered under his breath.

"I will," Cain said simply.

Brien raised a brow at Nazaire. "The challenge has been made. Do you accept?"

Nazaire pushed me at the two closest QCS vampires—Maxime and Rodrigo.

They grabbed me. Maxime's grip was impersonal, but my cousin's fingers dug painfully into my arm.

"You little idiot," he hissed in my ear. "What have you done?"

Cain growled and took a threatening step in our direction. Two QCS vampires were instantly in his face, blades to his throat.

He acted like they weren't even there. "Let her go," he ordered my cousin.

Rodrigo's chest puffed like the brainless rooster he was.

Maxime made an irritated sound. "Treat her with respect," he snapped at my cousin. "The challenge demands that."

"Blood-rat doesn't deserve my respect," he muttered.

I rounded on him, fangs bared. "I am *not* a blood-rat," I hissed. "He was the one holding a knife to my liver. That makes him the blood-rat. He has *never* treated me like his spawn. I'm only a tool to him, and a faulty one at that."

I meant every word. The scales had fallen from my eyes. I hadn't betrayed Nazaire. You couldn't betray someone who'd never deserved your loyalty.

I leaned closer to Rodrigo, fangs an inch from his neck. "And if you call me that again," I said softly, "you'll find out exactly how little I have left to lose."

His eyes widened—a flash, followed by a scowl—but he loosened his grip.

Nazaire was focused on Brien. "If I win," he said, "I'll be part of your hierarchy."

The primus dipped his blond head. "Correct."

"Ah..." Nazaire drew out the syllable like a hungry snake. "That would allow me to challenge you, wouldn't it, 'Primus'?"

Brien's lips lifted in a smile that should've made Nazaire shiver in his polished leather shoes. But he was too drunk on the fantasy of slaying Brien and claiming the title of Maritime Primus.

"I'd welcome it." Brien paused long enough to be insulting. "Enforcer."

Nazaire's eyes narrowed, but he let it pass, turning to Cain. "Then I accept."

"The challenge has been accepted," Brien announced. "Name your seconds."

"I name Lieutenant Talon as my second," said Cain, "and ask my primus and prima to serve as witnesses."

Talon stepped up beside Cain, broad-shouldered and formidable.

"We accept," said Brien.

Meanwhile Twilight inserted herself between me and Rodrigo. She took my arm. "I've got her," she told my cousin.

His mouth thinned, but he released me.

"You, too," she told Maxime.

He lifted a single, manicured brow. "I don't take orders from you."

Twilight exhaled through her nose—sharp, unimpressed. "Look, Nyx has got skin in the game, too. She's not going anywhere. He's her mate."

"Her mate?" Maxime sliced a considering look at me.

Nazaire's head whipped in my direction. "This is true?"

"No." I licked my lips. "I haven't—"

"Yes," Cain said at the same time. "She's mine."

"Not yet," I returned just as firmly.

Nazaire's lip curled. "So that's where you got the money."

"Money?" I echoed.

"That half-million you have in a Swiss bank account."

My mouth dropped, and he took that as guilt.

"That's right, I know everything. You've been passing intel to this lover of yours—selling your sire out to gain his favor. I knew the truth when you returned without Pascal and Lemaire."

"You're wrong," I said. "I took nothing from Cain, not a single cent. And Pascal and Lemaire were stupid enough to get caught by the Maritime Syndicate. I had nothing to do with that."

His upper lip curled. "Now you add lying to your sins? I should've staked you the night you first took breath."

At my side, Twilight went rigid. Cain inhaled, the sound loud in the charged silence.

But me? I felt only the faint echo of pain. I thought of telling Nazaire the truth—that the money came from my art, my "little hobby." But I honestly didn't care what he thought of me. Let him believe the worst.

"I disown you," he continued, his voice laced with scorn. "From this day forward, you are nothing to me. Nothing. The bond of sire to spawn is severed."

I braced for the familiar ache of rejection. But all I felt was a dizzying relief. I almost laughed with the weight lifting off my chest.

I was free. Nazaire had freed me in front of all of them, and he couldn't take it back. It was a victory I hadn't dared imagine.

I smiled—triumphant, unmasked. Letting my happiness show. Letting everything show. "So be it."

"Ass," Cain added in a low, carrying voice.

Our eyes met, and the room fell away. For a few seconds, there was only him. The man who'd surrendered to a rival enforcer for me. The man standing in the fire of a challenge because of me.

He hadn't chosen himself. He hadn't chosen his syndicate or his friends.

He'd chosen me.

How could I not choose him back?

My heart tumbled out of my chest and into his waiting hands.

"And yes," I said, my gaze locked with his, "I'm Cain's mate. I accept his mate bond. Whatever happens tonight, I accept that, too. His fate is my fate."

The words sealed it.

The bond surged so fast and hard, my chest jerked. Energy crackled between us. A thousand colorful threads wove themselves into a single, shimmering rainbow that pulsed from me to him and back again.

Something burst open inside me, brilliant and alive, a blossom made of light.

I brought a hand to my heart. How could I have believed I'd make Cain vulnerable, that I'd be a weakness others could exploit?

The mate bond didn't make you less. It made you *more*. Each of us reinforcing the other, our two energies twining into something strong and unbreakable.

Cain's strong throat worked. "I love you," my beautiful, dangerous man mouthed, uncaring of the roomful of syndicate vampires watching.

Nazaire turned to Brien, voice slick with contempt. "This lovesick fool is one of your lieutenants?"

I brought my hand down. In that moment, I almost felt sorry for my sire.

Cain had outmaneuvered him, devising the perfect way to severe my ties with both Nazaire and the QCS without igniting a blood feud. No one, even Régis Dussault, could cry foul if Cain won a public challenge witnessed by members of both syndicates.

And if my sire thought Cain would be easy game, he really was an ass.

Brien just lifted a brow. "Your second?" he asked Nazaire.

"Maxime. And my witnesses will be Rodrigo and Théo." He nodded at my cousin and another soldier.

"When and where?" Brien asked.

"Now. And the place will be the cemetery above." Nazaire pointed at the ceiling. "One blade only."

Brien glanced at Cain. "One blade only," he agreed.

"We accept," said Brien.

Talon bent to reclaim Cain's weapons. Nazaire snapped at Théo to collect the blades instead, but Brien cut him off.

"I know you're not insulting us by suggesting we'd break the challenge terms," he said coolly. "Because everyone in this room heard me and Cain agree."

Twin blotches of red colored Nazaire's sallow cheeks. "Of course not," he said, tight-lipped.

"That's what I thought," Brien replied.

35

CAIN

We headed back to the cemetery, Nazaire and two other QCS men in front, three more shadowing us from behind. Adrian carried Perla, a thick velvet throw tucked around her.

I locked my fingers around Nyx's, the terror from earlier still thrumming in me. I was still coming down from it, fighting the urge to snarl at anyone who came too close.

Sweet Lilith, I never wanted to live through something like that again.

Watching Nazaire turn on her—my mate—had nearly sent me over the edge. The other vampire's mouth had been set, his eyes like pools of black ice. The bastard had been willing—no, eager—to sacrifice his own spawn if it meant getting a chance at Brien.

It had taken every ounce of my control to bargain with him when what I wanted to do was rip off his fucking head and watch it roll across the veined black marble. But I'd forced myself to stick to the plan. It was the only way to pry Nyx loose from both him and the QCS.

The downside was that if I lost, Brien would be forced to welcome Nyx's snake of a sire into the syndicate as a lieutenant. It was a hell of an ask on my part, and I knew it. But we'd all agreed—

Brien, Twilight, Talon, and me—that if it came down to it, this was the best way to ensure Nazaire didn't survive the night.

We exited through the wrought-iron doors of a weathered crypt. Ahead of me, Brien and Talon swept narrow-eyed looks across the cemetery, assessing for threats the way other men breathed.

Nazaire strutted over the snow-laced grass in his fancy suit, arrogance clinging to him like a cologne. He was so damn sure he'd win. Yeah, he had a couple of centuries on me—and vampires grew in power as they aged—but I was a lieutenant in one of the largest, toughest syndicates on the continent.

Did he really think I'd go down easy?

Nazaire halted at a rectangle of frostbitten earth. His men fanned out, forming a ring around us. Adrian put Perla down on a bench and draped the throw around her shoulders.

Nyx cupped my face with both hands. "I love you."

My breath snagged. I caught her by the nape and took her mouth in a hard kiss.

"If this goes sideways," I said, "run to Talon. He'll take you somewhere safe."

She just looked back at me.

That's when it hit me—we'd mated. If I lost, I'd probably take her down with me. The shock to her system would be that great. And if she did survive, she'd be a hollowed-out shell of herself, like Brien's father after losing Lenore.

Fear squeezed my heart.

Her eyes darkened, and I realized she could feel it—my emotions bleeding into her the same way hers bled into me. She knew exactly how terrified I was for her.

She was afraid, too, but underneath was an unshakable confidence in me.

In us.

I swallowed hard.

Her fingers brushed my cheek. "You won't lose."

I forced a nod, projecting confidence with everything I had. Not because I believed victory was guaranteed, but because I refused to let her see the doubt clawing at me.

She gave me a last kiss and joined Perla on the bench.

Beside me, Talon stirred. "So, which blade are you using?"

"This one." I drew out my favorite, a long silver beauty that I'd used to stake both the guard and my opponent in the great room. A blood-red ruby, big as my thumbnail, shone in the ebony handle. Brien's parents had gifted it to me the day I'd become a made man in their syndicate.

He nodded approvingly. "Good choice."

"Yeah." I rubbed the pad of my thumb over the ruby. "It seemed fitting." I didn't add that I'd hoped it would come to a challenge, but I'm sure Talon guessed that part.

"I'll hold the others."

He held out a hand, and I passed over my switchblade and the other dagger. I'd agreed to one blade only. If the remaining dagger broke or was taken, I'd have to fight with fangs and claws.

Nazaire shrugged out of his suit coat, passing it and two daggers to his friend Maxime. He rolled his sleeves to the elbow, deliberate, unhurried, then lifted the blade he'd kept. Silver gleamed wickedly along its edge, the stainless handle carved with curling script that looked torn from some ancient book of magic.

Talon tapped his fist to mine and growled, "Now go take that fucker out."

"That's the plan." I looked past him to where Nazire watched me, his lizard-like eyes unblinking.

I let the corner of my mouth lift—a slow, deliberate mockery, the kind that said I wasn't impressed.

Talon joined the ring of vampires and dhampirs surrounding us, taking a spot opposite Brien and Twilight. Maxime remained in the center, ready to start the challenge.

I stole one last look at Nyx. She sat close beside Perla, an arm looped protectively around her friend's shoulders. Wisps of red had escaped her braid, curling around her face and throat. Beneath her straight-cut bangs, her brow was furrowed, her lips pressed into a line.

Even like this—tense, worried—she was beautiful, somehow both strong and fairylike at the same time. A firefly at dusk.

She caught me looking and smiled, quick and real. The tiny diamond in her nose twinkled at me.

I found myself winking back.

A rustle swept over the cemetery, and the hairs on the back of my neck lifted. A half-dozen vampires dropped from the skeletal trees, silent as falling leaves.

QCS men. I recognized a few from Brien's negotiations with their primus, Régis Dussault, about investing in a mammoth QCS casino. The newcomers sauntered forward, taking a place in the circle.

We all tensed. Brien's hands settled on his dagger hilts.

"More observers," Nazaire said with a sly glance. "Any objections?"

Brien inclined his head. "Not at all."

Then Dussault himself strode through the graves, boots whispering over the snow-crusted grass, dark hair slicked back from his face, eyes like polished stone—black, unreadable.

Talon's gaze cut to mine. I could practically hear him: *Called it.*

Nyx had warned us that the QCS primus might be using her sire as a proxy to strike at Brien. So we'd been aware this might be a trap, but had agreed it was worth the risk. Better to die in a fair fight than take a stake in the dark, the way Brien's mother had.

Dussault stepped into the circle opposite Brien. Unlike Nazaire, he wasn't tricked out in a designer suit. No, like us, he'd come dressed for war, twin daggers riding his hips.

"Brien." He inclined his head in a greeting that felt more like a threat.

"Régis," my friend returned, unsmiling.

Dussault rested his hands on his dagger handles, mirroring Brien. "I wasn't aware you requested permission to enter my territory."

"My apologies," Brien murmured for form's sake. "I was on a rescue mission. A friend of Lieutenant Cain's mate."

The other primus's brow furrowed. "Mate?"

I nodded proudly. "Nyx Nazaire has done me the honor of accepting my bond."

Dussault looked to her for confirmation.

She sat tall on the bench, shoulders back, chin lifted. "It's true."

His eyes cut to her sire. "You agreed to this?"

Nazaire's nostrils flared. "No. But she is no longer my concern."

"He disowned her," I said. "If I win the challenge, she belongs to me."

Dussault's frown increased. "Explain."

Maxime stepped forward, laying out the terms of the challenge.

It was highly irregular, and everyone there knew it. If Nazaire won, Dussault would lose an enforcer to the Maritime Syndicate. I braced for Nyx's primus to object, but instead he traded a long look with her sire before saying, "Very well. Proceed."

Brien's mouth bent down, his eyes meeting mine past Maxime's shoulder. Confirmation—Nazaire hadn't been acting alone. He'd been operating with Dussault's knowledge, if not his express permission.

Good. We'd forced him out into the open at least.

Maxime raised a dagger above his head, the blade glinting against the night sky. My grip tightened around my own dagger's ebony hilt. I dropped into a fighter's crouch, adrenaline surging. Across from me, Nazaire did the same.

Maxime's voice rang out. "Let the challenge begin!" He slashed the dagger down between me and Nazaire, and stepped back into the circle.

Nazaire circled me, eyes locked on mine. Watching and waiting for an opening.

I gave him three beats, then lunged, gambling it would throw off his rhythm.

It did.

He jumped back, evading the point aimed at his chest, but the edge kissed his deltoid, slicing through his white shirt and into his skin, delivering a jolt of silver to his system.

He grunted, spun, and came back at me a breath too late. I dipped right and he staggered past me. He recovered quickly and pivoted toward me with a snarl.

Around us, the circle erupted in jeers and cheers, but I barely registered it.

I could win this fight. That wasn't ego but an assessment born from years of sparring with Talon and Brien and the castle's old guard—Prosper, Donald and others. Nazaire might be two centuries old, steeped in power and politics, but I'd bet it was a long time since he'd engaged in a challenge.

He hadn't expected my hungry, streetwise way of fighting, and it was costing him.

I came at him again, a flying kick to his stomach. When he staggered backward, I sliced his cheek. Blood flowed down his face, darkening his silk collar.

He hissed and bared his fangs, attacking me in a flurry of movements that only another vampire could've countered. I danced and spun, our blades clashing, the dull clang of silver on silver the only sound in the now silent cemetery.

His blade got past my guard. I knocked it away at the last second and slid past him, both of us breathing hard now.

I shot left—and slipped on the icy grass, dropping to one knee. Nazaire launched himself at me, dagger aimed at my chest.

Instinct took over. I threw myself to the side, blade gripped in both hands and thrust upward. Nazaire was a beat too slow. The point of his dagger whistled past my chest, hit a frozen patch of earth and skittered out of his hand.

But my dagger found its mark, sliding beneath his ribcage and deep into his heart.

Nazaire's face twisted in shocked disbelief.

My smile was all white teeth and fangs. "You lose, Enforcer."

He spat something in French.

I pushed to my feet and wrenched the blade free. He swayed on his feet, blood and smoke pouring from the gaping wound. Black fire crawled over him, consuming him from the inside out. A final burst of heat and light tore through him.

He dropped to the frozen ground like a felled tree.

Nyx came to her feet, one hand pressed to her mouth.

Brien and Talon were at my side a moment later, clapping me on the back. I nodded, accepting their congratulations, my gaze on Nyx.

Mine, I mouthed.

Her hand fell away, and she gave me a smile that trembled at the edges. Then she glanced at her sire's body, crumbling to ash and charred bone, and the small smile vanished.

I guess she still felt something for the bastard, even after everything. The man had never understood what he had in her.

At my side, Brien raised my hand, proclaiming me the winner of the challenge. The Maritime vampires let out a cheer.

Brien grabbed me in a one-armed hug. "Thank you," he said for my ears only. "For my mother's sake."

I shook my head, uncomfortable. "Fuck your thanks. I did it for all of us."

"Thanks anyway," he said and released me.

Nyx shot across the graveyard, tears streaming down her face—but smiling again. She was still a couple of meters away when she launched herself at me.

I opened my arms and caught her.

36
NYX

It was done. I gulped in oxygen, my emotions a tangle of relief and sorrow and joy.

Relief that I was finally free of Nazaire.

Sorrow for the man he'd been—cold, calculating, incapable of love.

But threaded through it all was a wild, primal joy, so fierce I was shaking with it.

Cain had survived. He loved me. He'd claimed me as his mate.

It was as if my most secret painting, the story drawn only on my heart, had come to life.

Cain buried his face in my hair. "Don't ever do that to me again."

"Do what?"

"Let anyone put his blade to your throat. Or your fucking liver."

Laughter bubbled up in me. "I'll do my best."

"You'd better." His hands slid to my ass and squeezed.

I nuzzled his cheek. "Yes, sir."

He drew in a ragged breath. "Fuck, I need you."

Our mouths met in the kind of kiss where everything is fused, perfect—lips, bodies, hearts. When we broke for air, he frowned and swiped a tear on my cheek with his thumb. "You're crying. But I feel you—inside—and you're happy."

Only then did I feel the tears streaking my face. "I am happy—so happy. Just emotional."

His expression was both baffled and adoring, like figuring me out was going to be his life's work. "Okay."

"Cain," snapped Talon.

Silver flashed around us. Dussault and his people had us surrounded and were advancing. The Maritime people had their weapons out in answer.

"Fuck," Cain bit out. He shoved me in Perla's direction. "*Run.*"

My hand went to the dagger on my thigh. A glance at Perla told me she was all right, although she'd come to her feet, one hand on the back of the bench.

She caught my eye, and then my quiet, self-contained friend spat out, "Trou d'culs." Assholes.

Talon had already tossed Cain another blade. The four friends fought alongside James and Adrian.

Six against thirteen, and only a couple of the thirteen called this lair home. Dussault had clearly come not just to witness the challenge, but to take advantage of it. Nazaire must've contacted him as soon as he knew Brien was in the lair.

But for now, they'd left me alone. I eased the dagger from its holster and shot another glance at Perla. She brandished a silver switchblade she'd produced from somewhere, wordlessly letting me know she'd be okay. I nodded and circled the fighters.

Brien and Talon had each taken out a man already. Rodrigo and his friend Théo had teamed up against Cain. I slipped in behind them.

Cain's gaze flickered, although he was too smart to give me away. But he wasn't happy. I didn't need the bond to tell me he wanted me to run, not fight. To save myself.

To Hades with that. We were mates now. We lived or died together.

I focused on Rodrigo, and, drawing my blade up, slashed it down toward the base of his neck, aiming to severe his spine.

A dirty, vicious kind of fighting. I sensed Cain's surprise even as he stuck his blade through Théo.

Rodrigo ducked just in time and my blade sliced the side of his throat instead. A hot spray followed; I'd hit an artery.

Not good enough. It would weaken him, but if I didn't finish him off, he'd heal.

He spun and lunged at me, teeth bared. I threw up my arm, parrying his strike with my blade—and suddenly, Cain was there, driving his weapon into Rodrigo's chest.

He froze, shock widening his eyes.

Cain shot me a quick, toothy grin. *Got him.*

He jerked his blade from Rodrigo and together, we watched him crumple to the ground.

Out of the corner of my eye, I saw Twilight stake a man, too.

The odds were just about even now.

Then Talon called, "James! Behind you."

But it was too late. When I turned to look, Dussault had staked the Maritime enforcer from behind. He jerked his blade from James's back and crept toward Brien.

Twilight yelled a warning, but the tall blond primus had already swung around like he had eyes in the back of his head. He stalked forward, a dagger in each hand, a storm given shape and purpose.

"Was it you?" he spat out. "Did you order Nazaire to stake my mother?"

Dussault shook his head. "Order? No. But the enforcer was on Lilith Island with my permission."

"To do what?" Brien demanded between his teeth.

Dussault smiled. "Whatever he could get away with," he said, and attacked, one dagger aimed at Brien's chest, the other whipping toward his face.

Brien's daggers flashed, knocking one of the blades out of Dussault's hand and forcing him to fall back.

The weapon flew toward Cain. He snagged it mid-air and slid it into an empty pocket.

When Maxime objected, Cain rounded on him. "Shut the fuck up. Your primus broke the rules of the challenge, not us."

The older vampire scowled but backed off.

Around us, the fighting faltered as the clash between the two primuses hit like a shockwave—one of those instinctive, bone-deep signals that made everyone else pull back because the danger spiked. By unspoken consent, the two sides drifted to opposite edges of the clearing, giving the primuses space, all of us waiting to see how the battle played out.

Cain pulled me behind him. This time, I let him. He was on edge, torn between protecting me and watching his friend battle for his life.

I rested my hand on his lower back and edged sideways until I had a clear view of the fight.

Dussault circled left, Brien shadowing him. Brien lunged; Dussault twisted away. The fight erupted—Dussault all cool precision; Brien a relentless, fluid force. Their strikes blurred, nearly too fast to follow.

Then Brien shifted, paused. A tiny changeup in rhythm.

Dussault attacked, clearly believing he'd found an opening.

He hadn't.

Brien's blade caught Dussault's wrist mid-strike, cleaving it in two and sending his remaining dagger to the ground. His second blade took an upward arc that tore through his opponent's chest and burst out between his shoulder blades. For a few seconds Dussault hung there, impaled, face contorted in a silent scream.

"Burn in the noonday sun," Brien ground out, and yanked the blade free.

Dussault staggered, crashing to the frozen earth with a bone-jarring thud. His body convulsed once. He gave a single, inhuman groan that raised goosebumps all over my body, then stilled, blood blooming on his chest like a dark flower.

Brien stood over him, blades dripping crimson on the trampled snow. A thick smoke swirled around his long legs, fed by the slain vampires turning to ashes around us.

He snarled at what remained of the QCS upper hierarchy, his eyes rimmed a burning blue. "Anyone else?"

Every last one of them recoiled, Adam's apples bobbing. "No, my lord," they chorused.

Flames erupted from Dussault's mouth and chest, licking over his body like hungry tongues until his body was nothing but charred fragments of ash and bone.

Brien raised a blood-slick dagger high. "Quebec City is mine," he declared, voice echoing off the nearby mausoleums. "I claim it for the Maritime Syndicate."

The QCS vampires stood frozen, statues carved from fear.

Lowering the dagger, he eyed each one in turn, taking his time, making sure they knew he was noting their faces. Their stares stayed nailed to the ground.

Finally, he jerked his chin. "My people will be in touch. Now get the fuck out of my sight."

37

CAIN

I hooked an arm around Nyx's shoulders, keeping her close as the local vampires slipped away. Only Maxime remained. He cleared his throat, the sound loud in the night.

Brien's head swiveled toward him. "You have something to say?"

"I do." Maxime nodded at what remained of Dussault. "He—the primus—knew about your mother. Knew that Nazaire had staked her."

"And?"

"Nazaire had an...interest in Lenore." The information seemed dragged out of him, like what he had to say pained him. "He said your father had stolen her, that she should've been his mate, not Jules's."

Nyx stiffened against me. "What?!"

Maxime didn't seem to hear her. "And when Jules started gaining power, more than my friend ever expected—it was salt in the wound. In the end, he hated them both."

Twilight came up next to Brien, sliding an arm around his waist in wordless support.

Brien pulled her closer without looking away from Maxime. "So you're saying he staked my mother because he wanted her?"

The other vampire shrugged, a small, resigned gesture that carried more weight than anything he could've said out loud.

"No." Nyx straightened from me. "Maybe that's what he told you. He might even have started believing it. But this wasn't about Prima Lenore. This was about power."

A dark cloud scudded over the moon, like Luna herself was emphasizing Nyx's point.

"He knew he could never rise higher in the QCS," she continued, speaking slowly, like everything had finally locked into place for her. "Dussault was his age, and already had a lieutenant lined up to secede him. So he went after the Maritime Syndicate. I know he didn't expect Brien to take his father's place as primus." Nyx glanced at Brien. "Your father's lieutenant Prosper was supposed to slay you and ascend to primus."

Twilight nodded. "Prosper was counting on that himself."

Prosper had challenged Brien and lost. Brien spared him, but the lieutenant left Lilith Island anyway—a self-imposed exile that was better for everyone involved.

"So that was Nazaire's angle," I mused. "And I suppose he would've come for Prosper next."

Nyx spread her hands. "That's my guess. I don't have any proof, of course, but that's how his mind worked. Always scheming, figuring how he could turn things his way."

"Perhaps," Maxime allowed. He dipped his head in Brien's direction, half bow, half surrender. "Good evening, my lord. I'll make sure the truth of what happened here tonight reaches the right ears."

"Wait," Brien said as the other man started to turn away.

"Yes?" Maxime asked.

"Why tell me now?"

"You deserve to know. And maybe—" a self-deprecating smile curled over his lips—"I'd like a place in this new organization of yours."

"I'll consider it," was Brien's clipped reply.

"Of course. Now if that's all—?"

He waited for Brien's nod, then walked slowly, heavily, to the crypt we'd exited from. The rusty hinges groaned as he pulled it shut behind him. Two cardinals burst into flight, wings beating in panic. They disappeared into the sky and the cemetery fell still again.

Twilight slipped the daggers from Brien's grip. She wiped the blood on the grass, then held them out. He sheathed them without a word.

She glanced around at the rest of us. "It's getting late. We need to leave now if we want to be back before sunrise."

Adrian held up his phone. "Already messaged the drivers. They should be arriving just about...now." He indicated the two black SUVs pulling up to the cemetery gate.

"Thank you," said Twilight. "Can you help Perla?"

"Of course," he said.

"James's weapons," said Brien, turning toward where the enforcer had fallen.

Talon scooped them up. "I'll bring them back to the island."

Brien gave a tight nod. "We'll bury them at sea. James would've wanted that." The enforcer had loved to go sailing at night.

He and Twilight, headed for gate, arms around each other.

When I urged Nyx after them, she glanced at the lair, biting her lip. "My paintings."

"We'll have them sent," I told her. "But whatever else you have in there can wait. I'll buy you whatever you need."

She gave a small, telling shudder. "All I want is my paintings."

Adrian had already started off, Perla in his arms. We followed, climbing into the SUV after them. Brien, Twilight and Talon took the other vehicle.

We dropped Perla outside of the city at a medic she trusted, someone who could patch her. Adrian volunteered to stay behind and escort her personally to the island. He hovered over her protectively. She seemed not to notice, but when he insisted on carrying her inside, she winked at Nyx over his shoulder.

I smothered my amusement and helped Nyx back into the SUV. She settled against my chest with a tiny sigh.

Above us, the sky had cleared, bright with stars. We'd taken two choppers from the island, concealing them outside the city.

We had just enough time to make the three-hour flight home before dawn.

"Take us to the choppers," I told the driver. "And make it fast."

"Yes, sir," he said and accelerated onto the highway.

T he next night, it was still a few minutes before sunset when I felt Nyx's long, artist's fingers on my naked body—moving over my pecs, tracing my ribs, traveling down from my shoulders to my arms.

My eyelids were still glued shut, the day sleep keeping me under. But I knew it was her. The mate bond stretched between us, sparkling like she did. Not something I could see; something I felt. Heat and gravity, pulling us together.

The part of me who hadn't belonged to anyone—that feral, affection-starved boy—drank it in.

Mine.

I opened my eyes to find Nyx astride my hips, dressed in nothing but tiny red panties and a smile, her thighs sleek and warm against me, her clean scent flooding my senses.

Her mouth curved, slow and certain.

"Yours," she confirmed, like I'd said it aloud. "And you're mine."

She leaned forward, hands braced on my shoulders. Her curls tumbled forward, framing her pretty tits. "Thought I'd wake you up."

My dick sprang up between us, instantly, painfully hard. "Anytime," I managed, voice rough.

Her gaze searched mine, the heat giving way to something softer. "You're really happy about being mated to me?"

"You have to ask?" I slid my fingers into that wild, curling mass, cupping the back of her skull. "You're everything, woman—brains, beauty, talent. Plus you're *The* fucking *Haunt*. After that show in Paris, the whole world is going to know your work."

Her entire face glowed. "You mean that," she said, like she finally believed it.

I tightened my grip on her skull. "I will never lie to you, Nyx. Never. But how can you not know how special you are? You arrive somewhere and the whole damn place lights up. Why d'you think I call you *firefly*?"

"Yeah?" she asked, pleased.

"Yeah." I rubbed my lips over hers. She smiled against my mouth and we kissed—slow, unhurried, easy.

Then I drew back, voice stern. "Now let's talk about you and this plan you had to sacrifice yourself."

"Mm?" She fisted my dick, a firm hold that almost made me forget the lecture. But she wasn't getting off that easy.

"Distracting me won't work." I curled up and slapped her ass. "I nearly had a heart attack. When he threatened to stick you in the liver—"

I swallowed over the grit in my throat, reliving the terrible fear all over again.

She didn't release her grip on me. Smart woman.

"I'm sorry, mon coeur." She gave me an apologetic smile—and worked her hand up and down my erection. "But I'd do it again. You know I had to. You'd have done the same and we both know it."

Fuck. She had me there.

I narrowed my eyes at her anyway. "I will never be okay with you putting you in danger. You ever try something like that again—if you even think about doing it—and I'll spank that pretty ass of yours red."

She reached the tip and rubbed her thumb over the soft skin of the head, spreading the pre-cum around. "I'll make it up to you. I promise."

"Damn right." But I was focused on those graceful fingers and the wet spot I could see on the strip of red satin between her thighs.

She released me and brought my hand to her breast. "Touch me."

I pinched her nipple, a last punishment, enjoying her gasp and the spike of arousal that followed. Then I curled up, kissing the tip, soothing the hurt away. I wanted to turn her over, bury myself in her sweet, hot pussy. But she'd had a rough forty-eight hours. She didn't need me taking her like a greedy bastard.

"You ate?" I asked. "D'you need fresh blood?"

"I'm good," she said—and sent a rush of adoration through the bond, simply because I cared enough to ask how she was doing. Gods, Nazaire had done a number on her.

She rocked against my dick, and my breath hissed through my teeth. To Hades with being a good guy.

I fell back to the mattress, bringing her with me.

She caught my face in her hands. "I love you," she said fiercely. "So, so much." She kissed me hard, claiming me in her own way.

Warmth settled in my chest. A warmth that was still strange to me but that I was starting to recognize as happiness.

I poked at it like it might bite. Like it was some wild animal crouched low in the underbrush, watching me back. It didn't fight or recoil.

It just was.

Something I could trust.

Something I'd have forever.

I buried my face in Nyx's throat and let that good, happy feeling loose. "I love you, too."

"I know," she murmured, stroking my head. "I know."

The room around us faded—walls, shadows, the battle we'd fought last night—all dissolving until there was only her heartbeat thrumming against my chest. I slid my hands down her back, feeling the curve of her spine, the strength beneath her softness. She arched into me, her body fitting against mine as though it had always belonged there.

I kissed her mouth, her nose, her eyes. "You sure you're okay?" I asked.

"Yes." She squirmed against me, wet silk dragging over my hard flesh. "I want this, Cain. I need it."

"Yeah?" I smacked her butt one last time. "Then take off these damn panties."

✣ 38 ✣

NYX

It's true what they say about surviving something that should've killed you. You come out hungry—for life, for connection, for anything that proves you're still here.

I was so eager I tore the waistband of my underwear, tugging too hard in my rush, urgency buzzing through every nerve. Then I was back on top of Cain. I snagged a condom from the nightstand, rolled it on, and then sank slowly onto him, taking him inside one thick inch at a time.

"So good," I breathed and stilled, my forehead pressed to his. The faint scent of his skin—wild night air laced with something dark, spicy—wrapped around me. His fingers tightened at my nape, drawing me closer until we were touching everywhere.

I moved, and he answered, our bodies finding each other in a rhythm that felt instinctive, inevitable. I was used to Cain's focus during sex, his control. But this... this was different.

This was making love, raw and unguarded.

This stole the air from my lungs.

This changed everything, like stepping out of a sketch into a painting—lines flooding with color, shadows breaking open into light.

With each advance and retreat, I sank deeper, moving slowly

until I couldn't stand it anymore and sped up the rhythm. I lifted away from him to get a better angle, hands braced on his shoulders, hips jerking. He gripped my ass, slowing me down, and I whimpered until he sat up, bringing me against his chest, his lips to the hollow of my throat.

His fangs grazed my skin, sending a bolt of heat straight to my sex. "Just a taste," he said, like he thought I'd object.

"Gods, yes," I rasped. "Make me burn."

His answering growl rolled down my spine. He turned my head, exposing my neck, making me vulnerable in the best way possible—and then his fangs sank in.

I moaned his name and tightened my thighs around him.

He rumbled in pleasure—and released the aphrodisiac into my blood. Magic raced through my veins. I groaned, begged. Moving on him in pleasure-drugged waves as he sucked hard.

He swallowed, then drew on my throat again, driving me even higher. He gave a last, firm pull, then finished, licking the tiny punctures clean. Taking care with me as always.

He grasped my hips and drew me down hard, and I threw my head back, my hair tumbling down my spine. I exhaled his name, drawing it out. "Caaiinnn..."

"Right here," he murmured. "Always."

The world stilled. His eyes held mine, blue lightning flickering in their depths.

Then he lifted me up and dragged me down again, thrusting up to meet me. Once, twice, three times until I broke, grinding my pelvis against his, pinching my own nipples.

He cursed, a man pushed beyond his limits. "That's it. Take what you need. Bad girl. *My* bad girl."

Muttering hot, dark things until my climax exploded through me.

"Fuck," he groaned and jerked, following me into the fire.

Later we took a shower, taking turns washing each other between kisses and orgasms, Cain on his knees with me against the tiles, the hot water drenching us, as he licked me into delirium.

After, he had me sit on a stool in front of the bathroom

mirror while he dried and brushed my hair—long, slow strokes while I watched him in the reflection. He finished by putting the brush and hair dryer down so he could fluff my curls with his fingers.

A little bubble of amusement rose in my chest at how intent he was, like he had to make it perfect. "You're good at this."

He nuzzled my bare shoulder. "I love your hair."

"And I love you." I curled an arm around his nape, keeping him there, turning my face for his kiss.

That led to me on my knees on a thick towel, sucking him off.

"Because you need to know exactly who's in charge," he told me. But we both knew he just wanted my mouth on his dick.

We had a late dinner—blood-whiskey for him, wine and a rare steak for me—then curled up on the couch.

My belongings had been delivered to his apartment, and he took in the canvases stacked against the wall.

"We need to set up your studio," he told me. "You need sunlight, right?"

"Filtered," I said. Unlike him, I could take small amounts of sunlight, and I loved the heat on my skin, the colors of daytime. "But yeah. I prefer natural light."

"We can do that," he said. "And you already made room in my closet."

I bit back a smile. I'd seen how he'd eyed the clothes hanging next to his neat, black-and-white outfits.

"What about when all the clothes you ordered arrive?" He'd bought out an island store's stock in my size, and more was on the way from shops in London and Paris.

"We'll make room," he returned gamely.

I tapped my lips. "And I was thinking one of my paintings would look good on that wall." I pointed at the bare wall opposite the couch.

"You're going to make some changes around here, aren't you?" He didn't seem upset, just bemused.

I grinned. "A blank canvas."

He blinked, and I chuckled and kissed his cheek.

"Don't look so worried. I love this place—it's so you. I don't want to change that. But maybe a little color?"

He pulled me onto his lap and took my chin in his hand so he could meet my eyes. "Let's get one thing straight. It's not just mine anymore, it's ours. And I don't care what the fuck you do as long as I have you."

"Good answer," I said and somehow that ended up with me bent over the arm of his leather-and-chrome couch.

His voice dropped, rough and hungry. "Gods, I can't get enough of you."

"Then take me."

"Oh, I will," he said. "But first, I want to play."

My pants were jerked off, my panties following.

"Play?" I asked.

He slid a finger into my wetness and drew it out again, painting my clit with knowing strokes that made me gasp.

"Yeah," he said. "And I want some begging in there, too."

I turned my head so he could see my pout. "What if I don't want to?" I asked, poking the beast because it was so fun.

He dragged his teeth over my throat. "You'll want it," he said. "But just for that, I'm going to make you scream."

And he did.

EPILOGUE
CAIN

THREE MONTHS LATER My friends and I crowded around the large, cloth-draped painting in Nyx's new studio on the castle's second floor. A paint-spattered tarp covered the stone underfoot, and the air was thick with turpentine and linseed oil.

"Ready?" Nyx asked, and pulled the cover away, revealing the life-sized group portrait she'd been working on for the past month.

She turned back with that practiced smile I hated, pasted on to hide her fear that we wouldn't like her work. But then she straightened, shoulders squared, and dropped the smile, allowing herself to be unguarded, real.

She didn't need to worry. The canvas fucking glowed.

For a beat, the studio went quiet, broken only by Jude's babble, "Ya, ya, ya," his small voice echoing like a cheer.

Brien let out a low whistle, Twilight breathed, "Wowzer." Talon just stared, impressed.

Eden lifted Jude up to give him a closer look. "Look at you, you handsome guy. Just like your daddy."

I caught Nyx's face in my hands and kissed her hard. "It's perfect. Your best work yet."

The others closed in then, praising Nyx until she was flushed and grinning. I put my arm around her shoulders, smiling along with her.

Brien anchored the center of the canvas, sharp in an understated suit, green-eyed and compelling. Twilight leaned against him, painted nails resting on his chest, her short pink skirt flashing a middle finger at syndicate norms.

Talon stood on Brien's left, an arm slung around Eden, face stern, like he was daring anyone to question their bond. Eden was smiling at the dark-haired baby curled against her shoulder. Jude, six months old and a mini-alpha-in-training, clutched the collar of his mom's velvet dress with a fat fist—claiming before he could even speak.

That first week back on the island, Nyx had apologized to Eden. Eden, cool as ever, said she understood, had even thanked Nyx for doing what she could. Now the two of them, along with Twilight, were friends—sweating it out in workouts, dancing in the Bite Club and not-so-quietly dragging the Maritime Syndicate into the twenty-first century.

As for the portrait of me and Nyx? We stood on Brien's right side. She'd caught my restless energy and her own easy sensuality, the two of us part of the group and yet also our own unit. My hand clasped her nape and her head was turned so she gazed up at me, her hair spilling around her shoulders, a little smile on her lips.

Beneath our feet was a mosaic of a great white shark, and a swarm of fireflies encircled us like tiny gold stars. And Nyx being Nyx, a small green dragon coiled lazily around a vase on a nearby table, its ruby eyes gleaming with mischief.

Taken as a whole, it looked like we'd stepped into one of Nyx's stories. A modern-day fairytale about three brothers-in-arms and their fated mates.

And maybe we had. Twilight had reported that we—Brien, Talon and me—were trending on social media, rivaling the Kral Dark Angels for attention. They'd tagged us the Dark Hearts. Whatever the hell that meant.

Sweet Lilith, I was glad I lived on an island and not in New York like the Kral brothers.

I kissed Nyx behind the ear where I knew it would make her shiver. "They love it. You are so fucking amazing." I made it a point to tell her that at least once a day.

She let out a happy sigh and smiled up at me.

Brien was still gazing at the painting. "You want me to share it with the world, let me know. It's too good to hide on this island."

My beautiful, talented mate shook her head. She'd come clean to my friends about being The Haunt but had sworn them to secrecy.

"I don't need anyone but you four to see it," she said.

"Your choice." Twilight's grin was sly. "I bet the mystery is good for sales."

Nyx's lips twitched. "There is that."

Eden wasn't buying it. Her brow furrowed. "But that's not why you don't want anyone to know who you are, is it? This isn't about sales. You don't need the money, especially now you mated with Cain. You can afford to give your paintings away."

Nyx shrugged a shoulder. "Well, yeah. This way it's about the art. People don't filter it through what they know about me." She wrinkled her nose. "You know, my rep."

Twilight tossed her braid. "Because you're a hot female who likes parties and pretty clothes? Screw that. Who says a woman like you can't be a world-class artist or businessperson or even a damn doctor?"

Nyx laughed, and Twilight's grin flashed. "But hey, do your thing. We've got your back, one hundred percent." She flicked a glance at her mate. "Brien is still fan-boying over you."

He rolled his eyes skyward. "I am, of course, honored to welcome an artist of your caliber into the syndicate," he said, just this side of pompous—the way he always sounded when embarrassed.

Yeah, the dude was fan-boying hard.

He must've realized it himself because he grimaced and pivoted. "Why don't we hang the painting in that alcove outside the war room?"

"Perfect," said Twilight. "What d'you think, Nyx?"

Her smile widened. Through the bond, I felt her happiness, her sense of belonging. I squeezed her shoulder, taking her joy as my own.

"I'd like that," she said.

"That's settled then," said Twilight. "And if anyone asks, we'll tell them we took a photo and commissioned The Haunt to paint it."

Brien and Twilight left then for their nightly swim, but Talon and Eden stayed behind.

They exchanged a look, then Eden turned to Nyx. "We wanted to ask you something."

"Oh?" She glanced between them, puzzled.

Jude reached out for her, little arms stretching, voice babbling, "Nah, nah, nah." Kid had taken a shine to her. Smart kid.

Eden kissed his cheek and passed him over. "You know Jude's sponsor ceremony next week? We'd like you to stand with Cain as his godmother."

"Me?" Nyx cuddled Jude closer at the same time she shook her head. "But—"

"No buts," Eden said. "We think you're the best choice, and not just because you're Cain's mate. You're levelheaded, and if it ever comes down to it, I trust you to make decisions for Jude, not the syndicate. And he likes you."

She grinned at her son, who was gazing up at Nyx like she was the prettiest thing in the castle. Like I said, the kid was smart.

"Then I'd be honored," Nyx said. "I—thank you. I'll do my very best. Whatever he needs, I'll be there for him."

"We know," said Talon simply.

"And we should be thanking you," added Eden. "Now, if you'll excuse us, this little monster could use a nap."

Talon took his son from Nyx, and they left us alone in the studio.

Nyx slipped an arm around my waist. Together, we studied the painting. She turned to me, eyes shining. "We look like a family, don't we?"

I squeezed her shoulders. "We are a family."

Because the six of us—seven, if you counted Jude—weren't

about power or territory. Not really. The syndicate ran on that. We didn't.

We were something else. A brotherhood, first. Talon, Brien, me —bound by blood we chose, not blood we were born with.

And what Nyx and I had grew out of that same place. Not softer or gentler. Just deeper. The same loyalty, the same ride-or-die bond... only turned toward one person with everything I had.

Nyx touched my cheek. "I love you, Lieutenant Cain."

I hauled her close. "And I love you," I said, pressing my lips to her forehead. "Holy fuck, I love you." I kissed both eyes, then said it one more time against her mouth. "Forever."

That warmth, that happiness, flooded me. Filling the hollow places, burning out the dark.

It was familiar now, that rush, but one I'd never take for granted.

ALSO BY REBECCA RIVARD

Craving early access to my vampire romances and other shadow-kissed paranormal and romantasy stories? Join my newsletter for exclusive teasers, secret updates, special deals, and all the delicious behind-the-scenes details.

rebeccarivard.com/newsletter

THE VAMPIRE SYNDICATE

Gritty, twisty vampire mafia romance

Tempted

Pursued

Craved

Taken

Fallen

Hunger

Thirst

The Vampire Kingpin

VAMPIRE BLOOD COURTESANS

Steamy vampire romance set in Michelle Fox's Blood Courtesans World

Ensnared: Star

Compelled: Cerise

Learn more: rebeccarivard.com/vampires

THE FADA SHAPESHIFTERS

Dark shifters, seductive fae...

Stealing Ula (Prequel)

Seducing the Sun Fae

Claiming Valeria

Tempting the Dryad

Lir's Lady

Shifter's Valentine

Sea Dragon's Hunger

Saving Jace

Charming Marjani

Adric's Heart

Learn more: rebeccarivard.com/shapeshifters

ABOUT REBECCA RIVARD

USA Today bestselling author Rebecca Rivard read way too many romances as a teenager, little realizing she was actually preparing for a career. She now spends her days with vampires, shifters and fae—which has to be the best job ever.

Rivard's writing has garnered numerous awards including the prestigious PRISM, the RONE, and the Paranormal Romance Guild Reviewers' Choice Award. In addition, eight of her books have earned *InD'Tale Magazine*'s coveted Crowned Heart Review.

When she isn't writing, Rivard walks and bikes in the Chesapeake Bay area with her guitar-playing, storytelling husband. She loves to travel and is always on the lookout for mysterious castles, cobblestoned alleys and eerie cemeteries, many of which find their way into her plots.